"YOU'RE MAKIN' A BIG MISTAKE. WE'RE PINKERTONS. PUT DOWN THE GUN."

"Pinkertons? No shit!" Raider grinned.

The man moved slightly, shielding his partner. The second man whipped out a pistol and fired. Raider ducked and squeezed off the .44. The man's forehead exploded.

Something hit Raider hard, knocking him to the ground. Too late he realized a third man had edged around behind him. Raider was the only real Pinkerton in the group, and yet he'd just made a fatal mistake....

Other Books by
J. D. HARDIN

J.D. HARDIN

COLDHEARTED LADY

PLAYBOY
PAPERBACKS

CHAPTER ONE

Raider felt the train slow, hurriedly swallowed a last bite of sausage, and washed it down with coffee. Shoving up the window, he poked his head out and squinted up ahead. Cinders from the big Baldwin engine stung his eyes and he jerked back inside.

"Shit!" Raider groped for the linen dinner napkin and wiped it over his face.

"Mr. Raider, sir?" Someone drummed loudly on the compartment door. Raider stood, braced himself as the train ground to a halt, and slammed the heavy bolt aside. Lieutenant Graham and two troopers faced him.

"What the hell we stopping for? Anything wrong?"

"No, sir," said Graham. "Just taking on water."

Raider gave him a narrow look. "Isn't anything on my list about takin' on water."

"No, sir," Graham said stiffly.

Raider muttered under his breath, stepped back inside, and grabbed his Model 94 Winchester. With a quick look at the big iron chest bolted to the floor, he joined the soldiers in the hall and locked the door behind him. "This waterin' stop got a name?"

"Yes, sir. I think it's Cheyenne Wells."

Raider frowned. "I don't know any Cheyenne Wells in Kansas."

"We, ah—ain't exactly in Kansas, sir. 'Bout twenty miles into Colorado."

Raider glared, left the soldiers at their post, and stomped off angrily down the corridor. *Every raggedy-ass bluebelly on the train knows what's happening round here,* he fumed silently. *Everyone 'cept me and Doc, who are supposed to be running the show!*

It had been that way from the start, when Raider and his fellow Pinkerton operative joined the train in Chicago. They were supposed to be handling security, with authority straight from the top. Only, things hadn't worked out that way. Every colonel, big-shot railroad official, and half-ass engineer along the way had a finger in the pie. If they ever got to Denver in one piece . . .

Raider stopped at the mahogany-paneled door and knocked lightly.

"Rhagaraga-khussssh!" something roared from the other side.

Raider ground his teeth. As usual, he had no idea what the dumb son of a bitch was saying. "It's me," he called out. "Will you open the door, please?"

The panel clicked, then opened wide. The big Egyptian filled the doorway and glared down at him. Raider couldn't help backing off. Khalifi towered a good seven inches over his own six-two and made him feel like a dwarf. The man was built like a bull—380 pounds of brick-colored muscle from his bald head to his ridiculously tiny feet. "Miss Raman," said Raider. "If you're back there somewhere, I'd like a word with you."

The girl rattled off something in her own tongue. Khalifi went *"Rhoofa!"* and backed away.

"Miss Raman. Doctor." Raider nodded at the pair; with a wary glance at the giant, he stepped inside.

The girl's father grinned. He was a tiny little man, built like a bird. A bright red fez with a gold tassel was perched on his head. Raider couldn't imagine how this scrawny bag of bones could have sired a beauty like Neferti Raman. By God, Mamma must've really been a winner!

"Mr. Raider. You want something?" Neferti's enormous black eyes brushed him like ice. Raider flushed, pulled his gaze from her ample breasts.

"Uh—yeah. Just wanted to tell you an' your father we were—stopping. The train, I mean."

Neferti arched a brow. "Really? How interesting. I would never have noticed."

"Yes, ma'am." Raider swallowed. "Anyway, if you and the doctor would like to stretch your lovely—I mean, if you want to walk some . . ."

"An excellent idea," the girl said coolly. "Father. Will you join me?"

"I will be staying here, yes?" He showed Raider a mouthful of gold-filled teeth. "Is a most fine story on the marvelous Tabor Grand Opera House in your Denver city. You have seen this, Mr. Raider?"

"No, sir. It ain't exactly finished yet." He saw Dr. Raman was reading *The Great Divide,* a magazine that touted the wonders of Denver. Neferti stood, found her parasol, and tossed a black wing of hair over one bare shoulder. The giant Khalifi squeezed his bulk through the doorway and the girl followed. Raider moved after her, marveling at the tight little ass under the thin yellow fabric. *If the Union Pacific could put gears on that thing,* he decided, *we wouldn't* need *the fucking engine!*

Raider had thought of little else since he'd met the girl in Chicago. Clearly, she didn't care a thing about him. Not yet, anyway. Sometimes, real ladies took a little longer getting their skirts up than ordinary women and whores. Of course, sometimes it worked the other way around. No matter how long it took, Neferti was worth waiting for. What he could see of that olive and honey skin looked good enough to eat, and Raider figured it could only get better further down. Hell, she probably knew things girls in Tucson and Fort Worth hadn't even heard of!

Suddenly, a door sprang open ahead of Neferti. A man stumbled out, lurched solidly into the girl, and bounced her off the wall. Neferti cried out, slammed into Raider's arms, and sent him sprawling. Raider's head hit a brass spittoon bolted low on the wall. The girl's skirts flew up, showing a flash of bare legs.

"Wuups! Shorry 'bout that." Lord Eden Bade-Willis leered at the tantalizing sight. A dozen feet away, Raider caught the strong odor of cheap cologne and expensive French brandy.

"Lout!" screamed Neferti, angrily gathering skirts about her legs. "Stupid English lout!"

"Oh, I say now, let's not—*aaaaaark!*" A ham-sized fist closed about the Englishman's neck and lifted him effortlessly off the floor. His eyes widened in terror. Skinny arms and legs flailed air.

"Gabishab-kurf!" roared the giant. Tiny eyes glowed in

the skin-tight face. A knife flashed out of baggy pants and arced for Willis's throat.

Raider stared. The blade was fourteen inches long and curved like a snake. "Goddamn!" he shouted. "Hold it!"

"Khalifi—*no!*" snapped the girl.

"Huunnh?" Khalifi looked hurt. The blade stopped an inch from the man's chin. Neferti spoke sharply. Khalifi opened his hand and Willis dropped like a sack.

"Great Jesus!" breathed Raider. "Lady, you goin' to keep that thing around, you better get a leash for it!" Neferti glared. Powell Jamison, Lord Willis's aide, peered white-faced out the door. "Get him back in there and stay put," Raider said sharply. Jamison nodded dully and dragged the older man inside. When Raider heard the lock snap, he turned to the girl. "You all right, ma'am?"

"Oh, I'm fine," she said coolly. "Just—fine." Raider stuck out his hand. She jerked back quickly and shook him off. "I will *not* tolerate that man on this train a moment longer!" she flared. "Do you quite understand that?"

"Well, I—"

"Well, nothing!" The girl stood up and brushed her skirts. Dark eyes bored into Raider. "I have *warned* you. *All* of you. Right from the beginning of this miserable trip. That—*man* is an enemy of my people. His presence here is a slap in the face to Egypt!"

"Yeah, I understand," Raider started again. "I just—"

"*No!*" The point of the parasol jabbed Raider's belly. "You do not understand—*anything!*" Khalifi fingered his blade and growled ominously at Raider.

"Hey, what's the problem around here?"

Raider turned and saw his partner, Doc Weatherbee, bounding down the corridor, Lieutenant Graham at his heels.

"Oh, Mr. Weatherbee, I'm *so* glad you're here!" Neferti gave a grateful sigh and laid a hand on his arm.

"Now, now," said Doc. "Everything's all right, ma'am." He glanced at Raider. "What happened?"

"His lordship is hittin' the juice. We had us a little accident."

"It was no accident," the girl said stiffly. Her eyes flashed at the closed door. "That person deliberately—"

"All right," Doc said smoothly, leading her down the corridor. "Everything's going to be just fine now." Doc patted Neferti's hand and she leaned in against him, one lovely thigh brushing his leg.

Raider scowled after them. "Everything's goin' to be *just* fine," he mimicked. He fingered the knot on his head, winced, and kicked the brass spittoon off the wall. It bounced down the corridor, staining the thick red carpet.

The sun burned bright and clear over the scrub-covered plain. Raider squinted, stepped off the train, and peered down the tracks. Below the big water tower was a collection of tar-paper shacks. On one of the shacks a weathered sign spelled out CHEYENNE WELLS.

The soldiers were everywhere. Colonel Arthur's men knew their drill, he'd give them credit for that. Bluebellies circled the train in a long, ragged line, fifty men with carbines at the ready. Past them, a dozen soldiers on horseback plowed up the dust scaring gophers. Raider dug his heel in the ground, crushed a bed of ants, and stalked toward the head of the train.

Six cars trailed the big Baldwin engine and its tender. After the chair car for soldiers was a stable car for the mounts, and after that, the specially constructed mail car holding the treasures of Egypt. As usual at every stop, the soldiers had mounted a Gatling gun atop the car.

Past the treasure car was the elegant *City of Worcester*, borrowed from Jerome Marble for the occasion by the U.S. Government. Behind the *Worcester* was a Pullman sleeper, and behind that, a caboose for train personnel.

As Raider walked up the rails, soldiers gave him sour, disgruntled looks. He didn't much blame them. Fifty troopers were crammed together in one car from New York to San Francisco, sleeping on top of each other, eating canned beef and beans. They knew damn well how the people were living in the plush cars behind them. Instead of army rations, the party dined on fine wines, bluepoint oysters, stuffed roast quail, and New York ice cream. In Kansas City, Raider had nearly come to blows with a grizzled old sergeant who'd seen inside the *Worcester.* "No one asked you to join the fuckin' Yankee army," Raider told him in his best Arkansas drawl. The trooper turned beet red, and Doc and Lieutenant Graham had to pull them apart.

Raider spotted Doc and Neferti by the treasure car. The girl laughed and twisted her parasol, eyeing Doc from under long black lashes. The giant stood a few yards away, thinking about eating the big Baldwin engine. Doc puffed a Virignia cheroot and gave Neferti his best New York bullshit. The whole business irked Raider no end. Doc always dressed like a peacock, but he'd really gone crazy since the girl came into the picture. He brushed his gray derby six times a day, and put on a clean silk shirt every time Raider turned around. Today he sported a blue-flowered vest, a pearl stickpin, and a fine, English worsted suit with about six hundred buttons. Raider set his jaw and walked up between the two.

"Doc, I gotta talk to you. Right now."

Weatherbee raised a brow and tipped his derby. Neferti smiled back. Raider stared at the firm nipples poking through her dress. Doc walked off a few yards and Raider followed. "Rade, what is it?" Doc sighed. "We were having a very important talk about—"

"Come off it, Doc. You're trying to get in the girl's pants. Just like me. Don't give me any shit about talkin'. We got to do something about that maniac. The bastard's plain crazy. He's just dying to stick that curly knife in the Englishman's belly."

Doc looked at him. "Well, what do you suggest, Rade?"

"You want to *talk* to that girl about something, talk to her about that! Tell her to put a cage around her goddamn dog. We don't get to Denver with Willis in one piece, Doc, *you* can tell the President and Allan Pinkerton *and* the Queen of England we was too busy trying to screw that little Egyptian gal to keep him alive."

Doc looked pained. "Just because taking women to bed is all *you* ever think about Rade—"

"Yeah, yeah, I heard it all before." Raider stopped and

looked around. "Shit, where are the twins? I thought they were out here with you."

"I didn't see them," said Doc. "They're not inside?"

Raider groaned. He'd checked the *City of Worcester* and decided Willis's nieces had stepped off the train. If they hadn't, he knew where they were and what they were doing. The only question was, who were they doing it *with?*

CHAPTER TWO

Raider sprinted down the tracks past the treasure car and the *City of Worcester,* and swung up the steps to the sleeper. The sleeper was like none he'd ever seen. It had been specially built by George Pullman for a New York banker and was lavishly furnished with brass beds, plush carpeting, and gold-framed mirrors. Raider halted before the second compartment and pounded on the hand-carved door. Shrieks of girlish laughter answered his knock, followed by a protesting male bellow.

The door opened quickly and Louisa stood there stark naked, a wide grin on her face. Raider stared. He knew it was Louisa. Annette had a beauty mark under her chin.

"Oh, Mr. *Rai*der," she said, licking her lips suggestively. "What a pleasant surprise!"

"Uh, l-listen," Raider stammered.

"Don't listen, look. Oh, you are, aren't you?"

Raider was. It was impossible to do anything else. The twins were perfectly constructed for their favorite hobby: fucking everything in sight. Men, women, goats, chickens— whatever crossed their path. They were long-legged, full-breasted girls with corn-yellow hair and wicked blue eyes. Barely nineteen, Raider figured they might just make it to thirty.

"Hey, come on in," said Louisa. "We've got plenty of room!"

"Like hell we do!" shouted the man. "Get your ass out of here, mister!"

Louisa stepped aside and Raider saw the portly form of Colonel Harold J. Arthur on the brass bed. Annette was riding him like a horse, slim legs spread across his thighs. A duck-billed cavalry hat sat jauntily on her head. The colonel struggled valiantly to throw her off and cover himself, but Annette hung on like a leech, sucking his tool deeper into the curly patch of yellow.

Suddenly, Arthur's eyes went wide. He shuddered, gritted his teeth, and sank back exhausted. Annette shook hair out of her eyes and grinned at Raider. "You're next, fella!"

"Oh, *no* you don't," pouted Louisa. "This one's mine, lady."

Raider backed away. Louisa pressed him against the wall, fingers working quickly at his trousers. Raider's cock sprang to attention and the girl beamed. "Just let me get my mouth round that big old thing and we'll have us a ball!"

"Now, look!" Raider protested. He pushed the girl away and backed into a corner. "This—this here business has gotta stop. You hear me?" He glared at the twins. "You can't just—goddamn it, you got to quit this stuff!"

Annette looked puzzled. "Why?"

"Yeah, why?" echoed her sister. Her hand snaked back to Raider's pants.

"Damn it, stop that!"

Colonel Arthur pulled a sheet up to his chin. "Sir," he said shortly. "You have no right to break in here. This is a private affair!"

"*Private* is what you're going to be, mister!" Raider shouted.

Arthur purpled. "Good Lord—do you know who you're talking to? I'm a colonel in the U.S. Army. My third cousin is going to be the next President of this country!"

"I don't give a shit if you're the ghost of George Custer." Raider jabbed a finger in his face. "You pull this crap again and I'll go right to General Cleve in Washington. Try me, son."

Arthur's face turned white. Raider gave them all a withering stare. "We're stoppin' here awhile, in case any of you noticed. Be a good idea if you all got out and walked around some."

"I don't like to walk," Louisa said coyly. "What I like to do is—"

Raider turned, barged through the door, and stormed down the hall. "Fucking circus is what it is," he muttered. "Fucking cross-country circus!"

* * *

Raider and Doc had just wrapped up a Wells Fargo robbery in Albuquerque when the telegram reached them from the Pinkerton National Detective Agency. The message was short and to the point:

REPORT TO CHICAGO SOONEST.
—WAGNER

Doc and Raider were puzzled. In the four years they'd worked together, neither had been called to the Agency's main office.

"What the hell you figure we did?" asked Raider. It was some kind of trouble, he decided, and Doc agreed. If it was a new case, there were plenty of operatives closer than New Mexico.

A second message awaited them at Kansas City:

REPORT TO FRONT DESK, PALMER HOUSE, CHICAGO.
—WAGNER

"Hey, now, that's more like it," Raider grinned. "Bet there's some fine, high-class ladies stayin' at the Palmer House."

"Rade, what do you know about high-class ladies?" asked Doc. "And besides, it doesn't say we're *staying* there."

Doc was right. When they got in to Chicago they went straight to the Palmer House and left their names at the desk. The clerk told them to wait. Ten minutes later Supervisor Wagner himself walked into the lobby and guided them to a corner. Wagner had a face like a bull-

dog and a body to match. He nodded at Doc and sniffed at
Raider. "That all you got to wear, boy? You're in the city,
now, whether you noticed or not."

Raider looked puzzled. Hell, he was wearing what he
always wore. A good black Stetson, denim pants, and his
favorite leather trail jacket. There might be a little cow
dung on his Middleton boots, but so what?

Wagner got right down to business. "We got us a real
can of worms here, lads, and I don't want it screwed up.
Not any. Our client is the highest there is. The White
House. The office of the President himself."

Raider whistled, and Wagner gave him a look. "As you
likely heard in New Mexico, President Garfield was shot
a few weeks ago. That makes this whole business all the
more sensitive. The White House doesn't need any more
problems just now." Wagner paused a moment. "Either
of you ever heard of the *Nymph of the Nile?*"

"I saw an act in Topeka once—" started Raider. Doc
kicked him soundly under the table.

"The *Nymph of the Nile,*" Wagner said soberly, "is an
Egyptian statue. A statue of an, ah—unclothed young
lady. It is solid gold, and absolutely priceless. The *Nymph*
is part of an exhibit of Egyptian treasures traveling from
New York to San Francisco. The show stopped in Phila-
delphia, Washington, and Cleveland and it's here in
Chicago now. It leaves for Kansas City in the morning.
You two are in charge of security for the rest of the trip."

Raider looked blank. "That's it? We just guard this
treasure?"

Wagner gave him a weary smile. "Not quite, Mr. Raider.
We've already heard rumors that every outlaw west of
St. Louis has his eye on that train. Jesse and Frank James
are supposed to make a try for it, which is ridiculous.
Yesterday we heard Billy the Kid will definitely stage a
robbery in Kansas."

"That won't be real easy," Raider said drily. "Pat
Garrett killed him dead a couple of days ago."

"Exactly," said Wagner. "Nevertheless, *some*one is
likely to be foolish enough to try. That's why we've put

a special treasure train together, plus fifty soldiers under Colonel Arthur."

"Fifty?" said Doc.

"Fifty. Plus cavalry support units and a Gatling gun."

Doc ran a finger over his stickpin. "Mr. Wagner, you mind me asking—if they have all that firepower, what do they need Pinkertons for?"

"Good question. Even if you *don't* get robbed, you'll likely have your hands full. The real trouble is *in*side the train." Raider and Doc exchanged glances and Wagner went on. "There's a Dr. Raman on board. He's curator of the exhibit, a nice little fellow. His daughter, though, is an out and out radical. Hates the British. Wants to see 'em all dead and out of Egypt. Which is a little touchy, since Lord Eden Bade-Willis is also on the train. Political stuff between Washington and London. Not too good an idea if you ask me. Oh, he's a drunk, by the way," Wagner said absently.

Raider's smile faded. "Sure sounds like fun."

"Oh, I expect it will be." Wagner grinned unpleasantly, stood, and looked at the pair. "Be at the station at nine sharp in the morning."

"I, ah, guess we got rooms here, right?" said Raider.

Wagner looked pained. "Don't be ridiculous. Oh, one more thing. Bade-Willis has two nieces. Pair of little tramps. Make certain they do *not* embarrass the United States Government, Egypt, or Great Britain. And watch out for the giant."

Raider sat up straight. *"What* giant?"

"The Raman girl's bodyguard. Paroled killer, I understand. Murdered around forty men." Wagner's smile rested on Raider. "So far, anyway. Good day, gentlemen."

After two weeks in Kansas City, Raider grudgingly admitted Wagner was right. No one tried to steal the *Nymph of the Nile.* Arthur's troopers took it to a local bank at night and picked it up in the morning. Meanwhile, Neferti Raman set fire to the British flag in front of the hotel. Willis threw up on the governor of Kansas. A man winked at Neferti and Khalifi broke his arm. Annette and Louisa cornered a drummer and two bellboys, tied them to their beds, and kept them locked up nine days.

Afterwards, when they were back on the train, the treasure traveled in a special mail car. The *Nymph* itself was in an iron-clad crate bolted to the floor—the special responsibility of the Pinkertons.

"Doc," Raider said wearily the night the train left for Denver. "Why do you figure Wagner brought us up special from Albuquerque for this?"

"That's easy," said Doc. "Old man Pinkerton hates us. Didn't you know that?"

"Oh, yeah," said Raider. "I forgot."

•   •   •

Raider waited impatiently in the compartment he shared with Doc. He didn't have a watch and didn't need one—his stomach told him Weatherbee was long overdue.

Of course, he'd been shut up in worse places, Raider reminded himself. The *City of Worcester* was designed to take wealthy easterners on hunting treks to Wyoming, Colorado, and the wilds of Montana and the Dakotas. The carpeting was thick as grass, and the whole car was full of crystal chandeliers, gold-plated toilets, and enough mahogany to build a ship. It was as fine as any high-class whorehouse Raider had ever seen. All a man needed was that sweet little Egyptian gal and a bottle of good Maryland rye. If he could figure a way to toss Doc and that madman off the train . . .

Weatherbee pounded on the door and Raider let him in. "You sure took your goddamn time, Doc."

"I took an hour, exactly." Doc tapped the watch in his vest pocket. "If you had a proper timepiece—"

"Yeah, okay." Raider sniffed the air and frowned. "Doc, if I closed my eyes I'd think you was the prettiest whore in New Orleans. What the hell is that stuff?"

Doc set his teeth. "It's Eau de Paris Imported Lavender Toilet Water."

"Uhuh. *Toilet* water's about right. What's happening up front?"

Doc hung his scarlet vest and pearl-buttoned jacket on a

peg. "Lord Willis has passed out for the night. The twins are chasing young Jamison. Neferti and her father are having dinner."

"What about the monster?"

"Right there as ever. Where'd you think he'd be?"

"Kind of a average night, huh?" Raider strapped on his Remington .44, glanced in the mirror, and ran two fingers over his mustache. "What's for supper?"

"Grouse Macedonia, or Mutton with Caper Sauce. And a nice little Charlotte Russe."

"Who the hell's Charlotte Russe?" asked Raider. Doc picked up a marble bookend and Raider ducked out the door.

The twins were still at their table. Powell Jamison had fled to his room and Raider didn't blame him. Running from pretty girls wasn't exactly Raider's style, but Louisa and Annette pure scared the hell out of him. He'd never been raped before, and didn't intend to start.

The girls waved. Raider ignored them. They were modestly dressed for dinner, which meant only one or two nipples showed between them. Neferti's father was gone, but the girl was still eating. The giant lurked in the shadows. Raider nodded, started for a table past the tall, etched-glass doors.

"Mr. Raider—will you sit with me?"

Raider stopped, surprised. Neferti Raman had never even come close to being friendly. "Why—I'd be pleased to." He pulled out a chair and looked at her. Her skin looked like honey in the soft light, and her neckline was nearly as low as the twins'. Raider pulled his eyes away and blinked. A waiter set a plate before him immediately, and Raider sniffed at it.

Neferti frowned. "I know what you are thinking, Mr. Raider."

"Yeah? What?"

"The same as I am. That you would like to see a decent rare steak one night, instead of something buried in sauce."

Raider beamed. "Well, I'll be damned. I mean—you too, huh?"

Neferti looked at him and her smile faded. She glanced over her shoulder and looked earnestly into his eyes. "I must talk to you. It is *most* important."

"Well, sure. Go right ahead."

"That English bastard is going to kill me, Mr. Raider. Now. Tonight." Raider dropped a forkful of Macedonian Grouse.

CHAPTER THREE

Raider stared. "Miss Raman, I know there's bad blood between you and Willis, but—well, that's kind of strong, ain't it?"

Neferti's chin thrust out in defiance. "Mr. Raider—I am *not* making this up!"

"No ma'am, I'm sure you're not. It's just—how do you *know* he's going to try something like that?"

"Because he told me he was."

"Willis said that? When?"

"Just now. A few minutes ago."

"Did you tell Doc about this?"

Neferti shook her head. "It happened after Mr. Weatherbee left. Before you got here."

Raider thought about that. "Doc said Lord Willis had gone to bed. That he'd—"

"—drunk himself into a stupor," Neferti finished. "He did. I went back for something I'd left in my compartment. That's when it happened. Willis stuck his head out and said—" Neferti bit her lip. "I—can't tell you what he said."

"I kind of think you better, Miss."

"He—he said, 'You've got one coming, old cunt!' " The girl colored clear to her neckline and glared at Raider. "Are you satisfied now?"

Raider ignored her and sipped his coffee. "Was Khalifi with you?"

"Are you serious?" Neferti forced a laugh. "I would

have had him cut Willis in half! He was with my father
at the time. He'd asked for hot tea and I had Khalifi take
it."

"Has Willis ever done anything like this before? I mean,
come right out and threatened you?"

"No." Neferti shook her head. "Not in so many words."
She looked squarely at Raider. "Mr. Raider, you don't
really understand how things are between my country and
his, do you? He doesn't *have* to threaten me openly—his
very existence here is a threat. Britain and France are determined to swallow Egypt. They want all of Africa, and
Egypt's just the beginning. Any incident on this tour that
could embarrass my country—"

"Miss Raman," Raider interrupted. "Seems to me like
you gettin' killed would embarrass Willis's country a hell
of a lot more than yours."

Neferti's dark eyes blazed. "After your American press
got through with it?" she said hotly. "No, Mr. Raider—
it would simply be another incident involving 'Egyptian
savages.' I have *read* your newspapers. You always side
with your British cousins!"

"Well, now—"

Neferti gave him a withering stare, got up abruptly from
her seat, and stomped off to her quarters. Raider stood,
thought about following, and decided against it. Instead,
he pushed his plate aside and started back to tell Doc.
Annette and Louisa crossed the aisle swiftly and blocked
his way.

"Want to see something pretty, Mr. Raider?" Louisa
reached up, slipped her sister's dress off her shoulders,
and cupped a pink-tipped breast in her hand. "Doesn't
that look *delicious?*" She leaned down and planted a kiss
on the rigid nipple.

Raider flushed. "For God's sake, girls, leave me the hell
alone!"

The twins giggled. "We'll get *you* sooner or later."

"That's what I'm afraid of," mumbled Raider.

"I stopped off to see Willis but he was out cold, just
like you said," Raider told Doc. "Jamison said he'd been

there most of the time and didn't think the old man could've said any such thing."

Doc frowned thoughtfully. "But he wasn't there *all* the time."

"I guess not. What the hell you think of this business, Doc? Is she telling the truth or what?"

"I can't imagine why she'd make up a thing like that."

"You can't, huh?"

Weatherbee shot him a wary look. "What's that supposed to mean?"

"Aw, come on, Doc. Just because the lady looks better'n honey ice cream don't mean she's some kinda angel. You get a good look at her in Kansas City when she was lightin' that Union Jack in front of the hotel?"

Doc puffed fiercely on his cheroot. "All right, you made your point."

"I sure as hell did."

"I just *said* you did!" snapped Doc.

Raider eyed his partner, then threw back his head and laughed. "Goddamn, you sure want some of that bad, don't you Doc?"

Doc colored, jerked out of his chair, and lashed out swiftly with his right. Raider stared in surprise, slid under the punch, and caught a short left to the stomach.

"Shit!" Raider gasped, sucked in air, and stumbled to a corner. "Doc, what the hell's eatin' you? All I said was—"

Doc came at him, fists doubled in a classic boxer's stance. Raider shifted his feet. His partner was no street brawler, but Raider had a healthy respect for him. Weatherbee had a solid gold tooth as a souvenir of a previous encounter, but Raider had old aches and bruises to show their matches were anything but one-sided.

"Just calm down a minute," said Raider. "You're bein' too damn touchy about that gal." Doc didn't answer. He came straight on, feinting short jabs with his right. Raider had a better reach and lashed out with a left, brushing Doc's shoulder, then followed with a swift right to the jaw. Doc grunted, spit blood, and shook his head. Raider came on strong—Doc crouched under the punch and grabbed

Raider tightly around the waist. Raider twisted to shake him, tripped over a chair, and sent them both to the floor.

Doc sat up and wiped his chin. "Rade," he said soberly. "You ruined a perfectly good three-dollar vest. There's not a way in the world to get blood out of Chinese silk."

"Fuck your Chinese silk," Raider said flatly. "There ain't a way in the world to get my gut back in shape. You know I got stomach trouble, Doc."

"*That* doesn't come from fighting. It comes from filling your stomach with garbage like chili and hot peppers."

"Uhuh. And mutton with crapper sauce."

"That's *caper.*"

"Don't tell me what it tastes like. Look—" Raider pulled himself up to the bed. "You got a hard-on for that girl and you got a right to. I reckon I pushed you some."

Doc looked pained. "Don't you know any other way to put things?"

"Okay. You don't have a hard-on for her."

"I didn't say that."

Raider stood painfully, stumbled to his pack, and tossed a bottle of rye to his partner. Doc eyed it suspiciously. "I don't think I can handle that with this mouth you gave me."

"Sure you can. Just pull out the cork and—" Raider froze. The girl's scream cut through the rumble of the wheels. Doc dropped the bottle, jerked open the door, and ran down the car for the sleeper. Raider jabbed the .44 in his belt and made tracks after his partner.

Doc saw her, a flash of bare arms and legs, a sheet clutched to her breasts. "Neferti!" he shouted. She looked up, eyes wide with fear, and rushed into his arms. "Listen, what is it—what happened?"

Neferti's face twisted. Wood splintered down the corridor. Doc jerked up, saw the huge bulk of Khalifi burst through the door of his compartment. The giant blinked, saw Doc with his half-naked mistress. The tiny eyes went black with rage. A noise started in his chest and he came for Doc like a mad buffalo.

"Hey, just a damn minute!" Doc protested. "I'm not—

oh, *shiiiit!*" Khalifii plucked the girl out of his arms, picked
Doc up like a kitten, and tossed him through the etched-
glass doors at the end of the sleeper. Doc landed hard,
rolled down the aisle, and bounced off the wall.

"Hold it, you fuckin' ape!" Raider stepped over Doc and
leveled the Remington at the Egyptian's chest. Khalifi
paused, blinked at Raider, and growled.

"Khalifi!" Neferti said sharply. She spoke quickly in
her own tongue and the giant backed off reluctantly.

Raider bent down to help the girl. "You all right? What
the hell's going on out here?"

Neferti nodded dumbly, pulled the sheet about her, and
jabbed a shaky finger down the hall. "In—in there. My
room. A—a monster, a—" Raider moved fast. Colonel
Arthur stumbled down the hall. The twins peered wide-
eyed past their door. Raider swept by them all and poked
his head into Neferti's compartment. Something moved in
the corner and flashed toward him. Raider fired twice from
the hip and severed the rattler's head. Doc came up behind
him. "You all right?"

"Yeah, just great." He picked up the rest of the snake by
its rattle and stretched it up high. "Where do you suppose
that came from?"

"It sure didn't grow here. Someone went to a lot of
trouble to sneak it on board." Doc looked at Raider.
"Guess we better have a little talk with Lord Willis."

Raider pulled a towel off a chair, tossed it over the
still-twitching rattler, and kicked the bundle in a corner.
Doc walked down the aisle to where Arthur was helpfully
patting Neferti's bare shoulder. "The snake's dead," Doc
assured her. "Get in your father's compartment and stay
there. Have Khalifi sit outside."

Neferti tried to speak but nothing came out. She nodded
and let the giant lead her off. Doc turned to the colonel.
"You see any of this?"

"No. I heard the lady scream, saw her run down the
hall."

"Nothing else?"

"No, just you and Khalifi."

"Mr. Weatherbee. My goodness, what *happened?*"

Doc turned and stared. A tousle-headed Annette stood just outside her door, Louisa at her shoulder. Both girls wore black net stockings up to their thighs and nothing else. "Jesus!" said Doc. "Get back inside, all right?"

"Anything else?" Louisa's eyes twinkled mischievously.

"No, er—not at the moment, thank you." Doc shoved them back inside and shut the door. "Colonel—if you don't mind, it'd be a good idea to have a look around this sleeper."

"What are we looking for, Mr. Weatherbee?"

"I haven't the slightest idea. Maybe someone on this train who has no business being here." Arthur sniffed, showing what he thought of the idea, and marched down the hall.

Back in their compartment, Raider found the bottle Weatherbee had dropped, took a long swallow, and handed it to his partner. "Powell Jamison says he didn't come out in the hall 'cause he was scared to open the door. He's just a kid, Doc, and I think he's telling the truth." Raider looked disgusted. "I took a good look at Willis. Unless he's one hell of an actor, the son of a bitch is stiff as a board. I seen plenty of drunks in my time, and I'll tell you for certain he didn't toss that snake in there. Not this week."

"Then who did?"

Raider wiped a hand over his mouth. "I don't know. Whoever it was didn't want to hurt no one real bad, though."

Doc sat up straight. "With a five-foot diamondback? What the hell are you talking about?"

Raider reached in his pocket, pulled out a bloody handkerchief, and unwrapped it on the table. The rattler's severed head lay inside. Raider pried its jaws apart and showed it to Doc. "See that? Somebody's pulled the critter's fangs out."

Doc raised a curious brow. "They wanted to scare her but not kill her. That doesn't make sense, Rade."

Raider shrugged and took another drink. "Beats the shit

outta me. Like ol' Wagner said, we got a real can of worms here."

The train limped into Limon, Colorado, in the gray hours of dawn. Flash floods all the way to Denver had slowed traffic to a crawl and the treasure train followed a mile-long freight half the night. Arthur's troops spread out along the tracks, drawing the curious stares of the town-folk. Doc left Raider and found the telegraph office. The lines were still up and he sent a coded case report back to the Pinkertons' main office in Chicago. There was a message waiting for him at Limon. Mack Hooper, Pinkerton's veteran operative in Denver, reported everything was ready for the exhibit. Henry Lewiston of the First National Bank would have special wagons on hand to take the treasure to the exhibit hall, and the Denver police would lend their services to the Army.

Raider cornered Lord Willis at breakfast. The Englishman refused to join the others in the *City of Worcester* and had a meal brought in. Willis was appalled at Raider's story. "Why, by *God,* man," he sputtered. "You have no right to accuse me of such nonsense!"

"I ain't accusing you of anything," said Raider. "I want to know what happened last night."

"I got drunk, that's what happened," snapped Willis. "I get drunk frequently. So what, old boy?"

"So you didn't tell Miss Raman you were going to kill her. And you didn't toss a rattler in her room?"

"Of course not!"

"She says different."

"Then she's a bloody liar. Not a damned bit surprised, either." Willis cast a baleful, rheumy eye at Raider. The sharp points of his military mustache drooped on the ends, and his skin was the color of dough. "You obviously don't *know* the devils like I do," he said stiffly. "Damned Arabs, Egyptians—whole lot's a bunch of liars and thieves. Damned Middle East would go to ruin if we hadn't stepped in there, what? Don't know what's good for 'em, little brown bastards!"

Raider found it hard to think of Neferti Raman as a

little brown bastard. "Yes, sir. And you didn't see a thing, is that it?"

"Saw plenty. Always do." Willis grinned crookedly. "Way I drink, boy, see things you wouldn't believe. Join me in a little pick-up, eh?"

"Uh, no sir. Thanks just the same." Raider saw the breakfast tray was still untouched, and figured Lord Eden Bade-Willis would start on his real first meal of the day as soon as he closed the door behind him.

CHAPTER FOUR

The train was scheduled to leave Limon at ten, but didn't get moving till noon. Doc didn't like it a bit, but there was nothing he could do to hurry things up. Dark clouds filled the sky to the northwest, and the stationmaster reported flooding along Union Pacific tracks all the way to Denver. It was only a ninety-mile trip, the man told Weatherbee, but it might be a long one.

"I don't care for this," Doc told Raider. "If someone wants to hit us, this'd sure be a good time for it. We're goin' to be inching along like a snail looking for washouts."

Raider agreed. They stood on the narrow platform at the end of the Pullman sleeper watching the miles drag by. Colonel Arthur had special guards atop the caboose behind, and troopers on every car. The Gatling gun was mounted on the treasure car, and cavalry units scouted the country ahead.

"Arthur's all right," mused Raider. "A pompous little bastard more interested in fuckin' than fighting, but I guess he knows the ropes. Anyone'd be crazy to try to stop us, Doc. It'd take one hell of a crew of outlaws and a lot of 'em would end up dead."

"That never stopped outlaws before," Doc reminded him. "Not if they have something worth going after. Didn't you listen to Dr. Raman? That statue's something different—they haven't ever found anything like it. The old man told me a rich collector would pay maybe ten or twenty times what it's worth in gold, no questions asked. Which means we've got maybe a couple of million bucks in that box back there. Besides the stuff in the treasure car."

Raider scratched his jaw and gazed out at Colorado. "I dunno. Doesn't seem worth getting shot for."

At lunch, Raider and Doc searched the belongings of everyone on board. The passengers protested loudly, but the pair went doggedly ahead. Lord Willis's luggage unearthed enough whiskey to start a bar in Dodge. The giant Khalifi had a wicked collection of knives. The twins carried a red velvet box full of French photographs, silver chains, exotic wigs, leather straps and whips, and a few items neither Doc nor Raider could identify. Raider, who thought he'd seen everything, turned red at some of the pictures. "How the hell could you get in a position like *that?*" he asked in wonder.

Still, the search revealed no more rattlers, or anything else that would help identify Neferti's assailant.

At three in the afternoon, two of Arthur's horse soldiers galloped back to the train and reported logs and brush on the track a mile ahead.

"How bad?" asked Raider.

"Bad enough," said the trooper. "Take maybe half an hour to clear." He met Raider's eye and glanced at the colonel. "Sir, it don't look like any *natural* washout, either."

"Shit." Raider glanced warily at either side of the train. There were enough high red rocks and snaking gullies to hide half the outlaws in the West. He looked at Doc and Colonel Arthur. "Let's move. We're goin' to get hit."

In moments, the train screeched to a stop. Troopers poured off and took cover. Raider warned everyone aboard to keep down and away from the windows. Jumping to the tracks again, he jerked back to let Arthur and a dozen mounted troopers gallop by. Raider stared after them, then shook his fists at the riders. "Goddamn it, get those horses back here!" The cavalrymen disappeared down the tracks. Raider tossed his Stetson to the ground, picked it up angrily, and stomped up to the treasure train. Doc left two troopers and joined him.

"You see that?" snapped Raider. "Arthur's out playing Custer!"

"I see it." Doc shook his head and pointed north. "We're going to get a gully-washer in about twenty minutes, Rade. If water starts moving down those hills—"

Doc's words were lost as a hail of lead peppered the boxcar behind them. Raider jerked his partner to the ground, levered a shell into the Winchester, and snapped off three quick shots up the ridge.

"Come on," he shouted. "Let's get out of here!" Bullets sang at their heels. Smoke blossomed on the ridge and the troopers returned the outlaws' fire. Raider and Doc jumped in a gully and went flat. "Where the hell's that Gatling?" Raider muttered. Turning, he squinted back at the train. "Oh, shit, Doc—look at that!"

The outlaws were concentrating heavy fire on the Gatling gun. One trooper sprawled across the sandbags surrounding the weapon—his partner got off a quick rattle of fire, jerked up, and tumbled off the car. As Raider watched, two more troopers snaked up the side of the train. One reached the top, ran for the gun, and took a bullet in the leg. Shots dug wood all around him. He dragged himself to the safety of the sandbags and disappeared. The other soldier gave up and jumped to the ground for cover.

Raider muttered a curse, tossed the Winchester to Doc, and jumped out of the hole for open ground. Doc called after him but Raider didn't hear. The outlaws spotted him —knew where he was going. Shouts went up on the ridge and lead kicked dirt in Raider's path. Bullets sang past his head. One clipped a neat hole in his hat—another churned leather and burned his arm. Raider set his teeth, threw himself under the train, and rolled. Taking a quick breath, he started up the ladder between the cars.

The gunmen were ready for him. Raider ignored their fire and kept going. A bullet chunked wood between his legs, blew off the heel of his boot. Raider stumbled, ran the last few yards to the sandbags, and dived for cover.

The trooper looked up in surprise and shot Raider a painful grin. "Well, I'll be fucked. If it ain't Johnny Reb hisself."

"You!" Raider stared. It was the old Yank sergeant he'd nearly had to fight in Kansas City. "Shit—if I'd known who was up here—" He stopped, saw the man's bloody leg and the kerchief knotted around it. "How bad is it?"

"Bad enough." The sergeant spat and glared at the hillside. "I can feed this thing Reb, if you can fire it."

"We're up here," said Raider. "Let's get to it."

The sergeant dragged himself up with Raider's help and snapped in the vertical clip. Raider tossed a row of sandbags aside, swept the barrel across the ridge and turned the big crank. The Gatling coughed, shuddered, and spat fire. It was a new ten-barrel model and Raider pumped 450 rounds a minute into the rocks. The weapon wreaked havoc among the outlaws. Heavy-caliber slugs ripped up the landscape. Men crawled desperately for cover and the troopers below gave a ragged cheer.

Raider and the sergeant exchanged quick grins. The clip went empty and the sergeant shoved in another. Four men made a break for a big boulder. Raider jerked the gun around thirty degrees and sent a withering fire into their midst. The outlaws seemed to explode. When Raider looked again, there was nothing but bloody rags splattered about the rocks.

"We got 'em on the run!" shouted the sergeant. "Bastards are—holy shit, what was that!"

Raider shut his eyes as a sandbag blew itself apart by his shoulder. "Come from behind," he snapped. "Wondered when that'd happen." Raider lugged the heavy gun around and fired blindly into the landscape. Rifle and pistol fire answered, then another sandbag exploded. Raider cursed. Some asshole was curled up on the ridge with a Sharps, way out of the Gatling's range. He could sit up there all day and plunk away with the buffalo gun. "Keep your head down," he told the sergeant. Raising the barrels as high as he could, he turned the crank angrily and fired. It was a useless gesture and he knew it. The Gatling wouldn't even come near the sharpshooter.

He kept firing anyway—raking the hillside and keeping the other gunmen honest. Acrid smoke stung his eyes. He cranked until his fist ached and his arm went numb. The clip was empty. He jerked it out, threw it aside, and yelled at the sergeant for another. The sergeant didn't answer. "Goddamn it, I need a—" Raider glanced over his shoulder and bile choked his throat. "Oh, shit!" The Sharps had done its job, nearly taking the man's head off. Raider set his teeth and groped around for a clip. Suddenly, the boxcar shuddered on its wheels and sent him sprawling. Raider's ears rang. Another dull explosion came from the head of the train. Then another, close enough to rock the car beneath him. Raider cursed. Dynamite—the bastards were trying to blow the fucking train!

He ignored the Sharps and the gunmen behind him. Jerking up the Gatling he shoved it around again, jammed in a clip, and raked the hillside. Another dull blast shook the earth. He spotted an outlaw scooting down the side of the ridge. The man's arm arced back. Raider cut him in half. The dynamite dropped from his hand and exploded, blowing half the hill into the air. Dirt and rock rattled down on Raider's head. He wiped his eyes, gagged, and peered over the sandbags. Troopers were swarming up the hillside, chasing the outlaws out of their holes. Other soldiers drove the gunmen back on the ridge behind him. Raider started the Gatling again, firing from one side of the train to the other until all the clips beside him were empty.

Doc walked down the hill carrying Raider's rifle. Dusting off his custom-tailored four-button, he searched around for his derby and found it. His watch said only nine minutes had gone by since the outlaws had hit the train. He frowned, shook the instrument—it was hard to believe less than an hour had passed. Raider hobbled past the treasure train and walked toward him. Doc thought he was hurt until he saw the heel of his left boot was missing. "You all right, partner?"

"I guess," Raider snorted. He glanced down the track

where men were laying out dead and wounded troopers. "How many you think we lost?"

"Too damn many, Rade. There must have been seventy-five or a hundred men in those hills."

"There was. Somebody sure put some thought into this." Raider turned at the sound of horses. Colonel Arthur and his cavalrymen rode toward them from the head of the train. Arthur paused, peered about wide-eyed at the carnage around him, saw Doc and Raider, and spurred his mount forward.

"You're a little late," Raider said darkly.

Arthur's face clouded. "We were cut off," he said stiffly. "By God, sir, if you are insinuating something . . . !"

"You know a sergeant—big heavyset fellow 'bout forty?"

Arthur stared. "Mr. Raider, I cannot possibly know the names of every member of my troop."

"Didn't think so." Raider lashed out suddenly, caught the man by the belt, and jerked him off his horse. The horse bolted and Arthur slammed to the ground. Raider squatted and put a .44 to his head. "Get up," he said quietly. "You and me are climbin' that boxcar. It's time you got acquainted with your men."

The colonel paled. "Captain McCleod! Arrest this man!" he shouted hoarsely. Doc saw McCleod nearby. He was tending a younger trooper who was trying to hold his belly in his shirt. McCleod looked dully at Arthur, then turned back to his business.

Lieutenant Graham told Raider eleven troopers had been killed in the fight, and another dozen wounded. The soldiers found the bodies of nineteen outlaws, and Graham thought they might have found more if the rain hadn't started.

The debris on the tracks was cleared by six, and the train got under way for Denver half an hour later. Miraculously, no one was hurt on the train. The cars themselves were something else. Every window was broken. Crystal chandeliers lay shattered in a million pieces. Carpeting was chewed up with bullets and the fine mahogany paneling was full of holes.

Raider shuffled through the *City of Worcester* and shook his head. It looked like a Dodge City whorehouse after a fire. "Jesus. Old man Pinkerton ain't gonna be real happy about this. How much you figure this thing cost, Doc?"

"Fifty, sixty thousand, I guess. Why?"

"Just wondering how long it'll take us to buy a new one. That son of a bitch Wagner'll take it out of our pay for sure. You watch and see."

"I don't think he can do that, Rade."

"You don't, huh?"

"No. All he can do is fire us."

Raider relaxed. "Well, hell—something good comes outa everything, don't it?"

CHAPTER FIVE

When the train was some miles from the scene of the attack, Doc insisted on stopping again to let Denver know what had happened. Climbing a telegraph pole in the pouring rain, he attached his gravity battery-powered key to the line and found it dead. Either the outlaws had cut it or the floods had taken it out up ahead.

Colonel Arthur refused to send a rider. He wanted nothing to do with the Pinkertons and intended to have Raider arrested as soon as the train reached Denver. "Fine," Doc agreed. "The son of a bitch deserves it."

"I'm glad you see that," said Arthur, somewhat surprised. "Maybe I'll go easy on you, Mr. Weatherbee."

"I really appreciate it," Doc said graciously. "When I write General Cleve about the attack, and where you were when it happened, maybe I'll go real easy on *you*."

Arthur sat up straight. "Now just a damn minute!"

"Maybe the twins will go easy, too—when they talk to the *Rocky Mountain News*. Hell, even if your wife *sees* the story back in St. Louis she probably won't believe it."

Arthur's face went slack and the color rose to his brow.

In ten minutes, two cavalry troopers left the train riding
hard for Denver.

The train should have crawled into Denver at two in
the morning. Instead, three more washouts along the way
kept the party stalled while crews cleared the tracks.

Doc roamed up and down the sleeper and the *City of
Worcester,* trying desperately to bring order out of chaos.
Both cars were full of bullet holes and leaked like a seive.
The twins got loose and tried to rape the porter. Khalifi
Both cars were full of bullet holes and leaked like a seive.
decided young Jamison was after Neferti and chased him
down the hall with a knife. Colonel Arthur and Lord
Willis got roaring drunk. Doc prayed the case would end
soon. Maybe Wagner would give them something easy
next time. Like a shoot-out with Jesse and Frank.

Raider fell into a deep, exhausted sleep. He dreamed
of outlaws chasing him up and down the tracks. A faceless
man with a Sharps rifle met him at the end of a dark
tunnel. The barrel of the gun was as wide as a cannon.

Someone tapped lightly on the door. Raider sat up
straight, his body bathed in sweat. Blinking the sleep away,
he stumbled out of bed to snap the lock. Damn Weatherbee anyway. Looks like he could just—

"Mr. Raider," the voice whispered. "May I come in,
please?"

Raider stared. Pale light from the corridor touched the
dark tumble of hair over her shoulders. Her face was lost
in shadow; all he could see was a fleck of fire in her eyes,
the olive sheen of her skin. "M-Miss Raman?"

"Shhh! Please!" A finger came to her lips and she
slipped inside with a rustle of silk. "No one must know I
am here." She was close to him now and the strong woman smell assailed his senses.

"Is—anything wrong? Wait a minute, let me get some
light in here."

"No!" Her hand gripped his arm. She reached back and
Raider heard the lock snap. "Things are—different in my

country," she said hesitantly. "I could not—come to you openly. Let you know as as American woman might do."

Raider's mouth went dry. "Uh—let me know what, ma'am?"

"Do I have to tell you?" she whispered. "I am here. Don't you know what I want? Oh, my God, *please!*" The gown slipped off her shoulders and she came up against him. Her arms clawed at his back and the heat of her breasts burned his chest. Raider slid his hand under her legs and lifted her easily to the bed. She moaned beneath him, her tongue darting hungrily into his mouth. He answered her kisses, then moved down her neck to the full, swollen breasts. Neferti groaned. Raider sucked the stiff, thrusting nipples, teased them with his tongue. Neferti cried out, thrashed against him, and ground her hips into his hardness.

Raider spread her legs and felt the silky limbs press eagerly against his back. When he touched the wetness between her thighs she bit her lip, cried out, and shuddered against him. Raider shook his head in wonder. God A'mighty—all he'd done was touch her pussy once and she'd come in a second! He plunged his fingers in her again and again. She jerked against him, gasping for air, forcing him deeper and deeper inside. Raider slipped his hand out and grabbed his cock, guiding it quickly into the moistness.

Neferti reached down, pulled him out, and slid herself under his belly. Her black eyes danced in the darkness. "No, not yet." Her voice was a ragged whisper. She gripped his back, brought her head between his thighs and flicked her tongue at the end of his cock. "Fuck my mouth first, Raider. I want that—*please!*" She opened her lips and took him in hungrily. Raider's heart nearly stopped. For a shy Egyptian lady who could hardly stand him in the light, she was doing just fine in the dark. Her mouth circled his swollen shaft, kneading him tenderly, then fiercely, sucking the rigid tool against the flesh of her throat.

Raider nearly came a dozen times. The girl knew just how far to take him—when to stop him right at the edge and ease him back. Raider tried to force her. He was swelling near to bursting, the ache in his balls driving him crazy. Still, she guided him smoothly, expertly, down a path of her own. Finally, when she was ready, she pumped him hard once and flicked her tongue down the length of his cock.

Raider exploded. Everything inside him surged like a flood down her throat. Neferti shuddered, pulled him in harder, and drained him dry.

Raider fell back exhausted. "Damn, lady—you almost killed me. I didn't think you was ever going to stop!"

Neferti slid herself up beside him and purred into his ear. "Mmmmmmm, you were delicious, Raider. Absolutely delicious!"

"I kinda figured you Egyptian ladies—well, you know . . ."

"What, Raider?"

"Uh—knew different kinds of stuff. I read a book once about love secrets of the East. Hell, I guess it was all true."

"Oh, it is, it is." She gave him a throaty laugh and stroked her hand across his cock. "Like to see some more of those love secrets?"

Raider swallowed hard. "Yeah, uh—not for a minute, though. I need to sort of—"

"What?"

"Rest up some before we—*damn*, lady!" His cock sprang up straight again under her fingers. Neferti laughed and pulled herself up on his belly. Jerking his tool swiftly in her hand, she thrust it between her legs and rammed her cunt hard against his groin. Raider sucked in a breath. The girl wasn't playing this time—she knew where she was going and how to get there. The pressure grew in his balls again. He burst loose inside her. Neferti went stiff, gave a strangled little cry, and nearly shook him off the bed. With a sigh, she fell down limply into his arms. "Raider, that was—oh, God, I can't describe it!"

Raider grinned. "You don't have to. I was there, and it's nothin' that needs any words to it."

"You are a fantastic lover. You know that, don't you?"

"Well now, I don't know. I guess I am if you say so. You sure did surprise me, lady. You know that?"

"How, my darling?"

"Comin' to me like this. I mean, you haven't exactly been real warm and friendly up to now."

"Silly." She pressed a finger against his nose. "I told you. In my country, things are different. A woman who lets a man know how she feels in public is a—how do you put it?—loose woman? She would be shamed, and the man she wanted would have nothing to do with her."

"Is that right? Well, I'll be damned."

"I think it is much easier to get in bed with a man in America, yes?"

"Beats me," Raider said drily. "I ain't even *tried* to get in bed with a man."

Neferti laughed and sat up. "Just lie still. I must get back now."

"Hey, wait," said Raider. "Now that we've gotten better acquainted, let's get a little light in here. I already felt every inch of you, but I haven't seen a thing."

"Next time, all right?" He heard the gown slide over her skin. "You will see all of my body you want to in Denver. I *want* you to look at it, Raider. I want you to see my body lying naked—spread out on a bed just for you."

Raider's heart raced. "Hey, come back here, girl!" His cock started swelling again and he jumped off the bed to find her. The door opened and she slid through quickly, closing it shut behind her. Raider lay back on the bed, arms behind his head. "Well, I'll be damned!" He grinned smugly. "Don't know how I'm goin' to break the sad news to poor old Doc."

At dawn, a full troop of cavalry met the train and stopped it. Raider dressed quickly, splashed water in his face, and made his way outside. The sky was clearing, and ragged tails of cloud scudded off to the east into a brilliant sunrise. Raider stepped gingerly through dull pools of water and joined Doc. Colonel Arthur gave him a withering stare and marched away.

"The captain says we're not twenty miles from Denver," said Doc. "Arthur's boys must've really told 'em a story,

Rade. They figured we'd likely gotten hit again and were all dead back down the tracks."

Raider yawned. "I ain't surprised we're not."

Doc gave him a puzzled frown. "You look like hell, partner. You have a bad night?"

"Naw, not too bad," Raider said absently.

"Go on up and get some coffee in the car. I'm going back and get changed before we roll into Denver." He paused and looked Raider over. "You might do the same, friend. After the stories spreading around Denver, the whole town'll be out to see us. A shave and some clean clothes wouldn't hurt any."

"I ain't runnin' for office," Raider said acidly.

"Good. I'm sure relieved to hear that." Doc stalked off toward the sleeper and Raider climbed up to the battered *City of Worcester*. The place still looked like a battle-ground, but the Union Pacific porters were doing their best, and the coffee was good and hot. Raider took his cup to a table and joined Willis and Powell Jamison. Willis looked hung over, and Jamison had nothing to say.

The twins were nowhere in sight. Raider looked up as the door at the end of the car opened. Neferti walked in and Raider grinned. She smiled quickly and poured herself coffee. Lord, she looked good! Experience overshadowed imagination now, and he mentally stripped the red cotton dress past the pink-tipped breasts, tight little tummy, and long tapered legs. Picking up his cup, he walked over behind her. "Have a nice rest, Miss Raman?"

Neferti turned and looked at him. "Why—yes. Thank you, Mr. Raider."

"Thank *you*, ma'am." Raider gave her a broad wink.

The girl stared. "What in the world is *that* supposed to mean?"

"Hey, you don't *have* to do that now. No one's looking." He ran a finger lightly up her arm and down the swell of her breast. "By God, you got the softest skin I ever seen. All over, too."

Neferti gasped. Black eyes flashed and she slapped him hard. Raider blinked and staggered back. "Hey, I know it's broad daylight but you don't have to—" Neferti slapped him again, colored up to her brow, and stormed down the aisle. Raider stared after her. Hell, he thought angrily, she didn't have to play the game *that* serious. A man could lose a tooth like that!

Doc looked up as Raider entered the compartment. "You see the trousers to my brown suit anywhere? I can't—"

"No, I ain't seen your fuckin' trousers!" snapped Raider.

Doc looked at him. "What's eating you?"

"Nothing. Forget it."

"Whatever you think." Doc knelt down on all fours and groped under the bed. "Don't know where those fool pants could have got to. Had 'em just last— Well now, what's this little item?" He grinned and held the silky black wig up to Raider. "Part of your new disguise, friend?"

Raider's mouth fell open. Now why would Neferti wear a black wig? She already *had* a fine head of— Understanding came quickly and anger rose up to choke him. "Goddamn those bitches!" he roared. "I'll kill 'em. I swear I'll kill *both* of 'em!"

CHAPTER SIX

The train snaked into Denver at nine in the morning, winding northwest past the South Platte River and across Cherry Creek. The air was bright and clear, and the blue spine of the Rockies gleamed in the distance. Raider and Doc spotted the high clock tower of Union Station and, a moment later, heard a band strike up the ragged chords of a march.

Raider frowned distastefully at the banners, flags, and cheering crowds clustered about the tracks just ahead. "That sure don't help security, Doc. 'Bout a million goddamn people standing around gawkin'."

"Well, two hundred, anyway. But I know what you mean."

The train wheezed into the station, and the crowd went suddenly quiet. Cheers turned to a low rumble of awe and amazement. Denver knew about the outlaw attack, but no one expected a thing like this. The train looked like it had just rolled through the Battle of the Little Big Horn.

For the next half hour, the Pinkertons were lost in a babble of city fathers, police, and bewhiskered officials. Arthur's troopers unloaded the treasures of Egypt onto special wagons. Raider and Doc personally carried the *Nymph of the Nile* to a carriage, surrounded by carbine-wielding soldiers. Raider saw Lord Willis stagger into a carriage ahead, and glimpsed the towering figure of Khalifi plowing through a shrieking crowd of bystanders. Dr. Raman insisted on riding with the *Nymph*. Mack Hooper, Denver's Pinkerton man, crowded in with Doc and Raider, dragging a black-suited scarecrow behind him.

"Doc, Raider—this is Henry Lewiston of the First National. He's been a real big help to us."

Raider had worked with Hooper before and liked him. He was a plainspoken, heavyset fellow with a bulbous nose, sparkling blue eyes, and a mind like a trap. Lewiston was something else again. A loose-limbed, gangly man with a thatch of red hair, he looked more like a farmer than a banker.

"Real pleased to see you boys safe," Lewiston grinned, pumping everyone's hand. "By God—you sure had a time out there!"

"Yeah, we sure did," said Raider.

"Well, your troubles are over. You are now in the hands of the First National Bank of Denver."

"We're pleased to hear that," Doc said politely, exchanging a look with Raider. Police and cavalrymen cleared the street and the caravan left the station, moving south on Seventeenth, then west onto Blake. Lewiston kept up a lively chatter, much to Dr. Raman's delight.

"The station back there cost half a million," Lewiston announced proudly. "Just finished it last month. Got thirty-six thousand people here now—been the official capital since April."

"Please—where is famous Tabor Grand Opera House?" chimed in Dr. Raman. "I would see this, yes?"

Lewiston ignored him. "Got our first telephones in seventy-nine, two years ago. Damn things don't work good, but we've got 'em. Started stringing real electrical lights up last year—got the only generating engine this side of the Missouri."

Raman tugged politely at his sleeve. "Tabor House. We see this soon, yes?"

Lewiston frowned and leaned into Hooper. "Jesus, Mack, who the hell *is* this fellow?"

Doc decided Lewiston wasn't nearly as rattle-brained as he appeared. At least, he'd given a great deal of thought to securing the treasure. The bank was a sturdy three-story brick structure, and the vault was protected by a heavy steel door with an intricate combination lock.

"Put your minds at ease and enjoy the de-lights of Denver," Lewiston bragged. He stepped back and viewed his domain. "Let's suppose someone *could* blast through that door and get inside. Which they couldn't, of course. The treasure's here safe behind tempered-steel bars, just like you see in your finest prisons. Plus"—he moved swiftly to the caged portion of the room—"plus, a reinforced screen of steel mesh welded right to the bars themselves." He pounded his fist on the cage. "Take the best equipment and half a day to saw through this. And who's goin' to give them the *time*, gentlemen?"

"Henry, it looks real fine," said Hooper.

Raider eyed the rest of the room, where thick, banded packets of paper money and sacks of gold coins were stored openly in bins. "You don't mind me asking, how come you leave all *this* out? Seems like it'd be safer in that cage of yours. Hell, must be a million bucks just—layin' around."

Lewiston's head bobbed like a stork. "More than that, Mr. Raider. And to answer your question, we don't need a cage. It's safe right where it is. And," he added with a wink, "folks do like to take money *out* of the bank sometimes."

"Yeah, I heard that."

"Frankly," Lewiston said softly, "your exhibit doesn't *need* all that protection. But it looks good, doesn't it?"

After the others left, Doc stayed behind. Lewiston stationed two policemen in the vault in case he "needed any help." Doc figured it was a nice way of saying even a Pinkerton might be tempted to stuff a big wad of bills in his pocket.

Taking his Premo Senior camera out of its case, he set the instrument atop a tripod he'd brought with him and fastened it on securely. With chalk, he marked where the tripod touched the floor, and measured the distance from the floor to the camera. He'd taken several shots of the treasure in the bank in Kansas City. The pictures had come out well and would make good additions to the case report he'd send to Chicago.

After the straight-on shots, Doc stepped back, considered another angle, then decided against it. Weatherbee liked nice, neat pictures, and there was a pile of debris against the wall in question. Lewiston said a water pipe had been repaired there; he'd told the painters and plasterers to leave their tarpaulins and buckets where they were and finish the job when the exhibit left town.

Weatherbee took a last look at the treasures inside the cage. There were jeweled daggers, intricate necklaces and armbands, hawk-headed gods, and glittering vases of silver. All of them paled beside the breathtaking star of the show. Three feet high and fashioned of solid gold, the *Naked Nymph* was an awesome sight. The girl was young, no more than seventeen or eighteen. Her hands stretched boldly over her head, accenting the high curve of her breasts, slim waist, and delicately tapered legs. Her expression was haughty, yet openly sensuous. Raider had taken one look at the statue in Kansas City and shaken his head. "By God," he'd said. "That's a coldhearted lady, Doc." Doc wasn't all that sure. To him, the *Nymph* looked a lot like Neferti Raman.

The reception was in full swing on the third floor when Doc joined it. He looked for Neferti, couldn't find her, and spotted Raider across the room. "Hooper says he'll watch the folks up here, Rade. I'd like to get over to the hotel and look things over before our traveling zoo checks in."

"Shit, I'm for it," muttered Raider. "Too damn many people in here."

Downstairs, they got directions to the Windsor Hotel and started down Fifteenth. A policeman chased after them and caught them at Holladay. "You two Raider and Weatherbee? Better get back to the bank. Mr. Hooper's lookin' for you."

Raider and Doc exchanged glances and followed the officer. Hooper met them halfway, a concerned frown crossing his features. "Come on," he said soberly. "I've got a team waiting. We got trouble, boys." Hooper kept silent as he whipped the team across town to the exhibit hall. Doc and Raider followed him into the building, where several Denver police officers waited. "Morton, you tell 'em." Hooper motioned to one of the men.

The tall officer led them into the hall and across to the far side. Squatting down, he lifted a panel in the floor. "I sent for Mack when I found this. Some 'anonymous' friend left a note at the station tellin' us where to look." Morton stepped aside and Raider and Doc peered into the hole.

"My God!" Doc stared in disbelief. "Is that what I think it is?"

"Uhuh. Dynamite. Two more charges like this one along the wall. All real small ones, by the way. Fuse leads outside to some trash barrels."

"This don't make a lot of sense," muttered Raider. "Who'd want to blow up the treasure?"

"They wouldn't," snapped Morton. "The exhibit goes over there," he pointed past his shoulder. "Set these things off, though, and you'll get one hell of a frightened mob."

"Which would give some smart outlaws a chance to

make off with the *Nymph* and a couple of other goodies," Hooper finished.

Doc looked at Raider. "We have to tell Raman and Neferti. They aren't going to like it much."

"Neither is Chicago," added Raider.

"Mr. Morton," asked Doc. "How long will it take to make sure this place is clean as a whistle?"

Morton rubbed his chin. "All night, I reckon. But we can do it. I got an okay to use whatever men I need if it has to do with the exhibit."

"Good," said Doc. "If you need any Army help, let us know."

Morton gave him a testy smile. "If it's all the same to you, I'll do without. Okay?"

Back at the bank, Doc and Raider took Neferti and her father into a private office. Dr. Raman paled at the news. Neferti's face tightened, then her dark eyes blazed. "Why, *why?* Who is *doing* this thing!"

"Likely the same people who hit the train," said Raider. "Or maybe a different bunch. It's hard to tell right now."

"Morton of the Denver police assures us he'll have the hall safe for the exhibit by morning," said Doc. "His men are working all night. Hooper knows the man and you can be sure he'll—"

"Sure?" Neferti shook a tousle of hair off her cheeks and laughed. "Your Mr. Wagner and Mr. Pinkerton were *sure* no one would attack the train. Now you tell us you are *sure* the building will not blow up under the priceless treasures of my country!"

"Well, yes, but—"

Neferti drilled Doc with her eyes, turned around, and stalked back to the reception. Walking straight to the mayor, she grabbed a startled Robert Morris by his whiskers. "I spit on your city!" she screamed. "You are savages, barbarians! You will not see the treasures here. Never!" Leaving a wide-eyed crowd in her wake, she stomped out of the room and down the stairs.

CHAPTER SEVEN

Neferti's performance left the reception in a shambles. Denver was proud of its blossoming respectability. The tuxedo-clad merchants, bankers, and politicians had put out plenty in Washington to get the Egyptian exhibit. Now the whole thing was exploding in their faces—they'd look like fools to the rest of the country and didn't much like it.

Doc and Raider plowed through angry city fathers and got their party out of the bank. Mack Hooper commandeered two carriages and whisked everyone off to the Windsor. Harry Morton arrived a few minutes later; the policeman had a nose for trouble and wasted no time getting to it. Neferti, Dr. Raman, Lord Willis, and the twins were locked safely in guarded suites seconds before half of Denver swarmed into the lobby.

Seven portly gents followed Doc and Raider to their room. Raider promptly shut the door in their faces. Morton gave him an easy grin. "Well, boy, you just fucked yourself forever in Denver."

"Yeah?" snapped Raider. "How you figure that?"

"You don't slam the door on the Denver Club. Those fellows run this town, and 'specially the bunch you just pissed off."

Raider pulled a bottle of rye from his pack. "I been fucked in bigger cities than this. Goddamn bunch of—"

"Now wait a minute!" Doc held up a hand. Mack Hooper took a slug from Raider's bottle and handed it to a white-faced Henry Lewiston. "We're not going to solve anything tonight," said Doc. "Mr. Lewiston, I expect you're a member of this Denver Club, too."

"I was," moaned the banker. "I haven't checked the last five minutes."

"I think what we ought to do is let everyone simmer down till morning. If you would, get two or three of those

43

fellows together and we'll set up a meeting. I'll talk to Dr. Raman."

"Looks to me as if it's the daughter you better talk with," put in Hooper.

"We'll talk to both of them. All right?" Lewiston agreed, and Hooper escorted him out of the room. Morton left moments later.

"Well, shit," said Raider. "Now what?"

"I'll talk to the Ramans, though I doubt it'll do much good." Doc glanced at his watch. "It's after five. You want to meet later and go to dinner? The Windsor's the finest hotel in town. They have an excellent gourmet menu."

Raider screwed up a frown. "If it's all the same, Doc, I'll run out and scare up a steak. I've had about all the mutton and crapper sauce I can stomach."

Before he left the Windsor, Raider went to check on Lord Willis and the twins, leaving the Ramans to Doc. Willis was already in a stupor in his suite. Louisa opened the door to the twins' room and cheerily asked him in. "No thanks," snapped Raider. "I'm just checking."

"Ohhh, that is too bad," Louisa sighed breathlessly. "I thought you enjoyed the love secrets of Egypt, Mr. Raider. . . ."

Raider felt heat rise to his face at the near-perfect imitation of Neferti's throaty voice. "Listen, that was a dirty goddamn trick, Louisa!"

"I've got more dirty tricks than that. Want to see some?"

Raider fumed and stomped off down the hall.

He walked a block up Eighteenth from the Windsor and turned right on Holladay, still raging at the twins. Louisa was damn fine in bed, he couldn't argue with that. But her cute little act sure had fixed him with Neferti. *"I'm real sorry, ma'am—I thought it was you I fucked last night an' I guess it must've been someone else."* Now that'd help, wouldn't it?

Raider spotted a steakhouse, didn't like the looks of it, and walked on toward Twentieth. Abruptly, he was in the heart of Denver's red-light district, just a few blocks from the elegant Windsor Hotel. Jennie Rogers's famed whore-house was just across the street. Raider had been there several times and thought about stopping by. First, though, he had an empty belly to fill. The café to his right looked fine and he pushed through the doors and found a table.

After his second bite of steak, he spotted the woman. She was wolfing down a corn-fed slab of beef as big as his own. Raider liked the looks of her right off. She was a big girl, with flaming red hair, bright blue eyes, and a saucy mouth. Her green satin dress covered her body like the skin on a snake. When she looked up again, Raider grinned. The redhead smiled right back. Raider wiped up the last bit of steak grease with his bread, pushed his plate aside, and walked over to her table.

"Miss, if I'm not intruding, I'd sure like to buy you a cup of coffee."

"Make it a brandy and you're on," she told him.

By the second drink, he knew her name was Nancy and that she came from Cheyenne. Raider didn't ask what a good-looking woman was doing in Denver's seedy end of town, and didn't much care.

"I ain't going to be here long," he told her. "I'd sure be pleased if you'd show me around."

The girl arched a brow. "Mr. Raider, you wouldn't fool a lady, would you?"

"What do you mean?"

"I have an idea you're no stranger to Denver."

"Now just how did you figure that, ma'am?"

"'Cause you look like you been most everywhere twice."

Raider laughed. "Hell, I guess maybe I have. Three times, some places." When he called the waiter for an-other drink, the two men in the corner caught his eye. He pulled his gaze quickly back to the girl. Right off, he knew where he'd seen them before. They'd passed him outside the Windsor, and then again at the corner of Nineteenth. Twice was all right. Three times was one too many. Excusing himself, he stalked through the café and out the back door. There was a narrow alley there and an odorous outhouse. Raider flattened himself in shadow behind the privy and waited.

In less than a minute, the short, stocky member of the pair opened the door and quickly stepped outside. Raider let out a breath and drew his Remington. The tall man in the riding duster had gone out front, then. Likely, he was already circling around back. Raider squatted quietly, picked up half a brick and tossed it down the alley. The short man whipped around, jerked out a pistol and snapped three rapid shots into the dark.

Raider stepped from cover. "Over here, asshole." The man's eyes went wide and his gun arm shot out straight. Raider fired once. The man cried out, grabbed his shoulder and tumbled over a row of trash cans.

Raider backed into shadow and sprinted down the alley. The tall man appeared suddenly around the corner. The duster whipped aside. Light blossomed in the alley, followed by a deafening roar. Raider threw himself into a pile of garbage, rolled over, and snapped off a shot. The man jerked back. Raider cursed, pulled himself up, and started after him. Now he knew what the man carried under his duster—a double-barreled sawed-off, likely hung from his shoulder. It was an old outlaw trick—not something you'd figure in a big-city thief looking for wallets and watches.

Raider sprinted north toward Blake. The man was running hard a block ahead. A woman spotted his shotgun, shrieked, and jumped for cover. The outlaw yelled at her, turned, saw Raider, and ducked into an alley. Raider flattened himself against brick, heard a loud click, and knew the gunman had slipped two more loads into the weapon. Raider fired toward the darkness, leaped for the next doorway. The shotgun exploded twice. Buckshot whined past Raider's head. He turned in the alley and fired blindly, saw the man in the flash of his muzzle, and fired again. The man grunted, stumbled, disappeared in shadow.

Raider stopped. Bootsteps echoed down the alley. Raider reloaded on the run, cut down the alley to Twenty-first. The man would figure he'd follow, maybe hang back and wait. If he could cut around fast enough and come in behind . . .

Raider peered cautiously down half a dozen alleys. Fuming, he ranged up the street, glancing in restaurants, bars, and cheap whorehouses. Crossing Eighteenth again, he turned up Wazee Street and walked west toward Cherry Creek. Suddenly, Denver looked totally unfamiliar, and he realized where he was. This end of Wazee was called Hop Alley after the Chinese who lived there. They'd settled in Denver after the railroads let them go, and now worked as cooks, cheap labor, and laundrymen. Raider felt decidedly uncomfortable. The folks down here had no great love for white faces. A man had been beaten and lynched by whites in the big Chinese Riot just the fall before—hanged from a lamp post a few blocks away.

Quickly, Raider crossed Wazee and walked north toward Union Station. There was no use chasing the shotgunner. He was long gone for sure. In the morning, he'd talk to Harry Morton.

Raider stopped, suddenly remembering. Jesus, he'd left the good-looking redhead sitting in a restaurant on Holladay! If a pretty thing like that got away he'd never forgive himself. Turning on his heels, he sprinted back south. Half a block away he saw the place was still open and breathed a sigh of relief. Now, if the girl was still there—

The man stepped out of the alley, grinned broadly, and brought the shotgun up to his shoulder. Raider froze. The bastard had read his mind and doubled back! He reached for his gun and knew he'd never make it. Fire blossomed across the street. The shotgunner's hat blew off. He whipped around angrily, emptied one barrel at the stranger, turned the other on Raider. Raider's .44 barked twice and the outlaw folded. Raider crouched, saw Lieutenant Graham from the train racing over toward him. "I'm grateful you came along, soldier."

Graham squatted and stared at the gunman. "He's dead. What the hell happened?"

"It's a long story. I ain't real sure myself. Hang on here a minute." Raider pushed through the gathering crowd. The redhead was gone and no one remembered which way she'd headed. "Shit." Raider kicked open the door to the street. Four Denver policemen met him with drawn guns.

Harry Morton showed up at the jail an hour later, gave Raider a scathing look, and leaned against the bars outside his cell. "Welcome to Denver. What the fuck are you tryin' to do, friend?"

"I ain't trying to do anything," Raider snorted. "Get me out of here, Morton."

"You killed a man. Wounded another."

"They tried to kill *me*. I already *told* the fat policeman who put me in here!"

Morton sighed, called over his shoulder, and brought a guard. The guard opened Raider's cell and Raider followed the pair down the hall. Before he could ask more questions, Weatherbee and Mack Hooper burst through a door. "Goddamn it," snapped Doc. "What the fuck are you trying to do, Rade!"

"Morton already asked, Doc."

"Well, I'm asking again!"

"Sit down," said Morton. Weatherbee and Hooper sat. "You can go when you like," Morton told Raider. "Nobody's charging you with anything."

Raider stared. "Why the hell didn't you say so?"

Morton gave him a dirty grin. "You know how us lawmen are. Got to scare the shit out of folks." He perched on a desk and reached for a cigar. "We put some names to those two real quick. One's Curly Morris, and the dead one's Buckshot Ginty. Morris is small-time, but Ginty's been mixed up with the James Boys, Charlie Pitts, the Youngers—I don't know who the hell else."

Mack Hooper whistled. "You hooked you a big one, boy."

Morton gave him a black look. "I got an idea he did more than that. Ginty and Morris were both hooked up with T. C. Shipley, our local big shot, pimp, crooked gambler, and general asshole."

Raider scratched his chin. "So I'm running in fast company. What have they got against me?"

"Ginty and Morris were seen riding in last night from

the east." Morton looked meaningfully at Raider. "Where you boys came from."

Raider suddenly understood. "The damn train! They was out there?"

"I'd bet my hat on it." Morton gave him a broad smile. "You didn't make many friends with that Gatling gun, boy. Reckon you'll be getting some more callers 'fore you leave town."

CHAPTER EIGHT

Doc wished he was anywhere but Denver—with the possible exception of Chicago. He could imagine Allan Pinkerton's face when the papers hit his desk. Pinkerton liked publicity. The kind that read BRILLIANT OPERATIVES FOIL ROBBERY. He didn't much care for headlines like those in the *Rocky Mountain News*:

OUTLAWS SLAUGHTER TROOPS IN TRAIN MASSACRE

EGYPTIAN BEAUTY PULLS MAYOR'S BEARD

PINKERTON OPERATIVE KILLS GUNMAN
IN RED-LIGHT DISTRICT SHOOT-OUT

"Just great," Weatherbee moaned, stabbing a fork at the paper. "That's the one that'll do it, Rade. It just had to be across from a whorehouse, right?"

Raider set down his coffee. "Hell, Doc, I'm real sorry 'bout that. I wanted to gun him down in church, but the feller wouldn't listen."

Doc glared and attacked his eggs and bacon. He wished they'd had breakfast sent to the room. Everyone in town had flocked to the Windsor to get a look at the "fiery Egyptian" and the "Pinkerton shoot-out artist," or whoever the hell they could find. For the moment, he and Raider were it. Willis was still loaded. Neferti had vowed to stay in her room until the train left Denver.

"Not only that," he told Raider. "She's giving a damn interview. I tried to talk her out of it but she won't listen to anybody."

"Ought to make real interestin' reading," mused Raider.

Lewiston set up the meeting at Delmonico of the West, a few blocks from the Windsor. Doc was pleased at the chance to sample some fine gourmet dishes. Raider figured he'd get stuck with something buried in sauce and was relieved to find steak on the menu.

Harry Morton and Mack Hooper showed up, and Lewiston brought two influential members of the Denver Club. The meeting started off badly and went rapidly downhill. Lewiston's friends said they planned to sue Pinkerton's, the White House, Egypt, the Union Pacific, and the Queen of England if the exhibit was canceled. Raider said something about rich, fat-bellied assholes and the pair walked off in a huff.

Doc glared at his partner. "That was real fine, Rade. Every little bit helps."

"Frankly," sighed Lewiston, "I don't think you can hurt much at this point. Those fellows had their minds made up before they *got* here." Lewiston mumbled something about business downtown and left quickly.

"Well, nobody's left but us lepers," grinned Hooper. "I talked to the Union Pacific, Doc. They figure three weeks to get those cars back in shape. They're kinda wondering who's picking up the bill."

"Three weeks!" Doc set his teeth. "We can't wait three weeks. The exhibit's scheduled in San Francisco."

"She ain't canceled that?"

"Hell, no. She says San Francisco's 'civilized.' Not at all like Denver."

"Guess she hasn't seen the parts I been in," said Raider.

"*No* one's seen the parts you've been in. Hooper, we've got no choice. I've been trading telegrams with Washington all night. They say stall if we can but do what the Ramans want. It's their treasure."

"You know what I think?" put in Harry Morton. "I

think we're doing just what the *outlaws* want, whether we know it or not."

Doc frowned, then nodded understanding. "The thought's crossed my mind, damn it. That tip-off about the dynamite was a little too convenient."

"Someone wants that exhibit out of the vault and back on the rails where they can hit it," said Morton. "But, hell—what makes 'em think they can take it a second time?"

" 'Cause they damn near got away with it the first time," Raider said evenly.

Colonel Arthur found Doc in the lobby after lunch and led him to a corner. Doc was surprised to see the officer wearing civilian clothes. "Weatherbee," the colonel said coolly, "I don't like you *or* your partner, but I've got something somebody's got to see and I guess you're it."

Doc questioned him, but Arthur would say nothing. He had two horses waiting down the street, and Doc reluctantly mounted an ugly spotted stallion. Weatherbee hated riding horses. The only four-legged beast he could stand was his mule, Judith, who pulled the apothecary wagon he frequently used as a cover in the field. He hoped Judith was faring well in Albuquerque, and promised himself to get a telegram off to the stable keeper as soon as he had time.

Arthur crossed the Larimer Street bridge over Cherry Creek and led Weatherbee west toward the Platte River. Doc soon understood why the colonel had chosen horses instead of a wagon or carriage. Denver had plenty of seedy areas, but this was the worst. Raw sewage pooled in the unpaved streets beside tar-paper shacks, tents, and wooden crate houses. Dead dogs swelled in the roadway, and hollow-eyed street urchins roamed the alleys.

"Nice place, huh?"

"I'm from New York, Colonel. I've seen it all before. What the hell are we doing down here?"

"Just ahead." Arthur led his horse down a muddy alley and stopped before a clapboard shack. Doc followed him inside. The odor of stale sweat and bad food was over-powering. A stringy-haired young girl stepped from behind a ragged quilt curtain.

"This is Marcie," said Arthur. "One of my corporals picked her up in a bar on Wazee. She got drunk and said something the corporal thought was important. I think it is, too."

Marcie was clearly frightened, but she told Doc her story. She worked as a whore in one of T. C. Shipley's establishments. Shipley himself had come in last night and used the back room as a meeting place. Marcie had stepped outside in the alley to pee, looked in a window, and saw Shipley's guest.

"It was that pretty foreign lady," drawled Marcie. "The one that come on the train."

Doc sat straight up. "Neferti Raman?" He turned sharply to Arthur. "What the hell is this, Colonel?"

Arthur shrugged. "I have no idea, Weatherbee. When I heard the story, I asked myself, Why would the girl lie? I gave her two dollars for her time, but she'd already told the corporal everything she knew. She can't get a damn thing out of this 'cept a slit throat from Shipley."

Doc looked at the girl. "Marcie, are you *certain* that's who you saw? It couldn't have been someone else?"

"No, sir," the girl said dully. "It was her, all right. I seen her pitchur in the paper, and I was down to the station, too!"

On the ride back, Weatherbee turned to Arthur. "This doesn't make a bit of sense, Colonel. Why would Neferti have anything to do with a man like Shipley? Hell, how would she even *meet* him?"

"Hmmmph!" said Arthur. "Can't ever tell about foreigners."

"That has nothing to do with anything. She—"

Arthur cut him off and pointed northwest. Black, oily smoke rolled up to the sky.

"It's the railyards," said Doc. "Looks like the whole damn place is on fire!"

*   *   *

Raider knew it was useless, but he wanted to find the redhead. She was one of the best-looking girls he'd seen anywhere, and he didn't want to lose her. Walking down the center of town, he covered half a dozen bars, asked questions, and rode the cramped little wagons of the Denver Horse Railroad Company. Finally, he found himself near Union Station, remembered what Hooper had said about the cars, and decided to have a look.

The cars were sitting on a Union Pacific siding at the far end of the yard. There were no guards, and no workmen either. Raider thought that was a little peculiar. Still, there was nothing left to guard, and the railroad wasn't budging without money.

Climbing aboard, he wandered through the battered sleeper and the *City of Worcester,* then jumped down and headed for the treasure car. Surprisingly, it was still in good shape. It *looked* like hell, but the special reinforcing of sheet metal had kept the inside secure. Maybe they could—

Raider stopped. Footsteps crunched down cinder and gravel on the other side. Bending quickly, he saw two pairs of legs moving around the end of the car. Raider hoisted himself through the open door and rolled into shadow.

The two men stopped. Raider could hear their voices and, in a moment, the noise of tools banging lightly against the bottom of the car. What the hell were they up to? he wondered.

Raider listened, edged over to the door, and peered out. Afternoon shadow drifted over the yard. It was hard to see what the two were doing. One was crouched by the wheel; the other was on his back under the car. The banging stopped, turned into a low, grating sound like—like sawing! By God, thought Raider, that was exactly what they were doing. Sawing the fucking axle! Raider inched out the Remington, scrambled to his feet, and jumped to the ground. The man by the wheel jerked up, startled.

"Hold it!" snapped Raider. "You—slide your ass out nice and easy."

A face poked from under the car. The first man scowled at Raider. "What the shit you want, feller?"

"I was about to ask you."

"You're makin' a big mistake." The man shook his head. "We're Pinkertons. Put the gun down or you got trouble."

Raider grinned. "Pinkertons? No shit!"

The man moved slightly, masking his partner. The second man whipped a pistol from under his jacket and fired. Raider jerked back, squeezed off the .44. The man's face exploded. Something hit Raider hard, dropping him to the ground. Too late, he realized a third man had edged around the other side of the car.

Raider's face ground in cinders. The man pommeled him hard. Raider lashed out, tossed him aside. The other man was on him, grabbing for his gun hand. Raider pulled back, swung out blindly. The Remington's blade sight ripped the man's cheek. Raider turned, caught the big solid fist on the point of his jaw. . . .

His lids were heavy as lead. He took a deep breath and nearly choked. Reaching out blindly, his hand touched something hot. Raider jerked back, opened his eyes. "Jesus Christ!" Flames licked at the boards less than a yard away; thick smoke stung his eyes. Dragging himself up, Raider stumbled to the door of the car, threw himself to the ground. Hands reached out, grabbed his shoulders, and pulled him away from the heat. Raider sat up, shook his head, and coughed.

"You all right, partner?"

"Huh?" Raider gave Doc a stupid look. "What the hell are *you* doing here?"

"I was about to ask you. Here, let me give you a hand." Raider stood, blinked in awe at the sight. The whole special train was in flames. A team of horses galloped through the yard pulling a steam pumper. The area filled with shouting people. Raider quickly told Doc what had happened. Doc looked puzzled. "You sure you killed one of 'em?"

"Hell yes, I'm sure. I hit him right in the face, Doc."

"Then where is he?"

"He's not there? He's gotta be, unless they carried him off somewhere." Raider looked at his partner's face. "Hey, I'm not makin' this up. You know better than that."

"Rade—what were you doing here in the first place?"

"I was—remember that redhead I told you about? Well, I couldn't find her so I—Doc, come back here. I ain't finished yet!"

CHAPTER NINE

Raider had a painful burn on his hand and a fair-sized goose egg. An hour in a hot tub and a few slugs of Tangleleg cleared his head and brought back his appetite. Dressed, he was ready to search out a steak when Harry Morton and Hooper appeared.

"You can eat later," Morton announced. "I got a few questions."

"If you want, I'll order up something," said Doc.

"Thanks. You and me don't read menus the same. Harry, I already told you everything. There's nothing else to say."

"Yeah, there is, too." Morton pulled a pistol out of his pocket and dropped it on the table.

Raider picked it up and made a face. It was an old 1860 Starr, a double-action Army .44. "Someone sure ain't wasting any money on guns. You find it in the yard?"

Morton nodded and eased into a chair. "You don't see a lot of these anymore and I know who it belonged to. Shorty Hale from Topeka, one of T. C. Shipley's hands. I can guess who the other two were, not that it makes much difference." Morton looked thoughtfully at Raider and Doc. "They didn't have time to do what they came for, but they left their mark. If they'd kept their heads and just hauled Raider off and killed him 'stead of burning the evidence, we'd never have noticed a thing." Morton looked at his hands. "Not till that train got out in the wilds and the goddamn wheels fell off."

Doc lit a cheroot. "Makes sense with what we've been saying. They want to get that exhibit out of the vault and back on the rails."

Doc didn't much want to, but he had to tell Morton about the girl named Marcie, and what she'd said. Morton's eyes widened at the news. "Shit. You guys sure know how to make a man's day long."

"Doc," Raider said hotly, "if this comes from Arthur, it's a bunch of crap and you know it!"

"Rade, I don't like him either. But why would he set up a thing like this?"

Raider muttered to himself, but couldn't think of an answer.

Doc went with Morton to see Neferti. When she heard about her alleged visit to T. C. Shipley she turned red with fury and threatened them with Khalifi. Doc and Morton retreated hastily to the bar and joined Raider and Hooper. "I don't know what the fuck's going on here," Morton said angrily, "but I don't like it one damn bit." He poked a big finger in Doc's chest. "Find yourself a train, Weatherbee, and get this circus out of my town!" Mumbling to himself, he stalked out of the Windsor.

"He's got a point," said Doc.

"He's got more than that." Hooper lowered his mug of Tivoli beer and wiped suds off his mouth. "I've got sources in Denver, too. Some of them better than Harry's. Bad guys are drifting into the area like cats in heat. Hard-cases from Dodge, Cheyenne—hell, as far away as Texas. There's a little hole-in-the-wall bar out near Golden called Sally's. From what I hear, it looks like a wanted-poster convention. Something's brewing here, and I don't blame Harry for not liking it."

"Something to do with the treasure," said Raider.

"What else?"

"I still don't see Miss Raman working with this Shipley to steal somethin' that's already hers. It don't make sense."

"Doesn't it?" Hooper looked from Raider to Doc. "I

been doing a little reading, gents, and some of it *does* make sense. The girl's got a big voice in the rebellion going on back home. They're killing Frenchies and Englishmen by the dozen right now—only they're short of guns and ammo. Maybe the little lady's found a way to buy some. . . ."

Raider stared at his partner. "Doc, you're crazy as hell. I'm not goin' to let you do it!"

Weatherbee eyed himself critically in the mirror over his bed, inspected the false whiskers, then turned to Raider. "I don't see any other way, Rade. We'll never get to the bottom of this until we find what Shipley's up to."

"Shipley's too damn smart to show his face in that robber's nest."

"I know he is. But somebody'll be there who's right next to him. You can't do it, partner. A few of those boys know your face." Doc stepped into faded denims and worn boots, then slipped a greasy flannel shirt over his arms and stuck the Diamondback .38 in his belt. "How do I look?"

"Great," frowned Raider. "Like a New York Pinkerton in whiskers and a dirty shirt."

"Just what I was aiming for," said Doc.

•   •   •

Raider had lost his appetite, but grabbed a sandwich anyway and dutifully made his rounds. Willis was half sober for a change, playing cards with Jamison. Dr. Raman was asleep and Neferti wouldn't come to the door. The twins' door was unlocked. Raider opened it reluctantly and stepped inside. The room was empty. He muttered to himself and stalked down the hall. *That* wasn't good news at all. If they weren't fucking something in there, they were doing it somewhere else. He tried Arthur's room. The colonel glared at him and slammed the door in his face. Raider saw enough to know the twins weren't with him.

Raider dropped on his bed and stared at the ceiling. It was only 8:30, but he couldn't think of anything to do.

He was worried about Doc. Weatherbee was a good man, but playing around with hard-nosed outlaws was *his* business, not Doc's. Doc was better at making out case reports and taking pictures with his Premo Senior. He didn't have any idea how to talk to assholes like that.

The shot brought him straight out of bed. He knew he'd dozed off, but figured it couldn't have been more than a few minutes. He grabbed the Remington, jerked open the door, and sprinted down the hall. Lord Willis's door burst open. Jamison staggered out and crumbled to the floor. Raider bent down, grabbed him by the shoulders. "What happened? You all right?"

Jamison stared. His face was white and blood coursed out of his hair. "In—there—Lord Willis!"

Raider ran inside. Willis was sprawled on the carpet with his mouth open. For a moment, Raider thought he was dead. The bullet had slammed into his shoulder just below the collarbone. Raider ripped up a sheet, bound the wound tight, and turned back to the hall. Guests filled the corridor and Raider sent one of them for a doctor.

"What happened? You see anything?"

Jamison shook his head. "Jesus, is he dead? I—"

"No. He'll be all right."

"Someone—knocked. The fellow hit me."

"You recognize him?"

"No, never saw him before."

The doctor arrived with a Denver policeman. Raider told him to find Harry Morton and stalked back to his room to get a shirt on.

"Nobody saw anything," Morton said acidly. "They never do."

"Hell, I should have if anyone did. I was down the hall in a second."

Morton worked his mouth like he tasted something awful. "Willis is conscious. He wants Neferti arrested. Says she hired someone to kill him."

"What?"

"He can't make it stick. All it'll do is add a little more

stink round here. Like we needed some." Morton looked around. "Where's Weatherbee? He know about this?"

Raider glanced at the ceiling. "Doc's out for a walk. Always takes the air this time of the night."

• • •

Doc followed the narrow road straight west on his rented horse, past Arvado and on toward Golden. The strong smell of malt was in the air and he could see the lights of the big Coors brewery up north. A storekeeper gave him a frightened look and pointed the road to Sally's.

Doc almost missed it under the trees. A dozen horses were hitched outside and around the corner. Doc checked his beard and marched through the bat-wing doors. Every man in the room turned and glared. Doc swallowed hard and kept going. Hooper was right. They were the meanest bunch of bastards he'd ever seen outside of Yuma Prison.

"What the fuck *you* want?" growled the bartender.

"Whiskey." A dirty glass hit the rough plank bar, slopping half its contents. Two men got up and walked straight for Doc. One was bearded and fat. The other was tall and gray-eyed and stank of stale beer.

"This is kind of a private party, friend," grinned the tall man. "Finish your drink and move on."

Doc looked at him. "Got nothing against private parties."

The man's smile faded. "You got a name, boy?"

"Yep." The man waited. Doc calmly sipped his drink. He heard the sharp intake of breath, felt the man go rigid. Doc whipped the Diamondback .38 under the fellow's nose. *"Don't,* friend." The gray eyes went wide. Long fingers backed off from the .45. The fat man took a step away from the bar.

"Pull that and you'll draw forty pounds of lead!" raged the man.

"You won't hear it," said Doc. He snaked the man's weapon out of his holster and laid it on the bar. *Shit,* he thought. *Now what do I do with him?*

"What's the trouble, Charlie?" The man came up easily beside him and offered a wide smile. "Digger, take Charlie back somewhere and buy him a beer. That suit you, mister?"

"Suits me fine," said Doc. Charlie fumed and let Digger lead him off. Doc put his gun away and took a good look at the stranger. He was close to Raider's size and built just as solid. Friendly brown eyes flashed under a shock of yellow hair. He was better dressed than the others, sporting a burgundy vest Doc might have picked himself.

"Name's Butch Hackman. How about another drink?"

Doc stuck his hand out. "Folks call me—Alabama."

Hackman screwed up his eyes. "What part of Alabama you *from*, mister?"

"Mobile. 'Course I ain't been back in years."

"Figures. You don't sound much like a Southern boy. No offense."

"None taken." Doc forced a grin and lifted his glass. "Buy you one, Mr. Hackman?"

Hackman pretended not to hear. Warmth faded from his eyes, and he was suddenly all business. "What Charlie said is right. We don't get a lot of people here we haven't seen before. How did you get here and what do you want?"

"Work, if I can get it."

"Who said there was work here?"

"Shorty Hale." Doc mentioned the man Raider had shot in the railyards. "I saw him a couple of days ago."

"Uhuh. What kind of work did Shorty say you might get?"

"The kind I'm best suited for."

Butch didn't blink an eye. "Buy the man a drink," he told the bartender. "Enjoy yourself, Alabama. I'll get back to you." Hackman wandered off and Doc let out a breath. He didn't have to look around. He knew what Hackman was doing—asking everyone in Sally's if they'd heard the late Shorty Hale mention a dude named Alabama—one who sounded like he'd never been west of Cincinnati.

"Hi there, lil fella. Where the hell you been all my life!"

Doc turned and stared. The woman loomed over him

like a mountain. She was a good six-three, closing in on sixty, and carrying three hundred pounds of the ugliest female flesh Doc had ever seen.

"I'm Sally. Damn, you're cute. I'm gettin' horny just lookin' at you!" Sally giggled and hugged Doc to her. Breasts the size of Texas melons bounced out of her dress and smothered him. Doc came up gasping for air. "Come on." Sally grabbed his arm, "Let's you and me run out back and do some fancy fucking!"

Hackman laid a hand on Sally's shoulder. "Later," he grinned. "I'll save him for you, Sal."

"Oh, shit, Butch!"

Hackman drew him aside. "You really want a job, Alabama, I got one for you."

"I want one for sure."

"Fine." Hackman looked through him with eyes like ice. "Ride into Denver with Charlie and Digger. I want a lawman named Harry Morton shot dead."

CHAPTER TEN

Raider opened the door and stared. The last person he expected to find there was Neferti Raman. Without a word, she stomped past him and dropped into a chair. Raider looked at her. The girl was clearly seething inside. Anger flashed in her eyes; a vein throbbed in the long column of her neck.

"Mr. Raider," she said tightly, "I would like a drink if you have one."

"Uh, well sure. Got some pretty good rye here if that's—"

"Rye will do nicely." Ignoring the glass he offered, she snatched the bottle and took a long healthy slug. "Ah— much better. She caught his expression and laughed. "Don't look so surprised. I've had a drink before."

"I guess maybe you have."

Neferti studied him carefully. "If I ask you something, will you give me an honest answer?"

"I'll sure try."

"Do you think I tried to kill Lord Willis?"

"No. I never thought you had anything to do with it."

Neferti closed her eyes in obvious relief. "Thank you. That—means more than I can tell you." She let out a breath and stared at the wall. "I do *not* murder people. I would be pleased to see the bastard dead with all the rest of his kind, but I did not hire anyone to kill him. And I do not—*sneak* about in the night meeting criminals I never heard of!" Neferti's dark eyes smoldered.

"Hey, now, take it easy. You want another drink?"

She shook her head, stood abruptly, and stalked to the window. "I need help, Mr. Raider. I am in a strange country, and things are happening I do not understand. I—need someone who believes in me. Someone I can trust." When she turned to face him, she was a different woman from the one Raider had seen before. The anger was gone. The dark eyes had turned soft and lazy. Her mouth opened slightly; the full, sensuous lips were touched with moisture.

"Uh, Miss Raman—"

Her mouth curled in amusement. "That was a terrible joke of Louisa's. Did you really think it was me?"

Raider felt the heat rise to his face. "You—know about that?"

"Did you think those little sluts could *stand* not to tell me?" Neferti laughed. "Of course I know. Was she good?"

"Oh, come on now."

"Was she good, Raider?"

"Yeah she was good," Raider snapped. "What the hell are you doing, lady?"

"What does it look like?" She took a step toward him, reached up, and slipped the strap off her shoulder. A perfect little breast appeared, tilting up to a rose-colored nipple.

Raider's mouth went dry. He felt the swelling in his crotch and saw Neferti's eyes flick down to his pants. She bit her lips and smiled. "That morning, when you thought

I'd slept with you, I *had* to slap you. But when you ran your fingers over me like that . . ."

Raider walked away from her and took a long slug of rye. "Goddamn it, I been wantin' you right from the start and you know it," he said sharply. "Now you come in here actin' just like a—"

"A whore?" she finished. Anger flecked her eyes. "I want help instead of money. What's the difference how you pay it?"

"There's a lot of difference."

"Maybe you'd feel better if you tossed me a couple of Morgan dollars!"

"Yeah, maybe I would."

"Fine. Then let's get on with it!" Reaching behind her, she clawed the back of her dress and ripped it angrily down to her waist. Fabric tore, and the full skirts fell to her ankles. Raider gazed at the swelling hips, the dark patch of fur between her thighs, the lovely legs that seemed to go on forever. Pulling his eyes away, he jammed the Stetson on his head, crossed the room, and jerked open the door.

Neferti stared. "Wha—what are you *doing?*"

"I'm going out and get fucked, lady. There's something wrong with this. I ain't real sure what it is, but I don't much like it." Slamming the door behind him, he stomped off down the hall. "Ain't anyone going to believe this," he muttered darkly. "*I* sure as hell don't."

Denver had plenty of good whorehouses. Raider had sampled Mattie Silk's place and Bella Bernard's more than once, but he had a particular fondness for Jennie Rogers's parlor. Doc's weakness was gourmet food and fancy clothes; Raider had a soft spot for first-class houses of pleasure, and Jennie's was high on his list.

The famous madam was out for the evening, but several girls recognized Raider and greeted him enthusiastically. Raider grinned at them all, and finally settled on an old favorite. Cindy was a saucy-eyed blonde who claimed the longest legs in the world, and no man had argued with her yet. She hooked her arm through his and hurried up the stairs.

"Hold it, honey—I got first call on this one."

Raider turned and frowned at the girl below. *"Nancy?* Well, I'll be damned!"

The big redhead grinned broadly. "I'm not used to getting stood up, mister. You got some explaining to do."

"Not now he doesn't!" snapped Cindy.

"Hold it, girl. If there's anything left over, I'll call you."

"Well I never!" Cindy pouted and stalked down the stairs.

Nancy led Raider into a red plush room with a brass bed and a mirrored ceiling. Raider sat down on the bed. Nancy leaned back and looked at him, shook her head, and laughed. "Raider, honest to God—you look like your pa just caught you behind the barn. Surprised to see me here, right?"

"Uh, some, yeah."

"Disappointed? That I'm not a fine lady you bought a brandy for?"

"Hell no, I ain't disappointed!"

She turned and poured him a whiskey. "What happened to you, by the way?"

"I'll tell you all about it sometime. When we haven't got nothing else to do."

She caught his tone, set the whiskey down, and walked up to him. Without a word, she stepped out of her gown and let it whisper to the floor. Raider looked her over from head to toe. Neferti's little act had nearly driven him crazy. Seeing the redhead naked was all he could take. Picking her up in his arms, he tossed her on the bed and started throwing his clothes across the room.

Nancy's eyes went wide. "Lordy, you're *ready,* aren't you?"

"Damn near, lady." Tossing off his Stetson last of all, he jumped on the bed beside her and spread her legs. Nancy drew him into her and moaned.

"Why do I get the feeling this—isn't goin' to last long?"

"It ain't," said Raider, driving her into the mattress. "Not the first time."

"I don't know if I can—*stand* the second time!" she gasped.

Raider pounded her hard, running his hands over the soft ivory belly and the swell of her breasts. Nancy bit her lip and writhed beneath him, lashing her flaming hair across the pillow.

"Raider—Raider—I'm coming *hard!* I'm coming—NOW!"

Raider's cock swelled to bursting. His load rose up to surge into the nest of auburn hair. He held it back. Just one . . . more . . . thrust to make it right . . .

Nancy jerked away, nearly breaking his shaft in half. Green eyes flashed over his shoulder. "What the *hell* are you doing in here!" she screamed. "Get *out* of my room!"

Raider turned. Louisa and Annette stood wide-eyed and naked at the foot of the bed. "Shit. I don't believe this!"

"We were just watching," said Annette. "Oh, don't stop, please!"

"Nancy, what are they doing here?"

"They work here. Came in last night from Detroit."

"Detroit my ass." Raider stood on the bed and pointed to the door. "Get your clothes on. Right now!"

"What for?"

Raider roared. The twins squealed and ran. Tight little rears and coltish legs filled the door. Raider cursed, hopping about the room with one foot in his pants, groping for his boots.

"Mister," Nancy said sharply. "What the *hell* are you up to?"

"It's kinda hard to explain."

"I'll bet."

"Listen." Raider found his boots and stumbled for the door. "I'll get back as quick as I can."

"Don't fuckin' bother!" Raider ducked a full bottle of whiskey and slammed the door.

Girls and irate customers watched amazed as he dragged the half-dressed twins down the stairs and into the street. A carriage passed and Raider stopped it, tossed his screaming cargo inside. The driver paled. "Windsor, goddamn it!" snapped Raider. The man whipped his team into a trot.

Louisa and Annette were all over him. They weren't mad at all now and were eager for entertainment.

"Stop that," said Raider. "What the hell are you doing down there?"

"You *know* what I'm doing. Ohhh, look at that, Annette!" Annette squirmed out of his grasp. Raider grabbed for her. She peeled off her dress and tossed it out the window.

"Damn it now, you can't do that!"

"Sure I can."

Louisa's dress went out the other window. Raider went after her and Annette snaked her hands into his pants. "Oh, look, he's all hard!"

"Me first!"

"Shit. You had him on the train!"

"Windsor," called the driver. "I—thought maybe the back door, sir."

"Good thinking." Raider tossed a handful of coins behind him, clutched one blond head in each hand, and stumbled out of the carriage. There was a broad wooden door in the alley. Raider kicked it in with his bare foot. A cook looked up from a steaming kettle and stared. Two waiters ran into each other. The twins broke away and ran through the kitchen. Raider yelled after them, holding up his pants with one hand. His feet caught in a leg and he tripped. The pants fell to his ankles; he kicked them loose and kept running. The girls slipped through a small door and Raider leaped after them, caught two slim waists, and tumbled to the floor.

"Hah, got you now, damn it!"

A woman screamed. Then another. Raider blinked, looked up. The Grand Ballroom of the Windsor was filled with tables and people. Hundreds of people, in long gowns and boiled shirts. Raider spotted a colorful piece of cloth by his head and ripped it down, draped it around his middle and ran out of the room.

*   *   *

"Listen, I can explain this, Hooper."

Mack Hooper glared at him through the bars. "Good, Raider. I'd sure like to hear it. 'Cause I don't give a fuck about *your* job, friend. I've been with Pinkerton's fourteen years now, and up to two days ago . . ."

"Aw, shit." Raider kicked the dirty brick wall and sat down. "This hasn't got nothing to do with you, Mack."

"No? I'm the guy had to tell the governor what one of our people was doing stark naked with two bare-assed girls."

"What's the governor got to do with it?"

"Not much. It was his banquet, Rade."

Raider shut his eyes. "Well, sure. Why not?"

"Then there's running out of the ballroom with the Colorado flag over your ass."

"I did that?"

"No, of course not. I just—" Hooper stopped. Loud, angry voices rose from the front of the jail. A guard ran down the corridor and Hooper grabbed him. "What's happening?"

The guard shook him off. "Big shoot-out near Ed Chase's gambling hall. We got two dead and one comin' in." The door burst open and shouting, angry policemen shoved a ragged outlaw into the hall. His hair was a different color than his beard, and the beard hung half off his face. Raider thought he looked real familiar.

CHAPTER ELEVEN

The minute Hackman looked at him, Doc knew he was in trouble. The lazy smile in his eyes said the outlaw saw right through him. Butch might not know what he was, but he damn sure knew what he *wasn't*.

Doc kept his eyes straight ahead. On the road back to Denver, either Charlie or Digger was always behind him. What was the point of this farce? Doc wondered. If they meant to kill him, why not just gun him down in Sally's?

Not a man there would blink an eye. Doc cursed himself for a fool. The outlaws were gathered for something, and Hackman was surely their link to Shipley. But he hadn't learned a thing Mack Hooper didn't already know.

"Digger, I don't like this at all," Doc complained. "I came up her to make some easy money. Gunning down lawmen's the quickest way I know to get a rope around your neck."

The fat man scowled at him. "Just do what you're told and don't ask a bunch of dumb questions."

Charlie laughed. "Don't you worry your head about money, Alabama!"

"Shut up!" Digger said harshly.

Doc figured Digger was plenty cold-blooded, but at least he had a head on his shoulders. The gray-eyed man was something else. Charlie was mean clear through and wanted him dead. The only bright light Doc could see was Charlie's drinking. He sucked a bottle all the way from Sally's. With any luck, he'd fall off his horse before they got to Denver.

Digger led them to a small bar on Blake Street. The pair were clearly known there and the bartender brought whiskey and glasses. Doc looked around, puzzled. "What are we doing in here?"

"We're having a drink," said Charlie. "What's it look like?"

Digger leaned into Doc. "We're here 'cause the man we're after is across the street," he said quietly.

"Across the street?"

"Right. At the Palace. This Morton hangs out there."

Doc raised a brow. "And he's a lawman?" It didn't sound much like Harry Morton.

Digger downed his drink. "He don't gamble. He's got the hots for one of the dealers. Little lady named Alice with tits out to here." Digger spread his hands a good two feet from his chest.

"You sure he's there tonight?"

"He'll be there." Digger winked. "Leave the thinking to

me, Alabama. All you got to do is keep that little shooter of yours handy."

Doc saw Charlie's ice-cold eyes upon him. His heart jumped up in his throat and he suddenly understood what Hackman had in mind. Digger and Charlie would kill Harry. But he'd get the blame for it and somehow end up dead.

Doc knew about the Palace Theatre but had never been inside. It was a big, lavish room furnished with plush walls, giant chandeliers, and bosomy lady dealers. There was a stage at one end that gave the place its name, but gambling was the main attraction. Poker and twenty-one tables were ranged in back. Roulette, keno, wheel-of-fortune, and red-black outfits ran the length of the room beside the bar.

Charlie roamed off by himself and Digger stuck with Doc. "He ain't here yet," said the fat man. "We'll just mosey around."

Doc spotted an elaborate mahogany Will & Finck faro layout. Derby-hatted gents crowded ragged cowhands for a chance to "buck the tiger." Digger tossed a chip on the queen of clubs and lost. Doc passed the game by. Faro was a quick way to lose money. Likely, the pretty lady dealer had a prepared deck or a two-card dealing box on hand to up the house odds.

"Over there," Digger nudged Doc. "That's him."

Doc looked across the aisle and saw Harry. The busty brunette running the roulette wheel would be Alice.

"Wander over and put a bet down," Digger whispered. "Stick close to him."

"Where'll you be?"

"Right behind you, friend." Digger's hand dropped casually to his belt.

Doc ground his teeth. Jesus, these two were crazy as hell. They were going to do it right *here!* He'd have to warn Harry—without getting them both killed in the process. Doc spotted Charlie leaning against a column not three feet behind Morton. His hand rested easily under his coat. Any other time, Harry would have spotted the hardcases quick; now, his eyes were on the girl and nothing else.

Doc looked at the black and red numbers and laid a five-dollar piece on black 17. Alice dropped the ball in the wheel. It rattled around, bounced, came to rest on Doc's number. "Black seventeen," smiled Alice. "We got a winner, gents!"

Everyone glanced at Doc except Harry. Doc left the chips on 17. Alice spun the wheel. The ball settled easily into his number.

"A winner again!" shouted Alice. The other gamblers cheered. People from nearby tables crowded about. Harry Morton studied him curiously, shook his head, and looked away. Charlie gave him a mean-eyed look. This Alabama was suddenly the center of attention—not what he and Digger had in mind. Doc liked the idea fine. They wouldn't dare try anything now.

Alice glanced at a tall, well-dressed man at the edge of the crowd. The man nodded imperceptibly. "You—leavin' it on, mister?" she asked Doc.

"Uh, sure," said Doc.

A hush fell over the table. Alice dropped the ball. It chunked into 17 and the room went wild. "Jesus Christ!" Digger muttered behind him. Doc couldn't believe his eyes. One number twice was one thing, but three times— was that supposed to happen? A mountainous pile of chips moved in his direction. The tall man Alice had looked at moved up to him. "I'm Edward Chase, sir. I own the Palace. Looks like you've closed this table for the night. My congratulations."

"Uh, how much is in there?" asked Doc.

"At thirty-six to one, mister, I'd say about $244,000."

"What?" The cheroot dropped from Doc's mouth to the green baize table. He'd never played roulette in his life and figured he'd maybe won two hundred dollars.

"How would you like the money?" asked Chase.

"Just—hold it here for me, all right?" Charlie stepped behind him and jabbed a blade in his ribs. "Uh! I mean, cash, please." Chase gave him a look and walked off.

Charlie grabbed Doc's arm and led him out of the

crowd. "You sure scored us a pile, Alabama. Damned if you didn't!"

"Us?" What do you mean, *us?*"

Charlie showed yellow teeth. "You ain't that dumb, son."

"Shut up, Charlie!" Digger warned him.

"Hell, he already knows, Dig. So what?" The knife dug Weatherbee's ribs again. "Let's get that money, friend."

Digger stayed behind while Charlie and Doc collected a satchel full of bills. Charlie led him back to the rear and sniffed. "Where's Morton?"

"Kissing his girlie good-bye."

"Good!" Charlie's gray eyes beamed. He moved into Doc and jerked Weatherbee's .38 from his belt.

"Now just a damn minute!"

Digger clutched his arm. "Straight out the front, 'bama." Morton was a long block ahead walking east, maybe heading for the Windsor, thought Doc. Charlie quickened his pace, leaving Digger and Doc behind. Doc knew he had to move fast. Even if Digger tried to shoot him on the spot, he could yell a warning to Morton.

The lawman paused to light a cigar. Charlie stopped and pretended to look in a window. Morton walked on and Charlie sprinted back to Doc and the fat man. "There's a good alley right before sixteenth. I'll take him there." He smiled thinly at Doc. "So long, Alabama. Thanks for the pile."

Doc went stiff. "Move, feller!" Digger's pistol jammed his kidney. Ahead, Morton crossed the street. Charlie edged up quickly, keeping in shadow. Doc whirled on his heels, slammed an elbow hard in Digger's ample gut. Digger grunted. "Harry," yelled Doc. "Behind you!"

Morton jerked around fast. Charlie's pistol barked twice. The lawman staggered, kept going. "Get out of my fuckin' way!" cursed Digger. A ham-sized fist came up fast. Weatherbee ducked but caught the edge of the blow and stumbled into the street. Digger fired three rapid shots. Charlie crumpled to the street, snapped off a shot. Digger moaned and sprawled on his back.

Doc bent over the fat man. Blood spread in a widening

stain over his vest. "Digger?" Doc came close to his face.
"Who the hell's side are you on, anyway?"

Digger grinned against the pain. "I could—ask you the
same thing."

"I'm a Pinkerton, Digger."

"Goddamn. Ain't that a laugh? Tell Hooper . . . Tell
Hooper—it's the—bank."

"Hooper? You know Mack Hooper?" Doc stopped.
Digger's eyes went suddenly flat. Doc heard voices, footsteps pounding on the street. He looked up quickly. A
dozen Denver policemen ran toward him with pistols
and Winchesters.

"What *exactly* did he say?" asked Hooper. "Exactly,
Doc."

"I told you. 'Tell Hooper it's the bank.' Period."

"Shit." Hooper sat back and scowled at the wall.

"Why didn't you tell me you had a source in Sally's?"
Morton said angrily. "You've got no business keeping
that to yourself."

"I wasn't keeping it to myself. There wasn't anything
to tell."

"There is now," grumbled Morton. Wincing against the
pain, he moved his bandaged leg up to the chair.

"At least we know it's the bank and not the train," said
Raider. "That gives us a little head start."

"*You* keep out of this," warned Morton. "I haven't
even started on you yet!" He turned on Doc and Hooper.
"I know what your man said, Mack. I also know Butch
Hackman from back in Kansas. If he's in on this, he's
not fighting the Denver police and the U.S. Army to
break in no bank!"

"My man was dying," Hooper said bluntly. "Why
would he lie?"

"I haven't got the slightest idea," said Morton. "Get
out of here, all of you. I had about all the Pinkertons I
can stomach for one day."

CHAPTER TWELVE

"I'm real sorry, Doc. This isn't my doing, and you know it." Hooper jammed oversized hands in his pockets and stalked to the window. Doc set down his coffee and stared glumly at the two-page telegram. It was signed by Allan Pinkerton himself, and scathingly listed the sins of operatives Raider and Weatherbee. Doc figured it must have melted the lines between Chicago and Denver.

He didn't need to read it twice. Mack Hooper was now totally in charge of the case. Raider and Doc would take no action whatever "affecting the security of the Egyptian treasure." Halfway through the telegram, the old man gave them a clue to their future with the Pinkerton National Detective Agency. He began referring to them as "train guards" instead of operatives.

Doc wadded up the telegram and tossed it across the room. It landed near the morning edition of the *Rocky Mountain News*. The headlines screamed back at him in big bold type:

PINKERTON OPERATIVE, LOCAL LAWMAN, IN GAMBLING HALL SHOOT-OUT

NAKED PINKERTON AND UNCLAD BRITISH BEAUTIES ATTEND GOVERNOR'S BALL

Somehow, Weatherbee noted darkly, both stories managed to soft-pedal the facts. In the first, it sounded as if Doc had tried to gun down Morton instead of save him. The story on Raider failed to mention that he'd made an effort to get the girls back to the hotel. Readers could easily assume he'd taken the twins to a whorehouse, gotten them drunk, and hauled them into the governor's banquet.

"I ain't even sorry," fumed Raider. "It's about time I got me a decent job somewhere. Maybe my stomach'll settle down and quit hurtin'."

"Don't get all excited," said Doc. "We're not finished yet."

Raider stopped pacing and gave his partner a nasty smile. "Well, that's sure easy for you to say. *You* ain't hurting any, whatever happens. Jesus—a quarter million dollars and you don't know shit about gambling!"

"It's only $234,280," Doc said casually. "And if you'd read the regulations you'd know it isn't mine. You can't keep wages, winnings, or rewards you get on the job. Remember?"

Raider's face fell. "You can't? Hell, I was going to hit you up for a hundred."

Hooper held up a hand. "Look, gents, we're not solving anything like this. We still got a job to do."

Raider made a noise.

"Now goddamn it, Raider!"

"Sorry." Raider sank back into his chair.

"I talked to the Union Pacific people this morning," said Hooper. "They'll hook a mail car and a sleeper on the regular run to Cheyenne, Ogden, and San Francisco. That's the best they can do. We leave in the morning."

Doc and Raider came out of their chairs. "Shit," said Raider. "That's pure *askin'* for it!"

"Not really, now," Hooper said calmly.

Doc shook his head. "Washington will never go along with it."

"Ah, they already have, Doc." Hooper cleared his throat. "I got authorization early this morning. They figure some of Arthur's troopers on board will be—sufficient security."

Hooper's voice trailed off and Doc looked at him. "Was this your recommendation, Mack?"

"Yeah, my recommendation. Look, Doc—it's not going to make any difference. Those outlaws are going to hit the bank, not the train."

"We don't know that."

"Well, *I* know it," Hooper said hotly, "and I'm in—"

"Right," finished Doc. "You're in charge. Only I think you're making a big mistake, Mack."

Mack flushed. "Damn it, you're takin' this all wrong."

Doc started to answer. Someone knocked on the door and he rose to open it. Henry Lewiston walked in followed by Harry Morton hobbling on a cane. Lewiston didn't bother to say hello. He stalked awkwardly into the room, flailing his arms about. "L-listen," he stammered. "You people have g-got to do something! I've got soldiers and police swarming all over my bank. Customers are scared to come in. We can't d-d-do any business!"

"The protection's for your own good," said Hooper. "If nobody hits the bank today, we'll be out of your hair tomorrow."

Lewiston's mouth fell open. "Hit the *bank?* What do you m-mean hit the bank!"

"Haven't had time to tell you, Henry. We think they'll make a try for it."

"Oh my *God!*" Lewiston sank limply into a chair. "I w-want that junk out of my bank." His bony fists struck the chair. "I want it out *now!*"

"We can't take it out now," sighed Hooper. "Like I said—"

"First thing in the morning. First *thing,* Hooper!" Lewiston sprang up and bounded out the door.

Hooper let out a breath. Morton eased himself down and propped up his leg. "I haven't thanked you yet, Doc. You didn't have any goddamn business out there, mind you—"

"Should you be walkin' on that leg?" asked Raider.

"Hell no, I shouldn't. I ought to be home in bed. Only I can't do that with you bastards in town." He glanced soberly at Raider and Doc. "We found that Marcie girl early this morning. In a ditch down near the Platte. Throat cut from ear to ear."

"Damn!" said Doc.

"Shipley got to her. There's no way of telling how he found out, but he did."

"We still don't have a thing to link her with Neferti Raman," said Raider.

"No?" Morton gave him a scathing look. "Then why do you figure Shipley shut her up?" Raider mumbled to himself and poured a cold cup of coffee. "I got one more piece of news for you," said Morton. He raised himself up and hopped to the door. "That whole nest of outlaws cleared out of Sally's. Every last one of them."

"Son of a bitch!" said Raider.

"They're going to hit the bank." Hooper slammed a big fist in his palm. "I *told* you so!"

Morton shrugged. "Uhuh. Either that or stop the train between here and Cheyenne. Or in Utah or Nevada, maybe. Frankly, gents, I don't give a fuck *what* they do. As long as they do it outside Denver."

Lord Willis knocked on the door just before noon. "I want that bitch arrested," he told Doc. "By God, I will not put up with this sort of thing!"

"What sort of thing is that?" asked Doc.

Willis gave him a narrow look and set his teeth. "Don't give me that pained look of yours, boy. I know you side with the slut—you and your partner both." He glared at Raider. "I'm not finished with you, either. The twins told me how you forced them to—"

"Can it," said Raider. "What the hell do you want, Willis?"

Willis colored. "Neferti Raman has kidnapped my secretary."

"She's done what?" Doc shot Raider a look. "Now how do you know that?"

"Because he's missing. Whole bloody room is a shambles."

Raider and Doc followed the Britisher down the hall. Raider let out a whistle. "Doc, *something* happened here." Tables were overturned and a lamp was smashed against the wall. Powell Jamison's clothes were scattered about the room. Weatherbee leafed through a pile of personal papers but found nothing.

"Doc, take a look at this." Raider handed him the item and Doc turned it over in his hands.

"An *opium* pipe?" He frowned curiously at Willis. "Does this belong to Jamison?"

"Of course not!" Willis puffed up like a toad. "That bloody Egyptian dropped it when he stole poor Powell, you can bet on that!"

"You mean Khalifi?"

"Of course!" snapped Willis. "Damned degenerates. Into all sorts of deviltry."

"It ain't yours, is it?" suggested Raider.

"Goddamnit," Willis said sharply. "You know my vice, boy. I drink whiskey, like any decent man!"

Doc followed Raider down Wazee Street, glancing nervously over his shoulder. "This is a crazy idea, Rade. If Harry Morton catches us snooping around Hop Alley he'll have our hides."

"He's not going to catch us, Doc. Relax. We can't just sit on our asses doing nothing."

"That's what train guards do," Weatherbee reminded him.

"Well, I ain't one yet, and neither are you." Raider stopped, squinted up at a Chinese sign over a dingy shop.

"What are you going to do, ask directions to the nearest opium den?"

"I'm going to ask if they've seen Powell Jamison down here." Raider took a copy of the *Rocky Mountain News* out of his pocket. It was the issue covering the treasure train's arrival. Pictures of all the party were printed on the first page. "If he's been here, someone's seen him. They don't get that many white faces down here."

"I wonder why that is?" Doc said absently.

Raider ignored him and stalked into the shop. An ancient Chinese in a long robe stepped from behind a curtain. Raider held up his paper. "Uh, you seen this man? Him fella in picture?"

"No," said the old man. "Should I have?" Raider colored and backed out the door.

"He speaks better English than you do," said Doc.

"Shut up." Raider tried half a dozen more doors with no results. Starting back to the hotel, a young Chinese boy peeked out of an alley and motioned to them.

"You—looking for man?"

"Yeah," said Raider. "You know something?"

"Let me see picture." Raider showed him the shot of Jamison. "Ah—yes. I know him!"

Raider grinned at Doc. "Where? Where did you see him?"

"You have twenty-five cents, maybe?"

"Oh, sure." Raider dug in his pocket and handed the boy a coin.

"He was here. In Hop Alley. Last night. Came here with pretty girl."

Raider frowned. "Was he—anywhere near an opium den?"

The boy nodded eagerly. "Oh, yes. In opium den. Him and pretty girl."

"Can you take us there?"

"Sure. You have 'nother twenty-five cents?"

"Wait a minute." Doc took the newspaper from Raider, leafed through it, and folded the pages back to show a picture. "Have you ever seen this man? We have reason to believe he was here with the man and the girl."

The boy studied the picture thoughtfully. "Yes, I think so sure. He was here, too. Only he leave early. Have big fight with first man over who gets girl." He grinned widely at Raider and Doc. "I help plenty, huh?"

"Yeah, you sure did, kid." Doc showed the picture to Raider. "It's President Garfield, Rade. Somehow, I don't think he got off his deathbed in Washington to smoke opium with Jamison."

Raider colored. "Goddamn lyin' little bastard!" He turned angrily on the boy, who was already halfway down the alley.

Morton caught them coming in the lobby. "Where the hell you two been?" he asked suspiciously.

"Walking, taking in the sights," said Raider. "Any law against that?"

"Come on, you better see this." Turning on his cane, he led the pair out the lobby, through a long hall, past the kitchen, and outside. Half a dozen policemen were clustered about something at the far end of the alley.

Raider and Doc looked at Morton, then shouldered their way through the lawmen. Powell Jamison lay on his back in a pile of garbage. His face was twisted in a pale, tortured mask. His clothes had been ripped in a hundred places, and his body was covered with deep, ugly gashes.

"Holy shit," breathed Raider.

"He didn't get that from smoking opium," whispered Doc.

"Here's the weapon," said Morton, coming up behind them. "Look familiar?"

Doc and Raider stared at the curly fourteen-inch blade with the carved ivory handle. A gold Egyptian scarab beetle was inlaid in the hilt.

"Kinda dumb to leave that behind, wasn't it?" said Raider.

Morton made a face. "That fuckin' giant never impressed me as being real bright. I'm going up and get him down here right now. Washington and Cairo and whoever else can yell all they like. *No* one cuts people up like this in my town and gets away with it!"

"How many police you got in Denver?" asked Raider.

"Why?"

"If it's less than two or three hundred, I'd think twice about it."

"Shit!" Morton spat on the ground around his cigar. "He isn't any bigger than a sawed-off Ithaca. McLake? Get this body out of here. Booden—gather up five or six of your boys and find me a shotgun."

Raider and Doc stepped aside and Morton hobbled past them. A young officer ran out the kitchen door and nearly spilled the lawman. "Sir—you better come quick," he said breathlessly. "A bunch of goddamn outlaws are shootin' up the place!"

"The bank," cursed Raider. "Hooper was right."

"Oh, no, sir." The policeman shook his head. "They hit a Wells Fargo car out in the railyards!"

CHAPTER THIRTEEN

The sounds of gunfire reached them at the front of the hotel; by the time Raider and Doc got to Union Station, it was clear that a small war was in progress in the railyards behind. Morton spoke quickly to one of his officers, then turned grimly to the Pinkertons. "It's a Wells Fargo car, all right. Come in this morning from Kansas City with maybe half a million for a bank in San Francisco. They caught us nappin' because *nobody* is supposed to know when that much money goes through." Morton cursed through his teeth. "We had everybody guardin' that fucking bank of yours!"

"Wait a minute," said Doc. "If you pull those people from the bank— Harry, it could be a feint to draw us off."

Morton gave him a painful smile. "I've already pulled 'em off, Weatherbee. Don't you understand? The *treasure's* the feint. They suckered us in good."

Doc started to speak, but Morton walked off with one of his men. Police were pouring into Union Station, and Doc saw the first of Colonel Arthur's cavalry galloping up Seventeenth. "I don't like this," said Doc. "I'm going back to the First National."

"Huh?" Raider looked at him. "What for?" Weatherbee didn't answer. He ran off down the street.

Raider started around the side of Union Station. Lieutenant Graham galloped up and stopped beside him, three troopers in tow. The officer's face was bruised and he'd already lost his cap. "This isn't any hit-and-run operation," he said, catching his breath. "They got maybe a hundred men back there, Mr. Raider, and they're fighting more like soldiers than outlaws."

Raider followed him around the long lines of freights. Graham held up a hand and dismounted. Raider walked after him and peered cautiously between two cars. A bullet chunked wood at his head and he pulled back quickly.

"See what I mean?" said Graham. "Someone thought this out real good. They got two tracks on either side maskin' off the train with the Wells Fargo car. We can't even get close to them. It's like attacking a damn fort."

As Graham spoke, four Denver policemen broke from cover and made for the next line of cars. "Cover 'em!" Graham snapped to his men. The troopers raised their carbines and laid down heavy fire. The outlaws answered from between the cars and under the wheels. Raider caught movement, snapped off two shots with the Winchester. A man grabbed his arm and bolted for cover. The policemen made it halfway to the cars then ran into a solid wall of lead. One officer dropped, the others dragged him back.

"That isn't going to do it," said Raider. "They can sit there all day."

"Won't do 'em any good," cursed Graham. "We'll smoke them out eventually, and they got nowhere to go."

Graham's words brought Raider up straight. Damn it, they *did* have someplace to go, and he suddenly knew where. This was a well-planned operation—the outlaws wouldn't have dug a hole without leaving a way out. "Get your troopers and send a man back to Morton!" snapped Raider. "Come on, damn it—those assholes got a whole *train* under 'em and a handful of tickets!"

Graham stared, then barked an order to one of his men. Raider mounted up and trotted north, away from the action. Shouts of alarm went up behind him, followed by a ragged volley of shots. Raider brought his horse up short at the end of a freight. An engine was pulling toward him down the tracks, gathering a full head of steam. The car and tender were crammed full of riflemen. Raider emptied his Winchester then kicked his mount around fast. Bullets whined around him. One skinned the rump of his mare and the animal nearly threw Raider out of the saddle. He jerked up behind a rail shack. Lead chunked into the clapboard sides. Glass shattered, and a startled lineman came leaping out a window.

Graham and his trooper fired from a stack of rail

timbers. The train roared by belching smoke and gaining speed. Back of the engine and tender were two boxcars, the Wells Fargo car, and a caboose. Every car bristled with outlaw guns. Graham wasn't too far wrong, Raider decided. Close to a hundred was a pretty fair guess. He dismounted and collared the frightened lineman. "Where's that train headed, friend?"

"Those are U.P. tracks," he stammered. "Goes up to Brighton, Greeley, and Cheyenne."

"Get your ass back to the station and tell 'em to wire up there and sideline it fast!" The man took off, holding his cap to his head. Raider figured it likely wouldn't help. The outlaws weren't leaving loose ends around. They'd cover the switches up ahead till they got where they were going.

Graham came up beside him with a red-faced Colonel Arthur and a dozen cavalrymen. On their tail were Harry Morton and a string of mounted lawmen.

"I sent a man back to wire ahead," said Raider. "You likely passed him."

"Too late," snapped Morton. "All the fuckin' wires are cut going north."

Raider shook his head and fed shells into the Winchester. "They put some thought in this, Harry. They won't stick with that train long. There'll be horses waiting somewhere ahead."

"So they can haul out fast for the Rockies," Morton finished. "Colonel—if you don't mind, I'll ask you to take after 'em and keep the train in sight. Take my people who've got horses." Arthur nodded, and trotted across the yard to gather his men.

"Only thing that'll catch that train is another," said Raider.

"I know," Morton grinned. "I got one building up steam right now."

They spotted the plume of smoke south of Platteville. The outlaws had a good head start, but Morton's engine was bigger, and carrying only a single boxcar loaded with horsemen and Arthur's foot soldiers.

"They ought to be further along!" shouted Raider. He stood next to Morton in the engine, squinting out the open cab. "Maybe Arthur caught up with them!" Morton mouthed something Raider couldn't hear. Raider poked his head out the side again. The wind and smoke made it hard to see, but he had a good view of the relatively flat plains to the west of the train. Ahead, the country got rougher, but he could still see for miles. Something caught his eye to the left of the tracks. Three horsemen raced for the train, shouting and waving their arms. Suddenly, two of the riders pulled up short, raised their rifles, and fired off a volley. Stretching as far as he could, Raider saw answering gunfire on the tracks ahead. Something cold touched the back of his neck. He jerked back inside and shouted close to the engineer's ear. "Stop this goddamn thing—quick!" The engineer stared at him, then reached for the big handle.

Morton gave him a puzzled glance. Raider picked him up bodily and tossed him out of the cab, then shoved the engineer and fireman out the other side. Raider leaped, hit hard, rolled, and came up running. The flat hammer of the explosion lifted him up and slammed him to the dirt.

Raider stood, dusted himself off, and found his Stetson. Harry Morton sat up and bit his tongue. "Shit. I think you broke my other fuckin' leg."

Raider helped him up. The Baldwin engine lay on its side belching a screaming column of steam. The boxcar was off the tracks but still upright. Men and horses spilled out of the car and down the embankment. Graham reined in with a great plume of dust.

"Jesus—you fellows all right?"

"I guess," grunted Raider. "Wish to hell I had a medal or something for you, Lieutenant."

"We saw 'em planting a charge. Couldn't get there in time."

"You did enough," said Morton. "Stop any of them?" Graham shook his head and Morton took out a fresh cigar. "Well, gents, let's get moving. The fun ain't over yet."

*   *   *

Half a mile away, the tracks made a broad curve into a mountainous cluster of sandstone. It looked to Raider as if some careless giant had scattered marbles the size of houses over the landscape. The train had stopped in the middle of this cluster, and Arthur's men were trading shots with the outlaws.

"We can't get to them," fumed the colonel. "The rocks come right up to the tracks. We can't even see the Wells Fargo car."

"They're unloading it right there," Morton said thoughtfully. "They'll put the money on horses and keep us busy till they get a good start."

"Then we're wastin' time sitting here," said Raider.

"What've you got in mind?"

"Leave maybe ten men to keep them busy. We circle west and then north again and meet 'em where they're going."

Arthur frowned. "I don't much like it. They could just as easy take off east."

"I figure Raider's right," said Morton. "I can't make you take your troopers where you don't want to, Colonel. But I'd like to have you up there."

Arthur bristled and pulled himself up straight. "The *money* is *here,* mister. I am not sending my men chasing after shadows!

Raider gave him a nasty grin. "You sure got a nose for where the fighting *ain't* going to be." Arthur made a noise in his throat and went for him. Morton held him back, showing more muscle than Raider gave him credit for.

Raider rode point with Morton just behind. Fifteen horsemen armed with rifles and shotguns followed. Thompson, one of Morton's officers who knew the country, rode beside Raider. "Cut in here," he told Raider after half a mile. "The boulders thin out down below, and there's a dry riverbed just north. If I was them, I'd take off through there and keep good cover all the way."

Raider jerked his mount around at the man's words. He was certain they were doing the right thing, but the whole business gave him the creeps. If the rocky landscape gave them cover, it offered the same to the outlaws.

"Hold it," he said suddenly. The riders stopped. Raider trotted ahead with his guide. A high, craggy shelf yawned over the trail just ahead. The path narrowed alarmingly; only one horse could squeeze through at a time. Raider gave Thompson a wary eye. "Friend, that isn't the worst place for bushwhacking I ever seen."

Thompson shook his head. "It widens on the other side real quick. Not more'n ten yards."

"Yeah, well . . ." Raider hefted his Winchester and rode through slowly, craning his neck at the dark, soaring walls. He breathed a sigh of relief when the passage widened. Thompson pulled up beside him. "You see? It gets bigger real sudden li—"

The shot thundered through the narrow canyon. Raider's horse squealed and bolted. As he threw himself to the ground, he saw Thompson fly off his horse like a noose had jerked him up. An ugly fountain of red bloomed on his chest. *Shit*, thought Raider. *The son of a bitch with the Sharps is on my back again!*

•   •   •

Doc found Henry Lewiston in the lobby of the bank, wringing his hands and pacing back and forth like a stork. Lewiston spotted Doc and grabbed him by the collar. "Oh my God, what's *happening* up there?"

Doc shook him off. "The outlaws hit a Wells Fargo car. Everything all right in here?" He walked past Lewiston and peered around the bank. There were two policemen by the vault and he'd passed two others out front. "That's all? You've got *four* guards for the whole bank?"

Lewiston gaped at him and ran a hand through stringy red hair. "What am *I* supposed to do?" he said shrilly. "That's your job, Weatherbee! They all t-took off when the shooting started!"

Doc stood where he was and let his eyes touch the customers of the bank. There were nearly a dozen people doing business—mostly well-dressed men in derbys and dark suits. The kind of people you'd expect in a place like the First National. There were two or three women on hand, one with a baby in a carriage. A bewhiskered old gent leaned down to grin at the child.

As far as Doc could see, there wasn't a thing to worry about. Morton was right. The outlaws had dropped all the right clues to throw them off. They intended to hit Wells Fargo right from the start, while the police and Arthur's troopers were busy at the bank. Maybe the bandits who'd hit the train on the way to Denver were a different bunch altogether.

Something cold touched the back of Doc's neck. No, damn it, that didn't read right at all! Union Station was only four blocks from the bank. If they wanted to hit Wells Fargo, why not do it *before* it got into town—with no lawmen anywhere around?

The answer hit him like a blow to the gut. *If they stopped the train out of town, no one would leave the bank. The troopers and policemen would be right there!*

Doc ran back to Lewiston. "Get the vault closed, quick!" he said sharply. "Get everyone out of here and lock the front door."

Lewiston paled. "Wh-what for?"

"Just do it, damn it!" Lewiston gave him a blank look and loped off to the vault, Doc at his heels. The lady with the baby carriage blocked his way, and Lewiston stepped around her. The woman reached into the carriage, jerked out a sawed-off shotgun and jammed it in the banker's belly. "Hold it right there, friend," she smiled easily.

Doc turned, crouched, and grabbed for his .38 Diamondback. The nice old gent in white whiskers leaned down and stuck a .45 in his ear.

CHAPTER FOURTEEN

Raider crawled for cover. Gunfire rattled off stone walls and lead dug sand at his heels. He threw himself under a boulder, rolled, pulled his knees under his chin. The Sharps exploded again. A small crater appeared six inches away, stinging him with gravel. Raider cursed and drew himself into a ball.

Someone yelled to his right. Snaking his head around, he saw Morton and his riders burst through the narrow passage. A man went down, then another. Morton's horsemen stood their ground and peppered the canyon walls. The outlaws ducked long enough to let the last of the lawmen through. Raider grabbed his rifle, ran for the nearest horse, and threw himself into the saddle. Boulders offered cover thirty yards away, and he made for them fast.

"They're covering for the others," said Morton. "We got to get 'em out of those rocks or they'll pin us down all day." The lawman hobbled away on his bad leg, sending groups of men up through the boulders. Most met with a withering hail of fire and scuttled quickly to cover.

Raider studied the canyon. It was a maze of weathered stone and high croppings rising seventy-five or eighty feet to the west. The outlaws had all the best spots and needed few men to hold the lawmen. Morton was right. They could likely sit there forever.

Raider left his horse and snaked east through the boulders, away from the fire. Finding a narrow ridge that offered cover, he worked his way back the way they'd come, finally jumping four feet over the squeeze-through where the man with the Sharps had caught Thompson. He was on the west side of the canyon now, and made his way carefully. Ahead, he could hear the steady sound of rifles from the heights, and Morton's answering fire.

Raider stopped, crouched down to listen. In a moment he heard the heavy, distinctive boom of the Sharps. The man was straight up ahead, far down the canyon past the others. It was the same stunt he'd pulled when he'd blown the Yank sergeant's head off. With the greater range of his weapon, he didn't need to get in close.

Going to his belly, Raider inched his way forward, letting the rifle fire lead him. Raising up over a small rise, he saw the first outlaw, curled snug against the side of a boulder. Raider set his rifle aside and drew his .44. When the gunman squeezed off his next shot, Raider fired, the two sounds blending as one. The gunman slumped and lay still. Raider moved on. With luck, the other outlaws hadn't even noticed the extra shot.

The next man was forty yards ahead. Before Raider could fire, the gunman sensed him, jerking around. Raider shot him in the chest and sent him sprawling. A Winchester opened up loudly to Raider's left. Lead whined around him, pain knifed his side, and Raider folded. *Shit,* he thought darkly. *The son of a bitch was closer than I figured!*

The wound wasn't bad, but enough to slow him down. The bullet had hit the fleshy part of his waist just above the hipbone and he was bleeding like a pig. Setting his teeth, he ripped the front of his shirt and stuffed a wad of cloth against the hole. Pulling himself up carefully, he peered over the ledge. Lead grazed the band of his hat and he jerked back fast. The man knew he was there, and it'd be hell smoking him out.

Raider crawled quickly around the boulder, biting his lip against the growing pain. A shot smoked rock far above him. Another followed half a second later. Raider heard a sharp yelp of pain close by. Poking his head up, he saw the man he was after sprawled out dead not ten yards away. Raider grinned, mentally thanking whatever lawman had done the job.

Below and far to the right, he heard a ragged volley of gunfire and guessed Morton's men had surprised the main body of outlaws fleeing the train. The gunmen would have to fight their way through or fall back and meet Arthur. The colonel might see action yet, whether he liked it or not.

The hole in Raider's side was stiffening up bad. His feet were growing heavy, and every small boulder looked like a mountain. He knew the man with the Sharps was still on the ridge. He knew, too, that he'd never be able to climb that pile of rocks. *Fuck it!* he told himself, and sank down under a shady ledge to wait.

In a few moments, he heard the faint rattle of gravel overhead. A trickle of fine dust rained down, then a worn pair of boots. The man let go of his hold and dropped two feet in front of Raider. He froze, wide-eyed, reached for his pistol. Raider blew a hole in his head with the Remington. "You sure had that one coming," he said soberly.

For some reason, he was surprised at the outlaw's size. The awesome power of the Sharps had made him bigger in Raider's mind. He was a scrawny little man, hardly five feet tall. Raider picked up the weapon and weighed it in his hand. It was a fine gun, a .45-caliber buffalo-hunting rifle. It had a hooded front sight and leaf sights on the rear. A man who knew how to use such a weapon could hole up a thousand yards away and do one hell of a lot of killing.

Colonel Arthur strutted about the tracks, trying hard to look like George Custer. Like Raider'd figured, Harry Morton had driven the outlaws back in his lap, and the cavalrymen had picked them off easily. Raider stepped up in the Wells Fargo car with Morton. The car was empty, except for the bodies of two Wells Fargo guards, shot in the head.

"I lost nine good men out there," Morton said ruefully. "Traded 'em for 'bout forty of these bastards. Don't seem like too good a deal to me. We still got fifty or sixty hardcases on their way to the Rockies with maybe half the cash." Morton kicked the side of the car with his good foot. "Shit, Raider, they got a quarter-million bucks, and we got a fuckin' mess to clean up!"

"Crime pays real good, Harry."

"Don't remind me," muttered the lawman. "I see it every time I cash my goddamn paycheck." Raider wandered off and let a trooper tighten the bandage around his waist.

•   •   •

Now, when Doc didn't need them, there were plenty of policemen and troopers at the First National. Since there was nothing left to do, everyone rushed around the bank looking busy. Mack Hooper said, "I told you so" once, saw the murder in Doc's eyes, and didn't say it again. When Morton and Raider finally arrived, they were too tired to much care. Henry Lewiston locked himself in his office and refused to come out.

It had been the easiest bank job Doc had ever seen. There were six men and two women involved, all disguised as respectable ctizens. Three of the men had policeman's uniforms under their clothes. In seconds, they were stationed in front of the bank with the doors closed. The rest of the outlaws walked into the vault, sacked up the two million dollars sitting out in the open, and left. By Doc's watch, the whole affair had taken less than eleven minutes.

Doc showed Raider the vault, and pointed out the spot where the outlaws had tried to saw their way into the cage. Raider rubbed a finger over the saw mark. "Damn, they didn't even cut an eighth of an inch!"

"They didn't care one way or the other," snorted Doc. "Someone had a blade handy and gave it a try for the hell of it. We've been suckered real good, Rade. They never wanted that treasure in the first place. They wanted to empty the bank and pull every policeman and trooper out of Denver."

Raider scratched his chin thoughtfully. "They made a damn good try for it on the way up here."

"I've been thinking about that. I figure it was a real try, all right. But whoever's behind this didn't much care if it worked. What it did was scare the hell out of us. The exhibit got canceled, and we stored the treasure away in the bank, right where the outlaws wanted it."

Raider shook his head. "That doesn't make sense. We were going to keep the treasure here anyway."

"Yeah, but only at *night*," Doc reminded him. "This way, it was here in the daytime, too. Banks are a lot easier to rob when you don't have to blast your way through a vault and wake every lawman in town."

Raider had to admit he was right, and Harry Morton grudgingly agreed. It didn't sit right with the lawman to know outlaws had called the shots from the start, but there wasn't any other way to look at it.

"We still got some loose ends," said Morton, "and tyin' them up isn't going to be easy. If Butch Hackman was with those outlaws at the train, he got clean away. And I can't pin a damn thing on T. C. Shipley, even if I know he's guilty as sin. Shipley's the only one who can bring the girl into this, and he ain't likely to do that."

"Got to have the girl in it, don't you?" said Doc.

Morton turned red. "No, Doc, I don't *have* to have the girl in it," he said sharply. "She's there, though, isn't she? I've got testimony she was with Shipley—"

"From a dead whore."

"All right. From a dead whore. I also got this *unimportant* little matter of the Jamison kid, hacked up with something that sure ain't a Bowie knife."

Doc couldn't believe Neferti was guilty, and knew Raider didn't either. Still, he couldn't forget what Mack Hooper had said. The girl would likely give up the treasure to buy guns for the fight back home. If she'd do that, Doc reasoned, she wouldn't balk at taking cash from Wells Fargo or the bank.

Doc disappeared awhile, and when Raider found him again, he was back in the vault with his Premo Senior camera. "What the hell you doin' that for?"

"For the case report," said Doc without looking up.

"I didn't think railroad guards had to do case reports."

"Just leave me alone, Rade." Raider walked off, and Doc busied himself with the camera. He took several shots of the empty bins where the cash had been, then turned the camera around to shoot the treasure cage. Finding his old chalk marks, he set the points of the tripod exactly where they'd been, measured the distance from the floor to his lens, and shot several pictures. Finally, he moved the camera to the bank lobby and got a picture of the vault from the outside.

The bank was nearly empty when he left, and Doc's footsteps echoed over the marble floor. He knocked on Henry Lewiston's door, but if the banker was in there, he didn't choose to answer.

The giant Khalifi surrendered to Morton without a fight. Neferti Raman tagged along, screaming at Harry all the way. Morton questioned the big Egyptian and Neferti interpreted. Khalifi admitted the knife was his, but said he hadn't killed Jamison.

An hour after Khalifi and Neferti Raman arrived at the jail, a telegram came for Harry. In the strongest possible terms, Washington "suggested" that no charges be filed against any foreign nationals. The party was to be escorted to the train in the morning and dispatched to San Francisco with all courtesies.

Harry Morton was furious but did what he was told. He'd already talked to a few newspapermen and knew the next day's headlines. Great Britain and Egypt were ready to turn the business in Denver into an international incident. With a dying President on Pennsylvania Avenue and the government in an uproar, Washington didn't need extra headaches. Harry chewed his cigar and spit on the floor. *Shit,* he told himself stoically. *I can't even get a ten-dollar raise at city hall. I don't reckon I can fight the fuckin' White House.*

CHAPTER FIFTEEN

Doc and Raider got a telegram, too. It was only one line long this time, short and to the point:

PROCEED SAN FRANCISCO SOONEST
WITHOUT FURTHER INCIDENT.
—ALLAN PINKERTON

"Hell," said Raider. "That one's even scarier than the two-pager. I like it better when he gets all riled up. It's the stuff he *don't* say gives me the jitters."

"At least we seem to have our jobs back," noted Doc. "He doesn't say a thing about train guards."

"Of course we got our jobs," Raider said drily. "He ain't going to can us till we get to San Francisco."

*   *   *

In the morning, Harry Morton interrupted their breakfast and rushed them down to Holladay Street without a
word. Stairs led up from a shabby bar to a second-story
apartment. The rooms inside were lavishly furnished with
heavy drapes, plush carpeting, and every luxury imagin-
able. Neither a Morgan nor a Rockefeller would have felt
uncomfortable in T. C. Shipley's domain.

Denver's local crime boss was sprawled behind the
sofa in a blue silk robe. Shipley had been shot twice at
close range with a small-caliber weapon. Less than three
feet away, Butch Hackman lay on his back, staining a fine
imported rug a darker shade of red. Still clutched in
Hackman's hand was a pearl-handled Remington .41.

"Looks like these fellers had a fallin' out," said Raider.

"That's what it's *supposed* to look like," Morton said
acidly. Doc and Raider exchanged glances. Morton walked
over to Butch and saw the small hole in his chest. He
turned Hackman on his belly. There was a larger hole
in his back. It was the kind of wound a .45 makes at close
range. "Someone pulled a real cute trick here, gents." He
gingerly poked a pencil into the wound, spreading ragged
flesh aside. "Nobody'd even notice if they weren't looking
for it. A blade went in here first, in the small of the back,
then the killer shot Hackman from the front—figuring
to blow away enough flesh to cover the knife wound."
Harry stood up. "Now you two Pinkerton geniuses tell me
how Shipley stabbed Butch, shot him with a .45, then
walked over there and let Hackman kill him with a derringer."

"Wouldn't be easy," said Raider.

"Hell, no, it wouldn't. It's goddamn impossible is what
it is." Morton set his jaw. "There was someone else in here
with this pair last night. I ain't sure who did what to who,
but it took more'n two of 'em to do it. And I'll bet a five-
dollar gold piece the doctor'll find a real curvy blade did
that digging."

"You mean Khalifi," said Doc.

"No, I *don't* mean Khalifi. I had a man watching his
room all night and he didn't get out." Harry paused and
eyed them both. "I didn't have anyone on the girl, though.

I damn sure should have—she could've slipped in and out of the Windsor any time of the night."

"Oh, come *on!*" protested Doc.

"*You* come on, Weatherbee." Morton jerked up and stabbed a finger at Doc. "Every time I mention that cute little gal you and Raider hit the ceiling. Are you both fuckin' her, or just one of you?" Raider started for him but Doc held him back. "Go on," yelled Morton. "Get the hell out of here!"

Doc and Raider barely reached the Windsor before the lobby was swarming with police. In minutes, Neferti Raman, her father, the giant Khalifi, Lord Eden Bade-Willis, and Louisa and Annette were out of their rooms and on their way to jail. An hour later, four federal marshals walked into Harry Morton's office and quietly carried him off. Hooper learned their orders had come right from Washington, and passed the news on to Doc and Raider.

"Shit, I don't much blame Harry," said Raider. "Guess he's had about all he can stomach. He knew this would happen and went right ahead and did it."

"I found out something else, too. From an officer who works under Harry. They took everyone's room apart at the hotel. In back of Powell Jamison's closet they came up with a money belt stuffed full of bills. About ten thousand dollars."

Raider looked pained. "What the hell would he be doing with that kind of money?"

"It wasn't from the bank or the Wells Fargo job," said Doc. "He was already dead by then."

Hooper shook his head. "It wasn't from either one. Brand-new hundred-dollar bills."

"What you figure he did to earn that?" asked Raider. He shook his head at Doc. "This business isn't getting any easier."

"It is some," Doc said absently. "We're running out of people pretty fast. When they're mostly gone, we'll have a good idea who's running the show."

*   *   *

Neferti Raman caught up with Doc in the lobby and asked him to join her for coffee in the dining room. Doc was stunned by her appearance. In spite of what she'd been through, Neferti looked more sensuous and appealing than ever. Her dark eyes were warm and inviting, and Weatherbee had trouble keeping his gaze from the hollow of her breasts.

"That terrible man belived nothing I said," she told Doc breathlessly. "I did not lie to him, Mr. Weatherbee— I swear I didn't!"

"Well, I don't think Morton meant anything personal," Doc told her. "He's got a job to do and—"

Neferti colored. "Why does the blame for everything fall on Egyptians! My God—this British bastard is behind all this, don't you know that?"

"Miss Raman—" Doc cleared his throat. "I don't know much what to believe anymore."

"But you are ready to hold him blameless, yes?"

"I didn't say that."

Neferti's eyes narrowed. "Let me tell you something about this *Lord* Willis of yours. In spite of his fine airs and titles, he is broke." Neferti paused to emphasize her point. "Yes, flat broke. He has drunk up a small fortune and has nothing. I know this! *I* am accused of stealing, but no one looks in the pockets of the Englishman!"

"I didn't know about that," Doc admitted. "I kind of assumed . . ."

"Yes. Everyone has assumed." Neferti made a face. "Do you think Egyptians are idiots? Would I have Khalifi leave an *Egyptian* knife in Jamison? Willis planted it there. That is obvious to anyone but this foolish Denver policeman. Now they say that I myself went to this place and murdered two strong men. Bah—such nonsense!"

"Miss Raman. We're going to be on the train again tomorrow. I'm sure this whole mess will get cleared up soon."

Neferti's eyes softened. "Do you—really think so? Mr. Weatherbee, may I speak to you in confidence?"

"Well, sure."

"I am in a strange country and things are happening

I do not understand. I need someone who believes in me. Someone I can trust. Will you—help me, please?"

Doc's mouth went dry. The girl's strong, spicy scent reached him from across the table. The look in her eyes was one he hadn't seen before—not on this lady, anyway.

"Could we talk again later, do you think? Tonight, perhaps? I would be *so* grateful, Mr. Weatherbee. . . ."

CHAPTER SIXTEEN

"I talked to Mack," said Raider. "Harry Morton ain't going to lose his job or nothing. He'll just keep his head down good till things blow over." He grinned slyly at Doc. "According to Hooper, Morton's been around so long isn't anyone'd fire him. He knows where all the shit's buried, and where they hid the shovels."

Doc shook his head and studied the end of his cheroot. "If Harry's on ice, I have an idea the Shipley-Hackman business is good as dead, Rade. Our traveling companions are hands-off, and that doesn't leave anyone to talk to."

Raider sniffed and waved off Weatherbee's smoke. "Shit, Doc—the police are happy as clams. Like you say, we're shippin' all the prime suspects out of state. Nobody has to worry 'bout who did what to who. And who's going to miss the fuckers, anyway?"

Raider left and Doc frowned thoughtfully out the window. Whether his partner knew it or not, he'd put his finger right on it. An appalling number of lawmen, soldiers, and outlaws had traded lead in the last few days. Whores, Englishmen, and local crime lords were dropping like flies. There was plenty of money floating loose, if you knew where to look. Wells Fargo was out $250,000. The First National of Denver was two million poorer.

Now, Washington wanted the whole thing swept under the rug. Like nothing had ever happened. Even old Pinkerton himself was going along with the cover-up. In a way,

Doc couldn't blame him. It was the biggest story to hit the papers in years, and the Agency was getting plenty of publicity—all of it bad. Still, the whole affair made Weatherbee's blood boil. Washington and Chicago could forget the case, but he and Raider couldn't. "PROCEED SAN FRANCISCO SOONEST WITHOUT FURTHER INCIDENT." By God, if the troubles that had plagued them so far were "incidents," he was glad they hadn't run into any real *problems!*

Neferti Raman opened the door and greeted him with a warm and pleasant smile. Doc took a chair. The girl turned and poured him a brandy. "I am so grateful you could come. Our little talk this morning—I cannot tell you how it eased my mind, Mr. Weatherbee." She laid a hand on her breast and sighed. "I feel—safe, protected. You have swept my fears away!"

"Well, ah, I don't know if I did all that."

"Oh, but you have. Truly!" Neferti leaned toward him, bringing her shoulders together until the low bodice nearly bared her breasts. Doc blinked. The girl straightened, but made no effort to cover herself. "This trip has been a great hardship. The robbings and killings—the insults to my country. I am so confused! I mean no offense, Mr. Weatherbee, but—" Neferti paused and looked at her hands. "America is so different. All you want to do is make money and get bigger."

"Well now, that isn't all of it, ma'am."

"No?" Neferti's eyes flashed. "Where is your culture? Your art and your dance?" She paused and looked curiously at Doc. "Are you familiar with the dances of Egypt, Mr. Weatherbee?"

"Well, I've heard about 'em, of course."

"In all the wrong ways, no doubt," she said shortly. "In my country, a man does not view the flesh of a dancing girl with lust. He sees the *spiritual* meaning of the dance itself." She frowned thoughtfully, as if something had just occurred to her. "You are a man of breeding, Mr. Weatherbee. It is a thing you would appreciate in the proper manner." Without a word, she slipped out of her chair and vanished into the other room.

Doc shakily poured himself a brandy and downed it in one swallow. *Now* what the hell was she up to? He had an idea, but figured he was way off base. Neferti Raman might come on to a man, but she was a purebred lady. She sure wouldn't do something like that. Not right here in her own hotel room. The door opened. Doc gripped the arms of his chair and stared.

Neferti drifted in soft as a whisper, sank down before him in a ritual bow, and quickly swirled away. She was clothed in a wisp of airy material that did nothing to hide the naked flesh beneath. Doc caught a flash of pearls at her breasts and thighs, saw the tiny bands of gold around her ankles.

Neferti moved dizzily across the room, twisting the band of silk about her like captive smoke. She spun, darted, caught Doc with black and smoldering eyes. Pausing before him for an instant, she twisted her body from the waist and thrust her thighs tauntingly in his face. Then she was gone again, bare legs flashing, moving to a music Doc could almost hear. She whirled, sighed, gave a last graceful leap, and collapsed to the floor.

Neferti lay still a long moment, belly heaving for air. Finally, she came to her knees again, rested her thighs on her legs, and arched her back until tousled black hair swept the floor. Small beads of moisture clung to her dark olive skin. Her arms writhed like snakes above her head, curled down to her waist and brushed her thighs. Gently, she rubbed the silken garment against her legs and brought it slowly up the length of her body.

Doc felt his crotch swell at the sight. She was naked now except for the thin strands of pearls. Moving her hands to the hollow of her belly, she let scarlet nails rake a path across her flesh to the swell of her breasts. Her body trembled to a silent beat. Agile hands cupped her breasts, tore the pearls aside and sent them scattering across the floor. She squeezed the firm mounds lovingly, teased the rosy nipples between her fingers until they sprang up dark and rigid. Long fingers snaked down her belly into the silky black nest between her legs. Holding the moist lips aside, she slid the pearls from her thighs and slowly worked them inside her.

Doc had seen all he could stand. He threw his clothes aside and went to his knees between her legs. Neferti reached down, grabbed his swelling erection, and groaned. Her eyes rolled up and her mouth went slack. Doc sat perfectly still, letting her hands slide silkily over his cock. The girl's breath came faster. Doc reached down between her open thighs and slowly pulled the milk-white pearls out of her wetness.

Neferti trembled and went stiff. A thin cry escaped her lips and her belly jerked up to meet him. She came repeatedly, each convulsion greater than the last. Finally, she collapsed and went limp, her body slick with a fine coating of moisture. For a long moment she lay there, gasping hungrily for air. Doc spread her legs and thrust himself inside her.

"Nooooo!" Neferti jerked back, twisted away. "I—can't stand it! Not yet! I—!"

Doc didn't answer. Grabbing her slim waist, he twisted her roughly onto her belly. Neferti cried out, long legs thrashing against him. Doc grabbed the twin swells of her hips and plunged deeply into her cunt. Neferti's scream turned to a ragged moan of pleasure. Doc pumped her hard, slapping her hips against his belly. Neferti caught his rhythm and ground her ass up to meet him. Doc ran his hands down the lovely curve of her back, reached under her tummy, and squeezed her nipples. Neferti moaned, open lips twisting in pain and pleasure.

Doc was there, hanging on the edge with her. Moving his hands up to her waist, he gripped her hard, then rammed his tool violently into her pussy—again and again and again. Everything inside him exploded. Neferti screamed, her strong orgasm enfolding his own. With a last breath she fell away and sprawled on her belly. Doc leaned down and took her in his arms.

"Lady, I got to tell you—that was the most spiritually uplifting dance I ever saw."

Neferti gave him a shrill little laugh. "You see? You are a man of culture, just as I imagined."

He woke and saw her looking at him, chin perched in her hands. "I guess I dozed off a little."

"A terribly rude thing to do," she scolded. "You left me here with no one to play with."

Doc leaned down and slapped her naked ass. "From what I saw, girl, you don't really *need* any playmates."

Neferti grinned and showed tiny teeth. "Ah, you enjoyed the trick with the pearls, did you?"

"Hell, how could I do anything else? I thought you weren't ever going to stop coming."

Neferti rolled her eyes helplessly. "Neither did I!" She laid a finger on his lips and grinned mischievously. "You see? There are some things you Americans *can't* do with your marvelous machines and electrical lights. That is an old love secret of the East. Farther east than Egypt. It—ah, works better on me than it does on many women. I am—*extremely* sensitive down there, Doc. In case you didn't notice. All I have to do is *think* about touching myself."

"Uhuh. How does it work when someone else does the touching?" Doc ran a hand lightly over the feathery mound. Neferti's eyes went wide and she sucked in a breath.

"My God, Doc—you want me to *die* right here? After what you've done to me!"

Doc moved across the floor, grabbed two big pillows from the couch and stuffed them under her hips.

Neferti stared at him. "What—what do you think you're doing?"

Doc grinned, admiring the way her pussy rose invitingy up to meet him. "Fair's fair, lady. This is sort of a 'love secret' of the *West*." Spreading her gently with his fingers, he flipped his tongue lightly over the swollen little clit.

"Oh, Lord!" Neferti jerked back. "That is *not* a secret of the West and you know it!"

"You wait and see if it's not."

Neferti moaned and struggled to push his head away.

"I love it," she laughed nervously. "But I—told you—it's too *much* right now. Please!"

Doc reached under her hips, grabbed her wrists, and pinned them to the bed. Neferti saw what was coming and thrashed against him. Doc hung on. He jammed his head between her legs and thrust his tongue inside her. Neferti came the moment he touched her. Doc thought it was over, then saw it was just beginning. His touch triggered her off and Neferti couldn't stop. Her pussy convulsed like another mouth, throbbing violently against his tongue. Doc pushed harder, rolling his tongue rapidly around inside her. The girl's voice was a long ragged cry. Doc felt himself swelling, pulled away quickly, and emptied his load inside her.

He closed his eyes, took a deep breath, and looked down at her. His heart nearly stopped. "My God," he said aloud. "I've flat killed her!" With relief, he watched her breasts rise in a slow, easy rhythm. She was passed out cold, sleeping like a baby.

Doc wasn't sure what to do next. He'd bedded his share of women, but never fucked one unconscious. Were you supposed to hang around and wait, or what? It might be the courteous thing to do, but it would likely take all night. Doc lifted her off the floor and carried her limp form into the bedroom. For a long moment he looked at the naked, lovely shape stretched out on the bed. Bending down, he kissed the tips of her breasts. Neferti moaned in sleep and the pink nipples went rigid. Doc swallowed hard, covered her quickly with a sheet, and stalked into the next room to find his clothes.

Weatherbee was thankful Raider was out. Hobbling weakly to the bathroom, he filled the big tub with hot water and sank down with a sigh. After a good half hour he pulled himself out, wrapped a towel around his waist, and walked to the bedroom for clean underwear.

His hand stopped short at the drawer. It was a quarter-inch open and he knew he hadn't left it that way. Pulling it out slowly, he inspected his belongings. They were almost in place, but not quite. He knew it wasn't Raider.

If his partner had been looking for something to borrow he would have left the drawer in a shambles.

Doc quickly went through his other drawers, his valise, and his closet. Someone had clearly been over everything he owned. The Premo Senior camera, his telegraphy equipment—everything. Feeling about on the top shelf of the closet, he found his packet of case report materials. The intruder had leafed through them hastily, not even bothering to put things back in order. Maybe he took a while finding them, Doc decided, then made a quick job of it for fear he'd get caught.

Weatherbee took the material and spread it on the bed. What the hell was the fellow looking for? he wondered. Nothing was missing—every report and photograph was there. Doc paused, thought again, then moved back to his camera equipment. A low curse escaped his lips. Every damn plate had been exposed, then carefully put back in place! Whoever did the job had left tell-tale signs behind. If the intruder had known anything about photography, Doc would never have noticed.

What did the prowler want? What good would the pictures *do* anyone? A thought suddenly struck him and he walked quickly to Raider's pack. Digging around, he found the photographic plates and grinned. He'd given them to Raider at the bank and asked him to carry them back to the hotel. Inspecting the plates carefully, he was certain they were still intact. The prowler hadn't even bothered with Raider's things. That brought Doc up short. Someone had been here who knew them both prety well— what they wore, what belonged to each of them.

Still, he told himself, finding the plates untouched didn't tell him much. It didn't bring him one step closer to knowing what the intruder was after. Another thing bothered Doc, too. He didn't want to think about it, but there it was. Who could have known he'd be out of his room, thoroughly occupied with Neferti Raman? Like it or not, the girl herself was the only one he could think of.

Raider waited for Doc until his belly started growling, then walked out of the hotel after a steak. He found a café he liked, downed all the meat, biscuits, and mashed potatoes he could stand, then strolled contentedly down the street. In a few minutes he found himself at the long bridge over the South Platte River, turned around, and started back. The friendly light of a bar invited him in; he swallowed two quick whiskies and started for the hotel.

The man ducked into an alley a block ahead. Raider missed a step, inched his holster around instnctively, and kept going, letting his bootsteps sound on the street. Halfway to the alley he jerked abruptly into a doorway, flattened himself against brick, and rested his hand on the Remington.

Raider listened. The streets were nearly empty and there was no sound. Snaking the .44 out of his holster, he counted slowly to ten, then poked his head around the corner. The man froze barely three feet away, knew he'd been caught, and snapped off three quick shots. Raider jerked back, blinked against the bright flash of the muzzle, and heard lead chink brick. Boots retreated quickly down the street. Stepping from cover, he saw the man disappear in shadow. There was time for a quick shot but Raider let it go. *Shit,* he told himself soberly. *With my luck I'd hit him square in the head and have some more goddamn explaining to do.*

Raider walked in and screwed up his nose. "Jesus— something die in here, Doc?"

Weatherbee glanced up from his book. "I ordered up dinner. That all right with you?"

"Sure. What was it? Dead dog?"

"Liver and onions," Doc said absently. He stood and looked squarely at Raider. "Listen—what time did you leave here?"

"About six. Why?"

"I was gone till eight. Someone came in while we were both out and went through my stuff. Clothes, equipment, case reports—the whole works."

Raider made a face, "What for? They take anything?"

Doc shook his head. "No. And I don't know what for. But I sure as hell don't like it."

Raider sank into a chair. "I don't like getting shot at, either. It's getting to be a fucking habit."

Doc jerked around. *"Again? Where?"*

Raider told him what had happened. Doc cursed and kicked at a chair. "I'm sure as hell glad everyone thinks this mess is over, Rade. You know? Now we can just take it easy and have a nice train ride. Shit!" Doc stomped into the bathroom and slammed the door behind him.

Raider shook his head. Weatherbee wasn't given much to cussing, but when he did, he was flat serious about it.

CHAPTER SEVENTEEN

The Union Pacific from Kansas City broke down in Abilene and was seven hours late getting into Denver. It was nearly sundown before the train pulled out of town for San Francisco. The treasures of Egypt were loaded in a spare mail car guarded by eight of Colonel Arthur's troopers and Lieutenant Graham. The Union Pacific furnished a special car for Doc and Raider's party, one they used for traveling railroad officials. It was comfortable and well furnished, but a far cry from the luxurious *City of Worcester.*

Raider would have been happy to ride a cattle car if it would get them out of Denver in one piece. Doc was worried and thought they'd still run into trouble. Raider figured he might be right, but decided their luck was due to change. He looked forward to San Francisco. It was his favorite town next to New Oreans, and even if old man Pinkerton fired him on arrival, he was determined to enjoy it.

The train labored north past Brighton and Platteville. Raider felt an itch at the base of his spine when they entered the stretch of country where the outlaws had taken the Wells Fargo car. The wound in his side was still sore, and he wouldn't soon forget where he'd gotten it. Raider found fresh coffee, poured himself a cup, and wandered down the aisle. He didn't know where Doc was and didn't look for him. When Weatherbee had a burr up his ass, it was a good idea to leave him alone.

"Mr. Raider—please?" Neferti Raman beckoned him in as he passed her compartment. Raider was more than a little surprised. She hadn't even glanced at him since they'd had their little get-together. Damn, she looked good! There was a slight flush to her cheeks and a lazy, satisfied sparkle in her eye.

"Yes, ma'am, you need something?" He glanced quickly at the great bulk of Khalifi taking up a whole side of the compartment, then brought his eyes back to the girl.

"My father is not feeling well," she announced. "He is resting now but he is ill."

"You think he's comin' down with something? We'll be getting into Cheyenne late, but I'll sure find a doctor to look at him."

Neferti gave him an icy stare. "He is not ill in Cheyenne. He is ill *now*. There is undoubtedly a doctor on the train. Please find him immediately."

"Uh, sure. I could do that."

"Yes. I'm certain you can manage it." She gave him a quick smile and turned back to her book. Raider stalked out, biting his tongue. *Fuckin' stuck-up bitch.*

Lord Willis stepped out of his compartment and blocked Raider's path. "I need to talk to you. Now."

"Fine. Only it ain't going to be right now."

Willis stood his ground. "It's about Dr. Raman."

"What about him?"

Willis bristled. "We can't talk in the bloody aisle, man!"

Raider shrugged and stepped in the door. Willis clicked it shut behind him. "You know what's wrong with him, don't you? He's having an opium withdrawal."

Raider closed his eyes. "Come on, now. We're not going to start that shit, are we?"

Willis flushed. A tic started in his cheek and he sank to his seat. "By God, you never learn, do you?" He shot Raider a surly look. "How many people have to get *mur-*

dered before you understand they are not *like* us! Not like us at all, sir!"

Raider felt sorry for the man. He was a drunk and a general pain in the ass, but he'd taken young Jamison's death hard. Raider figured he had a right to feel the way he did. Only a few people had seen them off at Union Station. When everyone else was on board except Willis, a funeral wagon had brought Jamison's casket around and loaded it on an express car. A British flag draped the coffin, and Willis swore he'd see the body buried on English soil.

"Look," Raider said gently. "I know how you're feeling, but I don't think Dr. Raman left any opium pipe in Jamison's room. A scrawny little fellow like that wouldn't—"

Willis jerked up. "I didn't say he killed him, you idiot! Khalifi did that. Does everything the old man and the slut tell him to. Carries Raman's pipe for him. Won't let him smoke more'n the girl says." He gave Raider a sly look. "Raman ran out of the filthy stuff in Denver. Didn't know that, did you? Sent the assassin out to Chinatown to fetch more, I'll wager."

"Yeah, him and President Garfield," muttered Raider.

"What's that?"

"Nothing. You *see* him do any of this?"

"No. Didn't have to. Know damn well it's true, though."

"Yes, sir," Raider said politely. "I'll sure look into it."

The conductor told Raider there was no doctor on the train but he was welcome to look. There were seven cars full of passengers, and by the time Raider tried five, he was sure the conductor was right. There was no doctor aboard, but there was a little of everything else. Raider plowed through cowhands, drummers, old women, and mothers with squalling children. He paused between the sixth and seventh car for a breath of air. Jesus! He'd never seen so many ugly-looking folks in his life. A fat old lady kicked him in the shin, and two brats spit on him. In the last car, a middle-aged woman with stringy hair and thick glasses gave him a toothy grin when her husband wasn't looking.

Raider checked the last car and started back. Between cars, someone stepped out of shadow and touched his arm. Raider jumped. The girl laughed. "Damn, you sure are jumpy, friend!"

"Huh?" Raider squinted in the near-darkness. "Nancy? My God, what are *you* doin' here!"

"My ticket says San Francisco, Raider. Reckon I'll see if that's where the train goes." She caught his look and shook her head. "Hey, mister, don't go getting ideas. I'm not following you around, if that's what you thought. A girl'd be foolish to do that. I've seen 'bout all I care to see of Denver."

"You're not still sore at me, are you? Those goddamn girls—"

"Whoa, now." Nancy stopped him, glanced quickly at the car doors. Crossing her arms, she slipped the low-cut dress down to her waist and laid his hands on her breasts. "See? I'm not *real* mad, Raider. Or I won't be, if you can find that Pullman sleeper of mine in a couple of hours," she said, and gave him her sleeper number.

Raider's mouth went dry. "Damn—I reckon I can handle that, all right. We got some unfinished business, lady."

"Ummm. We do, don't we."

Nancy's breasts were full and hard, and rode high as a young girl's. The nipples sprang to life under his fingers. Raider felt a familiar stirring in his trousers. Nancy touched him and sucked in a breath. "Lord—not right here, Raider!"

"Why the hell not?"

"I—don't know. I don't guess I can think of a good—reason."

Raider quickly raised her skirts. He squirmed his hand between her legs, found the wetness there and poked two fingers inside. Nancy made a noise and came up against him. The door to the coach sprang open and a large woman with four children bumped square into Raider.

Raider backed off fast, covering Nancy. Nancy turned away to pull her dress up.

"We can see outside from here, dears," screeched the lady. "Now don't stick your head out, James—a pole'll knock it right off!"

Raider glared at Nancy. Nancy stifled a laugh behind her hand and hurried back to her seat.

Just past Greeley, the train began slowing. Before long it was creeping over level grade at a fast walking pace. Doc made his way forward from the party's special car, closed the door behind him, and pulled himself up on the railing between cars. He stood there a long moment, letting his eyes get used to the dark. Finally, he reached up, grasped a hold bar, and climbed to the top of the coach. Standing carefully, he walked the length of the car and jumped to the mail car behind. At the middle of the car he went flat and knocked twice, then once, on the ceiling. Someone answered from below, and in a moment he heard the lock click open and the door slide back. Grabbing the edge of the car, he lowered himself down until his legs dangled in front of the door. Two pairs of hands clutched him firmly and Doc let go.

"You all right, sir?" asked Lieutenant Graham.

"Fine, fine." Doc brushed himself off and blew soot off his curl-brim derby. "Sighted the freight yet?"

"No, sir. Ought to be coming soon." Graham gave him a worried frown. "You sure this is going to be all right, Mr. Weatherbee? I don't feel real good doin' something without Captain McLeod or the colonel's say-so." He glanced over his shoulder. "Neither do my boys."

Doc looked past the officer to the eight troopers at the far end of the car. "The order comes straight from General Cleve, Lieutenant," Doc said firmly. "You want to see the telegram, it's back in my room."

"I might want to do that," said Graham. "No offense, sir."

"None taken." Doc clapped him on the shoulder. "All right, let's get this show on the road."

*   *   *

Brakes squealed and the train ground to a halt. Doc could hear the engine monotonously chewing steam up ahead. The dark boxcar on the other track was only a few yards away. Doc jumped to the ground, knocked once, and the door slid back. Mack Hooper grabbed his hand and hopped to the railbed. The troopers quickly began passing the crates of Egyptian treasure to the other boxcar. Hooper had three men with him, all armed with Winchesters. The transfer took nine minutes, and when it was done, the mail car on Doc's train was full of large boxes that looked a great deal like the real crates, if no one looked too closely.

Hooper nodded to one of his men. The man hefted his rifle, sprinted up to the engine, then ran back and signaled Hooper. Immediately, the engine growled and belched steam, and the train jerked into motion.

"This better work," Hooper said grimly. "If it doesn't, there isn't any hole deep enough for you and me to crawl into."

"It'll work," Doc assured him, and jumped back aboard the mail car. As the train picked up speed, Doc faced Graham and his troopers. "I want to thank all of you for your help," he said. "Remember, you're under orders right from Washington to keep this to yourselves."

"Sir," a voice popped up from the shadows. "I don't guess we can ask where all that stuff's going."

"No, soldier, you can't!" snapped Graham.

"It's okay," said Doc. "I can't tell you where, soldier, but I'll say this much. By morning it'll be a hell of a lot closer to New York than San Francisco."

A few of the soldiers laughed, and Graham and a trooper boosted Doc atop the car before the train picked up speed.

Doc walked in and Raider stared at him. "What the hell happened to you? Been stoking fires up front?"

Weatherbee glanced in the mirror and started wiping soot off his cheek. "Stuck my fool head out and got a faceful," he muttered.

"Yeah? Got any idea why we stopped back there?"

"Conductor says we had a little schedule mix-up with a freight."

Raider was silent a moment. "Doc, is there something troubling you I don't know about?"

"No, why?"

Raider shrugged. "Nothing. Forget it." He stood, stretched, then plopped down again on the crate holding the *Naked Nymph.* "Miss Raman is all upset about the old man," he reported. "Says he's sick or something. Willis says he's comin' down off opium and that's what's wrong with him. I got no idea what the twins are doing, but I figure maybe they're fuckin' the colonel again."

Doc almost grinned. "Business as usual, right?"

"Uhuh." Raider studied the ceiling. "I got one more thing, too. Neferti Raman's got a look on her face I seen a couple of times before."

"What kind of look?"

"You know. Like someone pleasured her real good."

Doc's face colored. He turned quickly away but Raider caught him. "Well, I'll be a son of a bitch. Doc, you went and poked that lady yourself, didn't you?"

"Goddamn it, Rade!" Doc looked like steam might come out of his ears and Raider retreated quickly.

He knew Nancy was in the sixth car. Opening the Pullman door, he stalked down the aisle, blinking in the dim light. The curtains were drawn the full length of the sleeper. Raider heard half a dozen snores blending together. He studied the little numbers on each curtain, looking for Nancy's. It was either 17 or 7, he couldn't remember which. He stopped beside 7. "Nancy?" he said softly. "You in there?" No one answered. Raider carefully pulled the curtains back. The bed was empty. He moved quickly to 17. "Nancy?"

"Hmmmmmm?" someone muttered sleepily.

Raider grinned. "I'm comin' right at you, lady!" He jerked the curtains aside. The fat lady woke up, opened her mouth, and screamed. Raider turned and bolted out of the car.

CHAPTER EIGHTEEN

Cheyenne was only fifty-five miles from Greeley, but it took half the night to get there. The engine wheezed into town just before dawn, gave a final gasp, and died on the tracks. Doc left Raider sleeping and stalked up to talk to the engineer. The sour-faced railroader took him aside and pointed at the big Baldwin. "You know anything about trains?"

"Not a damn thing," Doc admitted.

"Then I won't waste my time or yours." He jabbed an angry finger at the giant boiler. "Some asshole's been messing with my engine. Isn't any other way this could happen."

Doc frowned. "Couldn't be a regular breakdown?"

"My equipment don't have no regular breakdowns, mister. If this has got anything to do with that business of stopping back at Greeley—"

Doc looked quickly over his shoulder. "You're not supposed to talk about that."

"I ain't likely to, am I?" The engineer spat on metal and made it sizzle. "I got a wife and a couple of kids. I don't need no more trouble than I got."

"Damn it," raged Doc. "It's just like I said, right? This thing isn't over, Rade. We're up to our necks in it and nobody cares!" He stalked angrily around the small compartment. "This isn't like old man Pinkerton. Or Wagner, either. They've got more sense than that."

Raider yawned and pulled on his Middleton boots. "It doesn't have nothing to do with Pinkerton, an' you and I know it. The government don't like the smell of something, they just dig a hole and bury it. That means it isn't happening no more."

Weatherbee didn't answer. He lit a Virginia cheroot,

jammed his derby on his head, and fumed out of the compartment.

By noon, passengers learned they'd be stuck in Cheyenne the rest of the day and maybe the next. There was no way to fix the engine without a new part from Denver. Word had been wired back south, but there was no telling when the part would arrive. Whoever had delayed the train had gotten what they wanted. Why, though? Doc wondered. What have they got to gain holding us up in Cheyenne?

Doc won the coin toss and took a room in the hotel near the station. Raider would sit on the *Nymph of the Nile* in the compartment, and Doc would relieve him later.

Neferti had a room down the hall, and after a quick lunch, Weatherbee looked in on her. "The doctor says there is nothing wrong with him," she said sharply. "This is not so. My father is ill—terribly ill." She sighed and sank down in a chair. "I am afraid, though, it is nothing a doctor can help."

"Now why would you say that?"

Neferti's dark eyes touched him. "I know my father, Doc. The sickness is not a thing of the body. He is deeply troubled, frightened of something. But he will say nothing. Not even to me."

Doc started to speak but changed his mind. If the old man was scared, it had something to do with the business at hand. Bringing up *that* subject would only set the girl screaming and stomping, and wouldn't accomplish a thing.

Doc took time to develop the plates he'd taken in Kansas City, then wandered back to the train to talk to Graham. The officer was polite but distant, and his troopers gave Doc surly glances. Weatherbee knew what was bothering them. Just across the street were good steaks, whiskey, and willing women. The soldiers were standing in the hot Wyoming sun guarding nothing but empty boxes, and didn't much like it. Doc prayed the train would get moving before one of them spilled the beans about Greeley. Arthur would bust a gut if he knew about that.

After wiring a long report to Chicago, Doc relieved Raider while his partner ate supper. Raider grumbled about spending the night on the train, but Doc wasn't about to let Rade talk him into one of his famous "deals." Not with Neferti Raman just down the hall. Of course, it was likely nothing would happen. With the old man sick, the girl would be sticking pretty close to her room.

He was barely in bed before she tapped lightly on the door. Neferti slipped in quickly. "Father's sleeping well and Khalifi's watching him," she whispered. "I thought— maybe you'd give me a brandy."

"Well, sure. Got some on the table here." Doc moved off and she pulled him back.

"This is foolish," she grinned, black eyes flashing. "I did not come here for brandy and you know it." Her arms slid tightly about his neck. "Doc—taste me again, please! I must have your mouth between my legs. I can't *stand* to do without that. Do you see what you've done to me?" She clung to him, her voice a ragged whisper.

Doc reached up and fingered hooks and buttons. The gown rustled easily to her ankles. Neferti shivered as his hand snaked over her body. Standing naked in the dark, she felt his mouth lightly touch her thigh, and came before he got any further.

Doc jerked up out of sleep. An unearthly roar shook the walls and stood his hair on end. He leaped out of bed, scrambled for his trousers and the Diamondback .38. "Great God A'mighty—sounds like a damn grizzly!"

"It—isn't." Neferti gasped, wide-eyed. "It's Khalifi. My God, they're after Father!"

Doc yanked open the door. A body flew past him down the hall and tore through a closed window. A ragged scream followed the shattered glass. Khalifi stood in the narrow hallway, tree-like legs rooted to the floor. A man lay crumpled at his feet, one leg strangely twisted. Another clung like a fly to his waist. Khalifi held a third by the neck, crushing his skull methodically against the wall.

"Khalifi!" Neferti barked a command in her own lan-

guage. The giant looked at her, blinked, and shook the
attacker off his waist. Doc saw a darting shadow and
yelled out a warning. A .45 thundered three times.
Khalifi roared, staggered back. His fist closed in pain
about the man in his hand. Doc heard the sickening snap
of bone and gristle. He raced past Khalifi, stumbled, got
to his feet. Boots raced rapidly down the stairs. Doc's
gun arm whipped out and he snapped off a shot in the
darkness. The outlaw turned, fired back blindly. Doc
leaped, hit the man in the belly, and sent him sprawling.
The man grunted, slashed out with the barrel of his gun.
Doc felt a sharp stab of pain, rolled, came to his feet,
and grabbed for the gunman's legs. The man cursed,
kicked out, and caught Doc square on the shoulder. Doc's
arm went numb. He stumbled up, saw the man fling the
front door aside and disappear.

Weatherbee came groggily to his knees, shook his head,
and threw up. Clutching the stair rail, he stumbled to the
second floor. Guests peered out of their doors, saw a
bloody giant stretched out in the hall, and quickly retreated.

"How is he?"

"He is hurt," Neferti told him. "He is strong, though.
I think he will be all right." She glanced up, brought a
hand to her mouth. "Oh, Doc! You've got *blood* all over
your face!"

"Yeah, I know. How's your father?"

The girl smiled tightly. "They did not get past Khalifi."
She looked fondly at the giant and spoke to him. Khalifi's
mouth widened in a crooked smile. Doc blinked in amazement. The son of a bitch had three slugs in him and was
sitting there grinning like an ape!

Feet pounded on the stairs and Weatherbee yelled behind him for a doctor. Blood was clouding his eyes and
he started back for his room, then stopped. "Neferti. What
the hell's going on here? If you've got any idea why someone wants your father dead—"

Neferti's eyes flared. "It is the British! I have told you
this before, yes?" She spat on the floor. "The pigs want
us dead—all of us!"

Yeah, well, of course, he said to himself. *Why did I bother to ask?*

Raider sat up at the knock and made a face.

"Rade, open up. It's Doc! Hurry!"

Raider staggered to his feet and pulled back the lock. The door ripped open and flung him back. A big fist caught him full in the face and slammed him against the wall. Raider choked, spit blood, and flailed out blindly. A blow grazed his head. He covered himself and jabbed in the right direction. The attacker made a noise and fell back. Another fist caught Raider solidly in the chest and it suddenly dawned on him there were two of them there in the dark instead of one. Jamming a foot against the floor, he pushed up hard, lifted the man up, and slammed him against the low ceiling. He sighed and went limp. The second man kicked out savagely, caught Raider in the belly. Raider folded, grabbed the man's arm. The outlaw tore out of his grasp and ran, taking half the door with him.

Raider went down on all fours, feeling for the man he'd dropped. His hand found a leg. The leg came suddenly alive, kicked him hard, and bolted out of the compartment.

Lieutenant Graham appeared in the doorway, a lamp in one hand and a pistol in the other. "Jesus! What happened?"

Raider picked himself up. "Beats the shit out of me," he snapped, grabbing up the Remington. "Neither of those bastards was Doc, I know that. Put a couple of guys on this door, will you? I gotta find Weatherbee."

Raider saw the crowd gathered at the front door of the hotel and broke into a run. Six men passed him carrying the giant on a spare door. "Holy shit!" Raider muttered, and sprinted up the stairs.

Neferti sat on the bed. Doc perched on a chair letting a black-coated man bandage his head. A man with a star on his chest stepped up and blocked Raider. "What the hell do you want?"

"It's all right," said Doc. "Show him your card, Rade."

Raider did. The marshal sniffed at it, handed it back, peered curiously at Raider's face. "Which end of this war was you in?"

"The other end." He looked over the lawman's shoulder. "One of the bastards sounded like you, Doc. That's why I let him in."

"I didn't do it," Doc said dully.

The marshal took Raider's statement and left, taking Neferti back to her room to talk to Dr. Raman. Doc filled Raider in quickly and Raider poured them both a brandy. "A man don't have to be too damn bright to figure this," said Raider. "They hit the train and here 'bout the same time. I know what they was after in our compartment. What the hell do they want the old man for?"

"He knows something we don't," Doc said flatly. "Whatever their reason, they want to shut him up. Khalifi killed three of them and the other two got away. Like always, Rade, we don't have anyone but dead bodies to talk to."

"What do you figure Raman knows, Doc?"

"I haven't the slightest idea." Doc touched his head and winced. "I reckon we better find out, partner. I don't think I can keep this up all the way to San Francisco."

Raider had a sure-fire method of sniffing out trouble: Go out looking for more. Whoever had gone after him and Doc had taken some hard knocks and lost a few drinking buddies. The first chance they got, they'd pour a little fire in their bellies. Then they'd start talking about next time they caught the poor fuckers who'd caused them pain.

He started at one end of the street and worked his way north, pausing in each bar long enough to order a drink and let everyone know who he was. For the most part, nobody cared. A few cowhands wanted to fight him just for the hell of it.

Raider recognized several passengers from the train who had nothing else to do. He spotted the stringy-haired woman with glassses who'd given him the eye the day before. Her husband was uglier than she was and Raider beat a hasty retreat.

The fifth bar was a step up from the others. Raider walked in, his eyes moving naturally to the best-looking woman in the room. Then he saw who she was with. Marching over angrily, he plucked Nancy out of her chair and stood her up. "What the hell you doin' with *that* son of a bitch?" he demanded. Colonel Arthur rose up indignantly and Raider sat him back down. "Don't push me, bluebelly—I ain't in the mood for it!"

Raider dragged Nancy aside. She jerked away from him and glared. "Listen, friend—I don't recall you and me gettin' married or anything."

"That's got nothing to do with it. Where'd you find that asshole?"

"He offered to buy me a drink. Which is more'n I can say for some people. What happened to *you* last night?"

Raider blew out a breath. "I couldn't find your goddamn bed."

"Hah! *That's* a new one!"

"It's the fuckin' truth."

"Fuckin' is what didn't happen. Remember? Jesus— what's the matter with your face?"

"I had a little accident."

"Not too little." Nancy ran a hand over her hair. "Okay. I give up. Want to buy me a steak?"

"Yeah. Only there's something I gotta do first."

"Oh, shit, mister!" Nancy's green eyes flared. "For a man wants to get in my pants, you're sure going about it funny!"

"Nancy—" The redhead gave him a withering look and stomped off.

The two men were paying no attention to him. Raider knew they'd followed him from the last bar. Downing his drink, he walked out of the bat-wing doors and squinted into the sun. A hundred yards down the street, steam was rising tentatively from the Baldwin engine. *Maybe they got the damn thing fixed,* he decided.

Without looking back, he cut across the dirt street and

wandered into the railyards. If the men were the ones he wanted, he'd give them a chance to take him. Stepping over three sets of tracks, he walked south and turned casually between a row of freights. The moment he was out of sight he broke into a run, squeezed between two cars, and hoisted himself up. The car was a flatbed stacked with raw lumber. It was broad daylight, but Raider figured they'd give it a try. If he was lucky he'd get the drop on them and avoid any shooting. He wanted live outlaws he could talk to, not dead ones.

Gravel and cinder crunched back of the car. Raider let out a breath and touched the Remington. A boot sounded just beneath his perch. He leaned out carefully and spotted a faded patch of denim. Now where the hell was the other one? In answer, the faint creak of metal sounded to his left. Raider froze. The second gunman had stepped on the ladder at the far end of the car. If he crawled up the stack of lumber, Raider would have to kill him. The other would take off, and there'd be no chance of winging him either.

He was running out of choices and took the only one he had. Edging to his left, he dropped quickly to the ground. The man in denim turned, started, whipped his Colt around fast. Raider hit him with the flat of his muzzle. The man's eyes glazed and he folded. Raider jerked back between cars as lead sang around him from above. Ducking under the flatbed he rolled over rails and came up running on the other side. The man found him, snapped off a shot. Raider's Stetson went sailing. The outlaw leaped off the car and sprinted for the end of the freight. Raider dropped to his knees and squeezed off two shots under the car. The gunman howled in pain and tumbled hard. Raider moved up fast and leveled the .44. "Hold it, asshole—don't even think about it!"

The gunman clutched his knee painfully in one hand, still gripping the Colt in the other. He gave Raider a lazy grin and brought up the pistol. Raider fired and hit him in the chest.

He stared at the dead man and ground his teeth. The son of a bitch was crazy to try a stunt like that. Any man in his right mind would've known when to stop. Jamming the Remington in his holster he stalked around the car.

Raider stopped and went rigid. The man in denim was up on his knees. He stared bleary-eyed at Raider, blood coursing down his face. The Colt in his fist was shaky, but it was aimed at Raider's head.

"Hey, now, take it easy, fellow." The man blinked. His finger tightened on the trigger. Two shots snapped in the hot air. The outlaw's gun went off and creased Raider's shoulder. The man sank to the ground and looked up at the sky.

"R-Raider, you all right?"

Raider took two broad steps past the flatbed and caught her. Nancy turned white and dropped the little derringer from her fingers. "I saw those fellows follow you and I—oh fuck, honey, I'm going to be sick!"

CHAPTER NINETEEN

Doc didn't like the look on the marshal's face. It reminded him of Harry Morton's satisfied grin when the train pulled out of Denver. The Pinkertons were leaving town again, taking their problems with them. Cheyenne had dead outlaws to bury and didn't much care how they'd got that way. Great. He and Raider had a brand-new craw full of questions and no answers to go with them.

The engine spit a great gout of steam and the train creaked to a start. Doc glared at the sun-baked railyard and started for his compartment.

"Shit, Doc—look at that bunch!" Raider pulled his partner back and pointed. At the last minute, six new passengers sprinted for the train and hoisted themselves aboard. Doc didn't need a second to guess their business. They wore their trade strapped low and heavy on their hips.

Weatherbee let out a weary sigh. "Rade, there can't be

two outlaws left between here and Dodge. Every damn one of them are after us."

The train picked up speed out of town and settled down for the long hot stretch across southern Wyoming. Ahead lay Laramie, Hanna, Rock Springs, and Green River—nearly five hundred miles of track between Cheyenne and Ogden, Utah. Plenty of room for trouble, Raider thought sourly. As a matter of routine, he checked out the Ramans, Lord Willis, and the twins. Louisa and Annette had made plenty of friends on the trip, and were nowhere to be found. They were the least of his worries now, and he didn't even bother to track them down. Willis was drunk. Colonel Arthur wouldn't answer his door. Dr. Raman was pale as a ghost, and Neferti sent the giant after countless pots of tea.

Raider couldn't get over the big Egyptian. For a man who'd swallowed several ounces of lead, he looked a hell of a lot better than Raider felt.

Later, he cornered the conductor and asked about the six gunmen who'd boarded the train in Cheyenne. They had tickets bought and paid for all the way to Ogden. Raider learned nothing more than that. Whatever they had in mind was likely scheduled for the next five hundred miles, but that was no help at all.

Lieutenant Graham found Raider in mid-afternoon. He looked worried and wanted to talk, but Raider put him off and went searching for Doc. Raider liked Graham fine, but wasn't real sure he trusted him. In his experience, even a good officer like Graham fell back on habit and did what he was told. In this case, that meant trailing after Arthur, a man Raider had no more use for than spit.

•   •   •

Doc stared glumly at the montonous horizon sweeping by. Something kept dogging the edge of his mind and wouldn't let go. He smoked two straight cheroots and snubbed them out, looking past the window and seeing nothing.

It was pretty clear why the train had been deliberately

held up in Cheyenne. Someone wanted to steal the *Nymph* and kill Dr. Raman, and figured both jobs would be easier to handle off the train. Doc understood the first part. But why shoot the old man? What the hell could he know that was worth killing over?

For some reason, Weatherbee's mind kept straying back to Denver and the intruder who'd searched his room. The whole business was a knot he couldn't unravel. What did the fellow want? What did he, Doc, know that no one else did? Something that would put the intruder in danger or expose him? If Weatherbee had anything like that, he had no idea what it was.

Once again, he spread out the contents of his valise— case reports, notes, photographs, the whole business. There was something there, he was certain. If he could only just *see* it. Tossing the papers aside irritably, he picked up the photographs and stared at them. The intruder had seen them all, except for the undeveloped plates he'd missed in Raider's gear. Doc put both pictures side by side and looked at them. The second shot was identical to the one he'd taken in the vault before the robbery. He'd made sure of that by hitting the same chalk marks and measuring the distance from the floor to the lens. It was a simple, straight-on shot—the treasure stacked neatly behind bars. There was nothing there that—

Doc stopped suddenly and stared at the two pictures. The before and after shots were exactly alike, only—Jesus Christ, they *weren't,* either! In the second picture, the *Nymph of the Nile* was turned slightly to the right. No more than an inch or two, but it had definitely been moved. Doc ground his teeth. That was downright impossible. The thieves had taken two million dollars from the bank but they hadn't even touched the treasure. *No* one had entered the steel-bar-and-mesh cage until the treasure was packed and loaded again for the trip to San Francisco. And that was *after* the robbery was over!

Still, the pictures didn't lie—no matter how hard Doc might want them to. No one had stolen the *Naked Nymph,* but they'd *moved* it from where it was—twisted it around a good two inches. And that didn't make a damn bit of sense. Grabbing up the two pictures, Doc bolted out of his compartment and headed for Neferti's room. Raider met him halfway there, and Weatherbee pulled him along without explanation.

"You have no right to do this," Neferti protested. "I am disappointed, Doc. My father is much too sick to answer foolish questions!"

"Neferti," Doc said evenly. "I don't want to make things any harder on him than I have to, but I think I've got a good idea what's *making* your father sick." Doc glanced at Dr. Raman. "I'm right, aren't I, Doctor? You know what happened back there in Denver—and why someone wants you kept quiet about it."

"No." Neferti shook her head. "I simply won't have this. He is too—"

"Wait, daughter, it is no use." Dr. Raman held up a trembling hand and beckoned Doc. "You are right in what you say," he said wearily. "It is true. I know these things."

"Father!" Neferti sucked in a breath.

"That's not the *Naked Nymph* Raider and I are guarding back there, is it?" Doc said quietly. "Someone took the real one and substituted a good fake."

"Yes, yes, this is true!" cried Dr. Raman. His features twisted in anguish. "I do not know how this can be—but it is so!"

"When was the switch made, Doctor?"

Raman shook his head. "I—don't know. Yes. It had to be while the statue was in the vault. It was—real when I placed it in there myself. I knew, though—the minute I packed the treasure to leave."

"And you said nothing, Father? Why? Why didn't you *tell* me?"

Raman's eyes rested on his daughter. "Forgive me, Neferti. I—thought you had somehow taken it. To buy guns to kill our enemies. This is foolish, I know. But I was frightened. If it was true, how could I let anyone know the statue was gone?"

Neferti looked soberly at Doc. "Do you think I had anything to do with this? Do you?"

"No. I think you might do a lot to further your cause. But I don't think you'd do this to him."

"Thank you." Neferti wet her lips and looked away. "You are right. I would not. Not to him." She sat down then and took the old man in her arms. Doc guided Raider quickly out of the compartment.

"Doc, what you're saying is fuckin' impossible, you know? Nobody could've got into that cage. There was guards on it night and day."

"Except during the robbery itself," Doc corrected.

Raider made a face. "And that was what? Nine, ten minutes? Not even time to make a half-ass try. You saw that little ol' saw mark on the bar."

"Rade, I know they didn't get in that way. The little mark you're talking about was put there to throw us off. Make us think they made a try for it and gave up. Did a damn good job of it, too."

"So we're carrying a fake all the way to San Francisco. Shit!" Raider let out a breath and scratched his mustache. "Well, at least the rest of the treasure's ridin' back there safe. I reckon that's better'n nothing."

Doc looked quickly away and hid his expression behind a cough. He couldn't tell Raider about that. Not right now, when everything else was falling apart.

Doc seemed certain Neferti had nothing to do with stealing the *Nymph,* but Raider wasn't all that sure. When you were fucking a good-looking woman, you started looking at her different. Doc was a damn good operative, but he was human like everyone else. Raider didn't imagine for a minute the girl had hired a bunch of killers to do in her own father, but that didn't take her out of the picture. Maybe she *did* take the *Nymph.* And someone else knew about it and wanted to get it. Couldn't there be more than *one* bunch mixed up in this business? There were sure enough people to go around. The whole thing gave him a headache. Nothing had made sense since he and Doc had left Albuquerque, and it damn sure wasn't getting any better.

Since there was nothing worth guarding anymore, Raider and Doc had supper together in the diner. Doc wandered back to their compartment, and Raider made his way up front. With any luck, he could get something going with Nancy. Every time they tried to hop in bed something got in the way. He was so damn horny for the redhead he could take her on all night.

Stepping into the dark between cars, Raider bumped squarely into two of the hardcases who'd boarded the train in Cheyenne. The taller of the two gave Raider a grin. "Sorry, mister. Didn't see you coming."

"Forget it," muttered Raider, and started around the fellow. The man shifted his weight and held his ground. "Now look, friend!" Out of the corner of his eye he saw the second man move. There's someone else behind him, Raider thought curiously. Another man, leaning over the— *"Holy shit!"* Raider's supper started up his throat. The tall man's hand snaked for his gun. Raider raced him for it—slammed the man hard into the wall, and ducked the big fist churning air above his head. Raider moved, kicked out savagely. The tall man grunted and slid to the floor. Raider squatted low, turned for the other man, saw a pale flash of white by the railing. Movement caught his eye and boots disappeared at the top of the car.

Raider pulled himself up and squinted down the long length of the train. The man was running low, making for the engine. Raider went to his knees, steadied himself, and squeezed off a round. The train jerked and the shot went wild. The man turned and fired back. Raider raised the .44 again. Smoke rushed at him and cinders filled his eyes. When he blinked again, the man was gone—lost behind a heavy veil from the engine.

"Okay, asshole, that works two ways," Raider muttered. "You can't see me, either." Steadying his boots against the swaying car and the wind, Raider moved after the gunman. Soot coated his throat and stung his eyes. He choked, spat, and stumbled on. Jumping two cars, he stopped and went flat. The engine made a narrow turn. Raider caught himself and nearly went over. Suddenly, the man came out of smoke and Raider fired. The gunman sprang into the air and flew off the car, his cry hanging back on the wind.

Raider stopped, looked ahead and over his shoulder. He sensed rather than heard the danger, dropped to the car and hugged it. The shotgun coughed twice, belching yellow fire. Lead rattled past him. Pellets stung his cheek and peppered the leather jacket. He hugged the swaying car, reached up and fired blindly into the dark. He knew what had happened and cursed himself for it. The man he'd left behind had come to and brought along his friends.

Lead dug splinters at his heels. Raider crabbed frantically down the car for cover. Heavy smoke gagged him. Jerking up suddenly, he ran the last few yards and dropped to the space between the first car and the tender. Hanging on with one arm, he quickly reloaded the Remington, then chinned himself up again. There were five of them, coming on fast. Raider squeezed off three shots. Two men dropped. The others sent him a ragged volley and scattered for cover. Raider's gun stitched a path behind them.

Quickly, he inched his way around the small railing on the side of the tender and jumped onto the engine. The engineer and firemen turned soot-black faces in surprise.

"Stop the engine, now!" Raider yelled above the noise.

The engineer shook his head. "No way, mister. I got a schedule to keep."

Raider came up against him. "Now you got a gun in your nose, friend. Think about it."

The train backed slowly down the track at a snail's pace. Yellow globes of light bobbed in the dark as men searched the ground on either side of the rails. After the first mile, they found two of the dead gunmen. Three miles farther was a third.

"Rade, that's got to be all of 'em," said Doc. "A passenger saw the other three make tracks when we stopped.

They'll steal horses somewhere and we'll never find them."

Raider gave his partner a hollow look. "Doc, trust me, will you? I ain't looking for no outlaws." He stalked off holding his lantern out ahead. Doc looked after him but said nothing.

Twenty minutes later, one of the searchers sang out and the lanterns came together in a single light. Raider squatted down, turned the body over and looked into the bloodless face of Lieutenant Graham. His open eyes were covered with dust and his throat was a ragged wound.

Colonel Arthur peered over Raider's shoulder, then shrank back quickly. "Jesus God!" He glared darkly at Raider. "One of my officers has been murdered, sir. You had better have a *damn* good explanation for this business!"

Raider shoved him roughly aside and stalked back to the train. Doc caught up and turned him around. "All right. You knew you'd find him back here. How come, Rade?"

" 'Cause I walked right in on them two slicing his throat, Doc. Right there between cars." Raider's voice was strained. "Shit—I didn't even know what I was seeing. There was someone else there in the dark, and then he kinda slid over the side and I caught this *look* from him. . . ." Raider stopped and gazed past his partner. "He had something to tell me this afternoon, Doc, only I didn't have time to listen to it."

"You tell anyone else about that?"

"Hell, no. I guess Graham did, though. Picked the wrong fuckin' person, too."

CHAPTER TWENTY

When the train pulled into Rock Springs at noon, Doc ran to the telegraph office and wired Harry Morton in Denver:

NAKED NYMPH IS FAKE. REAL STATUE STOLEN DUR-
ING STORAGE IN VAULT. CHECK CAGE THOROUGHLY.

—WEATHERBEE

Morton acknowledged the message. Doc paced the floor
a long three hours before the reply came through:

INVESTIGATION SHOWS EIGHT-INCH SQUARE OF STEEL
SCREENING NEAR CEILING CUT OUT AND SET BACK IN
PLACE. IMPOSSIBLE TO SPOT TAMPERING FROM
GROUND LEVEL. NOW WHAT?

—MORTON

"Rade," said Doc. "We've been suckered good. This
whole thing was set up long before the exhibit even *got*
to Denver. Someone *knew* the *Nymph* would be in that
vault, and figured just how to get it."

Raider looked puzzled. "Hell, Doc, even if they did,
that little square isn't big enough to crawl through. And
the statue was a good ten feet inside the cage."

"Doesn't matter. Whoever set this up figured a way.
Had plenty of time to work it out, too." Doc bit his lips
and frowned. "Rade—a pair of strong expanding tongs
would do it. The statue's heavy, but if you hung the tongs
from a good steel bar—" Weatherbee struck his palm
with a fist. "Of course—that's exactly how they did it!
Pulled out the real statue, then set the fake in its place."
Doc's smile faded. "Only, where did they put the damn
thing when they got it? They sure didn't carry it out. I
was there. All those people had were bags of money, and
the bags weren't big enough to hold the *Nymph*."

"As long as you're askin' yourself questions," Raider
said wryly, "where did they *get* those tongs you're talking about? They didn't take 'em into the vault, and they
weren't there after the robbery. Nobody could've—"

"The walls," Doc said soberly. "The damn walls!" He
turned on Raider. "Remember all the painters' equipment sitting around in the vault? They'd fixed a leaky
pipe a few days before, and Lewiston made them leave
all their stuff there so they could finish the job after the

treasure left the bank. There were buckets, tarpaulins—
a whole pile of stuff."

"And the tongs were hidden there waitin' for the outlaws," Raider finished. "Hell, the fake statue, too. They
put the tongs and whatever else they used back in the
pile when they were through." Raider looked pained.
"Shit. The real *Nymph* was there too, wasn't it? They
just left it in the trash and we walked all around it!"

"And the painters came in after we packed up the
treasure and simply carried the real *Nymph* out of the
bank." Doc's mouth fell open. "Lewiston," he said flatly.
"Henry Lewiston. Rade, it *has* to be him!"

"That scrawny little bastard? Come on, Doc—"

"Who else could it be? He knew the *Nymph* was coming, way in advance. Security for the tour was arranged
months before the exhibit left Egypt. And he had access
to the vault. No one else could have spent the time alone
in there to cut out that square. It was Lewiston who arranged for the painters, and worked up that fake leak
in the wall." Doc ran back to the telegraph office, Raider
trailing behind. Harry Morton had been putting two and
two together in Denver, and there was a message waiting
for them:

HENRY LEWISTON REPORTED ILL AT HOME SINCE
TRAIN LEFT DENVER. HAVE CHECKED RESIDENCE.
SUBJECT HAS FLOWN COOP.

—MORTON

Doc muttered a curse and quickly scribbled a message:

CHECK PAINTERS HIRED TO FIX WALL IN VAULT. BE-
LIEVE THEY ARE INVOLVED.

—WEATHERBEE

Morton's reply arrived half an hour later:

GUESS WHAT? NO RECORD OF PAINTERS. FAKE NAME.
FAKE COMPANY.

—MORTON

"We've been led around on a leash," moaned Doc. "Every step of the way. Lewiston worked with Shipley to stage that robbery on the way to Denver. It scared the Ramans into canceling the exhibit and putting the treasure in the vault long enough for Lewiston to get to it."

"Plus the two million bucks, *and* the Wells Fargo haul," Raider added. "Doc, there's a lot of little extras floatin' around on this job. You figure Lewiston did in Shipley and Butch Hackman? Kinda closing out the partnership?"

"Sure he did. Or had it done. That country-bumpkin banker act was a good one, Rade. He played the big feud between Neferti and Willis right up to the hilt and we fell for it. Killing Jamison and planting money in his room, taking a shot at Willis—the whole damn thing. And of course leaving those Egyptian knives lying around was the icing on the cake."

Raider stared out the fly-specked window of the telegraph office. "There's something we're forgetting, Doc. Lewiston wanted Raman dead so he wouldn't talk about the fake, and I reckon he had those dudes try to steal it off of me at the same time. Only there's someone a lot closer to all this than hired gunmen or Lewiston either. Someone who's been with us right from the beginning in Chicago and knows everything we're up to. Who went through your stuff tryin' to get that picture back? And who tossed a rattler in Neferti's room? There wasn't any *outlaws* ridin' in the *City of Worcester.*"

"Yeah, I know," said Doc. "It's one of our happy little group, only I don't know who the hell it could be. I'd give a double-eagle to know who Lieutenant Graham talked to yesterday afternoon. And what he wanted to tell you." Doc paused and picked at his cheroot. "Rade, there's something you got to know. I should have told you sooner, but I had a reason not to."

"Uhuh. I kinda figured."

Doc took a deep breath. "Remember when the train slowed at Greeley? I, ah—had Mack Hooper waiting there. We transferred the treasure to another boxcar."

Raider's jaw fell. "You did *what?*"

"I thought we'd get hit between Denver and San Fran-

cisco. It stands to reason they'd try to get the rest of the
treasure. There's some pretty valuable stuff there. Gold,
silver—"

"And you decided to leave me out of it. Goddamn it,
Doc—!"

"Now hold on a minute." Doc backed off. "I said I had
a reason, Rade. If something goes wrong, I'm responsible
for it and you aren't."

"Shit. Wagner'll figure I'm up to my ass in it anyway.
Where's the damn train now?"

"Going west like we are. A day or two ahead. Hooper's
riding shotgun. I told the soldiers it was going back east.
If any of 'em said anything—" Doc's words trailed off.
"Oh, shit, Rade!"

"Uh-huh. It likely got back to the same guy who
knocked off Graham. The little friend we ain't unmasked
yet."

"And whoever he is won't believe for a minute the
train's going east. Rade—I've screwed it up good, and
maybe I got Graham killed in the bargain." He stalked
back to the counter and penned another message. "Hooper's probably out of Utah already and into Nevada. The
least I can do is let him know what he's in for."

Raider caught his partner's expression. "Hell, Doc, I
might've done the same thing if I'd thought about it."

"Thanks. That's a big help." Weatherbee checked
freight schedules and figured Hooper's train was somewhere past Wells, Nevada, between Battle Mountain and
Reno. He telegraphed the railroad stops and lawmen at
those towns, and every shack on the way that had a wire
going in. Doc knew he'd have to wait till Ogden for any
kind of reply, and wasn't sure he could sit still that long.
He'd put Mack Hooper in a hell of a spot. Maybe he was
dead already—just like Graham.

After Rock Springs, Raider found it hard to look his
fellow passengers in the eye. One of them was clearly a
killer—someone who'd worked hand in hand with Henry
Lewiston right from the start. Someone he and Doc had
talked to a hundred times.

Raider ruled out Neferti first off. Whatever she might
be, she wouldn't harm her father. He'd seen the way she
looked at the old man, and you couldn't fake that. Dr.
Raman himself was too weak and Khalifi was too stupid.
Willis? Maybe, thought Raider. The Britisher was smart
enough to throw a false trail, and likely needed the money.
Still, Raider couldn't see him killing Jamison or anything
else bigger than a bottle. Louisa and Annette were too
scatterbrained to do anything harder than spreading their
legs. They were damn good at that, but it didn't add up
to murder.

Raider realized there were plenty of others on board
who'd had the opportunity. Colonel Arthur, maybe. Being
an asshole didn't brand you a killer, but the man had been
there all along. Still, so had a dozen of his troopers, men
who'd ridden the train all the way from Chicago. And you
couldn't rule out the railroad employees—train engineers,
porters, conductors, brakemen. Like the troopers, you got
used to seeing them around. They came and went as they
pleased and nobody noticed.

Raider shook his head and walked up to get dinner.
Hell, if you thought about it there wasn't anyone you
could really rule out. The whole business gave him the
creeps. He caught himself looking over his shoulder, wondering who was walking behind him.

At Evanston, a few miles from Utah Territory, Doc
learned from the stationmaster that Mack Hooper's freight
had passed through safely on schedule. There were no
more messages from stops ahead, but there was a long
telegram from Harry Morton:

DESCRIPTION AND HOLD ORDER ON SUBJECT FUGITIVE
SENT TO LAWMEN, RAILROADS, USUAL RECIPIENTS.
CLEAR EVIDENCE SUBJECT INVOLVED. POLICE INFOR-
MANT SAW HIM WITH SHIPLEY ON TWO OCCASIONS.
WEATHERBEE—WHERE IS HOOPER? PINKERTON OF-
FICE HERE SAYS HE IS UNAVAILABLE. REPLY IMMEDI-
ATELY.

—MORTON

Doc didn't like to lie to Harry, but the lawman was too far away to do Hooper any good. The wire he sent read:

THANKS FOR INFORMATION. KEEP UP GOOD WORK.
UNDERSTAND HOOPER IS ON SPECIAL ASSIGNMENT.
                                    —WEATHERBEE

Morton wouldn't like that, but it would calm him down for a while.

Ogden, in Utah Territory, was the end of the Union Pacific tracks direct to San Francisco. Here, Southern Pacific took over for the long 770 miles to the coast. Doc checked for telegrams and Raider bought Nancy a brandy.

The train moved north out of Ogden, circling the Great Salt Lake for the southwest haul to San Francisco. Raider watched the sun turn water into brass and scurried back to his own compartment. The train moved sluggishly north; small shacks and settlements dotted the railside, but the land was mostly empty. Raider found Doc busily scribbling another message.

"For what it's worth, Harry's sent out a bulletin on Lewiston," Doc said without looking up. "He knows Hooper's up to something, too."

"What'd you tell him?"

"I didn't tell him anything. What the hell *could* I tell him? Rade, I'm going to have to let Chicago know what we're up to."

"Includin' Hooper?"

"Including Hooper. It's been nice working with you, partner."

Raider started to speak. The train squealed suddenly to a halt, and he clutched at a wall to keep himself steady. "Shit, now what?"

Someone pounded urgently on the door. Raider answered and saw Arthur's scowling features. "You two better come and see this."

"See what?"

Arthur clamped his jaw shut and marched away without answering.

*   *   *

The short stocky man was raging at a conductor, his face growing redder by the minute. Raider recognized him right off. His wife was the stringy-haired woman with glasses. She was hunched over in a seat crying hysterically.

"What the hell's goin' on here?" asked Raider.

The stocky man answered. "That man attacked my wife!" he exploded. "Just—hit her right in the face and knocked her down! Damn—he could have killed her!"

"What man's that?"

"Could have *killed* her!"

"He dropped this when he jumped the train," said Arthur.

Raider looked at the thing and stared. It was a curly-bladed Egyptian knife. "He took after her with *that?*"

"The lady was going from one car to the other and this feller was standing there," the conductor explained. "Startled him, I reckon. Tried to hide something from her but she saw it."

"Tried to hide what?"

"Money," sobbed the woman. "Lots of it. And something shiny, like gold."

"Jesus Christ!" snapped Raider. Shoving his way through the crowd, he bolted down the aisle and jumped off the train. There was nothing to see but a scattering of small houses and a stack-pole corral. Raider sprinted around the shacks, gripping his Remington, then walked back to the tracks. Doc caught him and called him over. "He stole a horse, Rade. Two boys saw him. I rented us a couple of mounts."

"*You're* goin' to ride a horse, Doc?"

"Shut up. I'd ride a buffalo if I could catch up with that son of a bitch!"

Raider spotted him five minutes later, riding hard northeast toward the mountains, leaving a plume of gray dust in his wake. The way he was driving the mount he'd last another two miles and not much more. Raider slowed and let Doc catch up. There was no big hurry—the man had no place to go but flat open space.

"For a fella's showed a lot of smarts so far, he ain't using his head right now," said Raider. "Who do you figure it is?"

Doc didn't answer. He clutched the reins in one hand and his derby in the other. Raider held back a grin. "Circle on out to the right and don't press him. I'm going up ahead and come in on top."

"I expect he's got a gun, Rade."

"Well, shit, Doc, so do I."

Raider waited behind the low line of scrub. The rider was still coming fast, burning up dirt. Raider could hear the horse's labored breathing and see white flecks of foam on his mouth. It angered him to see an animal treated like that; there was no damn sense in it.

When the rider was fifty yards off, Raider pulled his horse around the brush, carefully aimed the .44, and fired two shots past the man's ear. The trick worked immediately. The fugitive jerked his reins straight back and sent himself and the mount tumbling over the landscape. Raider trotted up quickly, slid off his horse, and leveled the pistol. "Slow now, real slow, friend."

Doc reined in behind him. The man came to his knees and spit dirt. He blinked up at Raider and went white. "Damn—don't shoot me!"

"Why the hell not?" For a cool-headed killer, he sure didn't look the part. He was young, not more than twenty, dressed in a broad-checked suit. His arms stretched high and his whole body trembled. Raider looked curiously at Doc. "You ever see this dude before?"

Doc shrugged. Raider walked over and patted the man down for weapons.

"Y-you goin' to kill me, mister?"

"I'm thinkin' on it."

"I—didn't *do* anything," the boy protested wide-eyed. "Honest—I was just helping the lady out!"

"Doing *what?*"

"Helping her out. She give me this money—five hundred dollars. You can have it if you like. It's there in the bag!"

Raider told Doc to keep the boy covered and stalked over to the exhausted horse. There was a carpetbag hooked on the saddlehorn and Raider slipped it off and opened it. Inside was a small wrapped package and a roll of bills. Raider walked back and stuck the package in the boy's face. "Now. What's this shit about doing the lady a favor? What'd you hit her for?"

The boy's eyes widened. "I didn't hit anybody! Jesus! Her husband's trying to put her in the poorhouse and take all her money. She—she said if I'd mail the jewelry to her in San Francisco she could get away from him and I could keep the five hundred." The boy swallowed hard. "You got any water or anything?"

"No," snapped Doc. "This lady. What's she look like?"

"Tall, real gawky-looking, like a bird. Nice lady, but godawful ugly."

"Uhuh. And a short stocky husband," finished Raider. He tore the wrappings off the package. There were two heavy saucers from the diner inside, wrapped in newspaper.

The boy's eyes widened. "That ain't no jewelry!"

"That lady isn't any lady, either," Doc said warily. "Rade—you thinking what I'm thinking?"

"Shit!" Raider threw the saucers as far as he could. "It's Lewiston, Doc. Got to be. The son of a bitch put on a dress and rode the fuckin' train with us out of Denver!"

Doc started to speak. The sharp crack of gunfire carried over the flats, and Weatherbee stared at the bright gout of flame rising up from the train.

CHAPTER TWENTY-ONE

One end of the car was aflame; smoke from burning wood and upholstery curled up to the sky in a choking black cloud.

"Hell, that's *our* car," Raider shouted. "All our stuff's

in there!" Reining his mount in hard, he slid off the saddle and bolted for the far end of the coach. Suddenly, the rear door splintered open in his face. Raider jerked a hand to his eyes and backed off. A terrible roar came from inside. The giant Khalifi staggered through billowing smoke. Fire licked at his clothes. His face was a mask of pain and his eyes were filled with rage. In his arms he carried the limp form of Dr. Raman. Khalifi took two steps, stumbled off the platform, and sprawled on the ground with his burden.

Raider climbed the steps and pushed past the shattered door. The fire was nearly halfway down the car, but most of the smoke was sucking straight out the other end. Raider shouted, moved as close to the flames as he could, and quickly poked his head in the compartments that weren't burning. Moving back to his own quarters, he slammed the door against smoke, jerked open the window, and tossed his and Doc's belongings outside. Taking a last look over his shoulder, he crawled through the window and dropped to the ground.

"You okay?" said Doc.

"Yeah. What the hell's going on?"

Weatherbee helped him gather up their gear, and the pair moved quickly away from the blistering heat of the fire. The engine was moving now, pulling the rest of the car away from the burning coach and the mail car behind. Doc saw the troopers weren't even bothering to help—they knew there was nothing in the mail car to save.

"We were right," Doc said wearily. "That ugly lady was Lewiston. The bastard was right here with us all the time. Soon as we chased after the kid he and the stocky guy jumped the train and grabbed a couple of horses." Doc gave his partner a dark look. "Rade, they shot a couple of passengers and grabbed Neferti."

"Oh, shit. They took her *with* 'em?"

"Right. And the statue, which of course Lewiston was carrying, and I'll bet most of the money from the Wells Fargo job and the bank. Khalifi was with the old man or they'd never have gotten the girl. Lewiston stopped long enough to toss a lantern in the car to slow him down. Rade—we got to go after them. They haven't got much start."

"Not us, Doc. Me." Doc protested, but Raider stopped him. "You ain't worth shit on a horse, and you got stuff to do right here. I still figure someone'll hit Hooper's train if they can find it." Raider started gathering up his gear. Pausing a moment, he picked up the Sharps .45 he'd taken off the outlaw in Colorado. "I'll rent me a horse over there if they ain't all stole." Nodding at Doc, he stalked off to the corral.

The sun was nearly gone before the car burned out and was pushed onto a siding to let the Southern Pacific get underway again. Doc took time to walk up the tracks and hook his gravity battery-powered telegraph apparatus to a line. He tapped out a quick message to Harry Morton about Lewiston, and asked the lawman to forward information to Chicago.

Colonel Arthur was wating for him at the train. The officer's face was nearly purple, and Weatherbee knew he'd learned there was no treasure in the mail car.

"Goddamn it," he raged. "You had no business pulling a stunt like that! I want to *see* that so-called order from General Cleve, Weatherbee!"

"Sorry," Doc lied. "Got burned up in the train."

"Bullshit. You never had any order. Where's the shipment now?"

"On the way back east."

"I don't believe that."

"Believe what you like." Doc turned to go.

"I'll have your fuckin' hide for this!" Arthur yelled after him.

"Get in line," said Doc.

Dr. Raman was all right. All he'd done was swallow a little smoke, thanks to Khalifi. The old man was near hysterical about his daughter, and Doc assured him they were doing everything they could.

Khalifi had burns on his arms and shoulders that

would have put an ordinary man in the hospital. The giant wouldn't let anyone touch him and no one insisted. Doc passed him once, caught the look in his eye, and quickened his pace. He was squatting like a stone by the tracks, staring dumbly in the direction Neferti had disappeared.

When the train stopped briefly up the line, Doc ran quickly into the station. The message he'd feared all along was waiting for him. He read it and crumpled it angrily into a ball. Outlaws had hit the train a few miles inside Nevada. Hooper had a slug in his chest but was still alive. The gunmen had headed northeast over the badlands. Doc swallowed his pride and broke the news to Arthur.

The colonel barely repressed a smile. "Well, you fucked it up good, Weatherbee. Not a damn bit surprised."

"Okay, you got that in. I'm asking for help, Colonel."

"What kind of help?"

"I have to go after them. I don't have much choice. If they headed northeast they passed right above us and kept going. Nobody's going to stay in the badlands long if they can help it. I'm guessing Idaho Territory."

Arthur grunted. "That's a guess and nothing more. They could be anywhere, and you don't have a chance in hell of finding them."

Doc held back his anger. "I'm getting a horse and heading north, friend. You want to send a couple of troopers along, that's up to you."

Arthur said nothing, but half an hour later two troopers joined Doc at the local stable. Their names were Mason and Delaney, and it was obvious they didn't like either Weatherbee or the assignment.

Doc had few misgivings about leaving the train. There was still a killer aboard, but there was no way to unmask him without finding Lewiston first. Besides, who would he bother now? The game of setting Willis against the Ramans was over, and there was nothing left to steal.

Doc made a final stop at the station and got off a wire to Morton about the train robbery. At least, he thought miserably, he wouldn't be around for Harry's sizzling answer. Before the train pulled out, he checked in on Lord Willis and the twins, and talked to Dr. Raman. The old man pleaded with him to find Neferti.

"We're doing everything we can," Doc assured him again. "Raider's after him, and we've alerted lawmen all along the way."

"If anything happens to her—" Dr. Raman's eyes filled. "With Khalifi gone now, I'm all alone, Mr. Weatherbee. I—"

"Huh?" Doc sat up straight. "What are you talking about?"

"I—cannot find him. I thought he was sleeping, but he is gone! He is not on the train!"

●　　　●　　　●

Lewiston and his companion had a good two hours' head start. Raider saw they'd made the most of it—running their mounts into the ground and then trading for fresh ones twenty miles north. The girl was likely suffering for it, he decided. She didn't look like a lady who'd done much riding.

Ten miles from Idaho Territory, Raider pulled up short and took his bearings. To the east was Bear River and the Wasatch Range. The ragged peaks ran roughly north and south, with the Uinta Mountains cutting east and west right through them. It was wild country that pushed east into Wyoming and north through southern Idaho—a logical place to go if you were on the run. Yet, Lewiston had suddenly cut due west above the Great Salt Lake, heading into the desert. Now what the hell would he do that for? Raider wondered. It was killing country to ride through anytime, and especially in the heat of July. The land was a furnace, hot enough to drag down any man or horse foolish enough to venture into the salty wastes.

Still, Lewiston had chosen that path. The man was anything but crazy, and must have a reason for it. Raider turned west on the trail, already feeling the heat suck water out of his body.

＊　　　＊　　　＊

Lewiston's tracks disappeared late the next morning, blown away in the wind. Raider cursed and started criss-crossing, finally picking up the trail again in mid-afternoon. They were several miles north of the man's original path, and Raider decided hopefully the banker was coming to his senses and leaving the desert. If Lewiston didn't, Raider would. He knew what the land could do, whether his quarry did or not. The earth was so dry here it cracked and peeled in enormous flakes, like paint on an old building.

Raider followed the new trail a hundred yards, then stopped abruptly. Sliding off his mount he dropped to the scorching ground and peered closer. Jesus! His stomach tightened in a knot. One of the horses was gone. There were only two sets of tracks now. He guessed what had happened. The girl was slowing them down. She couldn't take the desert and they'd killed her and left her behind. Raider backtracked, picking up the trail again in a long gully, fearful of what he'd see. Two miles back he found it. The land dropped down to hide a muddy, near dried-up waterhole. Shaking his hat and shouting, he drove off the buzzards already picking flesh. They flapped away shrieking and Raider walked over to the body.

He knew already it wasn't the girl, and to his surprise saw it was the stocky man who'd played the role of Lewiston's husband. The birds had gotten to him, but it was clear he'd been shot in the chest. Raider climbed the gully and peered down the other side. Goddamn—*now* what? The short man's dead horse was there and two others besides—plus the riders to go with them. Both had the markings of gunslingers, but Raider had never seen either of them before.

The picture took shape slowly in his head. The two outlaws had waited at the waterhole several days. They had a tent to keep off the heat. There was an empty water tin, a few cans, and the evidence of several fires. Sometime earlier in the day, they'd met Lewiston and had a falling out. Lewiston's friend had gotten himself killed, and Lewiston had hauled off down the trail with the girl.

What the hell did it all mean? He and Doc had assumed

Lewiston pulled the business with the boy because they'd forced his hand—learned about the fake statue and put lawmen on the alert. Why, though? With everything else going on, he and Doc hadn't even thought about that. Lewiston had called attention to himself when he didn't *need* to. He could have simply walked off the train in his disguise at any stop and disappeared. Maybe, Raider decided, he'd found out about Doc's switch of the treasure at Greeley, and where it was going. He'd had plenty of time to wire ahead and tell his confederates the loot was on another train. The Southern Pacific tracks ran only eight or ten miles north of where Raider was at the moment. Was that what the outlaws were waiting for? It still didn't make sense. Lewiston could have reached them without calling attention to himself. There was something. Something else . . .

The truth hit him like a hammer. Christ, it was the girl. *He'd done it to get the girl!* The dumb son of a bitch had pulled a bunch of near-perfect crimes, then risked it all to steal Neferti off the train!

There wasn't a whole lot of logic to it, Raider decided— until you thought about Lewiston. Gangly and awkward, he likely had little luck with women outside of his head. Maybe he'd had his eye on that lovely little ass from the start—planned to take her off the train and do what he wanted with her.

A cold chill touched the back of Raider's neck. However Lewiston figured it, he sure had her now. And if Raider couldn't get to her first, Neferti might soon be wishing she was plain pig-ugly. A man like Lewiston would make her pay for every gal who'd ever turned him down.

Dirty water was better than nothing. Raider let his mount take all it was safe to swallow, then filled his canteen and the small wooden keg. When the sun started down he let the horse drink again, then moved off west. Backtracking had cost a little time, but Raider wasn't worried. The desert made everyone pay—Lewiston and the girl would have to stop.

Raider followed horse tracks north over the Southern Pacific rails and spotted the small campfire an hour after sundown. Leaving his mount in a shallow washout, he circled the fire until he was less than a hundred yards away. He could see two horses and Lewiston, and figured the girl was bound up somewhere out of sight.

There was little cover, only wind ridges and shallow hollows. He chose one of the hollows and bellied up slowly, working his way from one low spot to the next. When he was thirty yards off he saw men moving up on his right. Raider froze. There were four of them, sneaking in fast from the east. At first he thought they were Lewiston's men, then knew damn well they weren't.

* * *

Doc hated riding more than anything. Riding over land where the heat rose up in visible, choking waves was almost more than he could handle. The two troopers were veteran cavalrymen, more at home in the saddle than out. They took great joy in Doc's discomfort and grinned at him continuously. Doc didn't like either one, but Corporal Delaney was the worst. He was a lean, hard-bitten little man with close-set eyes and a pinched face. If there was a level stretch of ground, Delaney found a rocky ridge— for the sheer pleasure of watching Doc stumble over it.

Just after sundown they crossed into Idaho Territory and met rails going toward the Snake. The troopers watched curiously as Doc shinnied up a pole in his tight worsted trousers and red silk vest, the curl-brim derby perched atop his head. He quickly got off a message to Morton, letting the lawman know where he was headed, then climbed back down again, ripping his trousers in the bargain.

"There's a little town called Heely about six miles north of the Bear," said Mason. "Might be we could get a drink there and a place to stay."

Delaney glared at him. "Heely ain't worth shit. Isn't anything there but a bunch of drunk Nez Percé." He turned on Doc. "You want a town, mister, we better keep going northwest on to Spring."

"And how far's that?"

"Twenty, thirty miles."

"We'll try Heely," Doc said firmly, knowing his butt wouldn't make twenty miles.

"Suit your fuckin' self," muttered Delaney, casting a sharp eye at Mason.

Heely was all Delaney claimed it to be. A trail snaked off the road through spruce and ponderosa pine down to the Bear River. A collection of old trappers' cabins and canvas-covered sheds perched haphazardly on the water's edge. Blackfoot and Nez Percé Indians stood around the shack that served as bar and general store.

"What'd I tell you?" sulked Delaney. "Isn't shit here, mister."

Doc ignored him and questioned the storekeeper, asking if he'd seen anyone unusual going north.

"Unusual like what?" the man asked narrowly.

"Like armed men on horses, and maybe a heavy wagon."

"Yeah," said the man. "I seen 'em."

"You did?" Doc couldn't hide his surprise. "When? Did they come by here?"

"Rode through yesterday. Goin' north on the same road you come in on. 'Bout a dozen fellers and a big wagon. Tough-lookin' dudes."

Doc thanked the man. Mason and Delaney were bellied up to the bar wetting their throats. "Well, now—that's a piece of luck, right?"

"Yeah, ain't it?" Delaney said wryly. "A dozen armed outlaws and three of us. Kind of luck you always get in the fuckin' Army."

The three were on the road again by sunup, trailing the river north. The high peaks of the Wasatch tore a ragged line to the east under blood-red clouds. Both troopers knew the country well, and Mason pointed out Paris Peak to the north. "Had plenty of trouble up here three or four years ago," he said. "Big fight with Chief Joseph, then a lot of shit with Buffalo Horn in seventy-eight. If

Horn hadn't got killed, reckon we'd still be up to our ass in Indians."

Doc nodded. In spite of his discomfort, it was pretty country to ride through. The pines grew straight and tall, and there were plenty of elk and mule-tails.

An hour out of the settlement, Corporal Delaney pulled in his horse and faced Doc and Trooper Mason. "Reckon there's something we got to talk about," he said soberly.

"What's that?" asked Doc.

In answer, Delaney jerked out his revolver and calmly shot Mason through the head.

CHAPTER TWENTY-TWO

Raider's mind raced.

If he didn't move, the gunmen would never see him. They'd get Lewiston, though, and maybe Neferti would catch stray lead. If she didn't, he'd have four assholes to get her away from instead of one. Like it or not, he was on Lewiston's team for the moment.

Raider took them while they were still bunched up. The .44 roared, ripping away silence. A man cried out and dropped. Raider fired again. Rifles stitched a near-solid bridge over his head. Raider hugged dirt, backtracked fast down the draw. A quick glance told him Lewiston was wide awake—he'd scattered the fire, grabbed the girl, and melted into the dark.

Rising up cautiously, Raider caught two shadows— one straight on, the other off to the right. The second gunman was edging in close and Raider took him first. The man grunted, but Raider knew he'd missed. The other outlaw fired at the flash of Raider's muzzle. He flattened and spit dirt. Shit! It was the third dude he wanted, and that one was keeping quiet—waiting somewhere, or going after Lewiston.

Raider checked behind him, then sprang out of the hollow and threw himself over the low mound of dirt for his horse. Two Winchesters barked at once. A shadow jerked up out of the corner of his eye. White fire blossomed and pain sliced his back. Raider emptied his pistol, clawed for the saddlehorn, and kicked the horse in the ribs. The mount cried out and bolted. Raider went flat, let the animal have his head for a good quarter mile, then pulled up and reloaded the Remington.

In a moment he heard hooves cutting dirt. Raider set his teeth, slid off the horse, and urged it down flat. A running man was supposed to keep running. Raider didn't. He had no intention of losing Lewiston and the girl.

The gunmen thundered by him in the dark, three of them—so close he could smell their horses. Raider twisted, came to his knees, and fired. The first rider flung his arms up and flew out of the saddle. The second turned quickly, snapped off a shot. Raider winged him and sent him howling after the third. Kicking the horse up, he mounted and trotted off quietly back north.

A voice sang out far behind him. "Goddamn it, ride back to camp and get the others. I *want* that son of a bitch!"

Raider stopped short. Jesus! *What* others?

He knew the camp had been no more than two or three miles to the north. In less than twenty minutes he could hear them, coming up behind in a straight line. He knew what they had in mind—turn him back south and into the desert. For the moment, there was nothing he could do to stop them. There were too many riders and there was no good cover. The land was flat as a table and it wasn't all that dark anymore. When the sun came up, only distance would keep him alive. That meant letting them have their way and edging back south. They wouldn't have to kill him, then. The sun would take care of it fast.

Who the hell *were* they? Raider wondered. More than likely, they rode with the gunmen Lewiston had shot down at the waterhole. Were these the dudes who were supposed to take the treasure train? If they were, they sure as hell weren't working for Lewiston anymore. Raider figured the banker wouldn't get far after sunup. He didn't know shit about anyplace without four walls around it, and his luck had taken him father than he could expect.

He decided it was past ten—maybe nearly eleven. He'd stumbled on the depression just after dawn. It was a sink hole nearly twenty yards wide, curving gently down to ten feet deep—enough to hide both himself and the horse. The riders would have to come right up to it to spot it, just as he had. From fifty yards off it blended into the landscape, lost in blinding waves of heat rising from the salt flats.

The hole had seemed like a good idea at the time. He figured on staying there till the outlaws gave up and started back north. Now, though, he was trapped in the damn thing—frying in the shallow depression like an egg in a skillet. The gunmen had quartered the land all morning and showed no signs of stopping. Peering over the edge of his hole, Raider could see them, riding in pairs and fours slowly over the flats. Shit—the sun had to be getting to them. They couldn't stay out there forever!

Raider blinked against the brightness. His eyes stung and his skin was hot as fire. The gunmen looked like phantoms, sliding over mirrors of heat, sometimes halfway up the sky. He shook his head and squeezed his eyes. The desert played hell with a man's vision. Something might be thirty yards off or two miles away—it was hard to tell which. A few minutes before he'd seen three outlaws plodding along upside down across the horizon.

Backing down from the edge, he crawled to his canteen and let a few drops trickle down his throat. The water was full of salt and made him thirstier than ever. Somewhere in his flight he'd lost the wooden keg from the waterhole, and the canteen was near empty.

His lips were raw and split and his tongue was too thick to let him swallow. Bright red spots floated before his eyes. Raider knew what was happening to him. The heat was taking him fast, drawing all the moisture out of his body and draining him dry. A man could last in the

desert with good cover and water. Without it, he was a
dead man.

The horse smelled water, made a noise, and twiched its
dusty nostrils. Raider wet a kerchief and wiped it across
the animal's mouth. The horse sucked it eagerly, but it
wasn't enough. The poor devil wouldn't last much longer.
Raider knew his limits, and the mount's as well. Fuck the
outlaws. He had to get out of there and find water.

The horse stumbled, eyes rolling back in its head.
Raider jerked the reins and bullied him out of the hole.
He didn't even think about getting in the saddle. The
animal was doing well to stay on its feet. There was a
quarter cup of stale water in the canteen. He drank most
of it and gave the rest to the horse.

Raider walked north, keeping his eyes to the ground.
He couldn't think straight anymore and had no idea what
time it was. There was no use looking at the sun. The sky
was solid white from one horizon to the other.

The reins wound tight in his fist, jerking him to the
ground. Raider picked himself up, tried to focus on the
horse. The animal was finished. Raider lifted his saddle-
bag and the Sharps and walked on. He couldn't even give
the poor beast a bullet without giving himself away, and
he was sorry about that.

Raider's face was on fire.

He raised his head, the motion costing an agony of
effort. He was on the ground, he knew that much. Jesus,
how long had he been there? Forcing his raw lips open,
he sucked in a ragged breath of hot air. Got to—get up
now, he told himself. Can't just lie here . . .

Raider tried. His head wouldn't work with his hands.
He told them what to do but they wouldn't listen. He
cursed himself silently, trying hard to work up the anger
to live. One hand came to his face. Then another. He
squinted dully at the landscape. Suddenly, it didn't seem
as bright anymore. Maybe the sun was going down and
he'd make it.

Something moved. Raider tried hard to look at it. It swam out of the heat, took solid form and grinned at him.

"Still alive are you, asshole?" The voice forced a laugh. "Well, we can sure fix that." Raider heard the sharp, unmistakable click of a hammer, squeezed his eyes hard against the quick pain of the bullet.

Something rose up from the ground behind the gunman; a stone thrusting hard out of the earth. Raider heard a short, strangled cry of surprise. He opened his eyes and stared. The outlaw was hanging a foot in the air, eyes bulging, arms and legs flapping uncontrollably.

The body went limp and dropped like a rag. A shadow fell over Raider, turned him roughly on his back. Raider gritted his teeth against the sudden movement, stared up at the face looking down. It was a terrible, ugly face, eyes red and swollen, lips crusted with salt. Hands grabbed Raider by his shoulders and lifted him up.

"Rasha'huh? Neferti!"

Raider blinked. If the giant was an illusion, he was a damn good one. "Neferti," he said painfully. "That way. You understand?"

Khalifi grunted and dropped him roughly to the dirt. "Goddamn it," Raider yelled hoarsely. "You can't just— *leave* me here!" The giant marched stolidly over the desert. Raider stared after him until he was lost in waves of heat.

•   •   •

Doc stared down at the dark muzzle of Delaney's .45, his own hand frozen just above the Diamondback. "Don't even think about it," Delaney said through his teeth. The .45 jerked to the right. "Go on—get your hands away or I'll drop you right here!"

Doc gazed incredulously at the dead man. "You— *killed* him—just like that. What the hell for!"

Delaney grinned. "Nothing personal. Just wasn't in the cards for ol' Mason to go further." Keeping the Colt level, he kneed his mount up to Doc's and lifted the .38 out of his belt. "Cute little bugger. Ever hurt anyone with it?"

"Try me," raged Doc. "Goddamn it, what is this,

Delaney? You in with the outlaws, or just setting up business for yourself?"

The corporal spat on the ground and didn't answer. Holding the pistol in one hand and a length of cord in his teeth, he edged up behind Doc and bound his hands tight. Snubbing Doc's horse to a bush, he went through Mason's pockets, took his carbine and revolver, and kicked him down the river bank. Grasping the reins of Doc's horse and the dead trooper's, he stalked back to his own mount.

"Guess we better get moving, Mr. Weatherbee. Got a fair piece to go."

"And just where might that be?"

Delaney gave Doc a grin and climbed easily into the saddle.

In mid-afternoon, Delaney crossed the Bear River over a shallow bed of gravel and headed abruptly into the foothills of the Wasatch Mountains. Doc didn't know the country well, but recalled from maps he'd seen that they were still far south of the Snake River Plains. The country west of the mountains was fairly level, full of buttes, domes, and ancient lava flows. Old Fort Hall would be above them somewhere, and the Portneuf and Snake rivers.

There was no trail Doc could see, but the soldier clearly knew where he was going. Every mile east, the country got higher and rougher, but no one had come this way before them. If the outlaws who'd hit Hooper were headed where Delaney was, they'd taken another way in.

Weatherbee had no more doubts that Delaney was part of Lewiston's gang. He'd been one of the guards who'd helped switch the treasure at Greeley, and had quickly gotten word to Lewiston's confederate on the train. Maybe the corporal was the man who'd passed the word to shut up Graham before he could talk to Raider. Maybe—Doc cursed and shut his eyes against a swarm of gnats. "Maybe" doesn't mean shit, as Raider was fond of saying. He'd blown the whole thing, now—gotten Hooper shot up, lost the treasure, and put his own head in a noose. Doc had no illusions about his future with Delaney. The way he'd coldly gunned down Mason told him all he needed to know. The pinch-faced little corporal would keep him alive as long as he wanted to, and not a second more.

Shadows crawled up the high rock wall at Doc's shoulder. Thick boughs of pine turned a darker green. Delaney pulled off the path into a narrow defile, got off his horse, and shoved Doc's leg over the saddle without warning. Doc yelled and landed hard on his back. Delaney looked down at him, jerked out a knife, and cut his bonds. "Go over there and shit or do whatever you need to," he said.

Doc glared at him and moved off as far as he could. Delaney started pulling off saddles and whistling to himself, making a big show of ignoring his captive. He could afford to, Doc noted sourly. The walls rose straight up and there was no place to go.

Letting Doc run loose amused the corporal, and Doc played up to it as best he could. As long as he hung his head and looked scared, the man grinned and kept his bonds off. Delaney would be delighted if he made a run for it. He liked the idea of shooting people who couldn't shoot back.

"I don't suppose you can tell me where it is we're going?"

Delaney looked up from across the fire and set down his beans. "Isn't going to make much difference to you, mister."

"Why?" asked Doc. "Since I'm still alive, I figure you've got orders to get me somewhere in one piece."

Delaney's mouth tightened. "What the hell made you think so?"

"Because you enjoy your work too much. If you were going to, you'd have done it back there when you killed Mason."

"Goddamn—I can sure do it right now if you want!" He jerked the Colt from his belt, thumbed back the hammer, and leveled it at Doc's head.

"I don't think so." Doc tried hard to meet his gaze. "You'll keep me alive because someone told you to."

"Nobody tells me nothing," growled Delaney. "I do whatever the fuck I want." Still, he eased the hammer back and laid the pistol in his lap. Doc went back to his meal and didn't push the man further. He knew what he needed to know. The corporal would shoot him if he had to, but someone else wanted him alive—at least for the moment. Who? Doc wondered. Lewiston? One of Lewiston's silent partners?

Hopefully, Raider had already picked up the banker's trail and rescued Neferti Raman. With any luck, Lewiston might bargain to keep his head out of a rope, and lead lawmen up here to the Wasatch. More damn "maybes," Doc thought dismally. I'm sure stacking up a pile of them.

At first light, Delaney let Doc loose again for breakfast. Weatherbee shuffled about slowly, making a show of being stiff and sore from his ride the day before. The act wasn't that hard to pull off. Every muscle in his body cried out for a good week in a hot tub.

Delaney moved around camp checking his gear and horses, but made no effort to saddle up. Doc wondered about that, and didn't like it. If they weren't moving on, then someone was coming to meet them. That meant more people. And more people meant his chances of getting away would slim down to nothing.

Delaney squatted down, poured himself a cup of coffee, and showed Doc an ugly grin. "You sure look like shit, mister. Too bad we ain't got any fancy railroad cars for you to ride in."

"I don't much care for horses," Doc said absently.

"What a fuckin' shame."

"Do we have much farther to go?"

"Some. What difference does it make?"

Doc sighed. "Just asking, Corporal."

"Well, don't! I ain't interested in listening." Delaney raised the coffee to his mouth, blew on it, and glanced for a second into his cup. Doc's foot shot out and kicked the fire in the cororal's face. Delaney howled and clawed at his eyes. Doc flew at him, wrapped his hands around the man's throat and pounded his head into the ground. Delaney stabbed out blindly and caught Doc's nose. Doc felt cartilage snap. Pain cut like a knife through his skull. Delaney's knee came up for Doc's groin and Doc edged away from it. The motion gave Delaney leverage and Doc went sprawling. The corporal spotted his pistol and went for it. Doc came off the ground and rammed his head into the man's belly. Delaney grunted, air bursting out of his lungs. Doc hit him solidly across the jaw and Delaney went limp.

Weatherbee quickly gathered up the man's weapon and found his own Diamondback .38. For a brief moment he considered saddling up one of the horses, then thought better of it and sent all three mounts running out of the defile into the trees. Raider would make good use of a horse, but he could do better on foot. With a little head start he could lose himself in the mountains and they'd play hell finding him.

Binding Delaney up tight, he left the defile and started running back down the trail the way they'd come. He'd gone no more than a hundred yards when he stopped, froze, and dove for cover. Three seconds later, a dozen riders turned the bend and came up the trail straight for him. Doc kept low and watched them pass. The first man came within ten yards of him and stopped, sniffing the air and letting his eyes touch the landscape. Doc nearly stood up straight in surprise. He was out of uniform now, wearing denims and a worn hunting shirt. But Doc would have recognized Colonel Arthur's grim-set features anywhere.

CHAPTER TWENTY-THREE

Raider opened his eyes and wondered where the hell he was. A tree grew straight overhead. Thick clusters of needles blotted out the sky. Great, he decided—I'm dead. Either that, or out of the goddamn desert. Wherever he was, how the shit had he gotten there? The last thing he remembered was the giant stalking off over the flats and leaving him.

Painfully, he brought himself up on one arm and gazed around. It wasn't afternoon, now. Closer to mid-morning. Which meant he'd lost a good twenty hours somewhere. A narrow green valley snaked up to low foothills in the east. Beyond were high mountains and a brassy sky. Raider worked his lips and shrank back from the pain. They were raw and blistered and hurt like hell. His canteen lay a few feet away and he crawled to it eagerly. A big hand reached down and tossed it to him.

Raider blinked, looked up, and let his gaze travel the long length of Khalifi. The giant squatted down on his haunches and peered at him with tiny eyes. *"Neferti? Rasha-hunh!"*

"Yeah," said Raider. "Got you, partner." His own voice startled him. He sounded like a frog with a sore throat. The giant watched him as he brought the canteen gingerly to his mouth and took a deep swallow. He knew better but kept drinking. The cold water quickly knotted his belly and Raider gritted his teeth. "I guess it was you brought me up here, right? Well, I know you can't understand me, but I'm grateful."

Khalifi said nothing. Raising a sausage-sized finger, he pointed behind Raider's head and Raider turned. Stacked against the tree were his pack, the long Sharps rifle, and his pistol belt. "Neferti," the giant said, nodding eagerly, pointing first at the equipment and then at Raider and himself.

Raider nodded back. "Okay, I get the picture. Neferti. You and me, right? Fine, feller, we'll sure do that." He knew damn well why Khalifi had changed his mind and come back for him. Something in that tiny brain had told him he didn't know shit about where he was or where he was going. The man lying out there on the desert knew about such things and could take him to Neferti. Raider knew that was the only reason he was alive.

He was amazed at the man's strength and what he'd accomplished. Jesus—he'd carried about a hundred and

eighty-five pounds of limp flesh, a pack, and the rifle maybe forty miles, if they were anywhere near where Raider
thought they were. All that under a killing sun, and likely
no water at all. The son of a bitch wasn't bright, but he'd
thought things out the best he could. He'd brought along
the horse of the man he'd killed, but probably hadn't
thought of draping Raider over the saddle to ease his
burden. He didn't know how to do things like that—
horses and rifles were things men like Raider used, and
he wanted him to have what he needed.

Raider didn't feel like moving for another day or so,
much less sitting a saddle. Khalifi was eager to get started,
though, and kept growling and pointing at the horse until
Raider gave up. Short of shooting the giant about fifty
times in the head, there was no way to shut him up.

By late afternoon the country rose steadily toward the
Wasatch Range. Khalifi loped along tirelessly behind
Raider's horse, and Raider pretended he knew where they
were going. There was no use trying to tell the Egyptian
he didn't have the slightest idea where Lewiston had taken
the girl. If he'd slipped away safely when Raider fired on
the gunmen, he was undoubtedly headed northeast toward
less open country. That, of course, took in a hell of a lot
of Idaho Territory. He might be on their trail and he
might not—he sure wasn't going to tell Khalifi he had his
doubts. Every now and then he stopped, sniffed the air,
made a big show of following a trail. Khalifi seemed to
like that, and left him alone. What Raider was looking for
was people—a place to get a square meal and ask questions. Riding around playing Indian wasn't going to cut
it.

Just before sundown he found it—a small settlement
that didn't even have a name. They were willing to sell
him food and supplies at twice what they were worth, but
had nothing further to offer. It was a poor town, full of
pinched-face people getting by on nothing, and they didn't
like strangers—especially strangers with seven-foot giants
loping along behind their horses. Raider moved on quickly
and didn't make camp until the town was far behind. The

folks he'd seen there were so poor he was afraid they'd follow him and try to kill him for the horse and the rifle and his boots.

At dawn he ranged north, found the Bear River, and followed its course. He wished to hell he could find someplace with a telegraph so he could get in touch with Doc. Figuring out the time and miles in his head, he made a rough guess where his partner might be. Doc was worried about Hooper and the freight carrying the treasure and he'd be stopping when he could to wire ahead about that. By now, he'd alerted what lawmen he could find and there was likely help on the way—a posse, maybe, from right here in the territory, or soldiers up from Utah across the line. Maybe the best thing to do was quit moving north and turn back, he decided. Double back south and try to meet whoever Doc had sent to help him. It made a lot more sense than what he was doing. Hell, he could ride all over Idaho and never find a trace of Lewiston or the girl. The giant wouldn't like it, but Raider figured if he kept pointing ahead and saying "Neferti" Khalifi wouldn't notice where they were headed.

Twenty minutes later, Raider pulled his mount up fast and jumped to the ground. Going down on all fours, he picked sprigs of grass, sniffed them carefully, and moved a few yards to turn over a stone. Standing, he grinned broadly at the Egyptian. "Neferti! You understand? Neferti, that way!" He pointed excitedly back south. Khalifi's face clouded. Raider could see rusty little wheels turning around under the bald dome and figured the monster was going to jump him. Bending down again, he showed Khalifi the tracks. They belonged to a herd of antelope, but Khalifi was dutifully impressed. Raider let out a breath and climbed back in the saddle.

Khalifi woke him, clamping a hand over his mouth and bringing a finger to his lips. Raider nodded and followed him quietly to the edge of the clearing. They were gathered in small clusters on the bank of the river, twelve, fourteen riders and a heavy-bed wagon with packhorses tied on behind. Raider studied them a long moment, letting his gaze touch each of the riders. Suddenly he stopped, his hair standing on end. The moon was bright and he could easily make out the man's features. Great God A'mighty! It was Arthur—Arthur and a whole pack of outlaws!

After the first shock, Raider decided he wasn't too surprised. He'd never liked the man from the start, and his presence answered a lot of questions. Why Arthur had led his men out of the fight when the gunmen first hit the train, for instance. It also told him who had gotten Lieutenant Graham killed. That was a debt Raider meant to repay.

He didn't have to guess what was in the wagon. It was the treasure from Hooper's freight, no question about it. Khalifi went stiff beside him. The giant had finally recognized Arthur and decided he had something to do with Neferti. A low growl started in his throat and Raider touched him gently and shook his head. Suddenly, high-pitched voices came from the horsemen, and Raider squinted curiously into the dark. He could see them, now, two blond heads reflecting moonlight. Holy shit! He had the twins with him. The son of a bitch just couldn't leave all that pussy behind.

Raider studied the girls carefully and saw they hadn't gone willingly. They were bound together on a single horse, hands clasped tightly to their sides. Anxiously, he searched the faces again, looking for Doc. If he wasn't with the riders, his partner was likely dead or hurt bad. Doc wouldn't let Arthur get away without a fight. Maybe he'd found where the freight was, and asked Arthur to help. Raider's heart sank at the thought. Poor old Doc had walked right into it and gotten his head blown off.

Arthur's men quickly strapped the treasure onto packhorses, loaded the heavy wagon with stones, and rolled it into the river. A few minutes later, they splashed across the Bear and headed up into the mountains.

Raider thought fast. Arthur's party would have to stop for the night. Now, he knew right where to find them. He'd ride south and get help, even if he had to go all the way to the railhead. Arthur couldn't help leaving tracks and they'd be easy enough to follow. It was the best way to locate Lewiston and Neferti, too. If they made it north, they'd head for the same place Arthur was going.

"Look," he told Khalifi. "I don't think you're going to understand this, but I got to try. You—stay here. Okay? Me—I go—that way. *Comprende?*"

The giant clearly didn't. Even with Raider's elaborate gestures, the man's expression stayed perfectly blank. He stared dully at Raider, his mouth open, a drop of spittle collecting at one corner.

"Okay, asshole," Raider said irritably. "Try this. You go . . ." He pointed east. "Neferti gets dead. Got it? Neferti *dead* and it'll be all your fuckin' fault." Raider made a noise in his throat and ran a finger around his neck. Khalifi growled and came at him. "Wait, goddamn it!" Raider held up a hand. "You stay. Right here, see?" He made a big *X* on the ground with his boot. "You stay. Neferti *fine!*" He grinned and nodded his head to show how fine Neferti would be.

A glimmer of understanding crept over the giant's features. For the moment, that was all Raider could ask for. If the poor fucker took off over the river, there wasn't a damn thing for it. Raider didn't have time to argue.

The sky was dirty gray when Raider pulled up his horse and sagged in the saddle. The long night's ride on the heels of his trek in the desert had left him sore and bleary-eyed. He peered down through the thin line of trees and blinked away sleep. There were twenty, maybe thirty riders in the grassy hollow. Two or three downed a last cup of coffee while others scattered their fires and saddled up.

Raider looked them over carefully and a sudden smile spread his features. As the sky lightened, he could see half a dozen of the men wore bright shiny badges. By God, his luck was changing at last! He'd ridden right into the posse Doc or Harry Morton had put on his trail. Maybe Weatherbee was all right after all. Urging his horse down the hill, he trotted over to the first bunch of riders.

"Damn, I'm glad to see you fellers," he said. "Reckon I could have a cup of that coffee?"

The circle of men looked at him curiously. One returned Raider's grin, ambled over to meet him, and stuck a Smith & Wesson Schofield under his nose. "Billy—you ever seen this dude before?"

Raider's grin faded. "Hey, you got the wrong idea!"

The man named Billy walked up and looked him over. Raider saw his face, and all the heart went out of him.

"I know him," Billy said flatly. "It's the Pinkerton fuck that come on us when we was dumping that soldier boy off the train."

•   •   •

Doc saw Arthur, then spotted the twins bound on a big bay just ahead of the packhorses. He didn't wait to see more. When the riders were safely past he plunged into the thicket and made his way fast up the side of the mountain. In about five minutes they'd discover Delaney and know he was loose. Two minutes after that they'd be combing the whole country for him, and Doc didn't want to be anywhere close.

Hopefully, they'd figure a man on foot would make tracks fast—head down the trail to the Bear River and run south for help. Doc didn't intend to do anything of the sort. If he could cross the trail ahead he'd hole up on high ground, wait for riders to beat the bushes, then follow them wherever they went. Maybe Lewiston and Neferti were already at a hideout somewhere ahead. If they weren't, Raider had them. He'd make Lewiston talk, then lead a posse up to get Arthur and the rest of the outlaws. All Doc had to do was keep from getting caught, and hope for a chance to get the twins and Neferti out safe.

Even up close, the hideout was hard to spot. Built at the base of a high cliff, and sheltered by tall pines, it looked for all the world like a disorderly tumble of stones. From his perch up above, Doc watched the train of riders wind along the narrow ridge, pass the big boulder, then suddenly disappear. It had to be a cave, he decided. Or more likely a whole series of caves. They'd blocked up the entrance to look like the aftermath of an avalanche, leaving only a narrow, hidden passageway. There were probably several openings that would offer escape routes, maybe half a mile or more down the side of the mountain.

Okay, you've got 'em where you want 'em, Doc thought glumly. *What the shit are you going to do with them?* It was only late afternoon, but the temperature was already dropping fast. Doc pulled his collar around his neck and hunched up his shoulders against the wind. At this rate, he decided, he'd freeze to death about two hours after sundown. He was dressed for lunch at the Cheyenne Club, not for the goddamn mountains.

Thoughts of that marvelous establishment brought the aroma of delicious food to his nose. He hadn't eaten since Delaney's beans and bread the night before and there was a large hollow in his belly. Damn, thought Doc, the hallucinations are starting sooner than I figured. I can *smell* food cooking—real, honest-to-God food! Weatherbee craned his neck around the compass and sniffed. It wasn't his imagination, it was there, and not far off, either. Crawling carefully along the big rock, he inched his way south, following his nose. He found it not five yards away—a narrow cleft in the rock that dropped off into blackness. A thin wisp of smoke coiled up and disappeared, leaving the mouth-watering odor of bacon and fried potatoes.

Doc savored the smells. Clearly, he was right over the outlaws' cook-fire. They were down there, warm and safe, filling their bellies. Doc set his teeth and wobbled down off the rock. By God, there was no other answer. If he wanted to stay alive through the night, he'd have to get inside. Down there with Arthur and the outlaws. It was risky, but no more so than spending the night in the open without food or warm clothes.

It took a good three hours, but he found it. Doc thought Raider would be proud of him. He hadn't even looked for another way in, knowing that would take forever. The outlaws had planned their retreat well, and wouldn't leave doors standing open. Instead, he climbed down off the ridge, keeping low to avoid the sentries he knew were there, and started circling the area for tracks. If there was another entrance, it stood to reason there'd be a few tracks—horses or bootprints. He found what he was looking for in the soft ground below a small spring. It was only half a heelprint, but it was enough. The spring came from inside the mountain, and he followed it to a small hole just big enough to squeeze through.

The cave was colder than the weather outside, and Doc shivered. Still, that was a good sign, he told himself. The escape hole was far enough from the inhabited part of the cave to keep him from being discovered right off.

Doc felt reasonably safe for the moment. It was pitch black inside, and if he couldn't see them, they couldn't see him, either. All he needed to do was work his way toward a light, then stay well out of it.

The dim glow met his eyes past the first turn. He smelled the place long before he saw the torches sputtering in the wall and knew he'd crawled right into the communal outhouse. Doc's stomach was too empty for such a raw assault of odors and he nearly threw up on the spot. You were supposed to squat down and hit the stream that trickled through the little room, but few of the outlaws seemed to bother.

The discovery presented a real problem. If there were a lot of people in the place, the chances were good he'd meet someone head-on in the narrow tunnel leading farther into the cave. Still, there was nothing to do but chance it. Doc held his breath, stalked past the smelly piles, and plunged into the tunnel.

The next thing he smelled was horses. The tunnel opened up into a broad, high-ceilinged cave filled with mounts and bales of hay. Doc edged his way around the room, clinging to shadow. There was a choice of two passageways. Voices came from the one on his left. The odor of food came from the other. Doc didn't have to think twice.

It was a large, well-furnished kitchen, complete with

cookstoves and a whole wall of hanging pans. Doc was shocked at the sight. Someone had put a great deal of thought into this place, and brought all the comforts of home along with them. He'd seen smaller kitchens in big hotels.

The ceiling curved to a black fissure. A stovepipe led up to the top, and Doc guessed he was looking at the same hole he'd seen from above. He listened a moment, then crawled in quietly on all fours, grabbed a handful of beefstrips and bacon, and stuffed as many biscuits in his pockets as they'd hold. Still on his hands and knees, he backed out into the doorway toward the corral. A heavy boot kicked him squarely in the ass and lifted him into the kitchen. Doc yelled out in pain and surprise, crashed into the heavy stove, and clawed for his pistol. Twin hammers clicked and he froze, turned slowly, and looked into the ugly barrels of Corporal Delaney's shotgun.

CHAPTER TWENTY-FOUR

Raider shook his head, fingered his jaw, and spit out a tooth. The outlaw named Billy stood over him and grinned, fists still doubled in knots.

"Let him up, Billy."

"I owe the fucker, Lew!"

"Fine. You're paid up some, now. Lew stretched out a helpful hand to Raider. Raider shook it off and pulled himself shakily to his feet. Lew studied him curiously, chewing one corner of his mustache. He was a stocky, broad-shoudered man built low to the ground. His head was topped with short-cropped graying hair. Dark eyes and a broken nose dominated his face. "Looks like you found the wrong posse, friend. Real sorry about that." He nodded toward the fire. "Get yourself that coffee and we'll talk some."

Raider found himself a cup and filled it, ignoring the black scowls of the other outlaws. He could have kicked himself in the ass for getting sucked in by a dumb stunt like phony badges. It was a good trick when you had that many men riding, and he'd fallen right into it. If he hadn't been half asleep in the saddle . . . Shit, there was no use worrying about it now.

The man named Lew looked him over and rolled a smoke. "I reckon you already figured you're in big trouble, mister. These boys know who you are an' they don't much like you. Got any reason I shouldn't put a bullet in you right now?"

"I'm thinkin'," growled Raider.

Lew grinned. "Yeah, I would if I was you. I ain't real sure it's safe to pick *one* of those dudes to do the job. Too many of 'em wants it. Let's see . . ." He raised a stubby hand and started counting, squinting at the sky. "You played hell with that Gatling gun near Cheyenne Wells, took some good boys out when we hit Wells Fargo, and made a couple of more friends the other night on the flats." Lew shook his head and flipped his smoke away. "Damn, you sure walked into the wrong church, boy."

"Shit." Raider gritted his teeth. "If you're goin' to do it, do it and quit talking about it."

Lew looked surprised. "Ain't in any hurry, are you?"

"Kinda," said Raider. "This coffee isn't all that good, and I'm half asleep on my feet. Like to ask a couple of questions, though—just to set my head straight."

"Sure," Lew shrugged. "Why not?"

"First off, who the hell *are* you fuckers? I figured you was working for Lewiston, right up till you tried to kill him."

Lew's lazy drawl went flat. "We got a little score to settle with that bastard. Hell, not too little, either." He eyed Raider narrowly. "My last name's Hackman. I'm Butch Hackman's big brother. Butch had it set up with that dude Shipley in Denver to hit the train at Cheyenne Wells—make it look like we was goin' to take it right there. The other part of the deal was the Wells Fargo business, and we was in for a cut of the bank job." Lew made a face. "We was *supposed* to hit that E-gyptian treasure, too. Over in Nevada. Only someone else got to it first. Gunned down our boys at the waterhole waiting to meet someone to take us to it." Lew spat on the ground. "Shit. This fucker Lewiston set us *all* up—killed Shipley and Butch both after they was no more use to him. We figured that foreign gal was screwing things up."

"Yeah, so did we," said Raider. "When did you find out about Lewiston?"

"Same time you did. When he took off from the train dressed up like a lady. That asshole Army colonel's workin' with him. Knew that, didn't you? Had his own folks empty that boxcar right after it got out of Utah." Lew shot Raider a dark look. "Would've had that bastard Lewiston if you hadn't put your hand in, mister." He stood slowly, stretched, and hitched up his belt. "I got nothing against you personal, feller. Reckon you're doing what you're supposed to do. Let's get this over with, I don't take no pleasure in it." Lew's hand rested on the butt of his old Smith & Wesson.

"Hold it, now," said Raider. "I got one more question."

"Make it a short one—I ain't got all day."

"You know where Arthur took the loot from the boxcar? Where he's keepin' the cash from the Wells Fargo job and the bank?"

"Not yet. But we'll get the son of a bitch."

"You'll get him sooner if I take you to him," said Raider.

Lew stared a minute, then let his mouth curl into a grin. "Don't blame you for trying. I'd sure do the same."

"I saw 'em last night," Raider said evenly. "North of here on the Bear River. They had the treasure in a heavy-bed wagon. At the river, they dumped the wagon and put the stuff on packhorses. I was riding south to find some lawmen. I thought you was them."

"Huh-uh." Lew shook his head. "I ain't buying it."

"You would, though, if that wagon's right where I say it is. Shit, mister—you know what I'm doing. Everyone wants to stretch out livin' and I got something to sell."

Lew dropped his hand off the pistol. "All right. I'm plumb crazy for doin' it, but you bought yourself a day.

You know I don't need you after we find that wagon. I can follow tracks as good as the next man."

"Hell," grinned Raider. "I'll worry 'bout that when we get there."

Raider thought hard about a way to make the trip last, but came up empty. Lew Hackman didn't need any map to find Bear River. It was right there in plain sight; all he had to do was follow it north. He didn't really need Raider, either, and Raider knew it. If there was a wagon pushed in the river, he'd find it without help. Raider knew what the outlaw was thinking: The Pinkerton operative was either lying or telling the truth—either way, he'd bought another day and that didn't cost a thing. Raider figured Hackman would take it a step further: Any man with good sense held a card back to play later, and if there *was* something more, Lew aimed to get it.

Raider wasn't sure what that something would be. He had nothing else to offer, and Hackman wouldn't buy an empty sack. There was no use counting on Khalifi, either. The dumb son of a bitch had wandered off for sure by now. Even if he hadn't, Raider couldn't see him roaring out of the trees to strangle twenty or thirty outlaws.

Hackman's men waded out of the water and reported the wagon hadn't been in the river more than a day. Two riders splashed back over the Bear and said there were plenty of tracks leading up into the mountains.

Lew jerked his horse around to face Raider. "Well, I sure do thank you, Pink. Guess this is 'bout as far as you go."

Raider brought out the broadest grin he could muster. "Sure looks like it, don't it?"

Lew scratched his chin and screwed up his face. "For a feller 'bout two minutes off from a extry eye, you sure are a happy son of a bitch."

"So? What do you want me to do, Hackman? Scream and yell?" Raider laughed. "Goddamn it, you've got a head on your shoulders. Use it. Haven't you figured this gimmick yet?"

"Figured what?"

"You got maybe an hour or two 'fore you earn a hole in your head like mine." Raider nodded across the river. "Lewiston and Arthur have played this thing smart from the beginning. They fucked you, me, and everyone else— got a nice bundle of money and left you boys with nickles and dimes. Now, they just *accidently* left a clean trail to follow right to their front door, so you can ride in and take all that shit away from 'em. Makes real good sense, doesn't it?"

Hackman made a face. "What are you tryin' to say, mister?"

"Nothing. 'Cept I'll see you in hell before morning. Friend, you ain't going to get *close* to that crew. They didn't come this far to start getting stupid."

"Hmmmm," said Hackman.

"Aw, shit!" The outlaw named Billy pulled his mare up to Raider and glared. "This asshole's a *Pinkerton*, Lew. You know what he's trying to do!"

"Yeah, I do." Lew frowned thoughtfully. "Only trouble is, Billy, he's right."

"You don't want to kill him, I'll sure take the job."

Lew ignored him and looked warily at Raider. "Go on. Give me some more bullshit."

"If they're up there at all," explained Raider, "that trail'll end soon and take you somewhere else. Somewhere that winds back to the river and disappears, or leads up a nice blind canyon with some Winchesters waiting at the end."

"And how you figure on gettin' around that?"

"Have your men cross the river 'bout a mile up and wait there. You and me'll ride up the trail by ourselves."

"Like shit we will!" Hackman gave him a nasty look.

"Now, hold on!" Raider held up a hand. "If that hide-out's really up there, they'll gun down anyone climbing the trail in force. They won't likely bother two men. Not if one of 'em is me. Some of those dudes'll know me, and know what I am. If I'm carrying a white flag and riding with a man wearing a badge, I think they'll let us through. They've got three women up there, Hackman. An Egyptian and two English girls. Lewiston and Arthur'll figure I'm bargaining for them. That's close enough to the truth, too. If I was free that's what I'd have to do. Washington's been burnt on this business, and they'll shit for certain when they find we've lost those foreign nationals to a bunch of outlaws."

"None of this makes it any easier for the rest of my boys to follow," Lew pointed out. "If they got sentries out . . . "

"If they know where the trail is, your boys won't *have* to follow it. They can circle around and get rid of the sentries. Take some cigarette papers with you and drop 'em as you go. Isn't anyone going to notice."

Hackman stroked his chin again. "You're going to get me killed for sure, Pink."

"I ain't exactly got kin up there," snorted Raider.

* * *

Arthur poked a stick in the fireplace with his boot and gave Doc an amused grin. "In through the shithouse door, eh, Weatherbee? Not quite your rakish style, really."

"I don't see much *style* around here to worry about," said Doc.

Arthur's brow shot him a warning. "Corporal Delaney doesn't care for you, Weatherbee. Don't tempt me." The colonel walked away from the fire to an antique highboy and poured himself a brandy. Arthur's quarters had been an eye-opener for Doc. They were decked out lavishly with fine furniture and thick carpets. Gilt mirrors, tapestries, and oil paintings graced the cold stone walls. He'd only glimpsed the other rooms in the cavern, but what he'd seen was equally impressive. There was a dining room, complete with good crystal and china, just off the well-equipped kitchen. Doc guessed there were nice enough quarters for Arthur's outlaws somewhere down the tunnels.

Arthur caught his eyes and smiled. "Not too bad, eh? A step up from your everyday outlaw's cave." He lit a cigar and offered one to Doc. Doc refused. "Henry and

I started this place about four years ago. When we first went into business together."

"You mean the stealing business," Doc said bluntly.

"Exactly. The stealing business." Arthur raised his glass in a salute. "Here's to it. It has proven most profitable, Mr. Weatherbee. Most profitable, indeed. Henry knew where all the money was—I knew how it got from one place to another. Railroads, banks, warehouses—the works. Kept that fine detective agency of yours busy, too."

"Let me guess," said Doc. "You never used any of your own people. Just hired hands like Shipley and Hackman."

Arthur nodded. "And always through a blind, up to now. Treated them fair and square, too. Of course, we, ah—couldn't afford that luxury with Shipley and Hackman. Too much at stake. We're going out of business with this job, as you might have guessed."

"Mexico or Europe?"

Arthur's eyes picked up the flames from the fire. "That won't really matter to you, will it, Weatherbee?"

"No, I don't guess so. You going to do it yourself, Arthur, or let Delaney have the fun? Look—the government'll pay to get the twins back if they're not hurt or anything. You know that, don't you?"

Arthur threw back his head and laughed. "Weatherbee, you can't be serious. That's the quickest way in the world to get caught!"

"I'd help," Doc said firmly. "Give you a guarantee right now."

"You won't *be* here, friend. Don't you understand that?" Arthur looked down his nose, then sniffed at his brandy. "Besides, I'm looking forward to screwing that little Egyptian," he said blandly. "She any good?"

"She isn't *here* yet," Doc reminded him. "Or haven't you noticed? Lewiston isn't about to shake Raider. He's got a nose like an Indian."

"Oh, didn't I tell you?" Arthur pretended surprise. "He's already here. And the girl. I'm afraid your friend Raider the Indian is a *dead* Indian, Weatherbee."

Doc had no reason to believe him. Still, his stomach went tight at the man's words and he flushed with anger, knowing what Arthur had seen in his face.

The small room where Delaney dragged him was dry and reasonably warm. From the smell, Doc decided he was somewhere near the horse corral again. When the corporal left him, he struggled dutifully with his bonds, and knew right off there wasn't a chance in hell of getting loose. The rawhide cord was strong, and Delaney had done the job better than he had to.

Doc rolled over so he could see the dim glare of the torch in the tunnel outside. The rawhide was already numbing his arms and legs, and the thought of that sent a chill up his spine. If it was this bad already, he was in serious trouble. Unless he could loosen the cords and let the blood through, his limbs would be permanently damaged by morning.

The pain in his belly had turned to a dull, gnawing ache. Doc wondered if holding back food and water was Arthur's idea or Delaney's. Either of the bastards was capable of it, but Doc's vote went to Delaney.

Weatherbee was certain they were going to kill him. How and when was the question. If the colonel was keeping him alive, he had a good reason—something Doc was certain he wouldn't like. He'd seen a hint of that something in Arthur's eyes.

He woke in a cold sweat, felt the small hand over his mouth, and looked up at the girl. When he nodded, she took her hand away and came close to him.

"You—all right, Mr. Weatherbee?"

"Who is it—Louisa or Annette?"

"Annette. Golly, Mr. Weatherbee—you look just awful! I—is there anything I can do?"

"Sure. Cut me loose, get me a steak dinner and a good bottle of wine, a pistol, and a horse. Better make that two pistols. Big ones."

Annette bit her lip and looked hurt. "I don't think I can do any of that."

"That's okay," Doc assured her gently. "A knife'll do fine. I'll take it from there. Annette—do you think you can pull it off? I don't want to put you in danger or anything, but I've *got* to get out of here. Was it easy to sneak away? How are they treating you?"

Annette hesitated a minute. "It's—all right, I guess. I mean, you know what the colonel wants us for. We can do that, all right, but it's not much fun when you don't really *want* to."

"No, I suppose not. Listen, Annette. I know you're scared and it was a brave thing you did coming here. I don't want to frighten you any more, but you *have* to understand something. It isn't going to go on like this. Arthur and Lewiston aren't staying here. And when they leave, they'll kill us all. They have to. You know that, don't you?"

Annette's small mouth trembled. "Yeah, I guess so."

"Damn it, girl! You—" Doc took a deep breath and brought his voice back to a low, soothing pitch. "I'm sorry. Believe me, it's true. You've got to get me loose. You and your sister don't have a chance unless you do. Have you seen Lewiston? Does he really have Neferti with him?"

"He's here, and she is, too. I only caught a glimpse of them. She doesn't look real good." Annette paused thoughtfully. "Mr. Weatherbee, I don't guess I have to tell you what I am. Me and Louisa. You might not like me much but I never did anything to hurt anyone. I'm scared, mister. I've known a lot of men and done just about everything, but—that Lewiston is crazy. Just crazy as shit! I heard him tell Arthur what he's going to do to that girl. Jesus, I never *heard* of stuff like that! He's kinky as hell!"

Doc's hair stood on end. God, if the *twins* thought Lewiston was kinky . . . "Look—that's what I'm talking about. You got to get me loose. Maybe there's a knife lying around in the kitchen. A sharp piece of glass. Anything."

"I'll try. I—I really will."

Doc's heart sank. Her voice told him she really wanted

to, but didn't have the nerve for it. She'd never been in danger before—the idea of dying wasn't even real to her.

"Have you heard Arthur or anyone talk about Raider? He—told me he's dead, but I don't believe it."

Annette looked away from him. "He is, Mr. Weatherbee. For sure. I'm real sorry. Lewiston laughed out loud when he told Arthur. Raider saved him when some guys tried to kill him. Only the men got Raider instead."

A hard knot formed in Doc's belly. "Did he—see this? For certain, Annette?"

Annette didn't answer. Without a word, she turned and ran like a deer down the dark tunnel. Doc stared after her. It still doesn't mean anything, he told himself. Just because Lewiston said so. What kind of gunmen would be attacking Lewiston, anyway? Hell, they all *worked* for him! And if they were lawmen, they wouldn't be firing on Raider.

Doc tried to move his hands and feet. He couldn't even feel them anymore. By morning the damage would be done and they'd have to amputate to save his life. He laughed grimly at the thought. Who the hell was going to worry about that?

CHAPTER TWENTY-FIVE

Raider's eyes flicked nervously over the landscape. The narrow trail snaked up the steep curve of the ridge through scattered pines. There was little cover this high, and he imagined every outlaw within a hundred miles was watching him over the sight of a Winchester. Arthur had to have people out, had to know they were there. He felt like an idiot carrying the Sharps rifle with a goddamn hanky waving off the barrel. All it did was make a real fine target.

Still, Lew Hackman had bought the idea, and it had kept Raider alive. That's all it was for, and if Lew didn't know that, he was a fool. Raider had no intention of

walking into some robber's roost and bargaining with
the colonel or Lewiston. They'd laugh in his face, shoot
him on the spot, and worry later about his so-called
posse.

"I can smell 'em," Lew said behind him. "Those assholes are up there."

"I know they are," said Raider. "Lew, I'd feel a lot
better if you'd let me have my damn bullets back. You
might be wantin' some help if those fellers start shooting."

Lew chuckled to himself. "Figure I'll have a minute if
they do. Bound to shoot you first."

"Thanks," Raider said dully. "That's a comfort. You
was in the war, I guess. Looks like you might be old
enough."

"Took a ball in the foot at Gettysburg," said Lew.
"That was the end of it for me."

"You with Hancock or Pickett?"

"Pickett, of course!" snapped Lew. "I'm an outlaw,
friend, not a fuckin' Yankee!"

"Well, guess you can't be all bad," grinned Raider.

Lew Hackman was friendly enough, and willing to talk.
He told Raider about leaving a farm in Virginia and join-
ing the Army, coming back to find nothing left, getting
married, and losing his wife to smallpox. Raider almost
liked the man. He came from a farm himself and knew
what hardship was. He also knew fate could easily have
set him in the same boots as Hackman—the wrong side
of the law instead of the right. He knew plenty of men
who'd worn a badge and lost it, and others who'd given
up the gunslinger trade and earned their stars. It was a
thin line, and a hard one to walk.

Raider kept his eyes open, waiting for Lew to relax
a little and move up close. Hackman knew better than
that, knew what Raider was up to. He kept up a lively
line of chatter, but didn't give Raider the slightest chance
to jump him.

Not for the first time, Raider wondered what the hell
he'd do when they got wherever they were going. The

outlaws would either kill them real soon or step out and march them to the hideout. Raider wasn't sure which he feared most. Whatever happened, time was running out fast. He wondered what had become of Khalifi. And when a real posse would come thundering in to the rescue. Right about now would be a damn good time, he decided. It'd also be a good idea if whiskey was free and whores were two for a quarter. Only neither was likely to happen.

•   •   •

Doc heard the sound and opened one eye. It's Annette, he thought hopefully. She's got more guts than I gave her credit for and she's rounded up a knife. Suddenly, the torch flared in his face and he shrank back from the light. Corporal Delaney peered down at him and grinned through crooked teeth. "Well now, how you doing, ol' buddy?"

"How the hell you think?" grunted Doc. The smell of raw whiskey was strong on the man's breath. His eyes flashed in the fire, wild as a wolf on the prowl. He squatted down on his haunches, flicked a knife out of his belt, and brought the point up sharp under Weatherbee's nose. Doc flinched and Delaney laughed.

"Scared of me, ain't you?"

"Delaney, do whatever you came to do. I can't do much to stop you."

"Damned if you ain't right. Turn over, fucker."

"I *can't* turn over and you know it! I haven't got any damn feeling anymore."

Delaney shoved him roughly on his belly. "Shit, I'm sure sorry to hear that."

"Going to do it now, huh?"

"Hell, no," Delaney said gently. "You got me all wrong, friend."

"Uhuh. Sure I do."

Delaney leaned over Doc's hands, then moved to his feet. "There. You're free. That feel some better?"

For a moment, Doc felt nothing at all. He hadn't even realized the corporal had slashed his bonds. Then, suddenly, blood surged back to his hands and feet bringing sharp, agonizing stabs of pain. Doc bit his lip to keep from yelling.

Delaney threw back his head and cackled. "On your feet, mister. I got a score to settle with you, and we'll do it fair and square."

Doc stared through his pain. "Huh? What the hell you talking about?"

"Get up!" raged Delaney. "Come on, fight, you bastard. Your hands are free and I ain't got a weapon!" Delaney stepped up and kicked him hard in the chest. Doc groaned and rolled away. The movement sent new waves of pain through his limbs. Delaney danced around him, booted him in the kidneys, then slammed his foot down hard on Doc's legs. Doc let out a ragged scream. Delaney laughed and came at him again. Doc doubled up to cover himself and fought to get to his feet. His hands touched the floor and folded. Legs dragged uselessly behind him. Delaney knew he couldn't move and relished it.

Doc absorbed the blows as best he could. One part of his mind concentrated dully on his legs. Ignoring the pain, he pounded his feet viciously against stone, fighting to bring the life back.

Delaney worked on his head, kicked hard enough to hurt, easy enough to keep Doc conscious. Doc dragged up his arms to save his face. Delaney stepped on his fingers and ground them into the floor. The terrible, sudden hurt gave Weatherbee's body a strength he couldn't muster on his own. His back went stiff, arched into a bow. His legs snapped out against the agonizing assault on his senses and caught Delaney solidly in the groin. Delaney's face went white. His eyes bulged and his supper spewed out of his mouth. With a gasp, he sank to the floor of the cave and grabbed his vitals, jerking like a bug on its back.

Doc crawled toward him, pushed himself to his feet. He balanced a moment, took two awkward steps, sagged and fell on his face. Gritting his teeth he tried again. It was now or never and he knew it. If he couldn't take

Delaney out for good, the man would kill him or cripple him for life. Leave him broken, with a head full of jelly.

Doc's hands touched something hard, grasped it with bloody fingers. Delaney's knife! Doc fumbled for the hilt, tried to curl his fingers around it. Delaney stirred, shook his head, and wiped spittle from his mouth. Doc dragged himself to his knees. Delaney saw the knife and hurled himself at Doc with a curse. Doc stabbed out clumsily. Delaney hit him hard and the blade clattered away.

He could see Delaney's face, smell vomit and whiskey on his breath. Vaguely, he knew the corporal was straddling his chest. He could see the blows coming, slowly and deliberately. *Funny*, Doc thought hazily. *Can't be hitting me hard. Ought to hurt . . . Ought to hurt real bad . . .*

Doc didn't see or hear the two outlaws who pulled Delaney off, still screaming and flailing his fists. For a long time, he didn't even know Delaney was gone.

Weatherbee had no idea how long he'd been out. Delaney had come in the middle of the night, but that didn't tell him a thing. There was no daylight in the cavern, no way to judge the passage of time. Doc figured he'd lost a full day and maybe then some.

Everything hurt that could hurt. He didn't want to know what Delaney had done to him. Maybe his nose was gone, and his ears too. That was Delaney's style. A thought suddenly occurred to him and he almost laughed. If there was anything left of him, Delaney had saved his life. A whole night with the rawhide cords around his limbs would have left him a cripple sure. Maybe the corporal had taken care of that anyway. Maybe . . .

Something touched his shoulder and Doc flinched. The movement ripped his broken lips and he choked on blood.

"Jesus!" said a voice. "Delaney sure tore him up!"

"Delaney's a fuckin' animal," said the other. "Give him a little water 'fore we take him in there."

"Shit! *You* give him water, not me. They don't want this dude to have nothing."

"Don't matter, I guess. Poor fucker ain't going to last long."

Hands grabbed his legs and shoulders and lifted him off the floor. Doc felt only the start of it, then dropped off into darkness.

He smelled food.

The delicious, heady aroma of ham steak and red-eye gravy assailed his senses, started his juices flowing in his mouth, and knotted up his stomach.

Doc opened his eyes, tried to focus on the scene before him. Light and color swam together in nauseous, impossible patterns. Doc felt his stomach turn and closed his eyes. In a moment, he tried again. There was a table. A table with white linen. Good china and sparkling crystal. The plate before him was heaped with food. Clear, cold water danced in the crystal glass. Doc stared at it longingly, his parched throat begging for moisture.

"Ah, good—our guest's awake at last!"

Doc blinked and looked up. Colonel Arthur grinned at him across the table. He wore a fine, burgundy velvet jacket over a white ruffled shirt. His mustache was freshly trimmed and there was a good cigar between his fingers.

"Welcome back, Weatherbee. Thought you'd never come down to dinner. Don't mind if we went ahead, do you?"

It was hard to concentrate on the man's words. His head wasn't working right, or his eyes, either. It suddenly dawned on him that the twins were seated next to the colonel, one on either side. Doc blinked, brought them into focus. Even in his present condition, Louisa and Annette took his breath away. Their sensual beauty was startling. Blond hair poured like cream over bare shoulders; soft light brushed their naked breasts and sparked the golden pendants about their throats. Doc recognized the jewelry right off—two fine pieces from the Egyptian collection.

The girls looked back at Weatherbee, eyes wide with fear. Annette bit her lip and turned away. If his face looked anything like it felt, Doc figured he was a pretty scary sight.

Arthur caught the exchange between Doc and the girls

and grinned in amusement. "Really," he chided. "We *do* dress for dinner, Weatherbee. I'm afraid you're not properly attired." He turned to Louisa. "What do you think, dear?"

Louisa's mouth trembled. Arthur reached up, caressed her breast, then pinched the pink nipple hard between his fingers. Louisa's face twisted in pain. A tiny cry escaped her lips and the muscles in her throat went taut.

"Goddamn it," croaked Doc. "Leave 'em alone, you bastard!"

Arthur turned, the smile still pasted on his face. "Eat your dinner and shut up, Weatherbee."

"Sorry, I'm not hungry," Doc lied.

"Of course you are." Arthur pulled a pistol out of his jacket and aimed it across the table between Doc's eyes. "*Eat*, friend."

Doc caught the warning in his tone, saw his finger whiten on the trigger. Food and water would keep him alive, and he was past the point of pride. Just one drink of that water—

Arthur caught the surprise on Weatherbee's face and burst into laughter. Doc cursed him and strained against his bonds. His body was so dulled to feeling it hadn't dawned on him that he was strapped to the chair.

"Well, then," said Arthur. "Perhaps you're not as hungry as I thought."

Doc glared. "It's a long way from West Point to the sewer, Colonel. But you got there, didn't you?"

Arthur's face went slack. Doc knew his words had hit home, and didn't much care what it cost him. The colonel leaned toward him and forced a smile. "I wish we had time to *discuss* that, Weatherbee. Perhaps another day. I'd enjoy it immensely." Arthur looked up suddenly and Doc followed his gaze across the room. Henry Lewiston stood in the doorway, Neferti Raman at his side. Lewiston wore an ill-fitting blue suit, and all the wrong colors to go with it. His awkward frame made the clothes bulge in peculiar places; Doc thought he looked like a scarecrow fresh in from the field.

Weatherbee's glance slid quickly past Lewiston and

locked on Neferti. She was dressed in elegant green satin that lifted the swell of her breasts. Black hair framed her face and a velvet choker circled her throat. She was beautiful, an elegant lady dressed for a fancy ball, and the sight of her made Doc's hair stand on end. Neferti's beauty was dull, hollow. Her face was slack and her eyes stared vacantly into the room. *Christ, there's no life in her at all,* thought Doc. *She doesn't even know she's here!*

"What have you done to her?" Doc asked flatly as Lewiston and Neferti came in and sat at the table. "What's wrong with her, Lewiston?"

"Hummm?" Lewiston glanced up as if the question puzzled him. "Oh, the lady? Why, she *is* a little quiet tonight, isn't she?"

"Don't give me that shit. She's drugged. You've got her on something—what is it!"

Lewiston went stiff. "I don't *like* the way you're talking to me, Weatherbee," he said calmly. "You must n-never do that. You understand? I do not *like* t-to be yelled at."

"Weatherbee, shut *up*," Arthur said softly.

"What? What?" Lewiston turned on Arthur, eyes dancing. "D-did you say something, Arthur?"

"Not a *thing*, Henry."

Doc saw it then, the too-bright flecks of color in his eyes, the slight touch of moisture at the corner of his mouth. Too late, he knew he'd made a terrible mistake. Annette was right. Henry Lewiston was a man on the edge of madness, and Doc had inadvertently pushed him over.

Lewiston slowly pushed his chair back and walked around the table until he stood behind Doc. Doc felt bony fingers on his shoulders and swallowed hard.

"It's always been men like you," Lewiston told him. "I kn-know your kind, Weatherbee. You like to tell people what to do and I don't like to be t-t-told things. You understand that? Do you?" Lewiston's voice climbed the scale. He was a pouting child, now, frightened of the world and fighting back. "Everything goes r-real fine, and

then someone like you has to t-t-tell me to *do* something!"
Lewiston pounded Doc's shoulders. "I don't *like* it!"

"Ah, Henry," said Arthur.

Lewiston didn't hear him. Suddenly, his fists closed
on the back of Doc's chair and sent it sprawling. Doc
landed flat on his back, \bound feet in the air, arms
crushed beneath the chair. Lewiston's hands snaked to his
waist, stripped the wide leather belt from his trousers,
and stretched it over his head. The strap came down and
Doc screamed. Lewiston flailed him mercilessly, gasping
for air. The big silver buckle slashed Weatherbee's chest,
ripping and tearing his flesh. Doc squeezed his eyes against
pain and yelled at the top of his lungs. Lewiston's spindly
arms flew until he sobbed with exhaustion. Dropping the
belt to the floor, he stumbled to the table, grabbed Neferti
roughly, and pulled her out of the room.

"Jesus *Christ!*" Doc opened his eyes and sucked in
air.

"Told you to shut up," Arthur said drily.

"You—got yourself a real bedbug there, Colonel. *Goddamn!*"

"Henry has a slight—emotional problem," Arthur said
pleasantly. "Comes and goes."

"Oh, yeah? Is that what it is?"

"Baby," crooned Annette, rubbing her nipples against
Arthur's arm. "Can I, *please?*" She whispered in Arthur's
ear and the colonel grinned. "My God, you are a dyed-
in-the-wool freak, you know that, lady?"

"Uhuh. Just *hate* it, don't you?"

"Hell, get to it. I might like this."

Annette stood, stalked around the table, and stood
over Doc, long legs spread, hands on her hips. Biting her
tiny red lips, she winked at Doc and ran a finger through
the feathery mound between her legs. The finger moved in
sharp, rapid thrusts in and out of the wet pussy. Annette's
breath quickened. The hard little breasts rose and fell,
nipples standing dark and rigid. Annette cried out, threw
back her head, and bent to straddle Doc. Holding his
head in her hands, she thrust her cunt in his face, ground
it against his mouth. Doc cursed her and tried to jerk

away. Annette held him firmly between her thighs. Doc would have relished the experience some other time, but it was pure agony at the moment. Every thrust of the little whore's pussy sent new waves of pain through his head. Finally, Annette came again, trembled against him, and bounced off her perch.

"Mmmmmm, thanks honey," she grinned, then pranced back to the table, her ass swinging suggestively.

"Fuck you," choked Doc.

The guards threw him roughly into the cave, not even bothering to tie him. He didn't look like a man going anywhere soon.

Doc lay flat on the stone floor, gasping for breath. He didn't dare move. Breathing was bad enough. For the first time, he faced the grim truth and didn't back away from it. He was going to die right here. He'd never leave the cavern alive—they'd either starve him or beat him to death or both. At the moment, Doc didn't care which. If he could just have one drink of water—just one, he'd curl up and die peacefully.

A rock cut into his thigh and Doc shifted painfully to get it out. It wouldn't budge, and he stretched his hand under his belly to move it. His hands clutched the stone and he frowned curiously. Whatever it was, it sure as hell wasn't a rock. It wasn't under him, either, but in his pocket. Gritting his teeth, Doc reached down and brought the thing up to his face.

He didn't need the light from the tunnel. His touch told him all he needed to know. It was a small, one-shot .41 pistol, the first design of that model Mr. Colt had ever made. There was no question how Annette had carried it stark naked from the table. Doc grinned in spite of the pain. The girl sure had the cutest little holster in the world.

CHAPTER TWENTY-SIX

Raider and Lew Hackman inched their horses up the narrow run onto the ridge. A lone, ancient pine stood there, gnarled and twisted by the years. Past the tree, two wind-swept boulders came together to form a natural arch. When Raider and Lew passed through, the three gunmen were standing there waiting for them.

Raider reined in hard and heard Lew spit a curse.

"That's far enough, gents." The first man stepped up and leveled his Colt at Raider. His two companions stood off the trail. One had a Winchester, the other a shotgun. "You boys got to be crazy comin' up here, but that ain't no skin off my butt. Lay your guns down easy and step off them horses."

Raider didn't move. "We came to see Arthur and Lewiston," he said firmly. "We got business with 'em."

The outlaw looked surprised at Raider's name-dropping. For a brief second, he took his eyes off Raider and glanced over his shoulder. "Jess, ride on back to the—"

Suddenly, Lew opened up behind Raider. The Smith & Wesson barked three times. A shotgun roared and the man to Raider's right cried out. The second outlaw froze, leaped for better ground. Raider swung the heavy Sharps rifle from his shoulder and caught the nearest gunman solidly on the head, slid off his saddle, and scurried for cover. Lead stitched a path behind him. Lew Hackman was dragging himself painfully over gravel and Raider wrenched him roughly behind a rock. Hackman gave him a tight, ashen-faced grin. Raider scowled, clawed the man's pockets, and found his own .44s. "Dumb son of a bitch," he muttered, hastily loading the Remington. "What'd you open up for?"

"One of them bastards recognized me right off," said Lew. "Didn't have no choice. Used to ride with him in Kansas. How many of 'em left?"

"Two. I stopped the feller with the Colt but he's found

good cover." A bullet chipped stone by Raider's head. He answered it quickly, ducked down again. "You hit bad?"

"Naw, a bunch of shot in the leg is all, but I ain't walkin' nowhere."

"Great," Raider said testily. "Isn't neither of us riding, either. They scattered our horses good." Raider peered over the rock, glanced back at Lew. "Stay low and keep your eyes open. I'll do a little scoutin'."

Raider edged quickly back through the narrow archway and circled up the side of the hill. There were two of them, and one would keep Lew down while the other tried to work his way behind. The quickest path was up the draw, straight to the archway. One good shot from there would finish Hackman.

Raider waited. In a moment he heard the gunman. If he could take him without a hassle . . . The outlaw's boots appeared, then the rim of his hat. Raider pushed himself off the wall and hit the man hard with his right. The man jerked back, enough to soften the blow. His Colt jerked, came up for Raider's belly. Raider drove his left like a club and chopped the man's wrist, buried his right in soft gut. Air exploded in Raider's face and the man went down. Raider picked up the Colt, jammed it into his belt.

"Hold it, mister!"

Raider froze, knew he'd misjudged the pair badly. They'd both come up to flank him and caught him flat. Shit!

"Get up, Harry. Grab your fuckin' gun back." The outlaw stumbled to his feet holding his wrist, pulled the Colt off Raider, and backed away.

"Hang on to this one," he snapped. "I'll finish off the other dude."

"That one's mine," snarled Harry. "The son of a bitch shot Duke right through the head!"

"Hell, do it. I'll—"

The mountain of flesh dropped down behind them, silent as the wind. Two great paws clutched the outlaws' heads, cracked them together like eggs. Before they hit the ground, Khalifi snatched their collars and tossed them easily off the cliff.

Raider stared. The whole thing had happened before he could blink. "Holy shit—where'd *you* come from? Not that I'm complaining."

The giant had already forgotten the killings. Hunching down to Raider's level, he jabbed a big finger to the north. "Neferti! Neferti!"

Raider frowned thoughtfully. The damn fool was always saying "Neferti," but he wasn't asking now, he was telling, and Raider figured he meant business. "Look—you sayin' you know where she is? Is that it? Neferti—that way?"

"Huh! Huh! *Neferti!*" The tiny eyes blazed and Raider no longer doubted him. The giant didn't have sense enough to bluff—he meant exactly what he said.

Raider beat the bushes and rounded up a mount, then led it back to where Lew was. The outlaw saw Khalifi and his eyes went wide. "Jesus—where'd you find that!"

"It's a long story," said Raider. "Look. You and me got some fast talking to do. You're riding one side of the trail and I'm riding the other. Don't guess there's anything we can do 'bout that. I'm going in there and try to get those women out, and do whatever else I can manage. You want to ride down and get your boys, fine. I can sure use the help."

"That ain't the end of it," Lew said quietly.

"No, it isn't. You're looking for hides and I don't much blame you. Reckon I would too." Raider looked the outlaw squarely in the eye. "If I can, I'll try to take Arthur in, and Lewiston too if he shows up. And whatever loot's down there goes back where it belongs. I don't figure you'll see it that way."

Lew grinned. "Shit, not hardly. "You want to shove my ass on this horse, Pink? We'll be seein' each other again."

Raider squatted down beside the giant and squinted over the ridge toward the cliff. There was nothing to see there but red granite and a few scraggly pines—hadn't been, for the last half hour. Maybe Khalifi had imagined the whole thing, he decided. Figured he *ought* to find Neferti, and worked it out that way in his head. Still, the fellow had acted real sure of himself. . . .

"Uh! *Rasha!*" Khalifi punched him hard in the ribs and Raider sat up straight, brought his eyes back to the cliff. A head suddenly appeared there, growing right out of solid rock. Sunlight glinted on the barrel of a rifle. The head looked around, disappeared again. Raider grinned to himself. You could watch the place all day and not figure it, but once you saw where it was there was nothing to it.

Now for the hard part, he told himself—making sure Khalifi didn't fuck the whole thing up. "Look," he said slowly. "Sun up *there,* okay? Sun gets over *there,* you come runnin' like shit on a hill. Crack lots of heads, tear off their asses, all that stuff you do real good. Okay?"

"Huh?" Khalifi looked blank.

"Neferti," Raider said patiently, adding the magic word. "Tear up lots of heads for *Neferti* . . . when the sun is over *there.*"

Khalifi marveled at Raider's gestures. Finally, a small candle glittered somewhere in his skull. The man was going to help him crack heads. Khalifi understood that. And Neferti would be there to watch. All this would happen when the sun moved. He nodded eagerly at Raider. Raider let out a breath and started down the side of the hill.

Colonel Arthur stared at him, turned angrily on Lewiston. "Henry, you said this son of a bitch was *dead.* You *saw* those fuckers kill him!"

"I th-thought I did," stammered Lewiston.

"Well, you were wrong," snapped Arthur, "and I don't like this one goddamn bit. Harry"—Arthur nodded curtly at the man holding a gun to Raider's back—"you sure there was another one?"

"Mac heard gunfire and run up there an' found three of our boys. He took a shot at the guy but he was too far off."

"And he had a badge," Arthur said thoughtfully.

"Couldn't have been anything else?" The colonel made a face and scowled at Raider. "You either got guts or shit for brains walking in here, mister. What do you imagine I'm going to *do* to you?"

Raider shrugged easily. "Shoot me maybe, I don't know. That's kind of up to you. There's lawmen out there and a whole troop of your own cavalry. Those bluebellies aren't realy happy with you, Arthur."

"Fuck 'em!"

"All I'm doin' is bringing in the offer. The White House itself will back me up. You let the three women walk out of here with me and leave the Egyptian stuff behind. Take all the cash you want—that's yours. It's an automatic amnesty if you do."

Arthur laughed harshly. "Damn, you expect us to believe that?"

"He m-m-might be telling the truth," said Lewiston, concern creasing his features.

"I am, and you both know it. You been in on this from the start an' you know how itchy those boys in Washington are. You got the whole fuckin' United States over a barrel. They ain't real excited 'bout shipping those girls home in a box and losing the treasure in the bargain."

"I l-like the sound of that," Lewiston grinned foolishly. "The whole United St-st—"

Arthur shot him a look. "Henry, there isn't anyone out there except that bunch of boys *you* stirred up in the desert. This bastard's bluffing." Arthur turned quickly to one of his men. "Get some of the boys out there and look things over. I don't believe this dude, but it's easy enough to check."

"What should I do with him?" asked Harry.

"Kill him," Arthur said flatly. "The sooner the better."

"We might need him, you know," said Lewiston.

"What for? We already *got* a Pinkerton. Shit, save him if you like, Henry. I'm going outside."

When Arthur was gone, Lewiston turned to Raider. "I can do it to her anytime, you know."

"Huh?" Raider stared. "Do what? What the hell you talkin' about?"

"I can," Lewiston grinned. "I could stick my *thing* in her, and do anything else I w-wanted to. And nobody could stop me, either." He gave Raider a broad wink and stalked off in a lopsided gait.

"Holy shit!" Raider's skin crawled and hair climbed the back of his neck. The outlaw jabbed a Colt in his kidney and walked him out of the room.

Raider kept his eyes open, mapping the cave as he went. Somehow, he'd managed to keep a straight face at the news about Doc, but his stomach was heavy as lead. What the hell was his partner doing *here*? It didn't make a damn bit of sense! If Doc was really a prisoner, Raider had several hard facts to face. The lawmen didn't know where they were. There wouldn't *be* any posse thundering in to the rescue. All he had now was Lew Hackman and Khalifi. Raider didn't figure either would make much of a dent in Arthur's fortress.

"In there," said the guard, shoving Raider roughly into the small cave. "You can talk to your goddamn pal 'fore we—" The guard stopped short and gaped past Raider. "Luke, Hailey—get your asses down here," he yelled. "The son of a bitch is gone!"

* * *

Doc lay perfectly still, his eyes shut.

The guard sat in a chair under the torch, just outside the cave. For a while he peered in every few minutes, once even walking over quietly to stare down at his prisoner. Finally, he tired of that and quit coming in altogether. His captive was too far gone to worry about.

Doc waited.

The chair scraped stone. The guard glanced in, then bootsteps echoed down the tunnel toward the kitchen. Weatherbee gritted his teeth. Every ache and bruise screamed out in protest. He pulled himself up, grabbed the wall, and hung on, trembling all over as nausea shook his body. He had maybe five, six minutes at the most. No time to do anything. No way to find Neferti or the twins and get them out. Still, Annette had bought him a chance and he couldn't just lie there. Had to do—something.

Doc shook his head and tried to think. Stumbling down the tunnel in darkness, he dragged himself twenty yards and fell into the horse corral. Resting a moment, he moved sluggishly around the cave until his hand found the wooden troughs on the far wall. It took every ounce of control to keep from swallowing the stale water in great gulps. He cupped his hands and sipped slowly, a drop at a time. Finally, he plunged his head in and let the cool liquid soothe his face. A few yards down was a bin of oats and he stuffed half a handful into his mouth. It hurt like hell to chew, but Doc kept going, closing his eyes and relishing the taste. He'd never had anything better in his life.

After another swallow of water, Doc made his way around the horse cave, ignoring the tunnel to the outhouse and choosing the next. Two outlaws walked by and he went flat against the wall.

The first cave was empty. The second was filled with boxes. Doc blinked at the markings and saw they were the treasure crates from the exhibit.

The third cave was well lit by candles in silver holders. Rich tapestries covered the walls. There were tables, heavy chairs, and big bureaus. Doc looked to his right—and froze. Neferti Raman was spread naked on the oversized bed, arms and legs tied securely at the four corners.

Doc stumbled to her, ignoring his pain. "Neferti— Jesus, are you all right?"

Neferti squinted, screwed up her face. "Doc? 'ssat you? Can't—think real good."

"It's okay. He's got you on some kind of drug. Listen, what has he done to you, Neferti? I'll try to get you out. I can't—"

"No. S'all right," she said hazily. "He hasn't even . . . don' unnerstan' . . . Doc, he's not—"

"Don't talk. Look, I've got to leave you for a while. Find a rifle, something bigger than this damn thing."

"Have to . . . listen, Doc." Neferti bit her lip. Furrows

creased her brow and she struggled to gather her thoughts. "You have to—go, Doc. Right now. Whole place is . . . full of dynamite. Explo— Explosives . . ."

"Huh?" Doc leaned closer. "You mean *here*, in the cavern?"

"It's . . . whole thing'll just—" Neferti's voice faded and her mouth went slack. Doc stood. He wanted to cover her, but Lewiston would know he'd been there. Instead, he moved hurriedly out of the room and down the tunnel. He was getting dizzy fast, stumbling over his legs. They'd be after him soon. Shit, the guard was likely back already. Go through the corral, he thought dully. Crawl out the damn outhouse door and get help. Find Raider, maybe. Trying to pull something off by himself in the cavern was just plain crazy.

The man turned the corner, held up his torch, and froze. Doc jerked the little .41 Colt out of his belt, aimed it at the man's head, and pulled the trigger. The ancient gun shattered. Parts blew up and sparked the wall. Doc looked dumbly at his aching hand. Corporal Delaney grinned at him, laughed out loud, and doubled both his fists. . . .

"Doc! Damn it, Doc, you gotta wake up!"

Raider's face swam into focus. Weatherbee knew he must be dreaming. His partner wasn't here, he was dead. Dead somewhere in the desert. Arthur had said so.

"Doc, come out of it!"

Doc blinked, opened his eyes. "Rade? Uh—what the hell's happening? Is it over?" The room was nearly dark and he could barely see his partner's face.

Raider breathed a sigh of relief. "Doc, when that bastard brought you down here I thought you was dead."

"Not—real sure I'm not." He tried to move, sank back.

"Don't bother," Raider told him. "You're tied up like a fuckin' goose. So am I. Doc—we got to get out of here fast."

Doc laughed weakly. "Friend, I'm the escape king of

the Idaho caverns. Not real good at it, though. Usually get about thirty or forty yards."

"Shut up and listen a minute." Raider told him quickly about Hackman's big brother and the outlaws. "He's about the only chance we got. And even if he shows I ain't sure he'll do much good. Hell, I knew better'n to barge in here with a bluff. Seemed like a good idea at the time."

"No U.S. Cavalry, huh? Bugles, Gatling guns . . ."

Raider made a face in the dark. "Not any I know of. I thought *you* was bringin' 'em." Raider stopped. "Doc—you awake?"

"Uh, yeah. Think so. I feel like shit, Rade."

"You look like shit. Listen. You been here 'bout an hour. I don't think Lew's opened up on this place yet, but *something's* going on. There's outlaws running around like ants, carrying stuff out past where the horses are. Maybe I did some good and Arthur bought my story."

Doc shook his head. Something had suddenly occurred to him. "Rade, I forgot. I—found Neferti. She's all drugged up but she said something. Dynamite—she said the whole place is full of dynamite! Hell, they probably got the cavern wired to go up when they leave. Use batteries to set it off. That's what all the running around is about—they believed you, or figure Hackman's a real posse. We got to find that dynamite, Rade. I don't know how, but—"

"Doc," Raider said slowly. "Where do you think you are?"

"Huh? What do you mean? I'm right here, tied up like you. Damn, don't you understand? If that dynamite goes off, you and me and the girls have flat had it!"

"I already know where it is," said Raider. "You been out and aren't where you think you are. We're sittin' on it, Doc. About five or six hundred pounds of the stuff."

Khalifi tried hard to remember.

Thinking made his head hurt but he did the best he could. The man in the back hat said there'd be something up in the sky. He pointed right where it would be, too.

Khalifi watched patiently, but there was nothing to see except the sun. Still, he was sure the man was right. He'd wait, do what he said to do. When whatever was supposed to happen happened, he'd see Neferti again and make lots of men lie still. The man had said so and Khalifi believed him. If he didn't, he wouldn't sit there on the rock. He'd go in the little hole in the cliff and find someone he could squeeze real hard.

CHAPTER TWENTY-SEVEN

"Doc, listen—somebody's shootin' up there. Maybe ol' Lew's broke in. Doc, for Christ's sake!"

"Oh, yeah, Rade."

"Partner, you got to stay awake," Raider pleaded. "I know you been through plenty, but just hang on and we'll make it out of here."

Doc gave him a bleary look. "Just how we going to do that?"

"Shit, I don't know. But I'm not going to lie here and get blowed up if I can help it. I got a little of this rawhide working—not real good, though."

"Stuff's got to be battery-powered," Doc muttered absently. "Set it off with wires instead of a fuse . . . let 'em get off safe before they do it."

"What? Doc, I can't understand what you're saying."

"I'm saying we look for wires somewhere if we get a chance to. They'll have 'em laid around the explosives leading out."

"It's pitch dark down here. Even if I can pull loose of this stuff, how'm I goin' to do that?"

Doc didn't answer. From the sound of his breathing, Raider knew he'd gone under again. Lousy bastards— they'd come damn close to killing him. It was a wonder Doc was still in one piece. When the little pinch-faced corporal had brought him back and dumped him in the hole, Raider had been shaken at the sight of his friend.

Those bruised and battered features didn't look like Doc. It was someone else—someone he didn't even know.

Gunfire brought Raider up short. It was closer this time—inside the caverns, not too far down the tunnel. The rapid bark of pistols echoed through the cave, followed quickly by the cough of a shotgun. An outlaw shouted a curse. Another answered, and Raider heard the high shriek of a frightened horse.

Raider strained against his bonds, craned his neck to see into the tunnel. It was no use and he gave up trying —they were too far back in the cave. He concentrated on the rawhide, gritting his teeth against the pain in his wrists. Doc stirred and cried out. Raider tried to answer, but his partner only mumbled and went under again. Shit —if he *did* get loose, what was he going to do about Doc? He'd have to carry him out of the place and keep the Remington handy at the same time.

Suddenly, light flooded the cave and Raider blinked against the brightness. Henry Lewiston stood over him, pale eyes flashing, a crooked smile straining his features.

"You comfortable, Mr. Raider? N-need anything?"

"Listen, you crazy son of a bitch! Doc needs help. You can't just—" It was the wrong thing to say and Raider knew it. A little cry stuck in Lewiston's throat and he kicked Raider hard in the belly. Raider moaned and threw up on his shirt.

Lewiston cackled and kicked him again. "I don't l-l-like you," he said soberly. "I don't like you, m-mister!"

"Damn," croaked Raider. "I never would've guessed. You—" Raider strained against his bonds. "Hey, what are you doin' to him? Lewiston, leave him alone. He's flat had enough!"

Two gunmen crowded in behind Lewiston and bent over Doc. Lewiston held the torch in the hall while they turned Doc roughly on his stomach and slashed his bonds. Doc moaned. The pair dragged him past Raider out of the cave.

"Where you taking him?" yelled Raider. "He's hurt. Listen, you assholes—you want to hit someone, try a feller who can fight back!"

Lewiston didn't even look at him. The torch disappeared and Raider was alone again in the dark. Tears had never come easy, but his eyes clouded now. He knew for certain he'd never see his partner again.

* * *

Doc floated slowly up to consciousness and tried to make sense of what he saw. Torchlight flickered on stone overhead. Water clung to the surface in bright sweaty beads and splashed coldly on his face. Someone was dragging him along the tunnel. He could see his feet making furrows in the dirt, feel rough hands gripping his arms. Where were they taking him? he wondered dully. What had happened to Raider? Where had he gone?

Suddenly, the hands let go. Doc fell flat on his back. The shock brought him fully awake and sent fresh waves of pain knifing through his body. Something heavy dropped on his chest and Doc cried out. Opening his eyes, he saw the slim column of a neck stretched over his shoulder. A dark strand of hair curled down the neck. He traced it with his eyes to the full, swelling mound of flesh.

Doc squeezed his eyes, opened them again. His brain was going fuzzy for sure. It was still there, a beautiful little tit not an inch from his nose. It curved up gracefully, ending in a pink and rigid nipple. Doc gazed at it sleepily, trying to figure what the hell it was doing there.

"The horses are right outside," said a voice. "Let's get the hell out of here." The voice was somewhere above and behind him. Doc tried to find it. The burden on his chest kept him flat.

"All right. G-get 'em draped over those m-mounts. We can't w-wait around here."

Lewiston. Doc recognized the voice. Someone reached down and took the tit out of his face. Hands grabbed him again and dragged him over the floor. Darkness suddenly blazed into light and Doc squinted up at an open blue sky. Someone lifted him roughly, dropped his belly over a saddle. Pain hit him hard and nearly pushed him under.

"Luke, t-t-tighten that load on the packhorse. The strap's about to come off, damn it!"

"Mr. Lewiston, it don't *need* tightening. It's loaded up full and the strap won't take no more."

"Maybe we could leave some stuff here," the other voice suggested. "Shit, we got plenty. There's enough there to—"

"No!" shrieked Lewiston. "It goes w-with us, you understand? All of it!"

The man muttered to himself and Doc heard him shuffle away and do something to the horse. In a minute, Lewiston said, "Let's check inside. See if we c-covered the tracks good."

"I checked 'em. We're okay."

"Fine, L-Luke. Just check *again*, okay?"

Bootsteps receded. Doc heard a startled cry. "You son of a—" Two muffled shots reached his ears. Doc turned his head as far as he could around the rear of the horse. In a moment, Henry Lewiston appeared out of the dark cleft of stone. Neither of the outlaws followed.

•   •   •

Light blinded Raider again.

The dull muzzle of a .45 loomed up in his face, fell quickly away. Lew Hackman laughed. "You sure are a hatful of trouble, friend." He turned Raider over and slashed his bonds, bending close to the stacked boxes.

"Shit, Lew—get that torch out of here!"

Lew glanced up, threw the torch as far as he could into the hall. "Goddamn—there's enough stuff here to blow every bank west of St. Louis!"

"Yeah, well you ain't in no bank right now," snorted Raider. Standing, he rubbed feeling into his wrists, then squatted to feel along the walls. "Hold the light up but stay outside with it. I got to find something."

"I don't know what the hell you're looking for, but we ain't got time for it."

"I'm takin' time," Raider said flatly. "If I can't find the wires to this stuff, the whole fuckin' mountain's going to go and us with it."

Lew's face went slack. "That pile's *wired?* Jesus—what are we standing round here for?"

Raider ignored him. Scraping his hand around the edge of the explosives, he searched the rock wall and floor for a trace of the wires. In a few moments he knew the task was hopeless. Whoever had set the thing up hadn't meant to make it easy—the wires were clearly *beneath* the pile. Had to be. And there was no way to get to them without carefully moving every crate and powder keg aside. Raider figured that little job would take close to half an hour, even if he didn't blow himself up in the process.

"Shit!" Raider looked up at Lew. "There's no way. You better get your boys out of here fast. This place is goin' to get redecorated real quick."

"Where the hell you going?"

"There's folks still down here I got to get out. Got an extra pistol?"

"Use your own. Someone tossed your .44 and that cannon in the corner." Lew stuck the torch in quickly. Raider grabbed up his gunbelt and the Sharps rifle.

"I wouldn't hang around here long if I was you," said Hackman.

"Don't figure on it. Just got a couple of debts to settle."

"So do I," snorted Hackman. "See you in hell, Pink."

Raider had no idea where to look. All he'd seen of the place was the cave where the outlaws had tossed him and the little room with the dynamite. If he meant to find Doc and the girls there wasn't time for a guided tour. Deciding on the left instead of the right, he sprinted down the tunnel. Gunfire sounded a few yards off and he slowed his pace. Turning a corner, he stumbled over a dead outlaw. An empty sack from the First National in Denver was clutched in his hand. A few gold coins were stuck in the folds.

Bootsteps sent Raider against the wall. A man ran past him, fired his Colt into darkness and tumbled to the ground. Raider recognized him as one of Lew's men. The gunfighter saw him, grinned up painfully. "Shit. If it ain't our pet Pinkerton."

"You all right?"

"Hell, no."

Lead shattered stone over Raider's head. He ducked, peered past the corner, and jerked off a shot. The two men turned in mid-stride and crabbed for cover. Raider glanced back at the fallen outlaw. The man returned his stare and Raider knew he was gone.

A few yards up the tunnel he found Lewiston's quarters, then Arthur's and the lavish dining room. Lew's men had already been there and torn the rooms apart. There was no sign of Doc or Neferti or the twins. Hell, finding nothing was better than finding them dead.

Raider ran through the big kitchen into the empty horse corral. Gunfire sounded down a passage and he followed it. The tunnel led sharply upward, and horses and been there moments before. It suddenly dawned on him this was the same way he'd come in through the cliffside.

"Hey, Pink! Get your fuckin' head down!"

Raider squatted and crawled over to Lew. Hackman pointed up the passage where his men were pouring lead into the dark. "Those assholes got the way blocked good. Must be fifteen or twenty of 'em and they got all the cover. I sent some men round through the outhouse door to flank 'em."

Raider stared. "Jesus, Lew—you mean there's another way out of here? What are you sittin' here for—this place could go up any minute!"

Lew showed his teeth. "Told you we got some debts to pay. Besides, those bastards got money that belongs to me and I aim to get it."

"You're crazy. If anyone's got money it's Lewiston and Arthur. You're wasting time, Hackman. Those dudes didn't stay for the fighting—they're long gone, takin' everything they could carry."

Lew wasn't listening. "Where's this outhouse you're talking about?" asked Raider. Hackman nodded over his shoulder and bent to reload the Smith & Wesson.

Raider smelled the place long before he found it. In a minute he saw the torch by the small stream, and a slit of daylight behind. Holding his breath, he ran to the low crevice and inched his way through the hole. Late-afternoon sunlight touched the mountains. The sky was blood red. Gunfire rolled off the cliffs and tumbled down the ridge. Raider spotted the heavy pall of smoke hanging in the air to his right and knew Arthur's men were having it out with Hackman's.

He sprinted down the hill, boots slipping on gravel. Bracing himself with both hands, he reached the top and squatted next to a high stand of granite. Suddenly, a shadow peeled off stone, drove him to the ground. Raider came up fast, rolled the man off his shoulder. The man hit hard, grunted, came to his feet with a short blade in his fist. Raider clawed for his gun, saw it ten yards down the hill. The man grinned and came at him. Raider circled, watched the man's eyes. He was a gaunt, pinch-faced little man, hard and wiry, built like a spring. He was dressed in Army issue and Raider knew him. Delaney blinked, saw who Raider was, and showed his teeth.

"Sure is my day, ain't it? Nothing I like better'n cuttin' up Pinks."

"Come and do it, then," Raider urged him.

Delaney feinted, jerked back, whipped the blade dangerously close to Raider's cheek. Raider backed off. The man spat out a laugh. "Tore your partner up real good, mister. You know that? Broke him up *fine*, I did!"

The knife sang out again. Raider let it come, felt steel whisper under his arm and brought his left up solidly in Delaney's face. Delaney grunted. Blood flecked his nose and he stumbled to his back. Something clattered out of his belt and Raider picked it up. It was Doc's .38 Diamondback.

"Shit. It ain't even loaded," snarled Delaney. Wiping a sleeve over his face he sprang to his feet and drove the blade at Raider's belly. Raider stood his ground and pulled the trigger. Weatherbee's pistol barked like a dog. A small blue hole appeared like magic on Delaney's brow. Delaney looked surprised, sat back awkwardly on his ass, and slumped to the ground.

Raider stomped down the hill for his Remington, then worked back up the ridge. The men Lew Hackman had sent through the outhouse were pouring rifle fire at the base of the cliff, making a great deal of noise but doing little damage. Arthur's men had good cover and weren't interested in fighting. A few held back Hackman's crew while the others sneaked horses out of the line of fire and down the hill.

Raider prayed Doc was outside, even if Lewiston had him. If someone decided to blow that mountain— Motion caught his eye and Raider jerked up. Something white broke cover and flashed along the ridge overhead. Another figure appeared directly behind the first. Raider stared. Louisa and Annette, long legs flying, scampered bare-ass naked along the cliff, screaming their lungs out.

* * *

Doc hoped the ship would get where it was going before he threw up. It rolled from side to side, banging his bare butt against wood, his chest into something softer.

"Doc? *Doc!*"

"Huh?" Doc blinked. "Neferti? Hell, where are you?"

"What do you mean, where am I? Can't you *feel* me? Doc, come out of it. You're right next to me, about as close as you can get. We're—tied up to each other. Engaged, so to speak."

Doc shook his head. He could feel her now, almost see her. Thin stripes of yellow slanted down her arm from a crack overhead. Her cheek was next to his—hell, so was everything else. The heat of her body touched him all the way to his feet. "Seems like we've done this before," said Doc.

"Not like this we haven't," Neferti said stiffly. "Doc, I'm scared out of my wits. The man is crazy. I don't remember half of what happened back there and I hope I never do. I love being next to you, but trussed up naked under a wagon is *not* my idea of romance. Doc—that man is insane!"

"That's where we are—in a wagon?" Doc peered over his shoulder. "Yeah, like you said, under the floorboards.

Damn, I thought it was a ship. How long we been here?
I'm still a little groggy."

"An hour, maybe. He quit doping me up in the cave
and I *kind* of recall leaving. On the back of a horse."

Doc suddenly remembered. "Uhuh. Lewiston killed
the two guys who helped him load up. Nice fellow. Neferti,
I expect he's got the treasure, the *Nymph,* and most of
the money right in here with us. The son of a bitch doesn't
miss a bet, I'll give him credit for that. Probably got
wagons and teams stashed all over—" Doc stopped, grit
his teeth, and let out a groan. "My God, I've got to get
my brain working. He's back there—Raider. Tied up in
that damn powder room!"

"I know," Neferti said softly. "Lewiston told me. I'm
—sorry, Doc. I don't think there's anything you can do."

Doc started to speak. The floorboards tipped up suddenly and Lewiston grinned down from the driver's seat.
"How are you, children? Get a little nap, now, you played
real hard today at Granny's. We'll be home 'fore long and
get some supper."

The floorboards slammed shut. Dust settled on Doc's
face and his hair stood on end. Henry Lewiston was
dressed in a flowery cotton dress. A bright blue bonnet
framed the long red wig that hung to his shoulders. The
high, shrill voice sounded nothing like a man's.

• • •

Khalifi heard a noise.

It came from behind the canyon wall somewhere, over
the high crest of the mountain. He wondered what was
happening back there. Maybe the man wanted him to do
something. If he did, why didn't he come and say so? Or
put the thing up in the sky like he said he would? Khalifi
couldn't remember what the man had told him. He knew,
though, that he had better find Neferti. He hadn't seen
her in a long time. If he could find her, she'd say something nice to him.

CHAPTER TWENTY-EIGHT

"Listen," Doc said warily. "This fruitcake isn't pretending anymore. He's crazy as hell. *Granny's* house? Holy shit!"

"This is what I have been trying to tell you," Neferti said in his ear. "There is something—wrong with him, Doc. Something terribly wrong."

"Now that's the understatement of the year."

"No. I don't mean that. Something more. It's all so—hazy. I'm trying to remember."

"Is it something he—did to you, Neferti? Is that it?"

"Yes, that's it exactly! Only, I'm not sure he did anything at *all*. I was awfully frightened, Doc, and whatever he gave me made it hard to think straight. But there's—something. I can't put my finger on it, but it gives me the shakes to think about it."

The floorboards jerked up so fast both Doc and Neferti were startled. "You children *must* stop talking!" shrieked Lewiston. "That's not nice, you hear?" Turning away for a moment, he pulled the team to a halt, then clambered back to the bed of the wagon. Before Doc could protest, a thick wad of cloth was stuffed in his mouth. Seconds later, Neferti went silent as well. The floorboards banged shut, and Weatherbee was left to fume in the dark.

Doc wondered if Lewiston had seen something, or whether his infernal luck was running true. No more than five minutes after the gag went in his mouth, the sound of horses and muffled voices reached Doc's ears. The wagon jolted to a stop and a man spoke firmly to Lewiston.

"You see anything, ma'am? Anything at all? Horses, maybe—a whole bunch of riders."

"Not a thing," said Lewiston. "I been ridin' all afternoon and there ain't been anyone on the road 'cept you. Lordy, there's nothing *wrong*, is there? I'm all alone," he wailed. "Got no mister to look after me!"

"Now, now, don't you worry," the voice assured him. "Don't think you'll be bothered. Just stick to the road and get on home." In a moment, the horses thundered off, and Lewiston cackled after them.

Doc moaned and tried desperately to spit out the gag. It was the posse for certain—it *had* to be! Harry Morton had finally gotten the law moving and they'd passed right by. The crazy bastard had fooled them again with his old-lady act! Doc's heart sank. Whatever hopes he'd had of pulling himself and Neferti out of the fire died with the retreating hooves. Lewiston was home free and clear and there wasn't a damn thing they could do about it.

Doc cursed himself for being grateful, but couldn't help it. The cup of water and the small plate of beans and bread was better than the finest gourmet meal he'd ever had. He wolfed it down quickly before Lewiston changed his mind, ignoring the sharp jabs of pain in his belly.

"You okay?" he asked Neferti. "Like to order dessert or something? Coffee?"

Neferti gave him a look. "No. I am *not* okay. I am freezing to death." She shivered and hunched bare legs under her chin. "Doc, is he going to leave us out here like this? Naked without a blanket or anything? Do you have any idea how *cold* it gets here at night?"

"Maybe he'll bring us a cover," Doc said hopefully. "Hell, I don't know. You can't outguess a loony. He's gone right over the edge, lady. I don't think *he* knows who he is anymore."

Just before dark, Lewiston had pulled the team and wagon off the Bear River road and stopped in a little hollow. The area was surrounded by trees, and the campfire was impossible to see unless you came right on it. Weatherbee and Neferti were securely manacled together, Doc's right arm chained to the girl's left. Another set of manacles wrapped about the tall pine at their backs and ended at Doc's leg. They could stand and walk a few feet, but there was no place to go.

When Lewiston marched them out of the wagon and brought out the chains, Doc lost his temper and nearly got them both shot on the spot. The sudden, wild flash of anger in Lewiston's eyes warned him off. Clearly, he'd shoot them if the mood struck him. Without blinking an eye.

Doc put on his best front for Neferti. She was frightened out of her wits and had had all she could handle. He didn't tell her what he saw in Lewiston's eyes—the thing that prowled through the hollows of the man's mind, dark and musty and smelling of sour sweat. Lewiston had never touched Neferti. Doc was sure of that now. He'd stretched her out naked in the cavern, tied her to the bed, and simply looked at her, some dark, bizarre fantasy playing out in his head.

He liked to see her naked. But there was more to it than that. *He liked to see Doc naked with her.* That, and the fact that Lewiston *believed* he was a woman now chilled Weatherbee clear to the bone. Lewiston had plans for them. Both of them. And Doc didn't even want to think about what they might be.

*   *   *

For a moment, the sight of the two bare-assed young beauties nearly brought the small war to a halt. The two bands of outlaws stared at this wondrous sight, halted their business for a good three seconds.

Raider shouted at the girls. His voice was lost in a fierce volley of gunfire. He cursed, lost his footing on the slope, and went sprawling down the hillside, hands and knees raking gravel. By the time he answered the shots the man was gone. Raider caught a glimpse of him again through a thick stand of pine, bounding like a deer down the ravine. It's Arthur, he told himself darkly—god*damn* if it isn't!

A chill touched his spine and he knew where the colonel was headed. The wires trailed out of the cavern, probably buried under the soil. He'd have the box stashed far enough off so he could blow the place without risking his neck. Just like Doc said.

Bolting down the hill, Raider dodged lead from the

mouth of the cavern. Branches snapped in his face and thorns tore at his arms. He jumped a small creek, slipped on the stony bank, and ripped up his knees. Snaking down a dry gully, he saw Arthur again, squatted quickly with both hands on the .44, and fired twice into the trees. Arthur answered. The bullet snapped twigs at Raider's shoulder. The colonel scrambled up a small hill and fired again. Raider jumped for cover. His boot slipped, twisted on loose shale. Pain stabbed his leg like a knife. The .44 flew out of his hand, clattered on stone. He tried to stand, fell back clumsily on his butt.

"Shit!" he cursed. "Not now!" Bullets dusted the path behind him and he limped to cover. Clutching his leg, he squeezed it tightly and clenched his teeth. Arthur laughed, thirty yards above him to the right. Raider looked up and his throat went dry. The colonel pulled a squat wooden box up out of the dirt, opened it, and snaked out two long wires.

Raider measured the distance to his gun, knew he'd never make it. Arthur looked down, a broad smile of triumph on his face. He clutched the wires in his fist, brought them together—stopped suddenly and went rigid. Tossing the wires from him as if they were rattlers, he jerked a pistol from his belt and fired wildly into the brush. A terrible roar erupted from the hollow. Arthur squeezed the trigger until his gun clicked empty, tossed the weapon angrily, and backed off.

Khalifi lumbered up the hill, giant legs churning. Arthur crabbed sidewise, felt solid stone behind him, and went white. A scream started in his throat—Khalifi's ham-sized fists reached out to cut it off. With one swift motion, he lifted the colonel off his feet and drove his head into the stone wall. Arthur's skull split like an egg. Khalifi didn't stop. He rammed the bloody mess against rock, again and again, till there was nothing between his hands. Then, he raised Arthur high above his head, howled at the sky, and slammed the limp body down hard on the wooden box.

"Khalifi—no!" shouted Raider.

A sound like the end of the world burst out of the

mountain. A solid wall of air hit Raider, slammed him into the ground. Blood coursed from his nose and ears. The sky went dark as night; a black cloud of dirt and stone vomited out of the cavern and rattled down on the landscape.

Raider choked, wiped dust from his eyes, and stumbled up the hill, dragging his leg behind him. He kept his eyes away from Arthur, knowing what he'd see. Khalifi was twenty yards away, curled against the cliffside. Arthur had been a good shot, and Raider counted five holes in a four inch circle. Jesus! Raider shook his head in wonder. The son of a bitch had taken five chunks of lead around the heart and kept coming. At least, he could die like anyone else. Raider had never been certain of that before.

Half a dozen outlaws staggered about the blackened landscape. A man screamed somewhere, went suddenly silent. Raider knew the men who'd survived had been far from the hole in the mountain—no one inside had lived through that. Still, he knew he had to look. If Doc was in there, he'd have to find out.

The dust had cleared some and he could see his way with a torch. The fissure was twice as wide now, choked with heavy blocks of stone from the walls and ceiling. Raider saw two or three bits of flesh and part of a boot. Nothing else was left. Some of the tunnels were blocked completely; the caverns near the center of the explosion were sealed forever. Whoever was in there would stay there.

Raider found part of the horse corral and kitchen still intact and made his way though. His leg protested with sharp stabs of pain. At the far end of the cave he found a narrow passage that twisted toward pale daylight and he wormed his way through. The sun was down and night purpled the east. The cliffs towered straight up from where he was standing; a row of pines marched up the hill.

"Hi there, Pink."

Raider peered into shadow. Lew Hackman sat under a tree, a canteen held loosely on his lap. Raider squatted down beside him. "Shit—how come you ain't dead, friend?"

"Hell, maybe I am. I'm not real sure." Lew told him the fight at the other end of the cavern had gotten hot and heavy after Raider had left. He'd taken his men back past the main entrance to the outhouse door. Heavy fire had cut them off and they'd retreated to the far end and found the small fissure. "We was just about out when the son of a bitch blew. I still can't hear nothing."

"Where's the boys that was with you?"

Lew shrugged. "Lookin' for horses, I reckon. There's plenty of empties running round if you can catch 'em." Lew offered him the canteen and Raider took it. "You hurt or something?"

"Naw. Fucked up my leg is all." Taking off his jacket he tore strips of leather from the back and started binding the ankle over his boots. It wouldn't do much good, but if he took off the boot he'd never get it on again.

"I lost some good friends in there," Lew said sullenly. "Guess you got a man missing, too. Find anything?"

"There isn't nothing left to find."

"No. Not a lot." Lew looked up curiously. "I can't keep calling you Pink. You got another name?"

"Raider."

"Raider what?"

"Just Raider."

"Suits you," said Lew. "Listen, we can't squat here all night, friend. Going to get cold out, and hungry too. Maybe some of them horses—"

Raider cut him off. A party of riders was rounding the cliffside, just across the hollow. The horsemen came to a stop. Raider heard shells click in a dozen Winchesters. "Whoever the hell's down there, get your ass up here and keep your hands high. We're the law!"

Raider pulled himself erect and raised his hands. "Hold your fire," he called out. "I'm coming up!" He wasn't sure why, but he knew he was going to do it. "Just glue

204 J. D. HARDIN

yourself to that tree," he said without looking down. "I don't figure they know you're there."

"Goddamn," said Lew. "I won't say I ain't surprised."

"You and me both," Raider said drily, and limped up to the posse.

U.S. Marshal Dean McAllister was a leathery-faced lawman with water-blue eyes and a walrus mustache. He squinted curiously at Raider and spat a wad of tobacco into the fire. "Son, I heard a lot of woolly tales in my time, but you got the best." He scowled in the dark and shook his head. "I brung thirty-two men up here and killed three horses in the doin'. All you got left is 'bout ten raggedy-ass outlaws with no more bite in 'em than Monday-morning whores. Seems a waste, don't it?"

"I guess," Raider said absently.

"Where you headed from here? Back south? Ought to get that leg looked at when you can."

"I'll do that."

McAllister caught his tone and made a face. "Shit, boy, I'm rattling on and not thinking. You lost a friend down there and got plenty on your mind."

"Marshal, I'm not all that sure he was down there. Lewiston had time to get out. Maybe he took Doc with him. Isn't any reason why he should, but I got to keep thinkin' that." Raider stood and tried out his leg. "I'm taking one of those outlaw horses, and I'd be obliged if you can spare me a little grub for the road. I don't know where the hell to start, but I ain't real comfortable sittin' here."

"The grub you got," McAllister said soberly. "And as many of my boys as you need. I got an idea you don't want 'em, though."

"I do," said Raider. "But I'm scared to put too many men on this asshole's trail. He's crazier'n a hog, Marshal. If Doc or the girl's with him, I want them back alive."

McAllister scratched his chin thoughtfully. "Didn't see anything coming up, and we was sure keeping our eyes open."

"No one riding out, no sign of anything on the roads? They'd have to follow Bear River, unless they took off over open country. I don't much see Lewiston doin' that, even if he's running."

"Nothing," said McAllister. "Talked to a scrawny old bitch in a wagon. She come north ahead of us, and hadn't seen anything either."

Raider sat up straight. "A—scrawny old woman? Ugly as shit, with red hair, maybe?"

McAllister looked surprised. "Well yeah—how'd you know?"

"Jesus Christ!" said Raider.

•   •   •

Lewiston herded them back in the wagon at dawn without coffee or breakfast. In spite of the blankets they'd gotten the night before, Doc and Neferti were chilled to the bone. Weatherbee could hardly walk. Battered and bruised as he was, the cold night had nearly finished him off. Without Neferti's warm body, he was certain he'd never have made it. Doc couldn't remember holding a beautiful woman all night and doing just that—holding her. This time, he was grateful for the chance and so was Neferti.

By noon, the late summer sun had risen high enough to warm the wagon, and Doc stopped shivering. By pushing Neferti hard against the sideboard, he discovered he could crane his neck over her shoulder and peer out a small crack. Lewiston had left the Bear River road and taken off northwest across open country. The Wasatch Range fell behind, and by mid-afternoon they were riding over fairly level country.

"I think we're headed up to the Snake River," said Doc. "At least, that's what it looks like."

"What for?" asked Neferti. "Where is he *taking* us, Doc?"

"I don't know. Maybe he's got a plan and maybe he's just putting miles behind us. He's smart enough to stay off the road, and in that garb of his no one's likely to stop us." Doc paused a moment. "Neferti, I don't guess I have to tell you this. You know what we're into as well as I do. What I'm trying to say is, keep your eyes on me anytime he lets us out of the wagon. If a chance comes, I'm going to grab it. Just be ready to make the most of it."

Doc couldn't see her face, but he felt her stiffen against him. "No, Doc. If you try anything he'll kill you!"

"Uhuh. And if I don't, then what? What do you think he'll do then, Neferti?"

Neferti didn't answer.

The sun was low in the west before Lewiston brought the wagon to a halt. Doc had been watching periodically out of his peephole and knew they'd plunged into rough country again. Rugged, crumbling stone walls loomed up on every side; the dry riverbed beneath their wheels hadn't seen water in years. They were still south of the Snake River Plains, then. Maybe Lewiston wasn't headed there at all. Maybe he was cutting over west.

There were no trees, so Lewiston chained them to the wagon. Doc looked for a chance to jump him, staggering more than he had to to throw the man off. Lewiston knew better. He kept the pistol steadily on Doc and stayed well out of his way.

After he got a small fire started, Lewiston brought his prisoners the usual beans and bread and a little water. He hadn't said a word to them all day—not since the night before, if Doc remembered right. The man's silence gave Weatherbee the creeps. He was dropping further and further into his new role, retreating into something only he could see. He minced about the camp, humming and chuckling to himself, giving a chill imitation of a pinched-up farm wife.

When supper was over, Lewiston built up the fire and busied himself a few yards away from the wagon. Taking four long stakes, he drove them solidly into the ground, forming a five-foot square. When he was finished, he tied heavy strands of rawhide to the stakes and left the loose ends dangling. It finally dawned on Doc what he was doing. His skin crawled, and the beans and bread nearly rose up into his throat. He'd seen the Indians build a square like that, and knew what it was for. Lewiston was getting ready to play Apache.

CHAPTER TWENTY-NINE

Raider was up and in the saddle at first light, following the narrow road that snaked along the banks of the Bear River. Marshal McAllister's information had saved him time; the lawman knew exactly where he'd seen the wagon, and Raider went straight to it. There were horse tracks there and wheel ruts—the road was full of them. Which ones belonged to Lewiston? How the hell was he going to separate the right ones from the others?

Raider stopped, trying to guess the man's thoughts. Lewiston was crazy—not stupid. There was a great deal of difference between the two. He'd used the old-lady disguise twice now, but he had more tricks than that up his sleeve. Lewiston was a man who thought ahead—covered himself two or three ways. He'd stick to the Bear River Road as long as he needed to, maybe use the old-lady business to throw off anyone who figured it out. Let them *look* for old ladies headed north—while he went somewhere else. *Of course,* Raider thought glumly, *he could do just the opposite of that, too.*

Raider kept his eyes on the road, but he was more interested in those tracks that pulled off. Very few did —there was no reason to leave the road for rougher ground.

He found the spot around noon.

The wheels had moved over soft ground and he followed them easily to the hollow in the trees. Raider tied his horse well away from the campsite to avoid bringing more tracks into the area. The picture was fairly clear. The wagon had rested in the center of the clearing. Someone had made a fire and cooked over it. One meal, maybe two. There were crusts of bread about, beans tossed on the ground. Raider squatted, poked a finger in the white ash. There was no heat left, but that meant nothing. Only that the fire was older than the morning. The beans and bread told him something else. They were still too soft to be older than the night before.

For a while, the footprints puzzled him. There were three people, but only one wore shoes. Why the hell was that? Raider found the path to the pine tree and followed it. There were the man's bare feet, and a smaller set beside them. A woman's or a child's. Raider's eyes caught something and he bent to the base of the tree. Something hard had circled the bark, worn a little channel in the trunk near the ground. He wondered what it was, then saw the clear impression where a chain had pressed soft earth. Raider stood and stared at the tree. His heart beat faster and a chill touched the back of his neck. Jesus Christ—it *was* Doc and Neferti! Lewiston had chained them up naked to the tree all night. Chained them up like a pair of fuckin' dogs!

• • •

Doc could hear him moving around in the wagon, humming in his wierd falsetto voice. It sounded like he was rummaging through a trunk or a box, looking for something. "Listen," he whispered to Neferti. "I don't know what he's up to, but I don't much like it."

Neferti's eyes were wide as saucers. She sat hunched up on the sand, long legs drawn against her breasts, hands around her knees against the cold. "That—thing out there, Doc. What's it—for?"

Her eyes told him she'd already guessed. "It's a thing to tie people to, stake 'em out. I wish to hell I could say it's something else, but it's not."

"Oh, *God!*" Neferti bit her lip and trembled against him. "Doc—what's he going to *do* to me?"

"Look, just take it easy. I'm not going to let him hurt you."

Neferti blinked without expression. "You can't stop him. You can't do anything."

"I can try. If he—" Doc stopped. Lewiston jumped down from the wagon and stalked around to face them.

"Girl," he said sweetly. "Go sit over there, now. I have to talk to him and you *mustn't* listen." Lewiston shook a finger in her face. "Move, dear."

Neferti didn't budge.

"Go on," Doc said tightly. "Do as he says." Neferti crawled down the length of the wagon as far as her chain would go. Lewiston watched her, satisfied, then drew his pistol and kneeled behind Doc. The barrel touched Weatherbee's head. He heard the hammer click and flinched.

"Don't worry," Lewiston assured him. "I just want to make sure you pay *attention,* young man. Boys' thoughts *will* wander off sometimes."

"I'm—listening," Doc said drily. "You don't have to do that."

Lewiston ignored him. "I know you think I don't like you, but that's *not* so. You aren't being fair to me. I *do* like you. And I under*stand* why you do the things you do. Little boys can't help that. They're just made that way—different from little girls. You know about that, don't you?"

"Uh, yeah. Sort of," said Doc.

"Good." Lewiston let out a sigh. "Thank goodness I don't have to go through *that.* You *know* what kind of things you do."

"What—sort of things are you talking about?"

"You know," Lewiston chided. "Nasty things. You put your little tootie where it doesn't belong, *that's* what you do. I'll bet you'd like to put it in *her.*"

Doc swallowed. "Put my—what?"

"Your hard little tootie. You heard me, you bad boy. Bet you did it to her already, didn't you? When no one was looking. Poked it right in her little pink hole!"

Jesus, Doc moaned to himself. *Oh, Jesus!*

"That's all right." Lewiston patted him on the head. "I told you I understand." He leaned close to Doc's ear.

"I poked mine in a little girl once—when I was *him*. You know?" Lewiston stood, marched in front of Doc, and abruptly raised his skirts up to his waist. "See? I fixed it. Don't *have* to do dirty stuff now. You won't have to either!"

Doc stared. Food came up in his throat. There was nothing there. Just a patch of red hair, a tiny set of balls, and a long ugly scar.

•   •   •

The trail was easy enough to follow until the wagon left the hills and took off over hard, flinty ground. Raider pulled up his mount and cursed. He was still south of the Snake River, but the land was changing fast. Now he had no idea where Lewiston was headed. On up to the plains, east back to the mountains. Or maybe northwest. Raider discarded the east. He wouldn't go back to the Wasatch. North, though, or west. Shit—which one? If he picked the wrong path now he'd lose a hell of a lot of time. Too much. Maybe Doc and the girl didn't *have* any time. Turning his horse northwest, he trotted toward the Snake over the dry, windblown soil.

•   •   •

Lewiston added dry sticks to the fire. He didn't seem at all worried that anyone would see it. Doc figured he was probably right. Idaho Territory was an immense, rugged land. You could go for days, weeks, and still not see another soul.

Lewiston brought a cup of water to Neferti, then turned on Doc. "I don't think *you'd* better have any," he said thoughtfully, hands on his hips. "Don't want you to get sick or anything tomorrow." Lewiston pranced off, pulling the bonnet over his long red curls. Doc noticed he kept one eye on Neferti until she finished the water, making sure she didn't share any.

Neferti came up close to him and wound a hand around his waist. "Better watch it," Doc said grimly. "You know how little boys are. Might stick my *tootie* in your hole."

"Doc!" Neferti brought a hand to her mouth, appalled. "That is *not* funny! He's serious!"

"Hell, you think I don't know that? It's my tootie he wants to whack off. Listen—Lewiston's too smart to stay in the wagon. He'll set up his roll on the other side of the fire. Sleep facing him and make as big a hump as you can. Use my blanket to help. I'll get behind you next to the wagon. There's no way I can get these chains off, but I got to do something."

"Like what, Doc?"

"Hell, I don't know. I'll tell you when I do it."

Lewiston would come at dawn, Doc decided. Come for him and stake him out and it would all be over. If it wasn't for the girl he wouldn't worry. He'd take his chances with Lewiston—jump him, even if he got a bullet for it. Dying clean was a damn sight better than getting cut—he had no doubts about that. Only, the girl *was* there, and Lewiston would use her. He'd work on Neferti until Doc was ready to cooperate. Weatherbee didn't dare let it go that far. He had to stop Lewiston first, take him out for good before he had a chance to touch Neferti. Once he started on her it would be too late. Doc knew he'd give in and let Lewiston take him.

"You can't," she said flatly, guessing his thoughts. "I won't let you, Doc." Moving closer under the blanket, she wrapped herself warmly around him. "Anyway, what difference does it make? You think he's going to let me go—what*ever* happens to you?"

Doc saw the look in her eyes and grabbed her shoulders hard. "Now listen, damn it—there's *always* a chance. Don't forget that. You don't know what he's going to do. Don't go trying anything stupid. Leave the stupid stuff to me."

Neferti forced a grin, and went back to watching Lewiston.

Doc waited a long hour.

The fire burned low. Lewiston hadn't moved in a long time. Doc touched Neferti lightly, inched away from the warmth of her back, and crawled under the wagon. The chain was wound about the axle and the wheel. As he'd figured, there wasn't a chance in hell of getting it loose. Lying on his back, he reached up carefully and ran his fingers along the bottom of the wagon. The rough planks were nailed solid. He couldn't pull one off in a week, even if he could afford the noise.

For a while, he thought he could stretch the chain out far enough to reach in the wagon bed from the far side and find something to use as a weapon. Lewiston had already thought of that. The chain took him only halfway under the bed. If he wanted to look inside he'd have to stand up facing the fire. No good. Lewiston would wake up and spot him. Probably truss him up tight until morning.

He found the little nub near the center of the bed, poking through a crack between two planks. Working it with his fingers, he pulled out a full inch and a half and discovered it was leather. A harness—likely a piece of one that had been tossed in the back of the wagon. Doc pulled, slowly and carefully. The leather strip snaked out of the crack until he had a good three feet. Then the strip went tight. Doc had been waiting for that. Pulling gently, he could hear a faint bump from the bed. The harness was attached to something solid—a bit, maybe, or a rusty nail. It wasn't coming any farther.

Doc sank back and got his breath. He'd have to cut it. He *had* to have that damn harness! Stretching the leather as far as he could, he rubbed it for a long quarter hour against the metal band on his wrist. The leather was hardly bruised. *Great,* Doc sighed. *Back to basics, then.* Holding the leather between his fingers, he started chewing.

Doc and Neferti were already up, huddled under their blankets, when Lewiston woke and stalked over to them. The land was still dark, but a thin patch of gray touched the horizon. "All right," chimed Lewiston. "Let's have our covers, children."

"No," complained Neferti. "It's cold."

Lewiston's smile faded. "Toss me the blanket, dear."

"All right!" Neferti said hotly. Ripping off her cover, she threw it at Lewiston's feet. Doc tossed his on the pile and Lewiston nodded.

"Now. All ready for the big day?" He pulled out the pistol and aimed it at Doc. "Turn over. We have to get that chain off."

"What for?"

"Now you *know* what for," Lewiston sighed impatiently. "It's time. We *talked* about this, young man."

"You did. I sure as hell didn't." Doc sat where he was on the dry, powdery soil, one hand on his knee, the other casually touching the ground.

"Are you going to be a bad boy now? Is that it? If you are—"

Doc moved his little finger and Neferti screamed as loud as she could. Lewiston jumped, startled, swung the revolver away from Doc. Doc clutched the two ends of the harness and jerked hard. The loop, buried carefully under half an inch of soil, whipped over Doc's shoulder and stung Lewiston's face. Lewiston grabbed for his eyes and squeezed the trigger blindly. The shot whined over Doc's head. Doc lunged, going low for the man's legs. The chain jerked, pulled him up short. Neferti sprang on Lewiston's back, wrapped her legs around his middle and clawed at his eyes. Lewiston raged, hammered at her hands with the barrel of the pistol, then turned and slammed her hard against the wagon. Neferti sagged and went limp. Doc strained against his chains, caught Lewiston's skirt and pulled him off his feet. Lewiston shrieked, kicked out, and crabbed away. Doc hung on, gritting his teeth against the thrust of Lewiston's boots. Lewiston swung the pistol, missed, swung again. The barrel of the .45 caught Doc squarely on the side of his head. He held on grimly, shaking off nausea. Lewiston hit him again. Doc gave a last, hopeless cry and let go. Somewhere in the back of his mind, he knew the show was over.

•   •   •

Raider found the tracks again at dawn.
He stared at them a long moment, wondering if he'd

made a terrible mistake. They led straight up the dry valley toward nowhere. Did he have the wrong wagon? Was he following someone else now—a dirt farmer or a miner? Lewiston couldn't just drive the damn wagon over Idaho forever. He had to know people were after him.

Raider pounded his fist on the saddle and urged the horse on. If he was wrong, he'd likely killed Doc and the girl. There wasn't time to check out any more tracks than these.

* * *

Doc blinked up at a blood-red sky streaked with pink. Lewiston shook his head and made clucking sounds with his teeth. "That was naughty. *Very*, very naughty. I didn't want to hurt you—you *made* me do that."

"The girl, what'd you do to her?"

"I'm all right, Doc." Neferti's voice was strained, ragged. "Oh, God—please leave him alone. Don't *do* anything to him!"

"Take it easy," Doc told her. "Just take it easy, now." He couldn't see her but knew she was still chained to the wagon. Too far away. There was nothing she could do. Nothing anyone could do. His head throbbed from the blow and he could feel the strain where rawhide stretched his arms and legs.

"I must warn you," Lewiston said firmly. "This *is* going to hurt some."

"Really?" Doc said dully. "No shit?"

Lewiston's mouth puckered like an old lady's. "Don't talk nasty, now. You know I don't like that."

"Listen," Doc said hoarsely. "Don't talk to me about nasty, you crazy son of a bitch! Jesus—what *made* you like this? Didn't get any as a kid? Some girl turn you down? Good God, so what!"

Lewiston didn't hear him. He busied himself with something at his side, something Doc couldn't see. He heard the sharp clink of metal—a terrible, frightening sound. Lewiston laid a long strip of clean rawhide on his chest, then carefully lined up three shiny blades on his belly. Doc went rigid, shrank from the cold touch.

"God—what are you going to—do with those?"

"The cord ties off the blood," Lewiston explained casually. "See, that way, when I remove your thing for you . . ." He picked up one of the shiny surgical knives and showed it to Doc. "See?" He gave Doc a foolish grin. "It'll hurt some, but it's *real* sharp. And you won't have to do dirty stuff any more. I don't. It's *so* much nicer. You'll see." Reaching between Doc's legs, he pulled Doc's cock up straight and started winding the rawhide about the base of the shaft.

• • •

Raider stopped, let his eyes sweep over the landscape. The wagon tracks moved in a straight line past the low hill into the dry riverbed. The sun rose over his shoulder and Raider rode cautiously onto the flat. He knew he was close. He could feel it—smell the faint odor of woodsmoke on the crisp morning air. Someone was out there. Lewiston. It had to be Lewiston.

There was no cover at all now. Anyone looking in the right direction would see him coming for a mile. He came out of the shallow gully into the riverbed. Two dead saplings stood like warped poles stuck in the ground. Raider jerked his horse up fast, rose in the saddle, and squinted over the flat. His gaze took in the whole scene at once: The wagon. The girl. The naked man on the ground, the bizarre figure poised above him. Suddenly, the sun caught silver, a flash on the naked man's belly.

Raider's blood went cold. Sliding to the ground, he yanked the Sharps rifle off the saddle, pulled the curved lever, and checked the breech. Raider breathed a silent sigh of relief. The cartridge was still in there—right where it was when he took it off the outlaw. It was a powerful 45-90—ninety grains of powder and four hundred grains of lead.

Quickly, he flipped up the leaf-spring sight, rested the barrel in the crook of one of the dead saplings, and squinted down the riverbed. The Sharps Creedmoor would drop a buffalo at a thousand yards, but Raider wasn't after buffalo. His target was smaller, much smaller, and there was no damn time. No time at all. He didn't dare move closer. And if he missed . . . Raider twisted the sighting notch to 550 yards . . . 600 . . . back to 575. His heart pounded and his hands shook. The Sharps had a double-action trigger: Squeeze the rear trigger and listen for the tiny click that set the other, then touch the front trigger—touch it with a feather and it would go.

Doc screamed. His voice echoed over the flats. The silver in the figure's hand flashed down in a wicked arc.

The cord tightened at the base of Doc's cock. Doc cried out, shrank from Lewiston's touch. Lewiston grabbed the length of flesh, stretched it out, gave Doc a broad grin, whipped the razor-sharp blade between Doc's legs—

Sound cracked like thunder down the riverbed.

Time stopped—crawled like cold molasses. . . .

A dark blossom sprouted on Lewiston's brow.

The blossom grew, spattered Doc with red. Lewiston's mouth twisted in an impossible shape. The hand with the blade kept coming. Doc felt a quick touch of cold and closed his eyes.

Neferti screamed and couldn't stop. Doc stretched up as far as he could. Afraid to look, afraid not to. Lewiston lay five feet away between Doc's legs, the flowery skirt bunched up around his waist. Doc stared at the spot below his belly, knowing what he'd see. It was gone. He'd felt the pain.

A cry stuck in his throat. It was—still there! A hairline of red creased the shaft. A ribbon no more than a quarter inch long. Doc blinked at it, fell back, and passed out cold.

EPILOGUE

Raider woke up but didn't open his eyes.

Something interesting was happening. It was the same thing he'd been dreaming about—only the real thing was even better. His cock stood up straight and hard. Nancy held the swollen tip between two fingers. With another finger, she rubbed the arched back of the shaft in slow, lazy strokes. She was in no hurry. She knew where she was going and had all the time in the world to get there.

Raider couldn't stand it any longer. He opened his eyes, raised up on his arms, and grinned at her. "Sure is a fine way to wake up. Better'n a hot cup of coffee."

Nancy arched a brow. "Well, I sure as hell hope so. Isn't any coffee I know can do this." Sweeping red hair off her cheek, she opened her lips and took him in her mouth, letting the hard cock slide down her warm throat and back out again.

"Oh, Lordy," moaned Raider. "You're right as you can be, girl. That ain't no morning coffee."

"Doesn't *taste* like it, either."

"It ought to taste a lot like you. That's where I been keepin' it." Raider leaned back and looked at her. She knelt by the bed, flaming red hair brushing his belly and tumbling over her shoulders. Mid-morning light striped the pale yellow walls and touched the naked curve of her back and the swell of her hips. Raider could hear the sounds of San Francisco coming alive outside the hotel, but wasn't much interested. His attention was on Nancy, and what she was doing.

The girl pumped him hard, her hot little mouth full of fire. Raider gasped, thrust the shaft in deeper. Nancy stopped, her lips touching only the head of his cock, the pink tip of her tongue moving in slow, easy circles that drove Raider crazy. Nancy gave him a mischievous little grin, wrapped her hand around his tool, and jerked him

217

off fast. Raider came with a groan. Nancy opened her
mouth and took the load hungrily.

"Damn!" Raider fell back and let out a breath. "Girl,
how the hell am I supposed to get moving with you doin'
stuff like that? I'm too weak to lift a finger."

Nancy bounced up on the bed and draped herself over
his chest. "Mister, who said you was going anywhere? *I*
sure didn't. We got a lot of time to make up for."

"Seems to me like we did some fair catching up last
night," Raider said drily. " 'Bout six or eight hours'
worth."

"Ha! Got loosened up a little, is all. Reckon we're
ready for some serious fuckin' now."

"Serious fuckin'."

"Uhuh."

"That other stuff was just—"

"—loosening up. Getting the old juices flowing again."

Raider made a face. "Honey, you've 'bout sucked all
the juices out of me there is. There ain't nothin' left
to flow." Raider stretched, rolled over, and set his feet
on the floor. " 'Course, there's no reason we can't have
us some breakfast, then let me and Doc take care of our
business and see what happens after that."

Nancy snorted. "Mister, don't give me *that* shit. I
know what happens when you and that partner of yours
start doing *business*. Someone takes a shot at someone
else, and next thing I know you're off somewhere and I
don't get fucked."

"Hey, now—that stuff's all over. There isn't going to
be no shooting." Raider went down on all fours and
snaked his Middleton boots from under the bed. "Besides,
you haven't gone all that long without gettin' some, lady.
Don't hurt you any to wait an hour or so between—"
Raider raised up, his eyes level with the bed. "My God
girl—what the hell are you doing?"

"If you're not interested," Nancy said absently, "guess
I'll just have to go ahead by myself. Isn't anyone else
available at the moment."

Raider stared. Nancy's long, tapered legs were spread
wide, offering him a delicious view of the feathery ambe

nest. Two slim fingers held the pink lips apart, while another thrust deep into the moist pussy.

"Go ahead," said Nancy. "Don't mind me. Just get on about your business."

"Hell, reckon I know where my business is better than anyone." Raider came up off the floor and straddled her. Nancy gave a short little laugh, threw back her head, and scissored him with her legs. Her hands found his already rigid cock and eagerly thrust it into her warmth.

Raider rammed her hard, scooting her over the bed. Nancy sucked in a breath and pulled him to her, strong hands raking his back. Raider took her two firm tits in his hands and squeezed them. Nancy closed her eyes, reached up, and pinched her nipples and offered them to his mouth.

"Oh, God, suck on them, Raider—please suck on them hard! Harder! Suck my tits! Suck—my—*tits!*"

Nancy went rigid, arched her back off the bed. Her cunt jerked up to meet him, ground into his loins. Raider surged into her again. Nancy screamed, fell back with a sigh, and rolled her eyes to the ceiling. Raider pinched her nipples once more, licked each one, and grinned down at her.

"Serious fuckin', girl?"

"*Damn* serious, mister!"

Doc and Neferti Raman were at a corner table in the dining room. Both looked up and smiled broadly, as if they'd been there all day. Raider knew better. Neferti's dark hair was still tousled, and there was a smug grin on Weatherbee's face. "We, ah—figured you two'd be down soon," said Doc. "So we waited to order."

"Well, we sure do thank you," Raider said blandly. "Hope we didn't keep you more'n two or three minutes."

Doc flushed. Neferti glanced at Nancy and covered her laugh with a napkin. "We have a little time," Doc said quickly. "Woodmore isn't expecting us till eleven."

"You takin' good care of that stuff?"

"Doesn't ever leave my side," Weatherbee said soberly,

patting the two fat valises by his leg. "I'm not about to lose that money again, Rade. Don't think I could stand it."

"Hell, don't even talk about it," Raider said darkly. "I ain't goin' *near* no trains again. Not ever."

The Southern Pacific had brought them in from Ogden the night before, and Wells Fargo had quickly stored the recovered Egyptian treasures in its vault. A quick inventory showed less than a quarter of the pieces were missing. Dr. Raman was overjoyed to find that much—he'd never expected to see any of it again.

"He's feeling much better," said Neferti. "I think he'll be a lot happier, though, when we get back home."

"You're goin' ahead with the exhibit here, right?" asked Nancy.

"I don't think we could get out of town if we tried," laughed Neferti. "After what's happened, *every*body in California wants to see the *Nymph!*"

Nancy chewed on a piece of toast and winked at her. "Glad you'll be around. Soon as we get rid of these dudes, you and me'll find us some real *fun* fellers and do the town."

"Huh," scowled Raider. "Don't see how you could do better'n *us.*"

Nancy and Neferti laughed.

"Want to hear some *good* news for a change?" asked Doc. He lit a Virginia cheroot and blew a stream of smoke past Raider's head. "Lord Willis and the twins sailed last night at midnight. They're taking the long way home back to England."

Raider and the girls applauded. "I won't be real put out if I don't ever see those folks again," Raider said sourly. "'Course, those two girls was pretty little things I got to say that."

"Like hell you do." Nancy gave him a withering stare "You don't have to say anything of the kind, and it'd be a damn good idea if you didn't!"

Promptly at 10:45, two shotgun-wielding guards me Raider and Doc in the lobby of the hotel. The bank wa:

only two blocks away, but both the Pinkertons were glad for the escort. C. Clifford Woodmore greeted them warmly, escorted them to his office, and locked the door.

"I expect you fellows will be glad to get rid of that bundle. That's a lot of cash to carry around. You know how much is in there?"

"A hell of a lot," said Raider, hefting the two bags on the table. "Two, maybe three milion in big bills, I reckon, but we ain't had time to count it."

"All we did," explained Doc, "was pack up the money we found in Lewiston's wagon and sew the tops of the bags with rawhide. I'm sure there's some missing, but Wells Fargo and the First National in Denver ought to be happy. Considering they damn near lost it all."

"Well, then," said Woodmore. "Shall we get on with it, gentlemen? Open 'em up and I'll get a couple of tellers in here to do the counting."

Raider unfolded his Case knife, slit the rawhide cord binding the top of the first valise, and spilled its contents on the table.

Doc's mouth fell open. "Jesus—Christ!"

Woodmore gave the pair a long, penetrating look. "Is this some sort of a joke, gentlemen? If it is—"

"Shit!" Raider slashed the second valise open and turned it over. Like the first, it was stuffed with Wyoming and Utah newspapers.

"That's—impossible," sputtered Doc. "They—never left my side since Ogden!"

"They didn't have to," Raider said sourly. Poking through the papers, he came up with a filmy pair of black underthings edged in lace and held it up with two fingers. "It was those fuckin' twins, Doc. Louisa and Annette. Somewhere between here and Utah they fixed up two fake valises and slid 'em in right under our nose."

"But—when? Where? How in—!"

"Hell, how do I know? While we was sittin' in the diner, maybe. I expect one of them little cunts sidled up to us and giggled a minute while the other slipped a couple of phonies under our feet."

"Rade, what the shit are we going to do now?"

"I know what *I'm* going to do," Woodmore said stiffly. "I am going to get those two guards back in here before anything *else* gets stolen!"

"Now just a goddamn minute!" snapped Raider.

"Then I am going to find a couple of federal marshals to haul you two bastards off to jail!"

Raider went for him. Doc held him back. Woodmore stomped out of his office and slammed the door behind him.

"Shit," said Raider. "They're going to lock our asses up again, you know that, don't you?"

"Nobody's going to lock us up," said Weatherbee. "Not yet, anyway. Rade, how do you feel about a long boat trip?"

Raider stared. "What the hell are you talkin' about? I ain't going on no *boat* trip."

"Fine," Doc said wearily. "I'll take off after Willis and the twins. *You* go back to Chicago and tell Allan Pinkerton and Wagner how we lost two or three million bucks to a couple of nineteen-year-old girls."

Raider looked pained. "Aw, shit. Which way's the fuckin' dock?"

J.D. HARDIN

"THE MOST EXCITING
WESTERN WRITER SINCE
LOUIS L'AMOUR"

—JAKE LOGAN

___ 16840	BLOOD, SWEAT AND GOLD	$1.95
___ 16842	BLOODY SANDS	$1.95
___ 16882	BULLETS, BUZZARDS, BOXES OF PINE	$1.95
___ 16843	FACE DOWN IN A COFFIN	$1.95
___ 16844	THE GOOD, THE BAD, AND THE DEADLY	$1.95
___ 16799	HARD CHAINS, SOFT WOMEN	$1.95
___ 16881	THE MAN WHO BIT SNAKES	$1.95
___ 16861	RAIDER'S GOLD	$1.95
___ 16883	RAIDER'S HELL	$1.95
___ 16767	RAIDER'S REVENGE	$1.95
___ 16555	THE SLICK AND THE DEAD	$1.50
___ 16869	THE SPIRIT AND THE FLESH	$1.95

Myra Street

MYRA STREET was born in Scotland and trained at the Glasgow College of Domestic Science and at Atholl Crescent in Edinburgh. After qualifying, she moved to London to start her career as a demonstrator for a food manufacturer. Eighteen months abroad provided the opportunity to gain experience of continental food habits. She then moved into the editorial world as Cookery Editor to The Hamlyn Group. Although she is now teaching Home Economics at Harrow College, she still finds time to write cookery books as well as a regular monthly feature in *Homes and Gardens*.

Mixer and Blender Cookbook

Myra Street

Hamlyn Paperbacks

First published 1972 by
The Hamlyn Publishing Group Ltd.
Hamlyn Paperbacks edition 1978
Second printing 1979

Copyright © 1972 by
The Hamlyn Publishing Group Ltd.

ISBN 0 600 36314 7

Hamlyn Paperbacks are published by
The Hamlyn Publishing Group Ltd.
Astronaut House, Hounslow Road,
Feltham, Middlesex TW14 9AR

Made and printed in Great Britain by
Hazell Watson & Viney Ltd, Aylesbury, Bucks

Cover photography by Robert Golden
Line drawings by Elaine Hill

Contents

Useful Facts and Figures

Notes on metrication

In this book quantities are given in metric and Imperial measures. Exact conversion from Imperial to metric measures does not usually give very convenient working quantities and so the metric measures have been rounded off into units of 25 grams. This table below shows the recommended equivalents.

Ounces	Approx g to nearest whole figure	Recommended conversion to nearest unit of 25
1	28	25
2	57	50
3	85	75
4	113	100
5	142	150
6	170	175
7	198	200
8	227	225
9	255	250
10	283	275
11	312	300
12	340	350
13	368	375
14	396	400
15	425	425
16 (1 lb)	454	450
17	482	475
18	510	500
19	539	550
20 (1¼ lb)	567	575

Note When converting quantities over 20 oz first add the appropriate figures in the centre column, then adjust to the nearest unit of 25. As a general guide, 1 kg (1000 g) equals 2·2 lb or about 2 lb 3 oz. This method of conversion gives good results in nearly all cases, although in certain pastry and cake recipes a more accurate conversion is necessary to produce a balanced recipe.

Liquid measures The millilitre has been used in this book and the following table gives a few examples.

Imperial	Approx ml to nearest whole figure	Recommended ml
$\frac{1}{4}$ pint	142	150 ml
$\frac{1}{2}$ pint	283	300 ml
$\frac{3}{4}$ pint	425	450 ml
1 pint	567	600 ml
$1\frac{1}{2}$ pints	851	900 ml
$1\frac{3}{4}$ pints	992	1000 ml (1 litre)

Spoon measures All spoon measures given in this book are level unless otherwise stated.

Can sizes At present, cans are marked with the exact (usually to the nearest whole number) metric equivalent of the Imperial weight of the contents, so we have followed this practice when giving can sizes.

Oven temperatures

The table below gives recommended equivalents.

	°C	°F	Gas Mark
Very cool	110	225	$\frac{1}{4}$
	120	250	$\frac{1}{2}$
Cool	140	275	1
	150	300	2
Moderate	160	325	3
	180	350	4
Moderately hot	190	375	5
	200	400	6
Hot	220	425	7
	230	450	8
Very hot	240	475	9

Notes for American and Australian users

In America the 8-oz measuring cup is used. In Australia metric measures are now used in conjunction with the standard 250-ml measuring cup. The Imperial pint, used in Britain and Australia, is 20 fl oz, while the American pint is 16 fl oz. It is important to remember that the Australian tablespoon differs from both the British and American tablespoons; the table below gives a comparison. The British standard tablespoon, which has been used through this book, holds 17·7 ml, the American 14·2 ml, and the Australian 20 ml. A teaspoon holds approximately 5 ml in all three countries.

British	American	Australian
1 teaspoon	1 teaspoon	1 teaspoon
1 tablespoon	1 tablespoon	1 tablespoon
2 tablespoons	3 tablespoons	2 tablespoons
3½ tablespoons	4 tablespoons	3 tablespoons
4 tablespoons	5 tablespoons	3½ tablespoons

An Imperial/American guide to solid and liquid measures

Solid measures

IMPERIAL	AMERICAN
1 lb butter or margarine	2 cups
1 lb flour	4 cups
1 lb granulated or castor sugar	2 cups
1 lb icing sugar	3 cups
8 oz rice	1 cup

Liquid measures

IMPERIAL	AMERICAN
¼ pint liquid	⅔ cup liquid
½ pint	1¼ cups
¾ pint	2 cups
1 pint	2½ cups
1½ pints	3¾ cups
2 pints	5 cups (2½ pints)

Note **When making any of the recipes in this book, only follow one set of measures as they are not interchangeable.**

American terms

The list below gives some American equivalents or substitutes for terms and ingredients used in this book.

British	American
baked/unbaked pastry case	baked/unbaked pie shell
baking tin	baking pan
cocktail stick	wooden toothpick
cake mixture	batter
deep cake tin	spring form pan
frying pan	skillet
greaseproof paper	waxed paper
grill	broil/broiler
kitchen paper	paper towels
mixer/liquidiser	mixer/blender
muslin	cheesecloth
pastry cutters	cookie cutters
patty tins	muffin pans/cups
piping bag	pastry bag
pudding basin	pudding mold/ovenproof bowl
sandwich tin	layer cake pan
stoned	pitted
Swiss roll tin	jelly roll pan
whisk	whip/beat

Introduction

Mixers and blenders have come to stay. These invaluable aids fulfill a very definite need for today's busy housewife. Perhaps you own a mixer and blender and feel a little guilty at the thought that it spends too much time in a cupboard, gathering dust and taking up precious space. This book will show you how to make the fullest possible use of two very useful pieces of equipment which are not luxuries but essential requirements for the modern kitchen.

A blender is an incredibly versatile machine, a secret weapon in the kitchen which no cook can really afford to be without – particularly anyone who wants to cook with a minimum of effort. When using a blender you may have to bend some of the basic rules of cookery – yet this adds interest to the whole culinary art.

I have friends who say that nothing would induce them to use the blender for making mayonnaise mainly because they enjoy standing in the kitchen with an oil dripper, stirring in the sauce. A soothing and satisfying occupation, agreed. But with a blender you can save yourself ten minutes in which to sit down and relax – even more soothing and satisfying to the working hostess.

The blender is marvellous for giving you a variety of gourmet dishes at the flick of a switch – pâtés, pâté terrines, sauces, stuffings, and sweets – which would take so much longer using conventional methods.

If you use your mixer and blender in conjunction with other labour-saving equipment, time which would otherwise be spent in shopping or in the kitchen can be spent with the family. Remember to plan ahead. Several dishes can be cooked overnight in the automatic oven to save you long cooking sessions for several days. ❄ Again, if you have a home freezer, you can use your blender to take a lot of the effort out of cooking food in large quantities.

The blender can also help you save on food bills. All those odd little pieces that you hoard in plastic boxes can be made into sandwich fillings; leftover vegetables can be made into quick soups. Commercial convenience foods can be duplicated in your own kitchen – particularly those for babies and toddlers.

All in all, how did you ever live without your mixer and blender?

Expensively? With these useful kitchen aids cookery becomes less arduous and as a bonus you may even find yourself saving money.

Myrna Street

The star symbol ✳ throughout the text is used to indicate a hint on freezing for freezer owners, and helps to identify quickly recipes which freeze well.

Mixers

There are many types of mixer available to the housewife today and each type can be ideal for different family needs.

Before choosing a mixer it is wise to consider the growth or declining size of the family, the amount of use the machine will have, and the reason for the purchase. Many people buy mixers only to save time and effort with cooking whereas others want them to extend the range of their meals as well as saving work. Although any type of mixer is a great help in the kitchen it is obviously useful for the woman with several children to have a large machine with a stand to enable larger quantities to be made up at one time. A small hand mixer is ideal for cooking for one or two although many people prefer them to the larger stand models because it is possible to use them for beating and mixing in any bowl or pan. Small mixers can be used by holding in the hand or, for most models, a stand may be purchased.

Many people buy the mixer first and then return for the stand and some of the extras which are available. Several small models have extras such as slicers, shredders, coffee mills, and juice extractors as well as stands and bowls. Before buying a hand mixer do try to have a demonstration and see if it feels comfortable to use.

Before buying a table model, make sure you can find a permanent home on a stable surface. This piece of machinery is too heavy to heave in and out of a cupboard. People who keep mixers tucked away in a cupboard seldom use them for this reason.

Once you have decided on buying a mixer, make up your mind that it's going to earn its living. It is essential to have a demonstration before you buy. Then you can see how the machine is assembled, how it is used, and how the beaters are removed. This is most important as some manufacturers have not yet learned how to explain themselves to people like me who do not have a mind for things mechanical. Don't be like a friend of mine who confessed that she had to slip a bowl full of soapy water under the beaters to wash them as she couldn't work out how to remove them!

Your choice of machine will be a matter of personal preference and needs. But there are several golden rules to remember when buying a mixer which apply to both large and small.

1 Buy a machine which is adequate for the amount of use it will have. A cheaper, lighter one is not always a bargain if you intend to use it for heavy beating.

2 Make sure that it is easy to clean. Machines with blenders attached sometimes have bases which do not unscrew and it makes cleaning difficult if any food catches round the blades.

3 Read the manual supplied with the machine and follow the manufacturer's instructions if you want to obtain the best results and prolong the life of the machine. Most mixers and blenders need very little servicing.

4 Make sure any attachment which can be bought with your machine is really worth the space in the kitchen cupboard.

5 Read the recipe leaflet supplied with your mixer and use the correct speeds for similar recipes.

Attachments

The following attachments are available with many mixers.

Can opener I really could not be bothered to fix a can opener onto my mixer for the occasional can but a friend of mine finds it well worth while for opening the cans of dog and cat food which her menagerie of pets consume.

Shredder This is useful for soups and vegetables but I find my blender is much easier to use for crumbs, nuts, and coarsely chopping vegetables.

Coffee grinder If you grind your own coffee, you could use a blender. But the strong flavour of the coffee often lingers on. So it's best to use a coffee grinder.

Juice extractor Marvellous for health food addicts who want vegetable and fruit juices. I think it's a bother washing it afterwards unless you're going to extract pints at a time.

Mincer Thoroughly recommended to those who hang on to left-overs. With the mincer you can transform left-over meat and vegetables into delicious savouries. ❋ If you own a home freezer the mincer is invaluable for making fresh hamburgers out of stewing meat. A hamburger tastes all the better for being freshly ground.

Sausage fillers can also be bought with the mincer. So if you can get hold of sausage skins, you're all set for homemade sausage production. Personally, I'm prepared to leave this pursuit to people who wistfully hark back to the days when sausages really had a taste!

Bean slicer and pea huller Very useful if you have a large garden planted out with lots of beans and peas – especially if you want to prepare them for the freezer.

Dough hook Essential if you are baking with yeast. It takes care of all the heavy kneading.

Cleaning mixers and attachments

Keep your mixer clean by washing over with a damp cloth and then drying with a clean towel. Removable parts may be washed in warm soapy water and then rinsed in cold water. Do not use scouring powders on the metal parts.

Wash attachments as soon as possible after use to avoid staining from vegetables and fruit juices.

Do not dry parts in direct heat as plastic parts may warp.

DO NOT PUT ELECTRICAL PARTS IN WATER.

Hints for using the mixer

Creaming fat and sugar for cakes Lowest speed should be used to begin with, then increase the speed to about one fifth of the maximum speed of the machine, i.e., if your machine has 10 speeds continue on number 2.

Beating in the eggs At the same speed beat in the eggs one at a time.

Adding flour and fruit At this stage I feel that it is time for the mixer to give way to the human touch. I think it is safer to fold in your flour with a sharp edged metal spoon rather than take the risk of overbeating. However, if you are braver than I am you can reduce your speed to minimum and tip in all the flour. Switch on for a second, switch off and add fruit, again switch on only for a second.

Rubbing in fat to flour for cakes, scones, and pastry Cut the fat into the flour roughly and use minimum speed until fat is rubbed in to the fine breadcrumb stage. Beware of leaving your machine on at this stage as it will form a dough without liquid if allowed to go past the fine breadcrumb stage.

Beating egg whites for meringues Maximum speed is used until egg whites are stiff and fluffy.

Blenders

The blender is an extremely versatile piece of equipment which opens up new avenues to the ambitious cook. Dishes which take hours of preparation without a blender suddenly come within range. Here are a few points to consider before making your purchase.

1 A small blender, though useful for most grinding and chopping tasks, will only take a small amount of mixture at a time. Do not run beyond the time recommended by the manufacturers. You'll need to be patient and work with small quantities when making soups, stuffings, and sweets.

2 Whichever blender you choose, make sure it is easy to clean. Some won't unscrew, making it difficult to clean properly underneath the blades.

3 Find out the capacity of the goblet. If you fill it too full, you're liable to have your kitchen sprayed!

Cleaning the blender

Half fill with hot water and a drop of washing up liquid. Turn on to maximum speed for a few seconds. Empty the goblet and rinse. Use the same rules as you would for washing dishes. Rinse the blender first with cold water if it has been used for meat or egg mixtures which tend to turn solid in contact with hot water.

Hints for using the blender

With a well-stocked basic store cupboard it is amazing how you can make your own ingredients for cooking. In this direction, I am always finding new uses for my blender and getting out of a tricky spot when the shops are closed. Here are some of them.

Making castor sugar or icing sugar from granulated Put the granulated sugar into the goblet, not too much at a time, and run for a few seconds: until finely powdered for the castor sugar; until a dust for icing sugar.

Grating cheese Pop cubes of hard cheese into the blender a few at a time and grate until fine, using a medium speed (about 4). For this I usually wait until I have a few end pieces of cheese which are at the mousetrap stage. I then have a short grating session which keeps me going for sandwich spreads and sprinkling on top of finished dishes, like spaghetti and cauliflower. Store the grated cheese in an airtight plastic box in the fridge.

Chopping nuts Chop them finely or coarsely as the recipe demands, by popping in about 50 g/2 oz at a time, using a medium speed. You can also make ground almonds from whole ones.

Making fresh breadcrumbs Done in a trice! This banishes one of the most time-consuming operations in the kitchen without a blender. You can make as much as you like without effort for coatings and stuffings.

Make rice into flour Handy since rice flour is difficult to find in grocers. I like to use it in shortbread.

Grinding biscuits and cornflakes For flan cases, toppings, etc.

Making mayonnaise Use all the ingredients at room temperature and mayonnaise is yours in just a few seconds.

Making endless variety of salad dressings Only beware of leaving the machine on too long or the oil will emulsify.

Rescuing sauces with lumps You're saved with the flick of a switch!

Chopping herbs Wash and drain well before you start. ❀ I chop enough to store in the fridge or freezer in small plastic boxes and do enough herbs to last through the winter. You may need to add a little water to the herbs when chopping. Remember to drain well afterwards.

Sieving flour Literally in a second.

Grating citrus rinds Without grating your finger nails!

Making candied peel Feed through pieces about 2·5 cm/1 inch long and do 100 g/4 oz at a time in a large goblet.

Rubbing fat into flour Use for pastry and store in a plastic bag or jar in the fridge until needed.

Appetisers and Soups

Appetisers

There's quite a fashion these days for economical and informal entertaining, using dips, fondues, and pâtés served up with delicious crusty bread.

The dips are often served as a first course to a meal or with the drinks as the guests arrive. I find the latter an ideal arrangement when one is short of time. It also solves the problem of those hungry guests who arrive directly from work, having missed lunch, and who would otherwise fade away waiting for the main meal.

❋ Most appetisers and starters can be made well in advance and stored in the refrigerator or freezer until needed; both can then be garnished just before serving.

SALMON AND CUCUMBER DIP

METRIC/IMPERIAL

1 (198-g/7-oz) can salmon
50 g/2 oz cucumber
1 teaspoon lemon juice
1 tablespoon tomato purée
salt

freshly ground black pepper
150 ml/¼ pint double cream
To garnish
slices cucumber

Remove the bone and skin from the salmon and blend the flesh with the cucumber, lemon juice, tomato purée, and seasoning. When smooth add the whisked cream and fold in carefully. Turn into a bowl and decorate the edge with cucumber slices cut into quarters. Serve with crisp biscuits.

CHEESE AND PINEAPPLE DIP

METRIC/IMPERIAL

1 (340-g/12-oz) can pineapple
  pieces
450 g/1 lb cottage cheese

salt and pepper
2 tablespoons chopped chives

Drain the pineapple. Blend the fruit at low speed, then add the cottage cheese and continue to blend for a few seconds. Season and add the chives. Turn into a bowl and decorate with a few pieces of pineapple. Serve with small crisp biscuits.

ANCHOVY DIP

METRIC/IMPERIAL

1 (56-g/2-oz) can anchovies
juice of 1 lemon
8 tablespoons mayonnaise
  (see page 36)
6 tablespoons double cream

¼ small onion
several sprigs parsley
100 g/4 oz cream cheese
salt and pepper

Blend the anchovies with the lemon juice and add the mayonnaise, cream, onion, and parsley. Stop for a second and make sure all the ingredients are blended by pushing them round with a spatula. Switch on at medium speed and add the cheese in small amounts. Blend until smooth. Serve with crisps or small biscuits.

TUNA DIP

METRIC/IMPERIAL

6 tablespoons mayonnaise
  (see page 36)
1 (198-g/7-oz) can tuna
dash Tabasco sauce

1 tablespoon lemon juice
salt
freshly ground black pepper
2 tablespoons green olives

Make the mayonnaise as directed on page 36. Blend the tuna with the mayonnaise until smooth. Flavour with Tabasco sauce, lemon juice, and seasoning. Slice the olives and fold into the tuna mixture. Serve in a bowl, with crisps and biscuits.

AVOCADO DIP

METRIC/IMPERIAL

3 avocado pears
150 ml/5 fl oz soured cream
salt and pepper
few drops Tabasco sauce

juice of ½ lemon
1 (91-g/3¼-oz) can shrimps
To garnish
shrimps

Halve the avocado pears lengthwise, remove the stones, and scoop the flesh from the skin carefully. Put the flesh into the blender. Retain the skins if you wish to serve the dip in these. Add the cream, seasoning, Tabasco, and lemon juice. Put the top on the blender and blend at high speed until smooth. Add the drained can of shrimps and blend on low speed until the shrimps are chopped, but not pulverised, unless you prefer a completely smooth dip. I like to leave small pieces of shrimp throughout the mixture. Serve in a bowl, or pile back into the avocado skins, with the usual small biscuits. Decorate with whole shrimps if the dip is a party piece.

Variation

Use 6 tablespoons mayonnaise (see page 36) in place of the soured cream. For extra flavour ½ teaspoon curry powder can be added to the mixture.

SHRIMP DIP

METRIC/IMPERIAL

225 g/8 oz peeled shrimps
pinch cayenne pepper
2 tablespoons lemon juice
150 ml/5 fl oz soured cream

½ cucumber
salt and pepper
To garnish
shrimps

Sprinkle the shrimps with the cayenne pepper and lemon juice and allow to stand for at least half an hour. Put the cream and the peeled and cubed cucumber into the blender and blend at high speed for a few seconds, until smooth. Add the shrimps and blend until smooth, season to taste. Garnish with whole shrimps and a sprinkling of cayenne pepper. Serve with small crisp biscuits.

TOMATO AND EGG DIP

METRIC/IMPERIAL

6 tomatoes

6 hard-boiled eggs

10 tablespoons mayonnaise
  (see page 36)

1 teaspoon Worcestershire sauce

salt and pepper

Dip the tomatoes in boiling water, skin them, then blend the peeled tomatoes with the shelled hard-boiled eggs, mayonnaise, and seasoning. Serve in a small bowl. For extra flavour add ½ teaspoon curry powder to the mixture.

Variation

Cut the eggs in half lengthwise. Blend the yolks with the other ingredients and pile or pipe the mixture back into the egg whites.

CHEESY CHARLIES

Serves 4

METRIC/IMPERIAL

50 g/2 oz suet

300 ml/½ pint water

50 g/2 oz plain flour

2 eggs

50 g/2 oz cheese

salt and cayenne pepper

pinch dry mustard

Melt the suet in a saucepan. Add the water and bring to the boil. Add the flour and beat thoroughly with a hand mixer until the mixture forms a ball and leaves the side of the pan clean. Remove from the heat, cool slightly, and gradually beat in the eggs. Grate the cheese in the blender; beat in the seasoning and cheese. Drop teaspoonfuls of the mixture into hot oil or fat and deep fry until golden brown. Drain on absorbent paper and serve hot. Serve on sticks with drinks.

Variation

Substitute 50 g/2 oz chopped prawns for the cheese.

MOROCCAN STARTER

Serves 6

METRIC/IMPERIAL

150 ml/¼ pint olive oil
3 tomatoes
2–3 aubergines
4–6 courgettes

½ small leek
few sprigs parsley
½ teaspoon cumin
½ teaspoon cayenne pepper

Heat the oil in a heavy frying pan. Cut the tomatoes, aubergines, courgettes, and leek into 1-cm/½-inch slices. Cook the vegetables in the oil, a few at a time, until they are tender. As they are cooked transfer to the blender and add the parsley and spices. Add a little of the cooking oil and blend on a medium speed. Do this in several batches and when all the mixture is blended return it to the pan with a little more oil and allow to cook until the oil is absorbed. Cut into portions, serve hot or cold. This starter can also be served as part of an hors d'œuvre.

TARAMASALATA

Serves 4

To make this recipe without a blender all the ingredients have to be chopped and then ground with a pestle and mortar. Using a blender, a time-consuming but delicious recipe becomes as simple to make as a sandwich filling! ❀ This mixture freezes well.

METRIC/IMPERIAL

1 medium-sized boiled potato
1 clove garlic (optional)
225 g/8 oz smoked cod's roe
juice of 1 lemon

few sprigs chopped parsley
2 tablespoons olive oil
To garnish
lemon wedges or black olives

Put the potato in the blender with the clove of garlic and switch on for a second. Add the cod's roe, lemon juice, and parsley and blend together. The mixture can now be treated rather like mayonnaise. Switch the blender on at a low speed. Add the oil drop by drop until the mixture is creamy. If the mixture becomes oily add a little more lemon juice. Serve as a first course with hot buttered toast.

SAUSAGE SAVOURIES

Makes 30

METRIC/IMPERIAL

2 slices bread
few sprigs parsley
450 g/1 lb sausagemeat
1 teaspoon Worcestershire sauce
1 tablespoon tomato ketchup

salt and pepper

To coat

1 egg
fresh white breadcrumbs

Break the bread into small pieces and drop into the blender. Switch on for a few seconds until fine breadcrumbs are formed. Remove onto a plate then chop the parsley in the blender. Mix the sausagemeat, chopped parsley, sauces, seasonings, and crumbs in a bowl. Break the egg and beat lightly. With lightly floured hands form the sausage mixture into small balls. Dip in the egg then into the crumbs. Fry in hot oil until golden brown. Serve on cocktail sticks with a tomato (see page 41) or mustard sauce.

KIPPER STARTER

Serves 4

METRIC/IMPERIAL

225 g/8 oz kipper fillets
juice of 1 lemon
2 tablespoons double cream
salt and pepper

50 g/2 oz butter

To garnish

chopped parsley
lemon wedges

Remove the skins from the kippers (or use canned fillets) and put the flesh into the blender; switch on at medium speed. Add the lemon juice and blend until smooth; add the cream and seasoning and blend for a few seconds. Remove the mixture to a mixing bowl and beat together with the softened butter, using a hand mixer or a wooden spoon, until the mixture is really creamy. ❋ Because of the extra washing up involved in mixing this I always make up at least three quantities of this recipe and freeze two as this recipe freezes well. Serve with hot buttered toast.

PRAWN AND CRAB COCKTAIL

Serves 4

METRIC/IMPERIAL

mayonnaise (see page 36)
2 teaspoons tomato purée
few drops Tabasco sauce
1 tablespoon whipped cream
few drops brandy (optional)
100 g/4 oz prawns, shelled and
  deveined

50 g/2 oz crabmeat

To garnish
crisp green lettuce
lemon twist
whole prawns

Combine the mayonnaise with the tomato purée, Tabasco, whipped cream, and brandy. Stir in the prawns and crabmeat. Tear the lettuce into strips and line the bottom of the glasses. Carefully spoon in the shellfish mixture and garnish each glass with a twist of lemon and a whole prawn in its shell if possible. A little chopped parsley may also be sprinkled over the top. Chill before serving but please do not make up the cocktails too far in advance otherwise the lettuce will be soggy and the whole effect will be spoiled.

Glass sweet dishes can be used but as they tend to be on the large side, most people serve this starter in ordinary wine glasses.

Pâtés and terrines

Pâtés and terrines, served with thin toast or French bread, make delicious meal starters. The number of servings given here are for serving as a starter. If you want to serve a pâté as a light luncheon dish, or for a picnic in summer, you should allow twice the quantity to serve the same number of people.

✼ Pâtés freeze very well so several quantities may be made at once and the extra frozen. However, a better result is obtained if they are packed for the freezer in small portions rather than whole.

BACON AND LIVER PÂTÉ

Oven temperature
Pâté Moderate 180°C, 350°F, Gas Mark 4
Pastry Hot 220°C, 425°F, Gas Mark 7
Serves 6

METRIC/IMPERIAL

350 g/12 oz streaky bacon	100 g/4 oz chicken livers
1 onion	½ teaspoon pepper
1 tablespoon flour	1 teaspoon nutmeg
2 tablespoons milk	½ teaspoon salt
1 egg	200 g/7 oz puff pastry
2 tablespoons sherry	beaten egg

Remove the rind and gristle from the bacon. Set aside six rashers and cut the rest into small pieces. Put the onion, cut into eight pieces, into the goblet with the flour, milk, egg, and sherry. Run the blender on medium speed until the mixture is almost smooth. Add the chicken livers, chopped bacon, and seasoning gradually and blend until a smooth mixture is obtained. Line a 0·5-kg/1-lb loaf tin with the reserved bacon rashers. Pour the mixture into the tin and bake in a moderate oven for 40 minutes. Allow to cool for at least 10 minutes and then turn out of the tin. Brush over with beaten egg. Roll out the puff pastry thinly in an oblong shape which will accommodate the loaf shaped mixture. Enclose the bacon and liver terrine in the pastry and seal the edges with beaten egg. Cut several slits across the top of the pastry to allow the steam to escape and decorate with rolled out pastry trimmings in the shape of leaves. Brush over with beaten egg and bake in a hot oven until golden brown.

TERRINE OF CHICKEN LIVERS

Oven temperature Moderate 170°C, 325°F, Gas Mark 3
Cooking time 2 hours
Serves 6–8

METRIC/IMPERIAL

50 g/2 oz butter
1 large onion
1 small clove garlic
450 g/1 lb chicken livers
4 tablespoons chicken stock

salt and pepper
2 eggs
4 tablespoons dry sherry
150 ml/¼ pint double cream
12–14 rashers streaky bacon

Melt the butter in a frying pan and gently cook the roughly chopped onion, garlic, and chicken livers for a few minutes. Put into the blender with the stock, seasoning, eggs, and sherry. Blend at maximum speed until the mixture is smooth. Add the cream and blend for a few seconds. Line the bottom of an earthenware terrine or ovenproof dish with streaky bacon, allowing the ends to overlap the dish. Pour in the mixture, cover with the overlapping ends of bacon and cook for about 2 hours in a moderate oven in a bain-marie, or water bath. When cooked, allow to cool, chill then serve in the dish or turned out onto a serving dish.

COUNTRY PÂTÉ

Cooking time 1½ hours
Oven temperature Cool 150°C, 300°F, Gas Mark 2
Serves 8

METRIC/IMPERIAL

225 g/8 oz pig's liver
100 g/4 oz chicken livers
4 tablespoons white wine
1 clove garlic
1 egg
4 tablespoons double cream

salt and freshly ground black
  pepper
225 g/8 oz belly of pork
2 bay leaves
8 rashers streaky bacon

Cut the pig's liver into small pieces and put into the blender a little at a time with the chicken livers, wine, garlic, egg, cream, and seasoning. Mince the pork or cut it into small pieces and add to the mixture. Put into an earthenware bowl. Place the bay leaves on top and cover with the bacon. Cook uncovered in a cool oven, in a pan of water as directed in the preceding recipe, until the pâté comes away from the sides of the bowl. Serve with French bread or toast.

Note If you do not have a pâté dish or terrine improvise with a pyrex bowl or a 0·5-1-kg/1-2 lb loaf tin. This pâté improves with keeping.

SMOKED CHICKEN PÂTÉ

Serves 6

METRIC/IMPERIAL

225/8 oz smoked chicken	150 ml/¼ pint soured cream
rind of ½ lemon	50 g/2 oz butter
juice of 1 lemon	150 ml/¼ pint aspic jelly (optional)
1 tablespoon parsley	*To garnish*
salt	sprigs watercress
freshly milled black pepper	

Cut the smoked chicken into small pieces and put them into the blender. Switch on and run until the chicken is chopped. Peel the rind thinly from the lemon, add to the chicken with the juice, parsley, seasoning, and cream. Turn on at medium speed and add the butter gradually until a creamy mixture is obtained. Using a spatula put the mixture into six small ramekin dishes or one larger dish or bowl. If desired make up the aspic and spoon over the pâté just before the aspic is about to set.

Chill before serving and garnish with crisp watercress. Serve with toast or French bread.

Fondue

Serving fondues with wine at parties is now very popular as it is a fairly economical way of entertaining. It also adds to the fun for everyone to help themselves. Many people are given fondue sets as gifts and I always think it is sad that many are only used as ornaments. Cheese fondue is delicious and easy to make; on page 58 you will see how to use the fondue set for beef.

Safety rules for fondue parties Do be careful with the little spirit burners which are supplied with the sets. Take care to place the fondue in a safe place so that people wielding their forks will not be likely to have accidents. A non-inflammable surface should be used as a base for the fondue stand, e.g., Formica. Don't put piles of paper napkins next to it. Please forgive my caution but it is so easy to overlook these small details in the enthusiasm of using your new fondue set.

SWISS FONDUE

METRIC/IMPERIAL

450 g/1 lb Emmenthal cheese
225 g/8 oz Gruyère cheese
300 ml/½ pint dry white wine
1 clove garlic
2 teaspoons salt

freshly grated nutmeg
pinch cayenne pepper
2–3 tablespoons Kirsch
several French loaves

Cut the cheese into 1-cm/½-inch cubes. Heat the wine slowly in a saucepan but do not allow it to boil. Pour into the goblet and add the clove of garlic and a few cheese cubes. Turn on at a low speed. Add the remainder of the cheese gradually. Blend until smooth, stopping to make sure all the cheese has been pushed towards the blades. Pour into a fondue pot or heavy saucepan and stir over the spirit burner of the fondue set or a low heat on the cooker until thick. Season and stir in the Kirsch. Cut the French bread into cubes. Using long forks dip the chunks of French bread into the fondue and eat as soon as it is cool enough.

Soups

Home-made soup is ideal for growing families. It helps to satisfy
enormous appetites without stretching the family budget too much.
The blender takes all the hard work out of making soups. Vegetables,
meat, and chicken which sometimes accumulate in the refrigerator
can be used by popping them in the blender and adding the purée to
stock and milk.

Use the blender to add extra vegetables for flavour and quantity to
canned and packet soups.

❀ Time and effort can be saved by making larger quantities and
storing them in the refrigerator or home freezer. I have found some
foil bags for sale in my local freezer shop which are ideal for storing
soup.

For parties serve croûtons with your soups. Make these by deep
frying diced or small triangles of bread until golden and crisp.

AVOCADO SOUP

Serves 4

METRIC/IMPERIAL

1 large ripe avocado	300 ml/½ pint chicken stock
1 clove garlic	salt and pepper
300 ml/½ pint milk	150 ml/¼ pint soured cream

Peel the avocado, cut in half, and remove the stone. Cut the flesh into
four pieces and put into the blender goblet with the garlic, milk,
chicken stock, and seasoning. Blend at maximum speed until smooth.
Pour into a saucepan and heat, but do not boil. Stir in the soured
cream just before serving. This is delicious served chilled with a
garnish of sliced avocado.

❀ To freeze this soup, omit the cream and add just before reheating.

VEGETABLE SOUP

Serves 4

METRIC/IMPERIAL

1 small onion
600 ml/1 pint chicken or beef stock
1 carrot
1 turnip

1 stalk celery
3 sprigs parsley
150 ml/¼ pint single cream
salt and pepper

Put the peeled and roughly chopped onion in the blender with about 150 ml/¼ pint of the stock. Cover and blend for a few seconds. Gradually add the remaining vegetables, chopped, through the top, covering the hole before the machine is switched on. Put the puréed vegetables with the remaining stock into a saucepan and cook for 10–15 minutes. Pour the cream into the mixture before serving. This soup can also be served cold without any cooking.

Variation

Lentil soup Sauté all the roughly chopped vegetables in 40 g/1½ oz butter. Add 50 g/2 oz washed lentils and the stock and simmer for 30 minutes. Put the soup into the blender about 450 ml/¾ pint at one time. Reheat and serve. Stir in the cream before serving for cream of lentil soup.

SPINACH SOUP

Serves 6

METRIC/IMPERIAL

450 g/1 lb fresh spinach
outer leaves of a lettuce
3 spring onions
3 good sprigs parsley
1 teaspoon chives

50 g/2 oz butter
salt and pepper
½ teaspoon tarragon
900 ml/1½ pints stock
150 ml/¼ pint single cream

Put the first five ingredients in the blender. Cover the vegetables with water, cover, and run on high speed until vegetables are finely chopped. Drain through a sieve. Melt the butter in a large saucepan, add sieved vegetables and seasoning, and sauté for a few minutes. Add the stock and cook for 15–20 minutes. Stir in the cream before serving.

POTATO AND LEEK SOUP

Serves 4

METRIC/IMPERIAL

450 g/1 lb potatoes
2 onions
50 g/2 oz butter
generous litre/2 pints stock
1 teaspoon chervil

salt and pepper
225/½ lb leeks
150 ml/¼ pint soured cream
To garnish
chopped spring onions

Peel the potatoes and cut into rough slices. Chop the onions roughly, melt the butter in the soup pot, and sauté the potatoes with the onions for a few minutes. Add the stock, seasonings, and leeks and simmer until the potatoes are tender. Allow to cool slightly, mix with the soured cream, and put the soup through the blender at maximum speed. Serve hot or cold garnished with the finely chopped green spring onion tops.

Variation

Vichyssoise Substitute 600 ml/1 pint milk for 600 ml/1 pint stock in the recipe and use double cream in place of soured cream. After the mixture is blended without the cream, return to the saucepan and simmer for 20 minutes, add the cream, and serve well chilled, garnished with chopped chives.

LETTUCE SOUP

Serves 6

METRIC/IMPERIAL

450 g/1 lb potatoes
600 ml/1 pint stock
salt and pepper
1 large lettuce

600 ml/1 pint milk
2 teaspoons chervil
40 g/1½ oz butter
4 tablespoons single cream

Peel the potatoes and cut into medium-sized pieces. Cook in the stock with the seasoning until soft. Meanwhile wash the lettuce and remove the thick stems. Tear the leaves into pieces and add to the potatoes with the milk and chervil. Cook for 10 minutes, simmering gently.

Add the butter and allow to cool slightly before liquidising. Pour a little cream on top of the soup before serving. ❀ This soup freezes well but the colour darkens when it is reheated; however the flavour is excellent.

Variation

Watercress soup Substitute watercress for lettuce and garnish with fresh sprigs of watercress before serving

SMOKED FISH SOUP

Serves 6

METRIC/IMPERIAL

450 g/1 lb smoked haddock fillets 25 g/1 oz butter
2 onions   300 ml/½ pint milk
2 potatoes   salt and pepper
600 ml/1 pint water   parsley

Remove the skin from the haddock fillets, place in a pan with the roughly chopped onions and potatoes, cover with the water, and bring to the boil. Simmer gently until the vegetables are cooked; allow to cool slightly and put into the blender. Turn on at medium speed and liquidise until smooth. Heat the butter and milk in a saucepan, return the fish mixture to the milk. Season well and sprinkle with grated parsley.

BORSCHT

Serves 4

METRIC/IMPERIAL

225 g/8 oz cooked beetroot   600 ml/1 pint soured cream
½ lemon   *To garnish*
salt and pepper   beetroot diced very small
1 small onion

Put all the ingredients into the blender including the flesh of the lemon and a small strip of the peel; discard the white pith. Blend on maximum speed until smooth, serve chilled and garnished with diced cooked beetroot.

Dressings and Sauces

FRENCH DRESSING

METRIC/IMPERIAL

300 ml/½ pint oil
5 tablespoons wine vinegar
¼ teaspoon French mustard

pinch sugar
salt and pepper

Put all the ingredients into the blender and run for about 20 seconds at medium speed. Store in an airtight jar or bottle and shake up before using.

Variations

Garlic dressing Add 1 clove of garlic and 1 slice of lemon.

Herb dressing Add mixed herbs.

Parsley dressing Add 4 sprigs of parsley.

THOUSAND ISLAND DRESSING

METRIC/IMPERIAL

300 ml/½ pint mayonnaise
  (see page 36)
2 tablespoons tomato ketchup
½ small onion
1 stalk celery

3 sprigs parsley
¼ green pepper
1 slice canned red pimiento
1 hard-boiled egg

All ingredients except the hard-boiled egg should be blended at medium speed until the vegetables are chopped. Shell and quarter the egg and add it to the mixture. Blend until the egg is chopped. Serve with salads, steaks, hamburgers, and fish.

34

AVOCADO MAYONNAISE

½ avocado pear
juice of ½ lemon
6 tablespoons oil

salt and pepper
½ teaspoon sugar

Peel and roughly slice the avocado and place in the blender. Add the lemon juice and blend until smooth. Very gradually add the oil. Finally add the sugar and season to taste. Serve with tomatoes or eggs.

AIOLI

In order to make this successfully in the blender you must change the method for this famous sauce, which is so popular round the shores of the Mediterranean.

METRIC/IMPERIAL

2 cloves garlic
¼ teaspoon salt
1 egg

½ teaspoon water
300 ml/½ pint olive oil
1 teaspoon lemon juice

Put the peeled crushed garlic with the salt into the blender, add the egg, and switch on at high speed for several seconds. When the garlic is pulverised run the machine on low speed and pour in the oil in a thin stream. When the mixture thickens increase the speed slightly and add the remaining oil at a slightly faster rate. This sauce is meant to be very thick. Add the lemon juice very carefully when the sauce is removed from the blender. If it is added while the blender is running it may curdle. Serve with raw vegetables; it is also delicious with poached fish.

Variation

This can be made without egg by blending quarter of the oil with the garlic first.

MAYONNAISE

1 whole egg

salt and pepper

¼ teaspoon French mustard

2 tablespoons wine vinegar or
   lemon juice

300 ml/½ pint vegetable oil,
   preferably olive

For blender mayonnaise use the whole egg. Make sure all ingredients are at room temperature, i.e., do not use an egg which has just come out of the refrigerator. Put the egg in the goblet with salt, pepper, mustard, and 1 tablespoon vinegar, cover, and run on minimum speed. Pour in half of the oil very slowly while the machine is running Stop the motor and add the remaining vinegar or lemon juice, then switch on to maximum speed and pour in the remainder of the oil.

Note Mayonnaise can separate or curdle if the ingredients are not at room temperature or if the oil is added too quickly. However, all is not lost if this happens – simply begin again:

1 Pour the curdled mixture into a measuring jug.

2 Wash and dry the goblet thoroughly.

3 Break another egg into the blender, turn it on at minimum speed, and add the separated mixture slowly until the blades are well covered.

4 Now turn the machine up to maximum speed and add the remaining ingredients slowly. You may need a little extra oil.

Variations

Garlic mayonnaise Add 1 small clove of garlic.

Herb mayonnaise Add parsley, chives, or chervil.

Mixer mayonnaise Alternatively mayonnaise may be made with a hand mixer, using the sauce ingredients but only the *yolk* of the egg. Put the yolk of the egg into a small bowl with salt, pepper, and mustard. Turn the mixer to minimum speed and drop the oil in slowly. Add vinegar or lemon juice to taste at the end when a thick emulsion is obtained. Should the sauce curdle, start again with a completely clean dry bowl and beaters and another egg yolk. When an emulsion is formed with the egg and a little oil, add the curdled mixture as if you were adding the remaining oil.

COOKED SALAD DRESSING

2 eggs

2 egg yolks

2 teaspoons flour

4 teaspoons sugar

mustard

salt and pepper

300 ml/½ pint milk

1 teaspoon butter

4 tablespoons vinegar

Put the eggs, yolks, flour, sugar, mustard, salt, and pepper into a heavy saucepan large enough for the hand mixer to operate in. Beat on maximum speed until smooth. Put the saucepan on a low heat, reduce speed to medium, gradually add milk, and finally add the butter. Raise the heat and beat well, cooking until thick. Add the vinegar, remove from the heat and allow to cool. This sauce keeps in the refrigerator for a longer time than ordinary mayonnaise.

WHITE SAUCE

600 ml/1 pint milk

50 g/2 oz butter

50 g/2 oz flour

salt and pepper

Heat the milk and butter, then pour half into the blender. Add the flour and seasoning, switch on to maximum for a few seconds, then return to the saucepan with the other half of the milk. Cook over a low heat until thick.

Variations

Cheese sauce Add 100 g/4 oz grated cheese, a dash of mustard, and a pinch of cayenne pepper and blend with the basic sauce.

Mushroom sauce Add 100 g/4 oz mushrooms which have been sautéed in butter or blanched in boiling water.

Béchamel sauce Heat the milk slowly with an onion, a few peppercorns, and a pinch of nutmeg. Strain the milk into the blender and make as basic sauce.

HOLLANDAISE SAUCE

METRIC/IMPERIAL

225 g/8 oz butter   2 tablespoons lemon juice
1 tablespoon water   salt
1 teaspoon vinegar   freshly milled pepper
4 egg yolks

Melt the butter with the water and vinegar in a saucepan – *do not allow it to brown*. Put the egg yolks, lemon juice, and seasoning into the goblet and turn on at minimum speed. Now pour the melted butter into the goblet in a steady stream; the sauce should now be fairly thick. Serve immediately if possible. Alternatively, keep warm over a pan of warm water but stir continually as it tends to thicken at the bottom. Should you forget and allow the sauce to become thick return it to the blender and add a few drops of warm water and a few drops of lemon juice. Blend until smooth again.

    This sauce is delicious with fish and vegetables, especially asparagus.

BÉARNAISE SAUCE

METRIC/IMPERIAL

1 small onion or shallot   freshly milled black pepper
3 tablespoons white wine   few drops lemon juice
2 teaspoons tarragon vinegar   300 ml/½ pint hollandaise sauce
1 teaspoon fresh or ½ teaspoon   (see above)
  dried tarragon

Put the onion, finely chopped, in a saucepan with the wine, vinegar, tarragon, pepper, and lemon juice and allow to boil until the liquid is reduced to a few drops. Blend the mixture with the hollandaise sauce for a few seconds at maximum speed. This is delicious with chicken and meat.

BARBECUE SAUCE

METRIC/IMPERIAL

1 large onion	salt
½ green pepper	few drops Tabasco sauce
1 chilli pepper	1 tablespoon Worcestershire sauce
1 teaspoon mustard	4 tablespoons oil
2 tablespoons vinegar	4 tablespoons red wine (optional)

Chop the vegetables roughly and put all the ingredients except half of the wine in the blender until the vegetables are finely chopped. Use for basting chicken and pork. Serve the remainder heated with the remaining red wine as a sauce.

CREOLE SAUCE

METRIC/IMPERIAL

2 tablespoons oil	1 stalk celery
1 large onion	2 tablespoons vinegar
1 clove garlic	1 (198-g/7-oz) can tomatoes
1 green pepper	1 teaspoon sugar
1 chilli pepper (optional)	¼ teaspoon oregano

Heat the oil in a saucepan, add the roughly chopped onion, garlic, peppers, and celery, and allow to sauté gently for at least 5 minutes. Place the vegetables in the goblet and switch on at medium speed until the vegetables are finely chopped. Add the remaining ingredients and blend all together. Return to the saucepan and simmer for at least 10–15 minutes. Serve with shrimps, prawns, minced beef, or diced cooked meat, with rice or pasta, for an excellent savoury meal.

CURRY SAUCE

METRIC/IMPERIAL

25 g/1 oz butter	2 teaspoons curry powder
1 tablespoon oil	1 teaspoon tomato purée
1 carrot	salt
1 clove garlic	few drops lemon juice
1 small potato	300 ml/½ pint stock

Melt the butter in a saucepan, add the oil, and sauté the roughly chopped vegetables for about 5 minutes, stirring all the time. Turn up the heat and sprinkle the vegetables with curry powder; stir around the saucepan for a few seconds. Place the vegetables in the goblet and switch on at medium speed until they are liquidised. Add the tomato purée, seasoning, lemon juice, and some of the stock; switch on again for a few seconds. Return to the saucepan with the remaining stock and simmer for at least 10 minutes. Serve with fish, meat, or vegetables on a bed of rice.

TARTARE SAUCE

METRIC/IMPERIAL

8 gherkins	8 tablespoons mayonnaise
3 tablespoons capers	(see page 36)
	½ teaspoon lemon juice

Chop the gherkins and capers by putting them in the blender, switched on at maximum speed, for a few seconds. Add remaining ingredients and blend well. Serve with fried fish.

CUCUMBER SAUCE

METRIC/IMPERIAL

4 tablespoons soured cream	½ cucumber
4 tablespoons mayonnaise	½ teaspoon salt
(see page 36)	1½ tablespoons lemon juice

Mix the soured cream and the mayonnaise in a bowl. Place the other ingredients in the blender, having cut the cucumber roughly. Cover the blender and switch on until the cucumber is smooth. Add the blended cucumber gradually to the mixture in the bowl. Serve with cold fish.

PLUM SAUCE

METRIC/IMPERIAL

100 g/4 oz plum jam	pinch allspice
¼ teaspoon mixed herbs	2 teaspoons dry mustard
2 tablespoons vinegar	

Place all the ingredients in the blender and switch on at medium speed until everything is well blended. This sauce is delicious with roast pork, pork chops, or duck.

TOMATO SAUCE

METRIC/IMPERIAL

1 medium onion	salt and pepper
100 g/4 oz mushrooms (optional)	1 teaspoon sugar
1 (396-g/14-oz) can peeled	½ teaspoon oregano
tomatoes or 450 g/1 lb fresh	3 tablespoons tomato purée
tomatoes	150 ml/¼ pint red wine or stock
1 clove garlic	

Roughly chop the onion and mushrooms. Peel the tomatoes if using fresh and cut into two or three pieces. Put all the ingredients into the blender at high speed until smooth; you may have to liquidise in batches depending on the size of your machine. Simmer in a covered saucepan for 25 minutes. Use with fish, meat, pasta, or rice.

ORANGE AND CRANBERRY SAUCE

METRIC/IMPERIAL

1 orange	100 g/4 oz sugar
3 tablespoons water	225 g/8 oz cranberries

Cut the orange into about eight pieces, remove the pips, then put the sections into the blender. Add the water and sugar, cover the goblet, and switch on at a medium speed for about 10 seconds until the orange peel is coarsely cut. Add the cranberries and blend until the whole fruit begins to disappear. Do not completely pulverise the fruit. Serve raw, or simmer for 15 minutes. Chill before serving with roast poultry.

APPLE SAUCE

METRIC/IMPERIAL

2 large cooking apples	40 g/1½ oz sugar
3 tablespoons water	knob of butter
2 teaspoons lemon juice	

Wash, peel, and core the apples and cut into 2·5 cm/1-inch cubes. Put half the apple cubes with the water, lemon juice, and sugar into the blender and run on minimum speed until the apples are liquidised. Turn to high speed and add the remaining apples gradually. Melt the butter in a saucepan and add the apple sauce, cook for a few minutes, and then serve. ❀ This sauce can be kept in the freezer in small plastic jars.

MINT SAUCE

METRIC/IMPERIAL

fresh mint leaves   1 tablespoon boiling water
2 teaspoons sugar   2 tablespoons vinegar

Place all the ingredients in the blender and allow to run until the mint leaves are chopped into fairly small pieces. Allow to stand for at least half an hour before serving.

HORSERADISH SAUCE

METRIC/IMPERIAL

2 tablespoons horseradish or   1 teaspoon wine vinegar
   4 tablespoons finely grated   2 tablespoons cream
   bottled horseradish
300 ml/½ pint béchamel sauce
   (see page 37)

Chop the horseradish in the blender, add the other ingredients, and blend thoroughly. Heat through and serve with roast beef.

ORANGE BRANDY BUTTER

METRIC/IMPERIAL

50 g/2 oz butter   2 tablespoons brandy
50 g/2 oz castor sugar   rind of ¼ orange
50 g/2 oz icing sugar

Cream the butter and sugars together with the mixer until the mixture is pale and fluffy as in the first creaming stage of making a cake. Gradually add the brandy and finally the grated orange rind, mixing well. Pipe or pile into a dish and keep in a cool place until needed.

This hard sauce is delicious with Christmas pudding and mince pies. The orange rind can be omitted; or a mixture of lemon and orange rind is excellent served with a plain steamed pudding. As this sauce is rich very little is needed. ❀ If there is any left over it will keep well in the freezer.

RUM BUTTER

METRIC/IMPERIAL

100 g/4 oz butter

225 g/8 oz soft brown sugar

¼ teaspoon cinnamon

1–2 tablespoons rum

Cream the butter, sugar, and cinnamon together with the mixer until soft. Gradually add the rum and mix until the sugar and butter are well creamed. Store in small pots and serve with steamed fruit or sponge puddings. This butter sauce is also very good with mince pies.

CHOCOLATE SAUCE

METRIC/IMPERIAL

50 g/2 oz plain chocolate

50 g/2 oz sugar

150 ml/¼ pint water

1 teaspoon brandy or rum

2 tablespoons cream

Break the chocolate into pieces and chop finely in the blender. Dissolve the sugar in the water and bring to the boil, add the chocolate and stir into the syrup. Add the brandy or rum and the cream just before serving. This sauce is delicious served hot or cold with chocolate sponge pudding (see page 89) or ice cream.

LEMON SAUCE

METRIC/IMPERIAL

2 lemons

150 ml/¼ pint water

2–3 tablespoons sugar

Peel a thin rind from the lemons, put into the blender to chop finely. Put the water in a saucepan with the sugar. Squeeze the lemons and add 1 tablespoon strained juice to the sugar and water. Add the lemon rind and simmer until a thick syrup is obtained.

Variation

Substitute 2 oranges for the lemons to make orange sauce.

CUSTARD SAUCE

1 egg

2 teaspoons castor sugar

½ teaspoon vanilla essence

150 ml/¼ pint milk

Put the egg in the blender with the sugar and essence. Switch on to beat the egg. Bring the milk almost to boiling point. Strain into the blender, switch on for a few seconds. Return to the saucepan and cook very gently until the custard thickens. If any lumps appear through the sauce put back into the blender until smooth.

Fish

Fish can add so much variety to the menu that it seems a pity it is so often ignored. I think one of the reasons for this is that, for children, fish is something of an acquired taste and many mothers become tired of trying to persuade them to eat it. It is well worth persevering because fish can so often provide the answer when you are looking for variety, and some of the cheapest fish are the most nutritious.

In addition to the fish starters, dips, and sandwich fillings which can be made with the mixer and blender and are to be found in other sections, I have included the preparation of simple fish dishes, some of which can be served with a sauce from the sauce section.

With the blender, fresh or toasted breadcrumbs are readily available for coating fish, so much nicer than packaged crumbs.

Buying fresh fish

There is nothing more off-putting than fish which is not fresh. Modern methods of packing and transporting fish are excellent but sometimes we see some very tired fish in the shops. Avoid buying this as it only turns the family against what can be a most excellent meal.
1 A fish which has dull eyes and limp flesh is not fresh. The eyes should be brilliant and the flesh stiff.
2 The smell will be unpleasant when the flesh is really limp.
3 A finger mark on a fresh fish will disappear quickly; on a less fresh one it will linger.

FRIED FISH

Serves 4

METRIC/IMPERIAL

4 fillets white fish	1 egg
To coat	75 g/3 oz fresh white breadcrumbs
salt and pepper	cooking oil

Pat the fish fillets dry with a clean piece of kitchen paper, dip in the seasoned beaten egg, then dip in the crumbs. Pat crumbs into the fish firmly then dip back into the egg and again into the crumbs. This double coating gives an excellent finish to the fish. Pat the crumbs firmly onto the surface before frying. Use oil to fry the fish; there should be enough to cover the pieces of fish completely. It is advisable to store this oil separately and use again only for fish.

Allow the oil to become really hot. Test with a cube of bread if you are unsure. Put the cube into the fat and it should brown and come to the surface very quickly. Remember the fat will cool down quickly when the fish is added, so do not put too many pieces into the pan at once or the fish will be soggy. Fry until golden brown. Serve when crisp, garnished with lemon and parsley, and accompanied by tartare or tomato sauce (see pages 40 and 41).

CRISPY PLAICE CURLS

Serves 4

METRIC/IMPERIAL

225 g/8 oz long-grain rice	cooking oil
675 g/ 1½ lb plaice fillets	*To garnish*
50 g/2 oz flour	4 sprigs watercress
salt and pepper	4 lemon wedges
2 eggs	
175 g/6 oz fresh white breadcrumbs	

Cook the rice in boiling salted water (2 cups water to 1 cup rice) until the water is absorbed and the rice is dry and separate. Keep warm until the fish is cooked.

Skin the fillets or ask the fishmonger to do this when he is filleting the fish. Cut the fillets into strips. Dip the strips into the seasoned flour, shake the surplus flour away, then dip in beaten egg and breadcrumbs. Fry the strips in hot oil until crisp and golden brown. Drain well on soft kitchen paper.

Serve the fish on a bed of rice garnished with watercress and wedges of lemon. Accompany by tomato, tartare, or béarnaise sauce (see pages 41, 40, and 38).

SEA FOOD CREOLE

Serves 4

METRIC/IMPERIAL

175 g/6 oz peeled prawns
4 scallops
creole sauce (see page 39)
salt and pepper
225 g/8 oz long-grain rice

slice of lemon

To garnish

lemon wedges
parsley

Add the prawns and chopped scallops to the creole sauce and allow to simmer gently for at least 10 minutes. Season to taste. Meanwhile cook the rice in 450 ml/¾ pint boiling salted water. Add the slice of lemon to the rice while it is cooking as it adds flavour and keeps the rice white. Serve the rice in a heated serving dish, arrange the seafood down the centre of the dish, and garnish with lemon wedges and parsley sprigs.

KIPPER CAKES

Serves 4

METRIC/IMPERIAL

450 g/1 lb potatoes, peeled and
  boiled in salted water
3 tablespoons cream
25 g/1 oz butter
2 (198-g/7-oz) cans kipper fillets,
  drained, or 450 g/1 lb kipper
  fillets
2 tablespoons chopped parsley
salt

freshly ground black pepper
dash Tabasco sauce
2 tablespoons lemon juice
1 egg

To coat

flour
1 egg, beaten
dried breadcrumbs

Cream the potatoes in the mixer with the cream and butter until smooth. Blend the kipper fillets until very smooth and add to the potato with the parsley, seasoning, Tabasco sauce, and lemon juice. If using fresh kipper fillets remove the skins before blending. Beat well, then bind together with the egg. Form into croquette shapes. Flour, then dip in egg and breadcrumbs. Fry in deep fat until golden brown and crisp. Drain on kitchen paper and serve hot.

Variations

Salmon cakes Substitute 225–350 g/8–12 oz fresh or canned salmon. Salmon cakes made with the remains of a whole salmon make a most delicious breakfast dish.

Fish cakes Substitute 350 g/12 oz cod or haddock which has been poached in 150 ml/¼ pint milk. No cream is necessary. However, use the liquid in which the fish has been poached. Serve as a supper dish with tomato sauce (see page 41).

SALMON LOAF

Cooking time 45 minutes
Oven temperature Moderately hot
190°C, 375°F, Gas Mark 5
Serves 4

METRIC/IMPERIAL

75 g/3 oz fresh breadcrumbs	½ teaspoon celery salt
1 (226-g/8-oz) can salmon	2 sprigs parsley
2 eggs	pinch dried mustard
25 g/1 oz butter	pepper
1 slice onion	150 ml/¼ pint milk

Make the breadcrumbs in the usual way by pushing a few pieces of bread at a time into the goblet while the blender is running. Empty the crumbs out into a bowl. Put the remainder of the ingredients into the goblet and switch on at medium speed until everything is blended well. Pour the mixture into the crumbs and mix well. Bake in a greased 450-g/1-lb loaf tin in a moderately hot oven for about 45 minutes until golden brown. Serve hot with a sauce or cold with salad and cucumber sauce (see page 40).

FISH PIE

Cooking time about 20 minutes
Oven temperature Hot 230°C, 450°F, Gas Mark 8
Serves 6

METRIC/IMPERIAL

675 g/1½ lb filleted white fish	2 hard-boiled eggs
600 ml/1 pint béchamel sauce	225 g/8 oz tomatoes
(see page 37)	225 g/8 oz puff pastry or
salt and pepper	225 g/8 oz blender pastry
2 tablespoons cream	(see page 112)
½ teaspoon tarragon	

Cook the filleted fish (haddock or cod) for about 10 minutes in some
of the milk to be used for the sauce. Make up the sauce and add the
fish liquid and seasoning. Stir the cream into the sauce. Flake the fish
in the bottom of a pie dish, season well, and sprinkle with a little
tarragon. Pour over a quarter of the sauce. Chop the hard-boiled eggs
and sprinkle on top of the fish; add a little more sauce. Dip the tomatoes
in boiling water and remove the skins. Slice the tomatoes and place
in a layer over the hard-boiled egg; season well and cover with the
remaining sauce. Roll out the pastry, place on top of the pie dish, and
pinch the edges to make an attractive edge. Brush over with beaten
egg and cook in a hot oven until golden brown.

Variation

Cheesy fish pie Add a further layer by sprinkling grated cheese over
the sauce. Substitute mashed potatoes for the pastry. Cook 1·5 kg/3 lb
potatoes in boiling salted water until soft, drain, and then add 50 g/2 oz
butter and seasoning. Beat thoroughly with the mixer then add 1 egg
and 50 g/2 oz grated cheese. Beat until smooth and for a glamorous
finish pipe on top of the fish or spread over and mark in a pattern with
a fork. Sprinkle the potatoes with grated cheese and dot with butter.
Cook as directed above.

GRILLED SALMON

Oven temperature Moderate 180°C, 350°F, Gas Mark 4
Serves 4

METRIC/IMPERIAL

4 salmon steaks	*To garnish*
100 g/4 oz butter	4 tomatoes
freshly milled black pepper	1 (100-g/4-oz) packet frozen
hollandaise sauce (see page 38)	spinach
	4 slices lemon

Arrange the salmon steaks on the grill pan, score the flesh with a knife, and spread softened butter over each steak. Sprinkle with pepper. Make the hollandaise sauce. Halve the tomatoes and remove the insides (these can be used in a sandwich filling). Heat the frozen spinach, add a little cream after the spinach is drained if you feel extravagant. Mix the spinach with 2 tablespoons of the hollandaise sauce in the blender and stuff into the halved tomatoes. Pop into a moderate oven for 10–15 minutes. Now grill the salmon starting off under a hot grill and reducing after a few minutes to allow heat to penetrate the thickness of the slice. Turn over and baste with melted butter. Return to the grill to allow the underside to be cooked. Serve on a heated dish garnished with lemon wedges and stuffed tomatoes. Sauté or boiled new potatoes make an excellent accompaniment.

Serve the remaining hollandaise sauce in a sauceboat.

FISH MOUSSE

Serves 6

METRIC/IMPERIAL

225 g/8 oz boned white fish	4 egg yolks
15 g/½ oz gelatine	2 egg whites
1 teaspoon tomato purée	*To decorate*
salt and pepper	slices of lemon or apple
150 ml/¼ pint double cream	parsley

Steam the fish until cooked, melt the gelatine with a little fish liquid, allow to cool. Grease a 18-cm/7-inch soufflé dish. Tie a greased strip of greaseproof paper round the top. Blend the fish with the gelatine, tomato purée, and seasoning until smooth. Half whip the cream and add to the blended mixture. Whisk the egg yolks until thick, light, and fluffy. Fold the fish mixture into the egg yolk mixture. Lastly whisk the egg whites with the mixer until white and stiff. Fold into the fish mixture and pour into the soufflé dish. Allow to set in the refrigerator before removing the paper. Decorate round the edge with chopped parsley. Slices of tomato, cucumber, apple, or lemon can be used to decorate the top.

Meat

The mixer and blender make light work of meat dishes that need a lot of chopping and mixing. Stuffings can be made in the wink of an eye, allowing attractive dishes to be made easily with the more economical cuts of meat. Use the mincing attachment, if you have one, to help with the leftovers. In the blender you can make marinades which will tenderise and flavour the meat. Sauces can be made easily, giving new and exciting variety to your main meal of the day.

Use the following recipes as a guide, then start experimenting yourself.

Roasting Meat

When cooking meat dishes it is always better to preheat the oven. The chart below gives suggested temperatures and cooking times for roasting, together with some accompaniments which go well with each type of meat. The thermometer readings in brackets are what the meat thermometer will read when the joint is done.

❋ All roasts can be cooked directly from the freezer but the cooking time must be extended to allow the meat to cook right through.

TO ROAST	TEMPERATURE	TIME	ACCOMPANIMENTS
	Put all meat into a hot oven for 10–15 minutes 230°C, 450°F, Gas Mark 8		
Beef	Reduce to 180°C, 350°F, Gas Mark 4 (thermometer reading 60°C, 140°F rare, 71°C, 160°F medium).	15 minutes per 500 g/ 1 lb and 15 minutes over	Yorkshire pudding (see page 54) Horseradish sauce (see page 42) Thin gravy
Lamb	Reduce to 170°C, 325°F, Gas Mark 3 (thermometer reading 77°C, 170°F).	25 minutes per 500 g/ 1 lb and 25 minutes over	Mint sauce (see page 42) Medium thick gravy

TO ROAST	TEMPERATURE	TIME	ACCOMPANIMENTS
Pork	Reduce to 180°C, 350°F, Gas Mark 4 (thermometer reading 85°C, 185°F).	30 minutes per 500 g/ 1 lb and 30 minutes over	Sage and onion stuffing (see page 55) Apple sauce (see page 41) Thickened gravy
Veal	Reduce to 170°C, 325°F, Gas Mark 3 (thermometer reading 79°C, 175°F).	30 minutes per 500 g/ 1 lb and 30 minutes over	Veal forcemeat (see page 58) Bacon rolls Thickened gravy

Roast Beef

Cook as directed in the chart. There are several schools of thought on whether meat can be used straight from the freezer or whether it should be thawed out. My own experience with beef is that a well-hung piece of meat will cook well either way but meat which is not well hung will still be a little tough. This is not because it has been frozen, as many people seem to think. (Hardly any beef is allowed to hang long enough these days, as it is uneconomical for the butcher to take up space in his shop.) ❋ I have devised a foolproof method of obtaining delicious roast beef from my freezer; you may like to give it a try. It simply entails leaving the beef in a cool place for 24 to 48 hours, preferably uncovered, either before freezing it or after. This can be inconvenient but I think the result is worth it. A good piece of beef should have dark red flesh and firm yellow fat.

Gravy Pour off the fat from the roasting tin very slowly so that all the sediment and meat juices remain. Season the sediment which remains in the tin and mix well over the heat until it is dark brown. Add about 300 ml/½ pint stock (make up with a beef cube) and bring to the boil in the tin, stir well, and boil until a good flavour is obtained.

Pour into a gravy boat and skim any fat off before serving.

YORKSHIRE PUDDING

Cooking time 15–30 minutes depending on size
Oven temperature Hot 230°C, 450°F, Gas Mark 8
Serves 4

METRIC/IMPERIAL

100 g/4 oz plain flour	1 egg
pinch salt	300 ml/½ pint milk

Sieve the flour and salt into the mixer bowl, make a well in the centre, and break the egg into it. Add a little milk and beat with the mixer until a smooth batter is obtained. Gradually stir in the remaining milk with a spoon. To make the batter in the blender place the salt, egg, and milk in the goblet and switch on at minimum speed for 30 seconds. Remove the lid and pour in the sieved flour. Replace the lid and blend for a further 30 seconds. If possible, allow to stand in a cool place for at least 15 minutes before using. Pour the meat fat into individual patty tins or put 3 tablespoons into a shallow ovenproof dish. Allow the fat to heat until very hot and then pour in the batter and bake in a very hot oven for 15 minutes for individual puddings and 30 minutes for a large one.

Roast Lamb

Cook as directed in the chart. Lamb is particularly delicious when allowed to stand in a marinade as in the recipe for marinated leg of lamb; it can even be frozen in a marinade. Lamb can be cooked straight from the freezer quite successfully but it requires a longer cooking time and it should *not* be put into a hot oven initially.

Gravy Keep about 1 tablespoon fat in the tin with sediment and mix this with 1 tablespoon flour. Blend well and then continue as for beef gravy.

Roast Pork

Pork must be well cooked, therefore it is important to know the exact weight of the joint to ensure that it is cooked throughout. ❋ It may be cooked straight from the freezer but allow 1 hour per half kilo/per pound cooking time. Serve with thickened gravy as for lamb.

SAGE AND ONION STUFFING

METRIC/IMPERIAL

6 slices white bread	¼ teaspoon thyme
4 onions	few sprigs parsley
1 egg	salt and pepper
1 teaspoon sage	

Remove the crusts from the bread. Quarter the slices and make into breadcrumbs in the blender. Meanwhile partly boil the roughly chopped onions for a few minutes. Put the breadcrumbs in a bowl, then put the onions into the goblet with the other ingredients and blend until the onion is finely chopped. Mix together with the breadcrumbs and bake in a well-greased tin until the stuffing is firm and golden brown. Put the stuffing in the oven about 25 minutes before the pork is due to be taken out.

CROWN ROAST WITH APRICOTS AND ROSEMARY

Cooking time 30 minutes per 500 g/1 lb
Oven temperature Moderate 180°C, 350°F, Gas Mark 4
Serves 6

METRIC/IMPERIAL

14 chops formed into a crown roast	450 g/1 lb dried or 675 g/1½ lb fresh apricots
To stuff	salt and pepper
100 g/4 oz fresh breadcrumbs	*To garnish*
1 onion	1 (213-g/7½-oz) can apricot halves
25 g/1 oz walnuts	or several fresh poached apricots
1 egg	several sprigs rosemary
few sprigs rosemary	

Ask the butcher to prepare the chops into a crown. This roast is so popular now that most butchers are willing to do this if you give them a little advance warning. If you can persuade him to mince the scraps of meat which he trims away the mince can be used in the stuffing. Prepare the stuffing by making the fresh white breadcrumbs in the blender. Put into a medium-sized bowl ready for the other ingredients. Cut up the onion roughly and chop in the blender, and add the walnuts, switch on for a few seconds, then add the egg and the first lot of rosemary. When this is chopped add to the breadcrumbs in the bowl. Now chop the apricots roughly in the blender and add to the other ingredients with seasoning. Add mince if desired. This mixture should give a moist stuffing. If using dried apricots be sure to steep them in water for several hours before using them.

Now stuff the mixture into the centre of the crown, wrap tinfoil over the ends of the chops to avoid charring, and cook in a moderate oven allowing 30 minutes for each pound of meat. About 10 minutes before serving time place the halved apricots on top of the stuffing, brush with melted butter, and return to the oven. Decorate between the chops with a garland of rosemary. Cutlet frills can be put onto the ends of the chops when the foil is removed. Serve with roast potatoes and petit pois.

❋ **Note** The crown can be prepared in advance and frozen with the stuffing.

Variation

Serve the crown roast filled with new vegetables if you do not want to use a stuffing. The apricot stuffing is also delicious in a stuffed breast of lamb.

MARINATED LEG OF LAMB

Cooking time 1½ hours
Oven temperature Moderate 180°C, 350°F, Gas Mark 4
Serves 6

METRIC/IMPERIAL

1 glass red wine	several sprigs parsley
2 tablespoons chopped fresh mint	2 onions
1 teaspoon dried or a good sized	wedge of lemon
sprig fresh rosemary	3 tablespoons olive oil
1 teaspoon salt	1·5–1·75 kg/3½–4 lb leg of lamb
1 clove garlic	

Put the wine, mint, rosemary, salt, garlic, and parsley into the blender and switch on for a few seconds. Cut up the onions roughly and put into the goblet, then peel the rind from the lemon and add the flesh to the mixture (not the pith).

Blend on medium speed then reduce speed and add the oil. Put the leg of lamb into a casserole or a plastic bag, pour on the marinade, and cover or seal the bag. Allow to stand in a cool place or in the refrigerator for 12–24 hours. Remove the meat from the marinade but retain the mixture. Roast in a moderate oven for 1 hour. Pour the marinade over the roast and continue cooking for a further half hour. Carve the roast and serve the marinade mixed with the lamb juices in place of gravy. This makes a delicious main course for a special dinner party. ❊You can freeze the leg of lamb in a plastic bag with the marinade.

BEEF OLIVES

Cooking time 1½ hours
Oven temperature Moderate 180°C, 350°F, Gas Mark 4
Serves 4

METRIC/IMPERIAL

350 g/12 oz topside of beef	1 carrot
half quantity veal forcemeat	1 tablespoon flour
(see below)	300 ml/½ pint beef stock
2 tablespoons oil	salt and pepper
1 onion	

Ask the butcher to cut the meat into slices about 7·5 by 10 cm/3 by 4 inches in size and beat them flat. Otherwise buy the meat in a thick piece. Cut across the grain and flatten with a cutlet bat or wooden rolling pin. Make up the forcemeat and divide it equally amongst the slices of meat. Roll the meat round the stuffing and secure with a skewer or a wooden cocktail stick. Heat the oil in a heavy frying pan and brown the beef olives. Dice the onion and carrot and sauté the vegetables with the meat. Put the beef olives and vegetables in a casserole, sprinkle the flour into the frying pan, and mix with the meat juices. Add the stock and seasoning and mix well for a few minutes, then strain over the olives. Cook for 1½ hours in a covered dish in a moderate oven until the meat is tender. Remove the skewers before serving with mashed potatoes and the vegetables of your choice.

VEAL FORCEMEAT

METRIC/IMPERIAL

6 slices white bread	rind of ½ lemon
50 g/2 oz suet	salt and pepper
few sprigs parsley	½ egg

Make the bread into crumbs in the blender and empty into a bowl; add the suet. Chop the parsley and lemon rind in the blender, empty onto the breadcrumbs and suet, and add seasoning. Mix together with some of the beaten egg but do not allow the mixture to become too moist. Use for stuffing veal or beef or with poultry.

BEEF FONDUE

A fondue meal is fun as well as being easy on the hostess, but do be very careful with the fondue pot when it is full of hot oil.

Serves 4

METRIC/IMPERIAL

575 g/1¼ lb fillet of beef   cooking oil

Cut the beef into small cubes. Heat the oil in the fondue dish and keep it hot over the spirit burner. Each person cooks his or her own meat on the end of a long fork in the hot oil, and eats it with a variety of sauces and relishes. Tomato sauce (see page 41), curry sauce (see page

39), and béarnaise sauce (see page 38) are all excellent. Different mustards should be served, and a large bowl of salad and cheesy baked potatoes (see page 81) are delicious and easy to prepare.

MEAT LOAF

Cooking time 1¼ hours
Oven temperature Moderate 180°C, 350°F, Gas Mark 4
Serves 8

METRIC/IMPERIAL

10 water biscuits	1 small stalk celery
450 g/1 lb coarsely minced beef	1 small carrot
225 g/8 oz coarsely minced pork	2 sprigs parsley
1 large tomato	250 ml/scant ½ pint milk
1 small onion	1 egg

Crush the water biscuits and make them into crumbs in the blender. Keep the cover on while the machine is running. Empty the crumbs into a bowl. Add the coarsely minced beef and pork to the crumbs. Roughly chop the vegetables. Place the vegetables and remaining ingredients in the goblet and blend until the vegetables are finely chopped. Mix with the meat and crumbs. Put the mixture in a greased 1-kg/2-lb loaf tin and bake in a moderate oven for about 1¼ hours. Serve hot or cold.

SAVOURY MEAT LOAF

Cooking time 1 hour
Oven temperature Moderate 180°C, 350°F, Gas Mark 4
Serves 4–5

METRIC/IMPERIAL

450 g/ 1 lb minced beef	salt and pepper
50 g/2 oz fresh white breadcrumbs	few drops Tabasco sauce
1 medium onion	1 teaspoon Worcestershire sauce
1 (198-g/7-oz) can peeled tomatoes	1 egg
1 teaspoon tomato purée	

Brown the meat in a frying pan then drain off the fat and place the meat in a mixing bowl with the breadcrumbs. Sauté the roughly chopped onion in a little butter or oil; when it is cooled slightly place it in the goblet with the drained tomatoes, tomato purée, seasonings, and egg. Blend until smooth at a medium speed. Add to the meat and breadcrumb mixture and mix well. Put the mixture into a 0·5-kg/1-lb loaf tin and cook in a moderate oven for about 1 hour. Serve with tomato sauce (see page 41). ❀ Meat loaves freeze well but should be cut into portions first.

BARBECUED SPARERIBS

Cooking time 1½ hours
Oven temperature Hot 230°C, 450°F, Gas Mark 8, reducing to
moderate 180°C, 350°F, Gas Mark 4
Serves 4

METRIC/IMPERIAL

1–1·5 kg/2–3 lb pork spareribs   2 quantities barbecue sauce
(see page 39)

Put the spareribs in a roasting pan in a hot oven. Allow to cook for about 30 minutes then remove from the oven and brush with the barbecue sauce. Reduce the temperature to 180°C, 350°F, Gas Mark 4 and cook for a further hour, basting the spareribs frequently with the barbecue sauce. It is also advisable to turn the ribs from time to time. Serve the remainder of the sauce warmed with the spareribs. I usually serve a large mixed salad with this dish, and lots of paper napkins!

HOLIDAY PIE

Cooking time 25–30 minutes
Oven temperature Moderate 180°C, 350°F, Gas Mark 4
Serves 4

METRIC/IMPERIAL

450 g/1 lb finely minced lean beef   salt and pepper
1 onion   1 large can baked beans
300 ml/½ pint stock or water   450 g/1 lb cooked mashed potatoes

Brown the beef in a frying pan with a little fat if necessary. Chop the onion finely and add to the meat; add the stock and seasoning when the meat is browned and allow to cook for about 15 minutes. Pour

60

the meat into the bottom of a pie dish or shallow casserole and top
with baked beans. Make sure the mashed potatoes are smooth, beat
with the mixer with a knob of butter and a little milk until really
creamy. Spread over the surface of the beans, mark a design with a
fork, dot with butter if you like, and put in a moderate oven for
25–30 minutes.

Variation

Sprinkle the potatoes with 50 g/2 oz grated cheese before putting the
pie into the oven.

MACARONI TWIST SALAD

Serves 4

METRIC/IMPERIAL

225 g/8 oz macaroni twists
1 onion
1 green pepper
1 red pepper
225 g/8 oz salami

12 black and green olives
150 ml/¼ pint French dressing
(see page 34)
salt and pepper

Cook the macaroni twists until tender. Drain and wash with cold
water; allow to cool. Meanwhile chop the onion finely, deseed and
dice the green and red pepper, and chop half the salami into small dice.
Mix all ingredients together with French dressing, season, and pile
into a salad bowl. Serve with sliced salami and a green salad.

SWEET AND SOUR
MEAT BALLS

Serves 4

METRIC/IMPERIAL

450 g/1 lb minced beef or pork	3 teaspoons cornflour
seasoning	2 teaspoons soy sauce
3 green peppers	4 tablespoons vinegar
3 pineapple rings	2 tablespoons honey
Sauce	4 tablespoons chicken stock
1 clove garlic	2 tablespoons sherry

Make the seasoned minced beef or pork into small balls. Dip in seasoned flour (optional) and fry in hot oil until cooked and golden brown. Cut the green peppers into strips and boil for 5 minutes, drain. Cut the pineapple slices into 12 pieces. Blend all the sauce ingredients at maximum speed until the garlic is pulverised. Put into a saucepan with the green pepper and pineapple and simmer until thick. Arrange the meat balls in a heated serving dish and pour over the sauce. Serve with 225 g/8 oz cooked drained egg noodles or 225 g/8 oz cooked long-grain rice. It is also possible to buy bean sprouts in many department stores and supermarkets. These can be served as a vegetable by cooking in boiling salted water for about 4 minutes. Reduce heat and allow to simmer, drain when cooked but still crisp.

SPAGHETTI BOLOGNESE

Serves 4

METRIC/IMPERIAL

225 g/8 oz lean minced beef	grated nutmeg
tomato sauce (see page 41)	salt and pepper
225–350 g/8–12 oz spaghetti	Parmesan cheese
15 g/½ oz butter	

Fry the meat until brown then add the tomato sauce and simmer for at least 40 minutes. Cook the spaghetti as directed on the packet. The thickness may vary from brand to brand, but it will usually take around 10–12 minutes to be cooked *al dente*, as the Italians say. This means it is still slightly chewy, definitely not soft or mushy. A test for readiness is to bite through a strand and if the central core remains white the pasta needs a little further cooking. Drain the spaghetti into a colander when cooked, melt the butter in the saucepan, return the spaghetti to the saucepan, and shake well. Sprinke with grated nutmeg and freshly ground pepper. In Italy the spaghetti and sauce are often combined but this looks rather messy therefore it is better to serve spaghetti with the sauce on top, sprinkled with Parmesan cheese, and allow each person to mix his own together on the plate.

Variation

Spaghetti and seafood sauce Cook the spaghetti as above. Blend 3 peeled tomatoes or a 198-g/7-oz can with 1 peeled onion, 1 clove garlic, oregano, seasoning, and a little water. Simmer for 15 minutes, then add 100 g/4 oz shrimps. Heat the wine in a frying pan and add 600 ml/1 pint mussels, scrubbed and with the beards removed. Discard any mussels which will not close when given a sharp tap. When the mussel shells are wide open, sprinkle with chopped parsley. Add the mussel liquid to the tomato sauce. Serve the spaghetti with the sauce and surround the plate with mussels.

LASAGNE

Cooking time 30 minutes
Oven temperature Moderate 180°C, 350°F, Gas Mark 4
Serves 4

METRIC/IMPERIAL

175 g/6 oz lasagne	4 tablespoons cream
450 g/1 lb lean minced beef	salt and pepper
tomato sauce (see page 41)	Parmesan cheese
600 ml/1 pint béchamel sauce	
(see page 37)	

Cook the lasagne in boiling salted water, with a little oil added to the water, for about 15 minutes. Drain and rinse in cold water. Dry flat on a clean tea-towel. Fry the meat until brown, add the tomato sauce, and simmer for at least 30 minutes. Make up the béchamel sauce and allow to cool slightly before adding the cream. Butter a wide oven-proof dish which is at least 5 cm/2 inches deep, then put in a layer of meat sauce and a layer of béchamel. Now place a layer of lasagne over the sauce and continue to layer until everything is used, ending with a layer of meat sauce, topped with béchamel. Coat the surface generously with grated cheese. Cook in a preheated oven for approximately 30 minutes.

Poultry and Game

A really delicious roast bird is a dish which any cook can justly serve with pride. Interest and variety can be added to roast poultry and game by using marinades and stuffings. I feel strongly that the stuffing should be an integral part of the meal and not just a filler. Experiment with fruit stuffings for poultry, and use marinades to give flavour to frozen birds.

Since chicken is becoming one of the cheapest meats you have plenty of scope for experimenting with new dishes, and the blender takes the hard work out of stuffings and marinades.

To roast poultry and game

There is nothing more delicious than a simple meal of roasted chicken, pheasant, duck, or turkey. Sometimes a meal of this kind is more difficult for a new cook than a casserole or a dish which seems more complicated but has more explicit instructions in cookbooks. Here is a basic table with cooking times for stuffed poultry and game. In the chart you will find a guide for method and times for open roasting. If you are wrapping in foil then follow cooking times given on the foil packet.

TO ROAST	TEMPERATURE	TIME	PREPARATION
Turkey	220°C, 425°F, Gas Mark 7 for 15 minutes reducing to 180°C, 350°F, Gas Mark 4	20 minutes per 500 g/1 lb and 20 minutes over	Stuff the neck with veal forcemeat (see page 58) or chestnut stuffing (see page 68), up to 450 g/1 lb for a 6-kg 300-g/14-lb bird. Stuff the tail with 450–900 g/1–2 lb sausagemeat stuffing. Cover the breast with fat bacon. Baste.

TO ROAST	TEMPERATURE	TIME	PREPARATION
Goose	220°C, 425°F, Gas Mark 7 for 15 minutes reducing to 180°C, 350°F, Gas Mark 4	15 minutes per 500 g/1 lb and 15 minutes over	Stuff with sage and onion (see page 55) or a fruit stuffing (see page page 69). Baste.
Duck	200°C, 400°F, Gas Mark 6	20 minutes per 500 g/1 lb	Younger birds do not require stuffing but older, larger ducks are usually stuffed with sage and onion at the tail end. Baste.
Chicken	200°C, 400°F, Gas Mark 6	20 minutes per 500 g/1 lb and 20 minutes over	Stuff between the skin and flesh at the wishbone end until the bird is plump. Baste.
Pheasant	200°C, 400°F, Gas Mark 6 for 15 minutes, reducing to 180°C, 350°F, Gas Mark 4	40–50 minutes for small young birds, 1–1½ hours for larger older birds	Put a knob of butter inside the bird. Baste.
Hare	220°C, 425°F, Gas Mark 7 for 15 minutes, reducing to 190°C, 375°F, Gas Mark 5	1½–2 hours according to size	Stuff the body with veal forcemeat (see page 58).
Pigeon	230°C, 450°F, Gas Mark 8	Centre of the oven for 20–25 minutes Dredge with flour after 15 minutes.	Stuff with a mixture of 2 tablespoons breadcrumbs, 2 mushrooms, 25 g/1 oz butter, and the chopped pigeon liver. Cover breast with fat bacon. Baste well.

To truss a chicken

After stuffing a bird it is necessary to sew it up so that the stuffing remains inside. Most people buy ready-prepared poultry and game but it is important to know how to truss a bird after it is stuffed as this is one task you complete yourself. If you are intending to do this often it is as well to buy a trussing needle.

Thread a needle with about 46 cm/18 inches of string. Put the bird on its back, neck end nearest to you, and hold the thighs in an upright position. Put the needle through the top of one thigh behind the joint, bring it through the carcass and out through the other thigh. Turn the bird over then put the needle through the 'elbow' of the wing, bring it over the back and hold down the flap of skin, then bring it out through the other wing elbow. Take the string from the needle, pull the ends tightly, and tie with a double knot.

Now lay the bird on its back again and with about 30 cm/12 inches of string pass the needle through the skin which is being held over the the tip of the breast bone. Unthread and pass the two ends round the thick end of the drumstick, cross the string over the hole, and tie down tightly behind the tail. This means the legs are pulled down over the opening and the breast muscles are plumped up.

❋ Notes on frozen poultry

There have been several scares recently about food poisoning caused by eating poultry. The organism which causes this is present in both fresh and frozen poultry but is easily destroyed by ordinary cooking. It is therefore essential to thaw frozen poultry completely before cooking. A partially thawed bird may not allow the heat to penetrate sufficiently to kill off any bacteria which could prove dangerous. Therefore please do ensure that you follow the instructions which are normally on the wrapping of a frozen bird. This is especially important at Christmas when so many people are eating frozen turkeys. It is difficult for me to give an exact thawing time as this depends on the weight. Chicken pieces will therefore defrost more quickly than a whole bird. The best safety precaution is to plan ahead when using frozen poultry and allow it to thaw out overnight in the refrigerator. Do allow sufficient time for birds to cook through when they are being cooked on a spit, barbecue, or grill.

APPLE AND CELERY STUFFING

50 g/2 oz butter

3 rashers streaky bacon

2 onions

2 stalks celery

75 g/3 oz fresh white breadcrumbs

3 large cooking apples

small bunch parsley sprigs

2 teaspoons sugar

salt and pepper

Melt the butter in a frying pan. Cut the bacon into small pieces and fry until golden brown. Put into a bowl. Fry the roughly chopped onion and celery for a few minutes and in the meantime make the breadcrumbs in the blender. Tip the crumbs into the bowl with the bacon. Peel the apples and slice roughly. Put the onion and celery through the blender until finely chopped while the apples are frying in the frying pan. Add the onions and celery to the mixture in the bowl and lastly put the apples through the blender with the parsley and sugar until finely chopped. Finally mix all ingredients together, season well, and use as a stuffing or cook separately with duck or pork. This stuffing can also be used for a goose but a double quantity will be needed.

CHESTNUT STUFFING

450 g/1 lb fresh chestnuts

300 ml/½ pint milk or chicken stock

100 g/4 oz fresh white breadcrumbs

25 g/1 oz butter

3 rashers lean bacon

few sprigs parsley

rind of 1 lemon

1 egg

pinch thyme

salt and pepper

Boil the chestnuts for 2–3 minutes in water to soften the skins; drain and peel while hot. Simmer for 30–40 minutes in milk or chicken stock until soft; drain. While the chestnuts are cooking make the breadcrumbs in the blender and tip into a bowl. Melt the butter and fry the chopped bacon. Put the parsley, lemon rind without pith, egg, and seasoning into the blender and run on high speed until the rind is chopped. Add to the breadcrumbs in the bowl. Place a quarter of the chestnuts in the goblet and switch on at medium speed, add the remainder through the hole in the cap until chestnut purée is obtained. Mix all ingredients together and use to stuff the breast of the turkey.

Variation

Canned whole chestnuts can be used. 225 g/8 oz sausagemeat can be added if only one stuffing is required but many people like to have sausagemeat at one end and chestnut at the other. More beaten egg may be needed to make the stuffing moist.

CHESTNUT AND ORANGE STUFFING

METRIC/IMPERIAL

225 g/8 oz fresh white breadcrumbs	100 g/4 oz shredded suet
2 oranges	1½ teaspoons salt
1 (425-g/15-oz) can chestnuts	¼ teaspoon cayenne pepper
	2 eggs

Make the breadcrumbs in the blender. Peel the rind from the oranges thinly and grate in the blender. Squeeze the juice from the oranges and mix all ingredients together using the mixer. This quantity is sufficient for an 3·5-kg/8-lb turkey.

CREAMED SPROUTS

Serves 4

METRIC/IMPERIAL

450 g/1 lb sprouts	150 ml/¼ pint cream
4 rashers bacon	pepper

Wash the sprouts and boil in salted water for 6 minutes (4 minutes if they are tiny). While the sprouts are cooking, grill the bacon until crisp and keep warm. Drain the sprouts and put half in the blender, switch on at medium speed until they are chopped. Add the cream and pepper, turn on to medium speed, and add the remaining sprouts one at a time. Reheat and sprinkle with crumbled crispy bacon. Serve with pheasant with grapes.

PHEASANT WITH GRAPES

Cooking time 1 hour
Oven temperature Hot 230°C, 450°F, Gas Mark 8
Serves 4

METRIC/IMPERIAL

1 pheasant	20 whole walnuts
4 thin slices salt pork or bacon	1 tablespoon sugar
675 g/1½ lb seedless green grapes	2 tablespoons water
150 ml/¼ pint soured cream	*To garnish*
25 g/1 oz butter	grapes
1 tablespoon brandy	watercress
salt and pepper	

Remove the giblets, season the pheasant, and prepare it for roasting by wrapping in salt pork or bacon (if you buy the pheasant this may have been done by the poulterer); secure with string. Select a small bunch of the best grapes for garnishing. Put the remaining grapes, first removing the stems, in the blender and reduce to a purée. Remove 3 tablespoons of the grape juice. Add the soured cream, softened butter, brandy, and seasoning to the grapes and blend thoroughly.

Take a deep heavy fireproof casserole or saucepan and lay the walnuts on the bottom. Place the pheasant on top of the walnuts and pour the mixture from the blender on top. Cook gently for about 30 minutes. Put the sugar in a small saucepan with the water and allow to turn to a pale caramel, add the 3 tablespoons reserved grape juice, and pour the mixture over the pheasant. Continue cooking for a further 20 minutes. Meanwhile preheat the oven and when the pheasant has finished cooking take it out of the saucepan, remove the pork or bacon, and put it in the oven for a few minutes to brown.

While the bird is in the oven remove the walnuts, allowing them to drain first, and place them in the blender. Allow the sauce to reduce slightly. Chop the walnuts roughly in the blender. Serve the pheasant on a heated serving dish surrounded by chopped walnuts and garnished with grapes; pour the sauce over just before serving.

This is a marvellous dish for a dinner party and it can be partially prepared well in advance. Because you use the blender there is no messy sieving to cause extra washing up. Serve with small roasted potatoes and creamed sprouts.

CHICKEN HASH

Cooking time 1 hour
Oven temperature Moderate 180°C, 350°F, Gas Mark 4
Serves 6

METRIC/IMPERIAL

350 g/12 oz cooked chicken
1 (298-g/10½-oz) can condensed
chicken soup
2 potatoes
2 carrots
1 small onion
1 red pepper

2 sprigs parsley
sprig rosemary
salt and pepper
Crumb topping
2 slices white bread
40 g/1½ oz butter

Put the chicken and soup in the blender and run at maximum speed
until chicken is finely chopped. Pour into a saucepan and heat. Peel
the potatoes and carrots and chop roughly. Put into the blender and run
at medium speed until the vegetables are chopped. Add to the chicken
mixture. Peel and roughly chop the onion and red pepper and put
into the blender with parsley and seasoning. Run on high speed until
chopped. Mix all ingredients together in the saucepan, pour into a
buttered casserole, and bake in a moderate oven for 45 minutes.

Meanwhile make the topping. Clean the blender and use it to make
breadcrumbs; mix these with the melted butter. Sprinkle over the
baked casserole and cook for a further 10–15 minutes.

Variation

Leftover chicken gravy can be used instead of chicken soup. Serve
with tomato sauce (see page 41).

CHICKEN ON THE SPIT

Serves 4

METRIC/IMPERIAL

4 chicken portions
Marinade
1 onion
1 (198-g/7-oz) can tomatoes
1 teaspoon tomato purée
1 tablespoon lemon juice

¼ teaspoon rosemary
1 tablespoon soy sauce
3½ tablespoons oil
salt and pepper
2 tablespoons tomato ketchup

Season the chicken portions and put in a casserole or polythene bag. Roughly chop the onion and put all the ingredients for the marinade into the goblet. Blend until a smooth mixture is obtained. Pour the marinade over the chicken and allow to stand for several hours. ✳ This is an excellent way to use frozen chicken as it can stand in the marinade while it is defrosting. Thread the chicken pieces on the spit and paint generously with the marinade. Cook for 25–30 minutes. Paint the chicken with the marinade several times during cooking. Heat the remainder of the marinade with the ketchup and serve hot with the chicken. Serve with rice and a green salad.

FRUITED DUCK OR GOOSE

Cooking time 2–2½ hours
Oven temperature Moderately hot
200°C, 400°F, Gas Mark 6
Serves 6

METRIC/IMPERIAL

1 large duck, about 2·5 kg/5½ lb,
  or 1 small goose, about 3 kg/7 lb
stuffing (see pages 68–69)
Sauce
150 ml/¼ pint seasoned stock
  made from giblets
1 teaspoon Worcestershire sauce

1 (454-g/16-oz) can pineapple
  spiral slices
2 tablespoons sherry
2 tablespoons cornflour
To garnish
12 stuffed green olives
small bunch parsley

Make up the stuffing and put into both ends of the bird. Place on a trivet in a roasting pan and cook for 2–2½ hours in a moderately hot oven, according to the size. Remove some of the accumulated fat

72

from the pan, using it to baste the bird if necessary. When it is cooked, place on a hot serving dish and keep warm. Skim off all surplus fat, then pour the pan juices into the blender. Add the stock, Worcestershire sauce, the syrup drained from the pineapple, sherry, and cornflour. Retain three pineapple slices for decoration and add the remainder to the blender goblet. Cover and liquidise until smooth. Pour the mixture into a saucepan, bring to the boil, add the olives, cover, and simmer for 3 minutes. Cut the reserved pineapple slices in half, coat the edges of three halves in finely chopped parsley, and secure over the breast with cocktail sticks topped with olives. Surround the base of the bird with parsley sprigs and the remaining pineapple slices quartered. Serve the sauce separately.

CHICKEN PROVENÇALE

Serves 4

METRIC/IMPERIAL

4 chicken joints	1 teaspoon tomato pureé
50 g/2 oz butter	salt and pepper
2 cloves garlic	2 large sprigs parsley
6 large tomatoes, or	1 teaspoon oregano
1 (425-g/15-oz) can peeled tomatoes, drained	4 tablespoons sherry

Season the chicken joints and melt the butter in a heavy frying pan; add unpeeled cloves of garlic and the chicken joints. Allow to cook for about 15 minutes. Dip the tomatoes in boiling water one at a time and remove the skins, then put into the blender and chop finely. Add the tomato pureé, seasoning, parsley, and oregano, switch on to maximum speed for a few seconds. Heat the sherry in a ladle and set it alight with a match; pour onto the chicken and allow to burn. Add the blended mixture to the chicken and cook for a further 15–20 minutes until the chicken is tender and the tomato mixture is reduced. Arrange on a heated serving dish on a bed of rice and coat the chicken with the tomato sauce which is left in the pan. Serve with a crisp green salad.

Egg and Cheese Dishes

Eggs and cheese are a most important part of a well-balanced diet and with a little imagination they can add enormous variety to our everyday menus as well as saving money. Both products are comparatively cheap in relation to meat and fish, and although they have always been considered as ingredients for quick meals and snacks more people are looking at the possibilities of eggs and cheese in providing main meals. A combination of both can provide a most nutritious and exciting dish and the mixer and blender make even the more complicated dishes simple.

Omelettes

If you enjoy omelettes and pancakes it is wise to keep a pan specially for cooking them as it is important for really successful omeletes to use a pan with a good surface. Frying pans which have been used for bacon, eggs, etc., do tend to lose their surface. To prepare a new omelette pan, heat some oil in the pan until it is smoking hot, then wipe out with a piece of kitchen paper. *Do not wash* after use, simply wipe out with a little salt and kitchen paper. I have had one for eight years and I lock it away from the family and the Brillo pads as I know it will give me perfect omelettes and pancakes.

You can mix a plain omelette in the blender or with the mixer. Use the blender to make fillings and the mixer to make fluffy omelettes.

PLAIN OMELETTE

Serves 1

METRIC/IMPERIAL

2–3 eggs	freshly ground black pepper
salt	15 g/½ oz butter
1 tablespoon water	

Place all the ingredients except the butter in the blender and switch on to maximum speed for about 15 seconds. Alternatively, use the mixer. Mix the omelette just before cooking for the best results. Divide the butter into small knobs and allow it to melt in the omelette pan on medium heat. When the butter starts to froth pour the egg into the pan and allow the mixture to cook for about 10 seconds. Stir the egg mixture in the pan with the flat part of a fork once or twice, then lift the edge of the omelette to allow any uncooked egg to run onto the pan.

Tilt the pan away from you and fold the omelette over to the other side of the pan. You should now be able to tip the omelette out onto a heated plate by changing your grip on the handle of the pan.

Variations

Prepare the filling before making the omelette. Fillings serve 1.

Cheese omelette Grate 40 g/1½ oz cheese in the blender. Sprinkle the cheese onto the egg before folding the omelette.

Mushroom omelette Prepare 50 g/2 oz mushrooms by washing and slicing them, put into a pan in which a knob of butter has been melted. Allow the mushrooms to sauté for a few minutes then add 1 teaspoon flour, 2 tablespoons water, and seasoning. Stir on the heat until mixture is creamy; add a dash of Worcestershire sauce or a few drops of lemon juice for added flavour. Pour the filling into the omelette before folding.

Tomato and cheese omelette Grate 25 g/1 oz cheese, sauté 1 sliced, seasoned tomato in a little butter. Sprinkle the cheese on the omelette and place the tomato on the far side of the omelette before folding. Cooked diced bacon can be substituted for cheese.

Herb omelette Chop fresh chives and a few sprigs of parsley, thyme, marjoram, or tarragon, depending upon what is available, in the blender and then add to the omelette ingredients and make in the usual way.

SOUFFLÉ OMELETTE

Serves 1

METRIC/IMPERIAL

2 eggs
salt and pepper

2 teaspoons water
knob of butter

Separate the eggs and whisk up the egg whites in the mixer until
white and stiff. Season the egg yolks and add the water. Mix together
with a fork then fold the yolks into the whites gradually with a
sharp-edged metal spoon. Melt the butter in the omelette pan and
pour the mixture in. Spread evenly over the pan and cook until
almost set; the underside should be golden brown. Put the pan under
a preheated grill to brown the top. With a palette knife make a mark
across the centre of the omelette and fold over. Slide onto a heated
plate.

Variations

Savoury fillings can be added as for plain omelettes. Sweet soufflé
omelettes can be made in the same way by adding 2 teaspoons sugar
to the egg whites when they are beaten, and omitting the salt and
pepper. A little vanilla essence may be added to the yolks. Serve
sprinkled with castor sugar. Omelettes can be filled with jam, puréed
fruit, or small whole fruit and one omelette will serve two people as
a sweet course.

SPANISH OMELETTE

This omelette is not folded over but can be cut into wedges. Cook
in a large frying pan.

Serves 4

METRIC/IMPERIAL

2 potatoes
1 large onion
1 clove garlic
5 tablespoons oil

50 g/2 oz lean bacon
salt and pepper
5 eggs
1 tomato

Peel and roughly chop the potatoes, onion, and garlic. Feed them
gradually into the blender until they are grated coarsely. Heat the oil

in a frying pan, add the bacon, and cook until crisp; remove, allow to cool, and chop in the blender. Put the blender-chopped vegetables in the oil, season, and cook until soft. Pour off any excess oil from the vegetables. Add the bacon. Beat the eggs, pour over the vegetables, and stir until the omelette is just setting. Do not overcook otherwise the egg will be solid. Slice the tomato and place on the omelette, finish cooking under a preheated grill to brown the top, and serve cut into wedges.

This is a very substantial omelette and makes an excellent lunch or supper dish with a crisp salad. Alternatively, serve with a dish of green and red peppers which have been sliced and fried in butter with an onion and a clove of garlic until they are tender.

CHEESE SOUFFLÉ

Cooking time 25–30 minutes
Oven temperature Moderately hot
190°C, 375°F, Gas Mark 5
Serves 4

METRIC/IMPERIAL

40 g/1½ oz butter	1 teaspoon made mustard
25 g/1 oz flour	100 g/4 oz grated cheese
salt	4 egg yolks
cayenne pepper	5 egg whites
250 ml/scant ½ pint milk	

Prepare a 18-cm/7-inch soufflé dish by buttering it, and if desired sprinkle it with browned breadcrumbs.

Make a roux by melting the butter in a large saucepan, then adding the flour and stirring well. Season well, then blend in the milk with a whisk or put the whole mixture into the blender. Add the mustard and three-quarters of the grated cheese, then the egg yolks one at a time. This operation can all be done in the blender; at this stage return the mixture to the sauce pan if using the blender. In the mixer bowl whisk up the egg whites until just stiff. Then fold the whites gradually into the cheese mixture with a sharp-edged metal spoon. Pour into the soufflé dish and sprinkle with remaining cheese. Bake for 25–30 minutes in a moderately hot oven, serve immediately.

Variation

Pour the mixture over a layer of cooked fish, meat, or vegetables. This is an excellent way of using leftovers.

MUSHROOM SOUFFLÉ

Cooking time 35–40 minutes
Oven temperature Hot 220°C, 425°F, Gas Mark 7
Serves 4

METRIC/IMPERIAL

4 rashers streaky bacon	1 (298-g/10½-oz) can condensed
1 medium onion	mushroom soup
100 g/4 oz mushrooms	salt and pepper
25 g/1 oz butter	4 eggs
100 g/4 oz fresh white	
breadcrumbs	

Cut the bacon into thin strips. Chop the onion and mushrooms and cook gently with the bacon in the butter for 2–3 minutes. Place in a bowl with the breadcrumbs, soup, and seasoning. Mix well together. Separate the eggs and beat the yolks into the mixture one at a time. Place the egg whites in the mixer bowl and whisk on a high speed until just stiff – do not over-whisk as this tends to make them difficult to fold in and the soufflé will not rise well. Fold the egg whites into the mushroom mixture and turn into a 1-litre/1½-pint (15-cm/6-inch) buttered soufflé dish or straight-sided deep ovenproof dish and bake in a moderately hot oven for 35–40 minutes.

SPINACH ROULADE

This is a soufflé mixture which is cooked in a Swiss roll tin and rolled like a Swiss roll.

Cooking time 10 minutes approximately
Oven temperature Moderately hot
200°C, 400°F, Gas Mark 6
Serves 4

METRIC/IMPERIAL

4 eggs
225-g/8-oz packet frozen spinach
15 g/½ oz butter
salt and pepper
1 tablespoon grated Parmesan
   cheese

15 g/½ oz butter
1 tablespoon flour
salt and pepper
150 ml/¼ pint milk
grated nutmeg
2 tablespoons double cream

Filling
175 g/6 oz mushrooms

Strictly speaking a special paper case is used for a roulade but I find it is just as simple to line a 30 by 20-cm/12 by 8-inch Swiss roll tin as for a Swiss roll with oiled greaseproof paper. Allow 4-cm/1½-inch side pieces and cut into each corner carefully so that one piece can be folded over the other to form a neat mitre. Brush the paper with oil.

Separate the eggs. Cook the spinach as directed on the packet, drain, and put into the blender to purée, then add the butter, seasoning, cheese, and egg yolks one at a time. In the mixer whisk up the egg whites until white and peaky and fold into the spinach mixture with a metal spoon. Turn into the prepared tin and bake on the top shelf of a moderately hot oven for about 10 minutes or until firm to the touch.

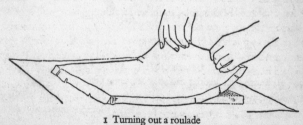

1 Turning out a roulade

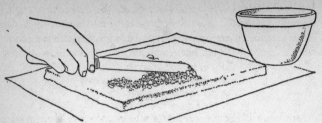

2 Spreading the roulade with filling

3 Rolling the roulade

Wash and slice the mushrooms and sauté in the melted butter in a saucepan. Remove from the heat and add the flour. Season and stir in the milk and nutmeg. Return to the heat, stir until thick, and add the cream when the mixture is again removed from the heat. Turn the spinach roulade onto a sheet of greaseproof paper, spread with the mushroom filling, and roll up. It can then be sliced as a first course, or larger portions make a delicious main course.

Variation

Meat and fish fillings can be used in place of mushroom.

WHISKY RAREBIT

Serves 2

METRIC/IMPERIAL

100 g/4 oz strong Cheddar cheese   cayenne pepper
1 tablespoon whisky   25 g/1 oz butter
1 tablespoon milk   2 large slices hot buttered toast
1 teaspoon mustard

Put the cheese in the blender to grate coarsely. Add the whisky, milk, mustard, and seasoning and switch on for a few seconds. Melt the butter in a saucepan over a low heat and empty the cheese mixture into the butter. Stir until warm and creamy – do not allow to boil. Pour onto the hot buttered toast.

Variation

Substitute 2 tablespoons beer for the whisky and milk. Alternatively, use 2 tablespoons milk, omit the whisky and beer, and add a few drops of Worcestershire sauce.

CHEESY BAKED POTATOES

Cooking time about 1 hour
Oven temperature Moderately hot
200°C, 400°F, Gas Mark 6
Serves 4

METRIC/IMPERIAL

4 large baking potatoes	4 tablespoons chives
225 g/8 oz cottage cheese	salt and pepper
150 ml/¼ pint soured cream	1 tablespoon grated cheese
50 g/2 oz butter	

Scrub the potatoes, mark with a cross, and bake in a hot oven until done (about 1 hour depending on size). Cut the potatoes in half and carefully scoop out some of the insides into the mixer bowl. Add the remaining ingredients except the grated cheese to the bowl and beat well with the mixer. When a smooth mixture is obtained, pile the mixture back into the potatoes and sprinkle with grated cheese. Pop back into the oven to heat.

These potatoes are marvellous as a snack if you are not on a diet and also delicious served with steaks or chops.

EGGS WITH SPINACH

Cooking time 25–30 minutes
Oven temperature Moderate 180°C, 350°F, Gas Mark 4
Serves 4

METRIC/IMPERIAL

1 (312-g/11-oz) packet frozen spinach	4 eggs
100 g/4 oz Cheddar cheese	4 tablespoons single cream
	salt and pepper

Cook the spinach as directed, drain, and cool. Divide between four buttered ramekin dishes. Grate the cheese in the blender. Break a whole egg carefully into each ramekin dish, put 1 tablespoon cream over each egg, season, and sprinkle with grated cheese. Place the dishes in a roasting tin which is quarter-filled with warm water and bake in a moderate over for 25–30 minutes.

SAVOURY ROLLS

Serves 4

METRIC/IMPERIAL

Filling	150 ml/¼ pint water
100 g/4 oz cooked chicken	salt
few sprigs parsley	50 g/2 oz plain flour
½ onion	Topping
knob of butter	50 g/2 oz grated cheese
Batter	

2 eggs

Put the chicken, parsley, and peeled and roughly chopped onion in the blender and chop finely. Empty into a saucepan in which the butter has been melted and cook gently until the rolls are ready. Put the eggs, water, and salt in the blender and switch on at high speed, then add the flour gradually while the blender is on. Rub the omelette pan over with oil, heat, then pour in a little batter to coat the bottom of the pan. When the underside is golden, turn out onto kitchen paper, cooked side up. Fill with the hot filling, fold the sides in, and roll up. When all the rolls are done, arrange in a serving dish, sprinkle with grated cheese, and brown under the grill.

Hot Puddings and Cold Sweets

Every family has a few favourite sweets and puddings but with the mixer and blender to take all the labour out of even the most elaborate party sweets, you can be more ambitious. Astound your friends with soufflés and meringues and the family with featherlight sponge puddings. Interesting textures and lovely toppings all add to the pleasure of making delicious puddings and sweets.

HOT SWISS TRIFLE

Cooking time 20 minutes
Oven temperature Moderate 180°C, 350°F, Gas Mark 4
Serves 6

METRIC/IMPERIAL

1 Swiss roll	2 eggs, separated
1 (213-g/7½-oz) can apricots	sugar
2 tablespoons custard powder	600 ml/1 pint milk

Prepare a buttered ovenproof dish.

Slice the Swiss roll and arrange around the sides of the dish, together with the apricots. Mix the custard powder, egg yolks, and 1–2 tablespoons sugar with a little of the milk; put the remainder on to heat. When nearly boiling pour onto the custard mixture, stir well, and return to the saucepan. Stirring all the time bring to the boil. Pour into the dish.

Whisk the egg whites stiffly then continue whisking while adding 3–4 tablespoons sugar. Pile on top of the custard. Bake in the centre of a moderate oven for about 20 minutes.

LEMON SUNSHINE PUDDINGS

Serves 4

METRIC/IMPERIAL

100 g/4 oz fresh white
  breadcrumbs
50 g/2 oz suet

100 g/4 oz castor sugar
grated rind and juice of 1 lemon
1 egg, beaten

Make the breadcrumbs in the blender with fresh white bread. Add the suet and sugar to the breadcrumbs and switch on for a second. Add lemon rind, juice, and egg and blend for a few seconds.

Transfer the mixture into four individual 150 ml/¼ pint plastic or foil pudding basins. Cover securely with lid, foil, or double grease-proof paper and steam or boil for 30 minutes. Turn out and serve hot with cream.

ZABAGLIONE

Serves 4

METRIC/IMPERIAL

4 egg yolks
50 g/2 oz castor sugar

5 tablespoons Marsala or sweet
  sherry

Whisk the egg yolks with the hand mixer until fluffy. Add the sugar and Marsala and beat the mixture in a bowl over a pan of hot water until it is thick, creamy, and the whisk leaves a trail. If using a stand mixer there is no need to whisk over hot water.

Serve at once in individual glasses, with sponge fingers.

APRICOT PANCAKES

Makes 8–10

METRIC/IMPERIAL

100 g/4 oz plain flour
pinch salt
1 egg
1 tablespoon oil
300 ml/½ pint milk

little oil to cook
3 (396-g/14-oz) cans apricot
  halves, drained
300 ml/½ pint apricot juice
3 teaspoons arrowroot

Sieve the flour and salt into the mixer bowl. Make a well in the centre and drop in the egg and oil. Switch the mixer on at medium speed and gradually add the milk to form a smooth batter. Heat a strong frying pan or omelette pan rubbed over with oil or dripping until it is smoking hot. Pour a small ladle of mixture into the pan and turn the pan until the mixture coats the bottom. Shake when mixture looks cooked or lift one corner with a palette knife. When nicely browned flip over, allow the other side to become golden, and slip onto a plate. Pile the cooked pancakes on a plate and keep warm in the oven.

Blend the apricot halves in the blender, reserving a few for decoration. To make the sauce, blend a little of the apricot juice with the arrowroot, bring the remainder to the boil. Pour onto the arrowroot and return to the pan; bring to the boil stirring well. Pile a little of the apricot purée on half of each pancake, fold the other half over, and arrange on an ovenproof dish. Decorate with the remaining apricots and pour a little sauce over each.

BLENDER PANCAKES

Serves 4–6

METRIC/IMPERIAL

Batter	Filling
250 ml/scant ½ pint milk	Orange brandy butter
rind and juice of 1 orange	(see page 42)
3 eggs	juice of 2 oranges
100 g/4 oz plain flour	2 tablespoons brandy
¼ teaspoon salt	1 tablespoon castor sugar

Pour the milk into the goblet, add the orange rind, cover, and blend until the rind is finely grated. Add the remaining ingredients and blend on medium speed until smooth, about 30 seconds. Heat the omelette pan and pour some of the mixture onto the pan until a thin pancake is formed. Cook until golden brown on each side. Fill with a spoonful of brandy butter, roll up, and keep warm on a heated serving dish.

Warm the orange juice, brandy, and sugar in a saucepan and pour over the pancakes just before serving.

FRUIT FRITTERS

METRIC/IMPERIAL

Fritter batter	4 tablespoons warmed water
50 g/2 oz plain flour	2 teaspoons salad oil
good pinch salt	1 egg white

Put the flour, salt, water, and oil into the blender, switch on at medium speed, and blend until a smooth batter is obtained. Beat the egg white until stiff and fold the blended mixture into the egg white with a metal spoon.

Apple fritters Peel and core medium-sized apples and cut into 1-cm/½-inch slices. Dust lightly with flour, dip into the batter, drain, and fry in hot oil until golden brown on both sides. Sprinkle with a mixture of cinnamon and castor sugar.

Pineapple fritters Cut thin rings of fresh pineapple and prepare as for apple fritters. Canned fruit may also be used.

Banana fritters Cut small bananas in half lengthwise and halve across the middle. Dip the bananas in lemon juice or lemon juice and rum, and treat as for apple fritters.

APPLE CRUMBLE

Cooking time 45 minutes
Oven temperature
Moderately hot 190°C, 375°F, Gas Mark 5, reducing to
180°C, 350°F, Gas Mark 4
Serves 6

METRIC/IMPERIAL

450 g/1 lb apples	225 g/8 oz plain flour
1 teaspoon allspice	150 g/5 oz butter
100–175 g/4–6 oz castor sugar	150 g/5 oz castor sugar

Peel and core the apples, slice thinly, and arrange in a greased pie dish in layers sprinkled with allspice and sugar. Soft brown sugar can be used with apples in place of castor sugar. Sieve the flour into the mixer bowl, add the butter, and mix into the flour until the butter is in small lumps. Add the 150 g/5 oz sugar and mix well. Sprinkle evenly over the fruit and level the surface with a palette knife. Bake on the middle shelf of a moderately hot oven for 15 minutes then reduce the temperature to 180°C, 350°F, Gas Mark 4 for a further 30 minutes. Serve with whipped cream, pouring cream, or custard sauce (see page 44).

Variation

Plums, gooseberries, apple and blackcurrant, or rhubarb can be used. Omit the allspice. Crumble mixture can be made up in large quantities and stored in an airtight jar in the fridge for some weeks. ❋ Crumble can be frozen successfully when cooked or uncooked.

APPLE PUDDING

Cooking time 35 minutes
Oven temperature Moderately hot
190°C, 375°F, Gas Mark 5
Serves 6

METRIC/IMPERIAL

2 apples	2½ teaspoons baking powder
2 eggs	1 teaspoon vanilla essence
150 g/5 oz plain flour	350 g/ 12 oz brown sugar
½ teaspoon salt	100 g/4 oz walnuts

Peel and slice the apples, drop into the blender, and chop roughly. Spread apples on the bottom of an ovenproof dish. Put the eggs, flour, salt, baking powder, vanilla essence, and brown sugar in the blender and switch on at medium speed for about 30 seconds. Switch off and add some of the nuts, blend until the nuts are chopped fairly small, and add the remaining nuts through the top of the blender. Turn the blended mixture over the apples, spread over the dish, and bake in a moderately hot oven.

UPSIDE-DOWN APPLE CAKE

Cooking time 40 minutes
Oven temperature Moderate 180°C, 350°F, Gas Mark 4
Serves 6

METRIC/IMPERIAL

2 cooking apples	100 g/4 oz butter or margarine
2 tablespoons soft brown sugar	2 eggs
25 g/1 oz whipped-up vegetable fat	100 g/4 oz self-raising flour
	1 tablespoon warm water
100 g/4 oz castor sugar	

Peel and core the apples, slice thinly. Sprinkle with lemon juice to avoid browning. Grease a deep 20-cm/8-inch tin, preferably one with a loose bottom. Mix the brown sugar with the fat in a small saucepan over low heat until the fat and sugar are combined; the fat should not be allowed to become oily. Spread this mixture over the bottom of the tin. Arrange the apple in rings starting at the outside of the tin until the bottom of the tin is covered with a neat pattern of apple slices. Cream the fat and sugar in the mixer until light in colour and creamy in texture. When the mixture is creamed sufficiently it will drop off the end of the beaters easily. Add the eggs one by one; a teaspoon of flour can be added with the second egg to prevent the mixture curdling. Add the sieved flour and fold in lightly with a metal spoon. Add 1 tablespoon warm water to the mixture before turning out of the bowl over the apples. Bake in a moderate oven for 40 minutes. Allow to cool slightly then carefully turn out onto a wire tray. Serve with whipped cream, custard sauce (see page 44), or ice cream as a dessert, or decorate with cream and use at tea time.

Variation

5 rings of canned pineapples or sliced canned peaches may be substituted for the apples.

88

STEAMED SPONGE PUDDING

Serves 4

METRIC/IMPERIAL

100 g/4 oz margarine
100 g/4 oz castor sugar
2 eggs
175 g/6 oz plain flour

2 tablespoons water
½ teaspoon salt
½ level teaspoon baking powder

Cream the fat and sugar with the mixer until pale and creamy. Add one egg and continue beating; add 1 teaspoon flour and then add the remaining egg. Add the slightly warmed water and mix well, scraping the bowl down. Sieve the flour, salt, and baking powder and fold in with a metal spoon. Put in a greased 1-litre/1½-pint pudding bowl and steam for 1½ hours. Alternatively, steam in a pressure cooker as directed by the manufacturers – usually about 25 minutes under low (5 lb) pressure. Serve with warmed syrup or lemon sauce (see page 43).

Variations

Lemon or orange rind can be added to the basic mixture and 1 table-spoon of either juice can replace 1 tablespoon of the water.

Cherry pudding 75 g/3 oz glacé cherries can be added with the flour.

Chocolate pudding Make 25 g/1 oz rice into flour with the blender, add 25 g/1 oz cocoa to it, and substitute for 50 g/2 oz of the measured flour.

Coconut pudding Add 75 g/3 oz desiccated coconut with the flour.

Ginger pudding Add 50–75 g/2–3 oz chopped preserved ginger and ½ teaspoon ground ginger with the flour.

Fruit pudding Add 75 g/3 oz sultanas, raisins, or currants.

Apricot pudding Stone and slice 450 g/1 lb apricots and place in an ovenproof dish in layers with 100 g/4 oz sugar. Make up the steamed sponge mixture and spread over the apricots. Bake for 45–60 minutes in a moderate oven (180°C, 350°F, Gas Mark 4). Serve with cream. Gooseberries, rhubarb, or apples are equally good.

CHRISTMAS PUDDING

Serves 14–16

METRIC/IMPERIAL

225 g/8 oz white breadcrumbs	225 g/8 oz currants
175 g/6 oz suet	225 g/8 oz sultanas
175 g/6 oz brown sugar	175 g/6 oz raisins
100 g/4 oz plain flour	50 g/2 oz peel
½ teaspoon salt	25 g/1 oz ground almonds
1 teaspoon baking powder	rind of 1 lemon
½ teaspoon mixed spice	4 eggs
¼ teaspoon nutmeg	300 ml/½ pint old ale

Make the breadcrumbs in the blender and empty into a large bowl.
Shred the suet in the blender and add to the breadcrumbs, add the
sugar, and mix well. Sieve the flour, salt, baking powder, and spice
into the bowl with the breadcrumbs. Add the cleaned fruit, ground
almonds, and lemon rind. The raisins and lemon rind can be chopped
in the blender if using large raisins. Mix all together with the mixer
add the eggs and ale gradually until the ingredients are well mixed
together. Grease three 1-litre/2-pint pudding bowls and fill three-
quarters full with the mixture. Cover well with a lid, two layers of
greaseproof paper, or a clean cloth, and steam for 8 hours. Alternatively cook one by one in a pressure cooker where they will take
about 3–4 hours under high (15 lb) pressure and about 40–50 minutes to
reheat, but check the weights of the puddings with the instructions
given with the pressure cooker. Serve with rum butter (see page 43).

COFFEE SOUFFLÉ

Cooking time 30–40 minutes
Oven temperature Moderate 180°C, 350°F, Gas Mark 4
Serves 4

METRIC/IMPERIAL

25 g/1 oz flour
25 g/1 oz butter
150 ml/¼ pint milk
2 tablespoons coffee essence

40 g/1½ oz castor sugar
3 egg yolks
4 egg whites

Grease a 15-cm/6-inch soufflé dish.

Make a roux in a saucepan by stirring the flour and butter together over a low heat for a few minutes. Add the milk and coffee essence and cook until thick. Should the sauce form lumps put it into the blender to smooth. Add the sugar, allow to cool slightly, and add the egg yolks one at a time. Whisk the egg whites with the mixer until stiff, fold carefully into the yolk mixture with a sharp-edged metal spoon. Make sure all the white is mixed in before pouring into the dish and baking on the middle shelf of a moderate oven for 30–40 minutes.

LEMON MERINGUE PIE

Cooking time pastry 15 minutes,
meringue 10 minutes
Oven temperature Moderately hot
200°C, 400°F, Gas Mark 6
Serves 6

METRIC/IMPERIAL

blender pastry (see page 112)
Filling
3 eggs, separated
225 g/8 oz castor sugar

3 lemons
40 g/1½ oz cornflour
300 ml/½ pint water

Make the pastry in the blender as directed on page 112. Use to line an 20-cm/8-inch flan ring and bake blind. Cool. To make the filling, place the egg yolks in a bowl with 75 g/3 oz of the castor sugar and whisk with the mixer over hot water until creamy. Grate the rind from two lemons, squeeze the juice from all three, and place in a saucepan. Moisten the cornflour with a little of the water, put the remainder of the water in the saucepan, and bring to the boil. Pour onto the corn-flour, return to the saucepan, and cook, stirring, until thick. Cool. Whisk in the egg yolks and sugar, allow to cool, then use to fill the baked flan case. Place the egg whites in the mixer bowl and whip with the mixer until stiff, fold in 1 tablespoon sugar with a metal spoon, pile meringue on top of filling, and place in a moderately hot oven until the meringue begins to crisp on top.

Variation

Fruit meringue pie Fill the flan case with stewed fruit, e.g., apples or blackberries. Top with meringue.

BITTER ORANGE CHEESECAKE

Serves 6

METRIC/IMPERIAL

40 g/1½ oz butter	1 orange jelly
75 g/3 oz digestive biscuits	2 medium oranges
1 dessertspoon sugar	350 g/12 oz cream cheese
100 g/4 oz chocolate	

Melt the butter in a small saucepan. Place the biscuits a few at a time in the blender goblet and run the machine until reduced to fine crumbs. Grease a 15–18-cm/6–7-inch deep cake tin with a loose base. Mix the crumbs with the butter and sugar then press into the base of the tin. Melt 75 g/3 oz of the chocolate in a bowl over hot water; pour over the biscuit base, spreading evenly, and leave until set.

Divide the jelly into cubes, place in the blender with 150 ml/¼ pint boiling water, and run the machine at a high speed to dissolve the jelly; pour into a bowl. Cut each orange into four pieces and put into the liquidiser gradually with 150 ml/¼ pint cold water; run for a short time at high speed.

Strain into the jelly then return all to the blender; gradually add the cream cheese and run until well blended. Half set the jelly then pour onto the biscuit base. When set, push up the base of the tin, carefully remove the base, and place the cheesecake on a serving dish.

To decorate, melt the remaining chocolate and place in a grease-proof paper icing bag, cutting off the tip. Pipe a design on top of the cheesecake, finishing with a slice of orange.

LEMON CHEESECAKE

Cooking time 1½ hours
Oven temperature Cool 150°C, 300°F, Gas Mark 2
Serves 8

METRIC/IMPERIAL

Crumb crust	300 ml/½ pint double cream
50 g/2 oz butter	3 egg yolks
75 g/3 oz biscuit crumbs	9 tablespoons lemon juice
50 g/2 oz sugar	grated rind of 1 lemon
¼ teaspoon cinnamon	100 g/4 oz sugar
Filling	1 tablespoon cornflour
225 g/8 oz curd cheese	3 egg whites
225 g/8 oz cream cheese	

Melt the butter in a saucepan, remove from the heat, and stir in the biscuit crumbs, sugar, and cinnamon. Press into the base of a 20-cm/8-inch loose-bottomed tin. Cool.

Place curd and cream cheeses, cream, egg yolks, lemon juice, rind, sugar, and cornflour in the blender and run at medium speed until smooth. Transfer to a bowl. Whisk the egg whites until stiff using the mixer and gently fold into the cheese mixture. Pour the mixture on top of the crumb crust and bake in a cool oven for 1½ hours, until set.

Allow to cool completely, preferably overnight, and turn out.

PINEAPPLE WATERLILY PUDDING

Serves 6

METRIC/IMPERIAL

1 (454 g/16-oz) pineapple cubes	1 teaspoon lemon juice
1 packet lemon jelly	few drops green food colouring
8 white marshmallows	few slices angelica
1 (170-g/6-oz) can evaporated milk	

Strain the syrup from the pineapple cubes into a measuring jug and make up to 300 ml/½ pint with water. Bring to boiling point, add the jelly, and stir until dissolved. Reserve half the quantity for the top of the mousse, leave in a warm place as it should not set too quickly. Dissolve 4 marshmallows in the remaining jelly. Liquidise the pineapple cubes, reserving a few for decoration. Put the evaporated milk and lemon juice in a bowl and whisk with the mixer on high speed until it will form soft peaks. Fold in the pineapple. Stir this mixture into the half-set jelly, mix lightly, turn into a bowl, and chill. Tint the remaining jelly green with a few drops of food colouring. If necessary, place the container in warm water for a few minutes first. Run the tinted jelly over the surface of the mousse. When this jelly topping has set, decorate with the remaining marshmallows, snipped round the edge to look like lilies with scissors dipping in icing sugar. Put a tiny piece of pineapple in the centre of each flower, and a leaf of angelica at the side.

ORANGE AND CINNAMON PIE

Cooking time 15–20 minutes
Oven temperature Moderately hot
200°C, 400°F, Gas Mark 6
Serves 6

METRIC/IMPERIAL

50 g/2 oz butter	water
100 g/4 oz plain flour	1 packet orange instant whip
25 g/1 oz castor sugar	300 ml/½ pint milk
25 g/1 oz chopped walnuts	*To decorate*
1 teaspoon ground cinnamon	angelica
1 egg, separated	candied orange segments

Have ready a 18-cm/7-inch flan ring or loose-bottomed sandwich tin.

Rub the butter into the flour and add the sugar, chopped walnuts, and cinnamon. Mix to a stiff dough with a mixture of egg yolk and water. Knead lightly and roll out into a round about 23 cm/9 inches in diameter. Line the flan ring, prick the base with a fork, and bake it in the middle of a moderately hot oven for about 15–20 minutes. Cool.

Just before serving make up the instant whip as directed on the packet. Stiffly whisk the egg white and stir it lightly through the whip. Turn this into the baked case and serve decorated with angelica and candied orange sections.

GOOSEBERRY FOOL

Serves 3–4

METRIC/IMPERIAL

150 ml/¼ pint thick custard, unsweetened

1 (538-g/1 lb 3-oz) can gooseberries

juice of ½ lemon

2 tablespoons double cream

1 egg white

Make the custard and allow to cool. Place the gooseberries and juice in the blender and blend until smooth. Sieve the purée into a bowl to remove the seeds, reserving 150 ml/¼ pint for the decoration. Rinse out the goblet and pour in the remaining purée, custard, lemon juice, and cream; blend well. Divide between three or four glasses.

Whisk the egg white stiffly with the mixer and fold in the reserved gooseberry purée. Swirl on top of the gooseberry fool in each glass.

RASPBERRY SOUFFLÉ

Serves 6

METRIC/IMPERIAL

175 g/6 oz sugar

4 tablespoons water

6 egg yolks

300 ml/½ pint double cream

50 g/2 oz castor sugar

225 g/8 oz raspberries

Tie a band of greased paper around a 18-cm/7-inch soufflé dish to come at least 2·5 cm/1 inch above the edge of the dish. Pour the sugar and water in a saucepan and boil until a syrup is formed. The syrup is ready when a long thread is formed when a spoon is dipped in the mixture. Put the egg yolks in a bowl over hot water and turn on the hand mixer. Add the syrup slowly while the mixer is running at medium speed. Cook for about 45–50 minutes in the double boiler until a thin sauce consistency is reached. Whip the cream until thick and add the castor sugar. Blend the raspberries until puréed, add to the whipped cream. Combine the two mixtures and pour into the prepared soufflé dish. Put the dish into the cold part of the refrigerator or the freezer. Remove from the freezer 15 minutes before required and serve decorated with fresh raspberries if available.

RASPBERRY WATER ICE

Serves 4

METRIC/IMPERIAL

175 g/6 oz granulated sugar   3 tablespoons icing sugar
200 ml/7 fl oz water   ½ egg white, whisked
1 kg/ 2 lb raspberries

Make a sugar syrup by dissolving the sugar in the water over a gentle
heat. Allow to cool. Put the raspberries in the blender, blend until a
purée is formed, add the icing sugar, and blend well. Pour in the cold
sugar syrup, blend again. Sieve into ice trays and chill in the freezing
compartment of a refrigerator or in the freezer. Do not allow the
mixture to become hard. Whisk the egg white until stiff, return the
chilled mixture to the blender and mix well, add the egg white.
Return to the freezer, stir from time to time until the mixture is set.
Serve decorated with raspberries and leaves. ❊ If you make a lot of
ice cream you can now buy a small electric machine to go inside the
freezer which stirs the ice cream all the time.

Variation

Pineapple water ice Substitute 1 large pineapple, peeled and cored,
for the raspberries and purée in the blender. Makes about 450 ml/¾ pint.

RASPBERRY COOLER

Serves 4

METRIC/IMPERIAL

1 (425-g/15 oz) can raspberries   *To decorate*
300 ml/½ pint milk   mint leaves
2–3 sprigs fresh mint

Place the raspberries and juice in the blender goblet and run at top
speed for a few seconds. Sieve the purée into a bowl. Rinse out the
goblet, pour in the purée, milk, and mint, and run the machine until
well blended. ❊ Pour the mixture into the ice trays or a bowl and
place in the freezing compartment of the refrigerator, or place in the
freezer.

Leave until just beginning to freeze, return to the blender, and mix until smooth. Replace in the freezing compartment and leave until frozen. Serve scoops or spoonfuls in glasses and decorate with mint leaves.

RASPBERRY SHORTCAKE

Cooking time 30–40 minutes
Oven temperature Moderate 170°C, 325°F, Gas Mark 3
Serves 8

METRIC/IMPERIAL

225 g/8 oz butter	1 raspberry yogurt
175 g/6 oz castor sugar	*To decorate*
350 g/12 oz plain flour	icing sugar
150 ml/¼ pint milk	raspberries
1 packet raspberry Angel Delight	

Beat the butter and sugar together until white and creamy; work in the flour. Knead the mixture lightly and shape into two flat rounds about 20 cm/8 inches in diameter.

Place on separate baking trays, crimp the edges, prick one well with a fork, and mark the other into eight wedge-shaped pieces. Bake towards the bottom of a moderate oven for 30–40 mintues. Sprinkle with castor sugar before quite cold.

Put the milk in a bowl, whisk in the raspberry Angel Delight, then stir in the yogurt. Put the shortcake base on the serving dish, swirl with the raspberry mixture, and arrange the shortcake wedges on top dusted alternatively with icing sugar and castor sugar. Decorate with fresh or frozen raspberries.

CHOCOLATE MOUSSE

Serves 4

METRIC/IMPERIAL

175 g/6 oz plain chocolate	*To decorate*
rind and juice of 1 orange	whipped cream
4 eggs	grated chocolate

Put the chocolate and orange rind in the blender and chop finely. Empty into a bowl and place over a saucepan of hot water, making sure that the water does not touch the bowl. Add the orange juice to the chocolate and allow to melt. Meanwhile separate the eggs. Remove the bowl from the heat and stir in the egg yolks one at a time. Whisk the egg whites until stiff, fold into the chocolate mixture, and pour into a serving dish or four individual pots. Allow to chill and decorate with whipped cream and melted chocolate.

CARIBBEAN RING

Cooking time 35–40 minutes
Oven temperature Moderate 180°C, 350°F, Gas Mark 4
Serves 6

METRIC/IMPERIAL

100 g/4 oz butter	1 level teaspoon baking powder
175 g/6 oz plain chocolate	small packet instant mashed
100 g/4 oz castor sugar	potato
4 eggs, separated	large can fruit salad
1 teaspoon vanilla essence	150 ml/¼ pint double cream

Grease a 1·75-litre/3-pint ring tin.

Melt the butter in a saucepan. Add the chocolate, broken into pieces, and stir over a gentle heat until melted. Remove the pan from the heat. Stir in the sugar. Beat in the egg yolks with a hand mixer, then add the vanilla essence, sifted baking powder, and the potato. Whisk the egg whites until stiff and fold into the chocolate mixture. Turn into the prepared tin and bake in a moderate oven for 35–40 minutes, until cooked. Turn out on a wire rack to cool.

Put the cake on a large plate. Drain off the liquid from the canned fruit and pile the fruit into the centre. Lightly whip the cream and fill a piping bag with a star pipe attached. Pipe five rosettes on the top and more round the base. Serve as a special pudding or cake.

Baking

Here the mixer comes into its own in a really big way, taking the hard work out of so many tasks – from kneading dough for bread to whipping up the lightest, fluffiest sponge you've ever tasted. Pastry can be made in the mixer or in the blender, as you like.

Cakes and pastries can be made in one step using the mixer. Whipped-up margarines and shortenings make these a great success. Grandmother may be horrified by such new-fangled sleight of hand but what a boon to busy mothers who have children's teas and family puddings to provide. ❈ Cakes freeze very well.

WHITE BREAD

Cooking time 30–40 minutes
Oven temperature Hot 230°C, 450°F, Gas Mark 8

METRIC/IMPERIAL

Yeast liquid	*Dry mixture*
15 g/½ oz fresh yeast	675 g/1½ lb plain flour
450 ml/¾ pint water	1 teaspoon salt
or	15 g/1½ oz lard
2 teaspoons dried yeast	
1 teaspoon sugar	
450 ml/¾ pint warm water	

Either blend the fresh yeast with the water, or dissolve the sugar in the water and sprinkle on the dried yeast. If using dried yeast allow to stand until frothy, about 10 minutes.

Sieve the flour and salt into the mixer bowl and rub in the lard. Pour in the yeast liquid and knead well with the dough hook until the mixture leaves the sides of the bowl clean, adding a very little extra flour if needed. Continue kneading with the dough hook until the dough is no longer sticky.

Place the dough in a lightly greased large polythene bag loosely tied, or in the mixer bowl covered with polythene or a damp tea towel. Allow to rise until doubled in size and the dough springs back when pressed with a floured finger. Rising times are adaptable to fit in with your plans but the best results are achieved by a slow rise.

Warm place: 45–60 minutes – quick rise
Room temperature: 2 hours – slower rise
Cold larder or room: up to 12 hours – slow rise
Refrigerator: up to 24 hours – very slow rise

Dough which has been risen in the refrigerator must be allowed to return to room temperature before shaping.

Turn the risen dough onto a lightly floured board and flatten firmly with the knuckles to knock out the air bubbles, then knead to make the dough firm and ready for shaping.

For a large loaf, stretch the dough into an oblong the same width as a 1-kg/2 lb loaf tin, fold into three, turn in ends, and place in the greased tin. For 2 small loaves, divide the dough in half, shape as for a large loaf, and place in two 0·5-kg/1-lb loaf tins.

Put the dough to rise again, by placing the tins inside a lightly greased polythene bag and allowing the dough to come to the top of the tin. It should spring back when pressed with a floured finger. Leave for 1–1½ hours at room temperature or longer in a refrigerator.

Remove the polythene and bake the loaves in the centre of a hot oven for 30–40 minutes until well risen and golden brown. Remove from the tins and cool on a wire tray.

Cooked loaves sound hollow when tapped underneath and shrink slightly from the sides of the tin.

✾ **Note** Bread can be frozen successfully if wrapped and sealed immediately it is completely cold. Thaw at room temperature allowing 2–3 hours for a large loaf. Bread can be thawed in the oven but tends to stale more quickly. Sliced bread can be toasted whilst still frozen.

WHOLEMEAL BREAD

Cooking time 30 minutes
Oven temperature Hot 230°C, 450°F, Gas Mark 8
Makes 6 loaves

METRIC/IMPERIAL

45 g/1¾ oz fresh yeast	20 g/¾ oz salt
900 ml/1½ pints tepid water	25 g/1 oz fat
1·5 kg/3 lb wholemeal flour	

Mix the yeast with half the tepid water. Mix the flour and salt together in the mixer bowl, make a well in the middle, and pour in the yeast mixture and the melted fat. Using the dough hook, gradually mix all ingredients together, adding the remaining water. Knead well with the dough hook until the dough is no longer sticky. Put the dough to rise in a greased polythene bag, mixer bowl, or greased saucepan with a lid for about 35–60 minutes in a warm place until it has doubled in size. Knead to knock out air.

Divide the dough into 6 portions and shape into rolls. Place in lightly greased 0·5-kg/1-lb loaf tins or on greased baking trays. Allow to rise again for at least 30–40 minutes. Bake in a hot oven for about 30 minutes.

PIZZA

Cooking time 20–30 minutes
Oven temperature Hot 230°C, 450°F, Gas Mark 8
Serves 4

METRIC/IMPERIAL

225/½ lb white dough which has had one rising	1 tablespoon tomato purée
	1 small clove garlic
olive oil for brushing	½ teaspoon fresh or dried thyme,
Filling	oregano, marjoram, or basil
25 g/1 oz Cheddar cheese	8 anchovy fillets
1 (198 g/7-oz) can peeled tomatoes	few black olives

Roll the risen dough into a long strip. Brush with oil and roll up like a Swiss roll. Repeat this three times. Oil two 15-cm/6-inch sandwich tins, or one 30 by 20 cm/12 by 8-inch Swiss roll tin. Divide dough if necessary, roll to fit tin, press in with the knuckles, and brush with oil.

To make the filling, grate the cheese. Place the drained tomatoes, tomato purée, crushed garlic, and herbs in the blender and using a slow speed mix until blended. Cover the pizza dough with alternate layers of tomato mixture and cheese, finishing with a layer of cheese. Place anchovies and stoned and halved black olives on top and allow to stand in a cool place for about 30 minutes. Bake in a hot oven for 20–30 minutes.

❋ **Note** Pizza freezes extremely well either in the uncooked state or cooked. The pizza can be frozen after the filling has been added or after cooking. Children love pizza but probably without the anchovies and olives. I substitute small rolls of bacon or cooked ham.

OVEN SCONES

Cooking time 10–12 minutes
Oven temperature Hot 220°C, 425°F, Gas Mark 7
Makes 10

METRIC/IMPERIAL

225 g/8 oz self-raising flour	1 tablespoon castor sugar
2 teaspoons baking powder	50 g/ 2oz margarine
pinch salt	150 ml/¼ pint milk

Sieve all the dry ingredients into the mixer bowl and cut the margarine into small pieces. Switch on the beater until the fat is rubbed into the flour. Add the milk and knead the mixture for a few minutes with the beater; do not over-knead, however. Turn onto a floured board, roll out with a lightly floured rolling pin, cut into rounds with a cutter. Put the rounds on a greased baking tray in the oven for about 10–12 minutes depending on the thickness of the scones.

Variation

Cheese scones Omit sugar, add 3 tablespoons grated cheese and a good pinch of dry mustard before adding the milk.

DROPPED SCONES

Makes 24

METRIC/IMPERIAL

225 g/8 oz self-raising flour   25 g/1 oz castor sugar
2 teaspoons baking powder   1 egg
pinch salt   350 ml/generous ¼ pint milk

Sieve the flour, baking powder, and salt in the mixer bowl. Sprinkle in the castor sugar. Make a well in the centre, drop in the egg and at least half of the milk. Switch on the mixer and beat until a smooth batter is obtained. Stir in the remaining milk with a metal spoon and allow to stand in a cool place for at least 15 minutes before using. Preheat a girdle or thick frying pan slowly on a moderate heat. Grease with a piece of dripping or cooking fat. Drop four dessert-spoons of mixture onto the girdle, allow bubbles to appear all over the surface before turning to allow top side to brown. Place in a clean tea towel or kitchen paper on a wire tray until cool.

PLAIN SPONGE CAKE

Cooking time 45–50 minutes or 20 minutes
Oven temperature Moderate 180°C, 350°F, Gas Mark 4 or
moderately hot 200°C, 400°F, Gas Mark 6

METRIC/IMPERIAL

3 eggs   75 g/3 oz plain flour
75 g/3 oz castor sugar   pinch baking powder

Use ingredients at room temperature and warm the bowl and whisk slightly before using. Grease and flour a 15-cm/6-inch tin which is 7·5 cm/3-inches deep, or two 20-cm/8-inch sandwich tins.

Break the eggs into the bowl, add the sugar, and whisk until the mixture is thick, very pale yellow, and fluffy. Remove the bowl from the machine, sieve in half the flour and baking powder, fold in with a metal spoon. Add the other half of the flour and fold in carefully. Turn into the prepared tin. Cook in a moderate oven for 45–50 minutes in the deep tin; sandwich tins take 20 minutes

Turn the cake out carefully onto a wire tray and allow to cool. Sandwich together with jam, sieve icing sugar on top. Alternatively fill with whipped cream and fresh or canned fruit.

WIZARD WONDER

Cooking time 1½ hours
Oven temperature Moderate 180°C, 350°F, Gas Mark 4

METRIC/IMPERIAL

175 g/6 oz self-raising flour
2 level tablespoons cocoa
1 level teaspoon baking powder
175 g/6 oz soft margarine
175 g/6 oz castor sugar

3 eggs

Topping

75 g/3 oz glacé cherries
40 g/1½ oz walnut halves
2 rounded tablespoons apricot jam

Grease a 1-kg/2-lb loaf tin. Make a lining using a double strip of greaseproof paper cut to fit the width of the tin and protruding at either end. Grease this paper lining also.

Sieve the dry ingredients together into a bowl, add the margarine, sugar, and eggs, and cream thoroughly with the mixer until the mixture is well blended. Spoon into the prepared tin, smoothing over the surface, and hollow out the centre. Bake the cake in a moderate oven for 1½ hours. Test with a skewer; the cake is cooked when the skewer comes out clean.

While the cake is cooking, prepare the topping. Halve the cherries and walnuts and put into a pan with the jam. Stir continuously, bring to the boil, and cook. Pour over the cake and leave in the tin until cold. Lift the cake out using the ends of the paper to help.

Variation

Small cakes Cook the mixture in a lined Swiss roll tin at the top of a moderately hot oven (200°C, 400°F, Gas Mark 6) for about 10 minutes. Turn out and allow to cool, then cut into shapes using shaped cutters. Decorate with butter icing (see page 115).

SWISS ROLL

Cooking time 7 minutes
Oven temperature Hot 220°C, 425°F, Gas Mark 7

METRIC/IMPERIAL

50 g/2 oz self-raising flour	50 g/2 oz castor sugar
2 large eggs	3 tablespoons jam

Sieve the flour and warm for a few minutes. Prepare a 15 by 25 cm/ 6 by 10-inch tin by lining with greaseproof paper. Allow enough to line the sides, cut into the corners, and mitre neatly. Warm the bowl and whisk for a few moments. Put the eggs in the bowl with the sugar, and whisk until the mixture is pale yellow and thick. Sieve the flour into the egg mixture and fold in with a metal spoon. Pour into the prepared tin. Cook on the second top shelf of a hot oven for 7–8 minutes. Turn out onto a piece of greaseproof paper cut the same size as the Swiss roll tin, which has been sprinkled with castor sugar. Trim the edges of the sponge, spread with warmed jam, and roll up tightly. Dust with castor or icing sugar.

Variations

The Swiss roll can be rolled without filling, then when it is cool unrolled and filled with whipped cream or butter icing (see page 115).

Party cakes Swiss rolls can be used as a base for several party cakes.

Yule log The most common one is the yule log when the roll is decorated on the outside with chocolate butter icing (see page 115) or melted chocolate. To suit the season a robin or sprig of holly will add the finishing touch for tea time around Christmas.

Engine cake The roll can be decorated with butter icing and liquorice all-sorts used as wheels and chimneys. Small children like the coal truck filled with smarties. This can be made by piping or arranging the icing with a knife into a small square at the back of the engine, then filling with sweets.

105

COFFEE MALLOW GÂTEAU

Cooking time 45–50 minutes
Oven temperature Moderate 180°C, 350°F, Gas Mark 4

plain sponge cake (see page 103)	6 tablespoons milk
12 marshmallows	chopped nuts
6 tablespoons black coffee	crystallised violets
1 sachet Dream Topping	

Make the sponge cake mixture according to the directions on page 103 and put in a 20-cm/8-inch deep cake tin. Bake in a moderate oven for 45–50 minutes. Turn out carefully and allow to cool.

Put the marshmallows and coffee in a small saucepan and melt gently. Leave to cool and thicken. Make up the Dream Topping with milk as directed on the packet and lightly stir in the coffee mixture. Split the cake through the centre and sandwich it together with one third of the coffee mallow mixture.

Assemble the gâteau by swirling most of the remaining coffee mallow mixture on top and around the sides of the cake leaving a little for the piped rosettes. Decorate the sides of the gâteau with chopped nuts and the top with rosettes and crystallised violets.

FUDGE CAKE

METRIC/IMPERIAL

25 g/1 oz stoned raisins	2 tablespoons drinking chocolate
65 g/2½ oz glacé cherries	225 g/8 oz wholemeal biscuits
3 tablespoons golden syrup	few chocolate buttons
100 g/4 oz butter	

Grease and line a 0·5-kg/1-lb loaf tin, using a double strip of grease-proof paper to fit the width of the tin and protruding at either end. Grease the paper. Soak the raisins in warm water for a few minutes, drain. Place the raisins in the blender. Reserve 4 cherries and place remainder in blender. Run on high speed until fruit is chopped, place in bowl. Place the biscuits in the blender and blend until mixture looks like breadcrumbs; place in bowl with fruit. Melt the syrup and butter in a saucepan, add the drinking chocolate, and pour over the dry ingredients. Press the mixture into the prepared tin; decorate the top with the remaining cherries and chocolate drops. Leave overnight then carefully lift out of the tin using the paper strips.

CHOCOLATE ORANGE CAKE

Cooking time 50 minutes
Oven temperature Moderate 180°C, 350°F, Gas Mark 4

METRIC/IMPERIAL

50 g/2 oz plain chocolate	pinch salt
175 g/6 oz butter	150 ml/¼ pint double cream
175 g/6 oz castor sugar	1 tablespoon milk
3 large eggs	3 oranges
150 g/5 oz plain flour	50 g/2 oz granulated sugar
25 g/1 oz cocoa	4 tablespoons water

Melt the chocolate in a small bowl over a pan of hot water, spread on a cool marble or Formica surface, and allow to harden. Make chocolate curls by pushing a sharp knife away from you over the surface of the chocolate.

Cream the butter and sugar together in the mixer bowl, beat in the egg yolks. Sieve together the flour, cocoa, and salt and fold in lightly. Whisk the egg whites until stiff and fold into the mixture. Turn into a greased and base-lined deep 20-cm/8-inch cake tin and bake in a moderate oven for about 50 minutes. Cool on a wire tray then slice into four equal layers.

Whisk the cream and milk together. Thinly peel the zest from one orange, then remove the skin and pith from all three oranges and cut the flesh into segments. Dissolve the remaining sugar in the water, add the orange peel, then boil until a thick syrup is formed. Remove from the heat.

To assemble the cake, spread the bottom layer of the cake with half the cream, place the second layer on top, and arrange orange segments over. Add the third layer, spread with remaining cream, and top with the last layer of cake. Spoon the glaze over the cake, decorate with chocolate curls, and dust with icing sugar.

This cake may be served as a sweet.

FRUIT CAKE

Cooking time 3–4 hours
Oven temperature Cool 150°C, 300°F, Gas Mark 2

METRIC/IMPERIAL

225 g/8 oz butter
100 g/4 oz castor sugar
100 g/4 oz brown sugar
1 tablespoon treacle
5 eggs
2 tablespoons brandy
275 g/10 oz plain flour
½ teaspoon allspice

½ teaspoon cinnamon
450 g/1 lb currants
225 g/8 oz sultanas
100 g/4 oz chopped peel
100 g/4 oz glacé cherries
50 g/2 oz chopped almonds
grated rind of 1 lemon

Cream the butter and sugars together in the mixer bowl until light and fluffy, using the mixer on medium speed. Gradually beat in the treacle and then the eggs, one at a time, adding a little flour with the last addition if necessary. Beat in the brandy. Sieve the flour with the spices and fold into the mixture; finally add the fruit, folding in gently with a metal spoon. Grease and line a 20-cm/8-inch cake tin and tie a band of brown paper round the outside. Place the mixture in the baking tin, stand on a piece of brown paper in the oven, and bake in a cool oven for 3–4 hours.

ORANGE CARAMEL CAKE

Cooking time 25 minutes
Oven temperature Moderately hot
190°C, 375°F, Gas Mark 5

METRIC/IMPERIAL

175 g/6 oz butter
175 g/6 oz castor sugar
grated rind of 1 orange
3 eggs

175 g/6 oz self-raising flour
orange butter icing (see page 115)
To decorate
few crystallised orange segments

Grease and line two 20-cm/8-inch sandwich tins.

Warm the mixer bowl and cream together the butter, sugar, and orange rind on a medium speed for about 2 minutes until the mixture is light and fluffy. Reduce the speed to low and add the eggs one at a time. Turn speed to high and beat well for 20–30 seconds, scraping down sides if necessary. Switch to low speed and add the flour, switching off immediately the flour is mixed in. Divide the mixture between prepared tins and bake in a moderately hot oven for about 25 minutes; turn onto a wire tray and allow to cool.

Sandwich the cakes together with a little of the butter icing, spread the remainder over the top and sides of the cake, and decorate with the orange segments.

CHOUX PASTRY

Oven temperature Moderately hot
200°F, 400°F, Gas Mark 6

METRIC/IMPERIAL

150 ml/¼ pint water	½ teaspoon salt
50 g/2 oz butter	2 teaspoons sugar
65 g/2½ oz plain flour	2 eggs

Pour the water into a saucepan, add the butter, allow to melt, and then bring to the boil. *Do not boil for too long before adding the flour.* Sieve the flour and salt onto a paper, sprinkle with sugar. Tip the flour into the boiling liquid and beat with a wooden spoon until the mixture becomes very thick and leaves the side of the pan. Allow the thick mixture to cool slightly, place in the mixer bowl. Switch on at a low speed and add the eggs one at a time. This beating process is very important as the lightness of the paste will depend on how much air is incorporated at this stage. To beat by hand is a very tiring process but the mixer makes it very easy. Beat in each egg thoroughly then switch the mixer to maximum speed for 30 seconds and the choux pastry is ready for use.

Prepare a greased baking tray and a 1-cm/½-inch meringue pipe in a forcing bag.

Chocolate éclairs Fill the forcing bag with the choux pastry. Hold the bag so that it is lying almost parallel with the baking sheet and force the pastry out in 6-cm/2½-inch lengths. Cut away from the pipe with a wet knife; leave about 4-cm/1½-inches space between each éclair. Bake in the centre of a moderately hot oven for 20–30 minutes. The éclairs should be crisp, golden brown, and dried through. Test by tapping the base – the pastry should sound hollow. Alternatively split them open; if there is any soggy inside return to the oven for a few minutes. Allow to cool, then fill with whipped cream. Dip the top into, or coat with chocolate topping made by melting 50–100 g/2–4 oz plain chocolate with 25 g/1 oz butter over hot water, or coffee glacé icing.

Cream puffs Pipe or spoon onto a greased baking tray in small rounds. Puffs will take 25–35 minutes to cook depending on the size. Allow to cool, fill with whipped cream, and dredge with icing sugar. Puffs may be used as a sweet, then they can be filled with fresh or canned fruit with cream.

Savoury choux buns Small savoury choux buns can be made by omitting the sugar from the mixture. Pipe smaller rounds for excellent cocktail savouries. Fill with a little white sauce mixed with shrimps, mushrooms, chicken, salmon. The cottage cheese and chive mixture used in the baked potatoes recipe (see page 81) is also an excellent filling. The salmon or tuna dip (see page 19) can also be used as a filling.

❈ To freeze choux pastry Choux pastry can be frozen baked or unbaked. To freeze unbaked pipe onto trays, open freeze for about 1 hour, then pack in foil, polythene boxes or bags. The frozen shapes can go straight from the freezer into the oven but allow an extra 5 minutes on the cooking time. The pastry shapes can be stored for about 3 months.

To freeze baked choux pastry, pack unfilled in a polythene bag or foil then in a polythene box. To use remove from the freezer and stand at room temperature for about 1 hour then pop into a moderate oven (180°C, 350°F, Gas Mark 4) for five minutes; cool and fill. Baked shells will keep frozen for at least 6 months.

❈ Notes on freezing pastry

All baked or unbaked pastry freezes well. Short crust pastry takes about 3 hours to thaw before it can be rolled therefore I can see little advantage in freezing it in a lump. It is much better to shape it into flans, pies, or tartlet cases becore freezing either baked or unbaked.

Fruit or meat pies can be made in foil dishes, plates, or flan rings. Put into the freezer uncovered but do not make holes or vents for the steam to escape otherwise the filling tends to dry out. When the pies are hard cover with heavy duty foil. Small pies can be removed from tins and stored in foil, polythene bags, or boxes.

Flan cases can be frozen in the rings or foil cases until hard; then remove rings, wrap in foil, and pack in a polythene box. Unbaked pastry stores well for 3 months.

To cook frozen shaped pastry Pies can be unwrapped and placed in a preheated oven; bake at the usual temperature allowing extra time for thawing. Cut vents on the top as the pastry thaws.

Flan cases will take about 25 minutes to bake 'blind' from the frozen state.

Cooked pastry pies and flans should be cooled quickly, left in the dishes, and packed in heavy duty foil. Freeze immediately when cool. Meat and fish pies will keep well for about 3 months, fruit pies last well for up to 5 or 6 months, unfilled pastry cases for about 6 months. Allow pies to thaw at room temperature for 2 hours before reheating.

SHORT CRUST PASTRY

METRIC/IMPERIAL

50 g/2 oz butter or margarine	1 teaspoon salt
50 g/2 oz white cooking fat	4 tablespoons cold water
200 g/8 oz plain flour	

Cut the fat into pieces and put in the mixer bowl, switch on at minimum speed. Tip the sieved flour and salt into the bowl and slightly increase the speed until the fat is broken up. Allow to mix until the mixture becomes like breadcrumbs; add the water and mix for only a few seconds until a dough is obtained. Turn out of the bowl onto a lightly floured board and use for either sweet or savoury dishes.

Variations

Sweet short crust Increase the fat content to 150 g/5 oz and put in the bowl with 2 teaspoons castor sugar. Mix the pastry with 1 egg yolk and 1 tablespoon water.

Cheese pastry Use 75 g/3 oz fat and make as directed, adding a pinch of cayenne pepper and dry mustard to the flour. When the mixture is like breadcrumbs, add 50 g/2 oz grated cheese. Mix well and bind with 2 tablespoons cold water.

BLENDER PASTRY

METRIC/IMPERIAL

200 g/8 oz plain flour
½ teaspoon salt

100 g/4 oz margarine or soft
cooking fat
2 tablespoons cold water

Put the flour, salt, and fat into the blender. Switch on for about 10 seconds. Stop and scrape down the sides of the blender with a wooden spatula. Tip out onto the table, make a well in the centre, and add 1 tablespoon water; when this is absorbed add the remaining water. If this seems too difficult tip crumb mixture into a bowl, add the water, and mix with a fork. Allow to rest in the refrigerator for a few minutes before using.

CRISPIE BARS

Cooking time 12 minutes
Oven temperatures Moderate 180°C, 350°F, Gas Mark 4
Makes 14

METRIC/IMPERIAL

65 g/2½ oz plain flour
25 g/1 oz castor sugar
50 g/2 oz butter
            Topping
25 g/1 oz margarine

1 tablespoon golden syrup
1 tablespoon sugar
1 tablespoon cocoa
25 g/1 oz rice krispies

Sieve the flour and sugar into the mixer bowl and using the mixer on medium speed rub in the butter. Knead lightly until mixture holds together. Roll into a 18-cm/7-inch square and bake in a moderate oven for about 12 minutes; cool.

Put margarine, syrup, sugar, and cocoa into a saucepan and stir over low heat until dissolved. Add the krispies and turn in the mixture until completely coated. Spread the topping over the shortbread and allow to set. Cut into bars when quite cold.

ONION FLAN

Cooking time 35 minutes approximately
Oven temperature Moderate 180°C, 350°F, Gas Mark 4
Serves 4–6

METRIC/IMPERIAL

Quick-mix pastry	Filling
175 g/6 oz plain flour	450 g/1 lb onions
½ teaspoon salt	40 g/1½ oz butter
75 g/3 oz whipped-up cooking fat	1 tablespoon olive oil
1½ tablespoons water	2 eggs
	150 ml/¼ pint double cream
	salt and pepper

Sieve the flour and salt in a bowl, cut the cooking fat roughly into the flour and add the water. Blend at minimum speed until the pastry is mixed to a firm consistency. Turn out onto a floured board, roll out, and line a 20-cm/8-inch pie plate or flan ring. Prick the bottom of the flan, fill with baking beans, and cook on the second top shelf of a moderate oven for 15 minutes.

Meanwhile, cut the peeled onions into rings and sweat in the butter and oil until transparent and soft – do not brown. Beat the eggs with the cream, season well. Arrange the onions in the flan and cover with the cream and egg mixture. Bake in a moderate oven until golden brown. This flan is delicious hot or cold and makes a marvellous hot starter on its own.

Variations

Quiche lorraine Beat 1 egg and 1 egg yolk in a bowl with 25 g/1 oz grated cheese 150 ml/¼ pint milk, and seasoning. Melt 15 g/½ oz butter in a saucepan and slowly cook 2–3 slices bacon, chopped, and 1 small onion, chopped, until golden brown. Add to the egg mixture, pour into the pastry case, and cook as for onion flan.

Bacon, egg, and tomato flan Mix 2 eggs, 50 g/2 oz grated cheese, 2 tablespoons milk or thin cream, and salt and pepper with 2–3 rashers of bacon, chopped and cooked, and pour into the pastry case. Cover with sliced tomatoes and cook until set.

COCONUT HEAPS

Cooking time 15 minutes
Oven temperature Moderately hot
190°C, 375°F, Gas Mark 5
Makes 12

METRIC/IMPERIAL

75 g/3 oz butter
75 g/3 oz castor sugar
1 egg
100 g/4 oz plain flour
1 tablespoon cocoa

1 teaspoon baking powder
50 g/2 oz desiccated coconut
1 tablespoon milk
Filling
butter icing (see page 115)

Cream the butter and sugar together in the mixer bowl, then add the egg, beating well. Sieve together the flour, cocoa, and baking powder and fold into the mixture. Stir in the coconut and mix to a soft dough with the milk. Place teaspoonfuls of the mixture on greased baking trays and bake in a moderately hot oven for about 15 minutes. Cool on a wire tray. Sandwich together in pairs with the butter icing.

SHORTBREAD

Cooking time 20 minutes
Oven temperature Moderately hot
190°C, 375°F, Gas Mark 5

METRIC/IMPERIAL

200 g/8 oz butter
100 g/4 oz castor sugar

200 g/8 oz plain flour
100 g/4 oz rice flour

Mix the butter and sugar together with the mixer until light and creamy then, using the mixer on a slow speed, gradually work in the flour until the mixture holds together. Knead the dough lightly with the hands and form into two 20-cm/8-inch cakes on a greased baking tray, or press into two greased 20-cm/8-inch loose-bottomed sandwich tins. Pinch the edges and prick all over with a fork Put into a moderately hot oven and bake for 20 minutes until pale golden.

MARMALADE COOKIES

Cooking time 15 minutes
Oven temperature Moderately hot
200°C, 400°F, Gas Mark 6
Makes 30

METRIC/IMPERIAL

100 g/4 oz margarine	25 g/ 1 oz drinking chocolate
100 g/4oz castor sugar	200 g/7 oz self-raising flour
2 eggs	50 g/2 oz rolled oats
2 tablespoons chunky marmalade	

Cream the margarine and sugar together in the mixer bowl then add the eggs one at a time, beating well. Add the marmalade. Sieve together the drinking chocolate and flour and fold into the mixture lightly using a metal spoon. Roll teaspoons of the mixture in the oats and place on greased baking trays. Bake in a moderately hot oven for about 15 minutes, then decorate with pieces of marmalade peel.

BUTTER ICING

METRIC/IMPERIAL

100 g/4 oz butter	flavouring
200 g/8 oz icing sugar	

Cream the butter in the mixer bowl until white and fluffy, sieve the icing sugar and add to the butter, beat with the mixer until well blended. Beat in the flavouring as required.

Variations

Orange butter icing Add 2 tablespoons orange juice and a little grated orange rind.

Lemon butter icing Add 2 tablespoons lemon juice and a little grated lemon rind.

Coffee butter icing Add 1 tablespoon instant coffee blended with 2 tablespoons boiling water.

Chocolate butter icing Add 2 tablespoons cocoa blended with 2 tablespoons boiling water.

Mocha butter icing Use both the coffee and chocolate flavourings together, with just a half quantity of each.

FONDANT ICING

METRIC/IMPERIAL

450 g/1 lb icing sugar
1 large egg white

2 tablespoons liquid glucose

Place all the ingredients in the mixer bowl and beat until the mixture is well blended together and forms a 'dough'-like lump, leaving the sides of the bowl clean. Turn out onto a board, lightly sprinkled with icing sugar, and knead until soft and pliable. If you intend to colour the icing, knead in a few drops of colouring at the beginning of kneading. This icing is applied as almond paste in that it is rolled and cut to fit the cake.

ROYAL ICING

METRIC/IMPERIAL

3 egg whites
juice of 1 lemon, strained

675 g/1½ lb icing sugar
1 teaspoon glycerine

Place the egg whites in the mixer bowl and beat on high speed for about 30 seconds. Gradually beat in the sieved icing sugar and lemon juice until the mixture stands in soft peaks. Add the glycerine to prevent the icing from becoming too hard. If you intend to pipe with the icing a little more icing sugar will be needed.

ALMOND PASTE

METRIC/IMPERIAL

225 g/8 oz ground almonds
275 g/10 oz icing sugar
1 egg white

2 teaspoons orange flower water
few drops lemon juice

Mix together the almonds and sugar in the mixer bowl, add the remaining ingredients, and, using the mixer on a slow speed, blend until a smooth paste is obtained

Meringue

This is a mixture of egg white and sugar which can be cooked by itself shaped as shells, rounds, or baskets, or used as a topping on puddings.

MERINGUE 1 *Suisse*

This mixture is usually used for meringue shells which are filled with whipped cream, or as a topping for pies.

Cooking time 1 hour 20 minutes
Oven temperature Very cool 130°C, 250°F, Gas Mark ½
Makes 12–16

METRIC/IMPERIAL

4 egg whites
225 g/8 oz castor sugar

300 ml/½ pint double cream

Prepare two baking trays by brushing with oil and then dredging with flour. Alternatively line the baking sheets with non-stick silicone paper. Put the egg whites in the mixer bowl and beat until quite stiff, the mixture should stand up in peaks. Whisk in 4 teaspoons sugar until the mixture becomes more glossy. Sprinkle the remaining sugar into the mixture and fold in with a metal spoon. Shape the meringue mixture into shells with two spoons and place on a prepared baking tray. For a more professional finish put the meringue mixture into a piping bag with a plain nozzle and pipe into rounds. Dredge with castor sugar and bake in a very cool oven for about 1 hour, changing the trays round to avoid the meringues becoming brown.

Piping meringue rounds

After about 1 hour the meringues will be set; lift them gently from the trays with a palette knife, press the flat bottom to form a hollow, then return to the oven to dry for a further 15–20 minutes. Cool on a wire rack. Fill with whipped cream and sandwich together in pairs just before serving.

MERINGUE 2 *Cuite*

This is a firmer type of meringue which is hard work to make by hand but is quickly done with the mixer. It is really easier to handle than the softer mixture and even an inexperienced cook will find it easy to pipe as it holds firm for longer even in a warm kitchen.

Cooking time 50–60 minutes
Oven temperature Very cool 130°C, 250°F, Gas Mark ½
Makes 6 small baskets or 1 large

METRIC/IMPERIAL

4 egg whites   2 drops vanilla essence
240 g/8½ oz icing sugar

Put the egg whites in the mixer bowl and whisk until foaming but not quite stiff. Add the icing sugar 1 tablespoon at a time until the mixture is stiff and shiny. To test lift a little mixture up and if ready it should retain its shape as it falls back onto the mixture. Put the mixture into a piping bag with a large plain pipe and pipe as shown in the drawing into 6 baskets. Bake in a very cool oven for about 50 minutes.

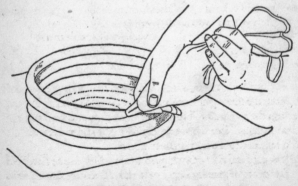

Piping the walls of a basket

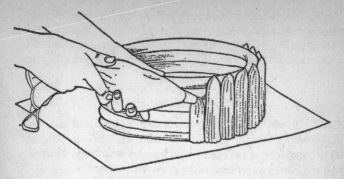

Vertical piping to complete the wall

Alternatively pipe into a large basket. Fill with fruit and cream or ice cream and fruit and serve as a dessert.

Note The meringue takes some time to become thick so do not be worried if it seems to look runny. I find it takes about 5 minutes in my large mixer using a whisk.

HAZELNUT MERINGUE GÂTEAU

Cooking time 1 hour
Oven temperature Cool 140°C, 275°F, Gas Mark 1
Serves 6

METRIC/IMPERIAL

4 egg whites	300 ml/½ pint double cream
250 g/9 oz castor sugar	*To decorate*
100 g/4 oz hazelnuts	8 hazelnuts

Grease and line two 20-cm/8-inch sandwich tins with greaseproof paper. Make the meringue as for meringue suisse (page 117). Put the hazelnuts in the blender and blend until finely chopped. Fold into the meringue mixture after the sugar, divide the mixture between the tins, and bake in a cool oven for about 1 hour.

Allow to cool and fill with whipped cream which can be flavoured with a few drops of vanilla essence or brandy. Decorate the top with piped cream rosettes topped with a hazelnut.

VACHERIN

Cooking time 1 hour
Oven temperature Cool, 140°C, 275°F, Gas Mark 1
Serves 6

METRIC/IMPERIAL

5 egg whites

275 g/10 oz castor sugar

225 g/8 oz fresh strawberries

2 tablespoons sugar

300 ml/½ pint double cream

Grease three baking trays and line each with a round of oiled grease-proof paper 20 cm/8 inches in diameter. Whisk the egg whites until stiff, add 1 tablespoon of castor sugar, and continue whisking until the meringue takes on a more shiny appearance. Fold in the remaining castor sugar with a metal spoon. Divide the mixture and spread over the oiled papers. Alternatively, pipe in a spiral shape with a piping bag and plain nozzle. Bake in a cool oven for about 1 hour. Do not allow to brown.

Reserving three strawberries for decoration, slice the remaining strawberries and sprinkle the sugar over them, Whip the cream and mix half of the cream with the strawberries. Sandwich the meringue rings together with the strawberries and cream and decorate the top with the remaining whipped cream and strawberries (see cover photograph).

Eating for Health and Beauty

Nearly all of us decide at some time to go on a diet. This is usually brought about by discovering that one's dress size has gone up one or the favourite trousers no longer fasten. It is depressing to have a weight problem and it should be tackled at once – the longer you keep it the more it seems to become! Sensible slimming for healthy adults means cutting down the intake of food overall, and making sure you eat plenty of proteins and less starch. If you are eating 2500 calories a day and you are putting on weight this means the body is unable to use all the calories and is storing the excess as fat. No amount of machines or exercises will alter this fact radically.

The blender takes the sweat out of preparing many low-calorie dishes. Fresh vegetables and fruit not only help one to slim but give a bonus of a clearer skin and brighter eyes. Don't be caught napping next holiday time, stay trim by having a low-calorie day once or twice a week. These recipes are also helpful if you are entertaining.

SPEEDY BREAKFAST IN A GLASS

Serves 2

METRIC/IMPERIAL

2 eggs
300 ml/½ pint chilled orange juice

2 tablespoons powdered milk
artificial sweetener to taste

Put the eggs, orange juice (frozen juice is excellent), and milk powder in the goblet. Turn on at maximum speed until the milk powder is dissolved. Add sweetener to taste.

GAZPACHO

Serves 4–6

METRIC/IMPERIAL

1 clove garlic	1 tablespoon salad oil
1 small onion	1 tablespoon wine vinegar
5 large tomatoes	several sprigs parsley
½ cucumber	600 ml/1 pint water
2 green peppers or 1 green and	*To garnish*
1 red	1 dish diced green or red pepper
1 slice white bread	1 small dish diced cucumber

Peel the garlic, onion, tomatoes, and cucumber and chop roughly, then put into the blender, switch on, and allow the vegetables to be chopped finely. Add the roughly chopped peppers gradually while the blender is running at medium speed. Add all remaining ingredients except the water and mix well. Add as much water as the blender will take and mix thoroughly, transfer to a bowl, and chill well before serving.

CHEESE SOUP

Serves 6–8

METRIC/IMPERIAL

2 onions or 4 spring onions	225 g/8 oz processed cheese
1 large carrot	25 g/1 oz flour
3 stalks celery	salt and pepper
300 ml/½ pint chicken stock	900 ml/1½ pints milk

Chop the onions, carrot, and celery finely in the blender with some of the stock. Pour into a saucepan and add the remaining stock. Simmer for about 10 minutes. Meanwhile wash and dry the blender. Grate the cheese in the blender, putting in cubes a few at a time. Add the flour, seasoning, and half the milk to the grated cheese and run for a few seconds on high speed. Add the contents of the blender to the vegetables, stirring all the time until the mixture begins to thicken. Lower the heat and add the remaining milk. Serve immediately, garnished with chopped parsley and croûtons. This soup is an ideal nourishing lunch-time snack. Use skim milk if you are on a strict diet.

YOGURT SOUP

Serves 4

METRIC/IMPERIAL

rind of ¼ lemon
2 tablespoons lemon juice
1½ tablespoons sugar or
  equivalent artificial sweetener
2 (150-ml/5 fl-oz) cartons low fat
  natural yogurt

1 egg
pinch cinnamon
pinch salt
50 g/2 oz seedless raisins

Put the lemon rind and juice into the goblet and blend until the rind is finely chopped. Add the sugar and half the yogurt, switch on for a few seconds. Add the remaining ingredients and run the machine until the raisins are roughly chopped. Chill thoroughly before serving.

CAULIFLOWER FLUFF

Serves 4

METRIC/IMPERIAL

1 cauliflower
1 onion
50 g/2 oz butter
2 tomatoes
½ quantity white sauce
  (see page 37)

100 g/4 oz grated cheese
salt and pepper
4 eggs

Divide the cauliflower into florets and put into boiling salted water for about 7 minutes. Peel and slice the onion and sauté in the melted butter. Peel and slice the tomatoes, add to the onion, and allow to sauté for about 3 minutes. Make up the white sauce and add half the grated cheese, season well. Drain the cauliflower, arrange in a fire-proof dish and cover with the onion and tomato mixture, and top with the sauce. Separate the eggs and beat the whites stiffly with the mixer. Spread the egg white on top of the cauliflower, make four little holes in the white, and drop the yolks into the holes. Sprinkle with the remaining cheese, season again, and grill until golden brown.

DESERT ISLAND SALAD

Serves 3

METRIC/IMPERIAL

12 dates
2 tablespoons desiccated coconut
rind of ¼ orange
1 piece crystallised ginger
3 oranges

1 banana
50 g/2 oz seedless grapes
lettuce

To garnish

4 slices orange

Put the stoned dates, coconut, orange rind, and ginger into the blender, switch on at maximum speed for 10 seconds. Peel and slice the oranges and banana, add to the blender, and switch on until the fruit is really finely chopped. Add the whole grapes and serve on crisp lettuce leaves, garnished with slices of orange.

Note This salad is delicious with roast duck.

STUFFED PEAR SALAD

Serves 4

METRIC/IMPERIAL

2 tablespoons blender mayonnaise
  (see page 36)
225 g/8 oz cream cheese
½ slice lemon
2 tablespoons milk

4 ripe pears
lettuce or endive
lemon juice
50 g/2 oz chopped nuts

Put the mayonnaise, cream cheese, lemon, and milk in the blender and switch on for about 30 seconds until smooth. Peel and halve the pears and arrange on salad greens which have been sprinkled with lemon juice. Fill the centre of the pears with the cream cheese mixture and sprinkle with chopped nuts. The nuts can be chopped in the blender.

SLIMMERS' LUNCH

Serves 1

METRIC/IMPERIAL

1 carrot   6 slices cucumber
1 tomato   slimmers' dressing (see page 127)
6 florets cauliflower

Cut the carrot into sticks and the tomato into wedges, arrange the vegetables around the dressing.

CHINESE VEGETABLES

Serves 4

METRIC/IMPERIAL

3 tablespoons oil   2 teaspoons soy sauce
4 stalks celery   1½ tablespoons cornflour
½ small cabbage   4 tablespoons stock or water
2 large onions   salt and pepper
2 carrots   100 g/4 oz bean sprouts
150 ml/¼ pint vegetable stock or
  water

Put the oil in a pan. Roughly chop all the vegetables except the bean sprouts in the blender a few at a time – *do not liquidise*. Add the vegetables to the heated oil and sauté for about 5 minutes. Pour in the stock and bring to the boil, simmer for a further 5 minutes. Blend the soy sauce, cornflour, 4 tablespoons stock, and seasoning until smooth and pour over the vegetables. Season and cook for a further few minutes, stirring from time to time. Add the bean sprouts and continue cooking until they are hot. This can be served with rice or noodles to non-dieters.

TOMATO MOULD

Serves 4–6

METRIC/IMPERIAL

300 ml/½ pint tomato juice

15 g/½ oz gelatine

2 thin slices unpeeled lemon

1 tablespoon lemon juice

2 tablespoons tomato purée

1 slice onion

½ medium-sized cucumber

1 tomato

1 teaspoon vinegar

salt

lettuce

Heat half the tomato juice and put into the blender with the gelatine for about 10 seconds. Add lemon pieces, juice, tomato purée, and onion, switch on until finely chopped. Add remaining ingredients and blend until all ingredients are liquidised. Allow to cool until the mixture starts to thicken then pour into a 1-litre/2-pint oiled mould and chill until firm. Unmould onto a bed of shredded lettuce. Serve with tuna, salmon, lean meat, or cottage cheese.

WHEAT GERM NUT LOAF

Cooking time 50 minutes
Oven temperature Moderate 180°C, 350°F, Gas Mark 4
Serves 6

METRIC/IMPERIAL

175 g/6 oz pecan nuts

2 stalks celery

1 carrot

350 ml/12 fl oz milk

½ onion

3 eggs

40 g/1½ oz plain flour

1½ teaspoons salt

pepper

100 g/4 oz grated cheese

90 g/3½ oz wheat germ

Line a 1-kg/2-lb loaf tin with greased aluminium foil.

Blend the nuts until chopped, pour into a bowl. Put the roughly chopped celery in the blender and chop, empty into a saucepan. Next chop the carrot roughly and turn into the saucepan. Put the milk, onion, eggs, flour, salt, and pepper into the blender and switch on for several seconds. Pour the smooth mixture on top of the celery and carrot and cook on a low heat until the mixture thickens. Add the cheese, pecans, and wheat germ, mix well. Pour into the loaf tin and cook in a moderate oven for about 50 minutes. Allow to cool for several minutes before removing from the tin. Serve with salad and cheese and pineapple dip (see page 20).

SLIMMERS' DRESSING

METRIC/IMPERIAL

100 g/4 oz cottage cheese   salt and pepper
½ onion   150 ml/¼ pint skimmed milk
2 tablespoons lemon juice

Put all the ingredients into the blender and run until the onion is finely chopped and mixture is well blended. Use as a salad dressing and as a dip for raw vegetables.

SOURED CREAM DRESSING

METRIC/IMPERIAL

150 ml/¼ pint soured cream   pinch dry mustard
1 tablespoon lemon juice   pinch cayenne pepper
2 tablespoons mayonnaise   salt
  (see page 36)   1 teaspoon dill

Put all ingredients in the blender, switch on to medium speed until everything is mixed. Chill before use.
    This dressing is delicious on tomato salad or with a fish salad.

FROSTED COFFEE

Serves 2

METRIC/IMPERIAL

2 teaspoons instant coffee   2 tablespoons non fat powdered
2 drops vanilla essence   milk
3 ice cubes   artificial sweetener to taste
200 ml/7 fl oz cold water

Put all the ingredients into the blender and switch on at medium speed until the mixture is smooth and the ice is crushed.

SLIMMERS' COCKTAIL

Serves 2

METRIC/IMPERIAL

rind of ½ lemon or lime
4 tablespoons fresh lemon or
   lime juice

6 ice cubes
150 ml/¼ pint cold water
artificial sweetener to taste

Put the lemon rind and juice in the goblet and blend until finely chopped. Add the ice cubes and switch on until finely crushed; pour into glasses and add sweetener to taste. This is a refreshing drink and a change from reduced calorie soft drinks, and when the diet is serious it is better than nothing!

For Babies and Children

I know that it is easier and quicker to open a convenient little can or jar for junior but it is extravagant on the days when you are having food which is easily made suitable for the baby by blending. It also means the baby is used to family meals and flavours. Many mothers wonder why toddlers refuse food when they are old enough to join the family for meals. Usually this can be traced back to only eating prepared baby foods. It is easy to introduce new flavours with the blender because familiar and favourite flavours can be mixed with new ingredients. It saves money to blend one's own baby foods and this is important to most people now – after all one pays quite a lot for those glass jars!

For older children the blender makes light work of sandwich fillings for lunch boxes, tea time, and parties, and helps you make speedy puddings.

VEGETABLES, MEAT, OR POULTRY FOR A BABY

Serves 2

METRIC/IMPERIAL

3 tablespoons milk or stock   pinch salt
100 g/4 oz cooked drained
   vegetables, meat, or chicken

Make sure the knife, board, and blender are spotless. Cut the meat into 1-cm/½-inch cubes, put all ingredients into the blender, and switch on until very smooth. Store unwanted food in a sterilised plastic box until the next day. Do not prepare more than 2 days' food. For toddlers, make a coarser texture.

CHICKEN SAVOURY FOR TODDLERS

Serves 2

METRIC/IMPERIAL

100 g/ 4 oz diced cooked chicken   40 g/1½ oz cooked rice or potato
1 tablespoon cooked vegetables

Put all ingredients into the blender and blend roughly, do not allow
vegetables and chicken to become completely smooth. Season according to child's age. Heat through before serving.

BEEF DINNER FOR TODDLERS

Serves 2

METRIC/IMPERIAL

100 g/4 oz lean cooked beef   ½ tomato, skinned
2 tablespoons cooked vegetables   1 tablespoon milk
1 small potato, cooked

Put all ingredients into the blender and blend until correct texture is
obtained – smooth for very young children, slightly coarser for
toddlers. Heat through.

Note For older children the above recipes can be made with raw
food and then cooked in a covered saucepan until the meat is cooked.

BANANA DESSERT

Serves 1

METRIC/IMPERIAL

1 small banana   3 tablespoons milk or made up
3 tablespoons baby cereal   baby milk

Peel the banana, put all ingredients in the blender, and switch on until
smooth.

APRICOT APPLE DESSERT

Serves 6

METRIC/IMPERIAL

225 g/8 oz dried apricots   50 g/2 oz sugar
1 apple

Allow apricots to soak for several hours. Put in a saucepan, cover with water, add the sugar, and stew. Peel, core, and roughly chop the apple and add to the apricots for the last 15 minutes. Cooking time will be around 25–30 minutes altogether. Allow to cool slightly, turn mixture into the blender, and liquidise until smooth. Divide into portions. ❋ Some may be frozen for future use in small plastic containers or plastic bags. Do not serve frozen.

APPLE CUSTARD

Cooking time 40 minutes
Oven temperature Moderate 170°C, 325°F, Gas Mark 3
Serves 3

METRIC/IMPERIAL

200 ml/7 fl oz hot milk   1 tablespoon honey
½ apple, peeled and cored   1 egg

Put all ingredients except the egg into the blender and switch on until the apple is liquidised – about 30 seconds. Add the egg and switch on for a few seconds to blend the ingredients well. Pour into three greased ramekin dishes and place in the roasting tin or a casserole quarter-filled with water. Bake in a moderate oven for about 40 minutes.

RAISIN RICE PUDDING

Serves 3

METRIC/IMPERIAL

150 ml/¼ pint milk   1 egg
65 g/ 2½ oz cooked rice   50 g/2 oz seedless raisins

Put all ingredients in the blender until smooth, then bake as for apple custard.

BABY DESSERT

Serves 2

METRIC/IMPERIAL

3 tablespoons syrup or fruit juice   1 teaspoon honey
100 g/4 oz drained cooked fruit

Make the syrup by dissolving 2 teaspoons sugar in 2 tablespoons
water. Put all ingredients into the blender and run until very smooth,
Apples, apricots, oranges, bananas, peaches, or blackcurrants are
suitable.

SANDWICH FILLINGS

Savoury spread Cut one skinned tomato into portions and put into
the blender with 25 g/1 oz melted butter and seasoning. Blend on
medium speed then drop 100 g/4 oz roughly chopped meat (ham,
chicken, corned beef, etc.) into the goblet a little at a time. Older
children sometimes like a little tomato ketchup for flavour.

Egg and cheese Cream 25 g/1 oz luxury margarine or butter with
2 shelled hard-boiled eggs 100 g/4 oz cream cheese, and seasoning
using the hand mixer.

Cheese and tomato Grate 100 g/4 oz cheese in the blender, then add
3 peeled and quartered tomatoes, salt, and pepper.

Salmon or tuna spread Blend 1 (198-g/7-oz) can with 1 teaspoon
vinegar, salt and pepper, 1 tablespoon tomato purée or ketchup, and
$\frac{1}{4}-\frac{1}{2}$ peeled thickly sliced cucumber.

Sausage pinwheels For these you need an uncut loaf which is then
sliced lengthwise. Remove the crusts and flatten the slices slightly
with a rolling pin. Spread with butter or marmite or cheese and
tomato spread. Place a cooked sausage at the end of the slice and roll
as for a Swiss roll. ❋ The rolls freeze well at this stage. To use cut into
slices.
    Gherkin pinwheels can be made by spreading the bread with
salmon or tuna spread and rolling around 2 gherkins.

JELLY WHIP

Serves 4–6

METRIC/IMPERIAL

1 packet jelly   1 small can evaporated milk
600 ml/1 pint water

Make up the jelly with 600 ml/1 pint water which is just under boiling temperature. Stir until dissolved, allow to cool, then pour half of the cool jelly (almost at setting point) into the mixer bowl with the evaporated milk. Whisk until fluffy and thick. With half the remaining jelly line a mould by pouring about 2·5 cm/1 inch into the bottom of the mould. When the jelly is set pour in the whip mixture, allow to firm up for 10 minutes, then add the remaining jelly in a layer on top. Turn out when set. Any flavour of jelly can be used and the whip can be served on its own or with fruit and cream.

Note The jelly may be made up with juice from a can of fruit. Dissolve the jelly in 150 ml/¼ pint boiling water, then make up to 600 ml/1 pint with the fruit juice.

DANISH PUDDING

Serves 4

METRIC/IMPERIAL

450 g/1 lb cooking apples   25 g/1 oz Demerara sugar
175 g/6 oz fresh white bread   150 ml/¼ pint
50 g/2 oz butter

Wipe the apples, remove cores, and cut into slices. Place in a saucepan with a very little water and cook until soft. Place in the blender and run until a smooth purée is obtained. Clean the blender. Make breadcrumbs with the bread and fry in the melted butter until golden, stirring constantly. Add the brown sugar. Sweeten the purée to taste but be careful not to over-sweeten. Put alternating layers of apple and breadcrumbs into a glass dish, ending with a layer of breadcrumbs.
Whip the cream and decorate the top of the pudding.

Drinks

The blender makes delicious drinks for every occasion from children's milk shakes to sophisticated cocktails. Experiment with your own favourite fruits and flavourings. Crushed ice for your drinks is always available at the flick of a switch.

CHOCOLATE MILK SHAKE

Serves 2

METRIC/IMPERIAL

300 ml/½ pint milk   3 teaspoons drinking chocolate
1 teaspoon sugar

Put all the ingredients in the blender and run on maximum speed for 30 seconds.

Variations

Add 1 scoop ice cream to each glass. Different flavourings for milk drinks can be used for milk shakes. Add 1 tablespoon raspberries or strawberries to a plain milk shake mixture in the blender. This is also delicious with ice cream.

LEMONADE

METRIC/IMPERIAL

2 large lemons   50 g/2 oz sugar
900 ml/1½ pints cold water

Wash the lemons. Peel the rind off and put it into the blender. Now peel the white pith away and discard, put the fruit of the whole lemon in the blender. Cut into pieces if using a small machine. Add some of the liquid and the sugar then blend until the fruit is puréed. Strain into a jug and add remaining water; add ice cubes and slices of lemon just before serving.

Orangeade Use 450 ml/¾ pint water to 2 oranges and reduce the sugar, or omit, unless you have a sweet tooth.

TOMATO COCKTAIL

Serves 4

METRIC/IMPERIAL

450 g/1 lb ripe tomatoes or
   1 (425-g/15-oz) can peeled
   tomatoes
1 stalk celery

salt and pepper
2 teaspoons lemon juice
1 teaspoon sugar

Put all ingredients in the blender and switch on to maximum speed for 30 seconds. Sieve into a saucepan and simmer for a few minutes. Add a few drops of Worcestershire sauce if liked and chill well before serving.

PINEAPPLE APRICOT PUNCH

Serves 30

METRIC/IMPERIAL

1 small jar maraschino cherries
1 (283-g/10-oz) can apricots
3 tablespoons lemon juice

1 bottle dry white wine
2·25 litres/4 pints pineapple juice

Put the drained cherries, retaining a few for decoration, and apricots in the blender, add a little apricot juice and lemon juice. Blend until the fruit is liquidised. Mix with the remaining ingredients in a punch bowl. Serve with small ice cubes and cherries floating in the punch.

PINEAPPLE CIDER CUP

Serves 30

METRIC/IMPERIAL

1 orange	600 ml/1 pint soda water
1 lemon	2·25 litres/4 pints cider
1 (340-g/12-oz) can pineapple	*To decorate*
pieces	maraschino cherries
12 cherries	slices of orange
150 ml/¼ pint sherry	

Peel the rind of the orange and lemon very thinly and put in the blender with a little pineapple juice; switch on until the rind is finely chopped. Remove the white pith from the orange and lemon. Cut a few orange slices for decoration and put the remainder of the orange and the lemon into the blender with the pineapple pieces. Switch on at maximum speed and allow to liquidise. Empty into the punch bowl, add the cherries and sherry. Pour in the soda water and cider just before serving. Crush some ice in the blender and add crushed ice to the punch; decorate with slices of orange and maraschino cherries. More cider can be added.

SHERRY OR BRANDY FLIP

Serves 1

METRIC/IMPERIAL

1 egg yolk	1 teaspoon sugar
125 ml/scant ¼ pint sherry	nutmeg

Put all the ingredients together in the goblet and blend for 10 seconds. Grate some nutmeg on the top. I have an elderly relative who has a small blender only to make the daily flip – she swears it gives her all her zing!

WHISKY SOUR

A gorgeous summer drink. A measure is your choice!

Serves 4

METRIC/IMPERIAL

5 measures whisky

2 measures lemon juice

2 tablespoons sugar

2 ice cubes

Blend all ingredients together for about 20 seconds. Strain through a small nylon sieve into a jug or glasses. Garnish with lemon slices and maraschino cherries if desired.

CHAMPAGNE COCKTAIL

Serves 8

METRIC/IMPERIAL

4 ice cubes

juice of 1 lemon

3 drops Angostura bitters

2 measures brandy

1 bottle champagne

Put the ice cubes into the blender, pour in the lemon juice, bitters, and brandy, and switch on until the ice is crushed. Strain into glasses and top up with champagne.

Index